THE GHOST TRAP

THE GHOST TRAP

A Novel

K. Stephens

A LeapLit Book
Leapfrog Literature
Leapfrog Press
Teaticket, Massachusetts

A LeapLit Book
Leapfrog Literature

Published in 2009 in the United States by
Leapfrog Press LLC
PO Box 2110
Teaticket, MA 02536
www.leapfrogpress.com

Distributed in the United States by
Consortium Book Sales and Distribution
St. Paul, Minnesota 55114
www.cbsd.com

First Edition

Library of Congress Cataloging-in-Publication Data

Stephens, K. (Kaley)
  The ghost trap : a novel / K. Stephens. – 1st ed.
    p. cm.
  ISBN 978-0-9815148-7-1 (alk. paper)
  1. Lobster fishers–Fiction. 2. Maine–Fiction.
I. Title.
  PS3619.T476765G47 2009
  813'.6–dc22

    2009027436

Printed in the United States of America

To Mainers and the salt that binds them.

THE GHOST TRAP

ONE

Most days he woke up, his body twisted with the kind of ache that made him suck his back teeth before sitting up in the dark. But nothing hurt today, not even the distorted muscles in his back, and so it was already shaping up to be a fine day. Even with a heaving sea, a day fine and blue. Dirty blond whiskers haunted his face as he gunned his boat to cruising speed, smacking against the chop with a steady thud, past a rocky outcrop and out of the harbor. Past the first green can, Little Island on the right, past Sawyer Fernald's strings and up beyond the ledge with four runty spruce trees. He knew this route as blindly as a commuter in morning traffic. His family's territory was a three-mile-square area studded with little islands: Seal Rock, Squirrel Island, Sawyer Light and Decker's Gut. The previous year, some of these islands were profiled on the Internet and Decker's Gut had been sold to a prince in Bahrain. People had gotten angry about that—a library in Rockland had been vandalized. Hundreds of tiny islands on an atlas had been scratched out like the eyes of an ex-lover in a photograph.

A fumbling crackle on the VHF radio tipped him off that she was trying to call.

"Jamie—hellooooo. Where am you?" Anja had no radio protocol, never did. The VHF scorched with static, distorting her words.

Jamie wiped bait off his hands, pulled the mike off the clip.

"Anja," he said and had to say it once again. "Keep your mouth off the mike. Say it slow."

"I can't get the fucky vacuum cleaner to work." People thought it was so funny to hear Anja swear, but hearing it every day to describe everything (pass the fucking toast, where the fuck is my other sock?) wore him down, especially because it was the word he heard over and over in the harbor to describe every little thing. ("Did you see that feckin' guy's boat?" "If they were in my feckin' harbor, I'd feckin' fuck 'em up." "Christ, I feckin' 'ma-jin.")

"Anja, did you plug it in?"

"Yes, Jamie! It is plugged in and everything and when it goes turned on, it goes. . . ." (And here she made a sound like a lawn-mower running over a stump, further torqued by her inability to keep her mouth off the mike.)

"Anja—I can't figure it out from here." At that moment he was headed toward a craggy scruff of islands that delineated his family's fishing grounds. "I'll be back at three—we can look at it then."

"But it needs it now, Jamie. And I've got to make the vacuum go, then I need to scrub the pot on the stove or else my whole day will be ruined!"

That part was true, for her routine—maybe two tasks—*would* take an entire day. For after she got through making her lists, strategizing how best to maneuver the vacuum through the house (straight rows? or cross-hatch?), perhaps jotting her feelings about it down in a special notebook, forgetting that she had planned to vacuum at all, then realizing about midway through the morning—yes, indeed, she had planned to vacuum—he would've already finished a day of wrestling 300 traps over the wash rail.

"Jamie you didn't not leave me a note this morning," Anja said. Even over the distortion of the radio he could hear the pout in her voice. Every morning, he left her a note, something to cheer her day. *Don't eat too much cheese—I'll get home usual time, love ya love ya love ya.* Or *I'll check the propane later, we'll grill out, have a fine day, love ewe, J.*

"Yeah I was kind of running late this morning," he said, his thumb releasing the button. When he got up at 4:30 every morning, the poetry wasn't always there.

"You can give me one now?"

"What, a note?"

"Yeah huh, just a little one?"

The snow on the radio blew hard, a voice interrupting, "I'll give ya a note sweet cakes." Big Steve being funny. They were on an open channel, everyone on the water could hear.

"Anja," Jamie said, leaning against the wheel. "Kinda busy right now, I'll make up for it when I get home."

"Oh."

Jamie's eyes rose to the canopy. His thumb pushed in the mike button and he began to mumble through an old ballad.

> "Awake, awake, you drowsy sleeper,
> Awake and listen to me
> There's someone at your bedroom window
> A-weeping there most bitterly."

"Hey Eugley," a man's high voice interrupted. It was Thongchai. "What you feckin wasting your life on the water for? You got all that raw talent, you could be on American Idol."

The VHF snorted with more comments. Big Steve's voice. "I thought it was kind of ten-dah." Jamie resisted nailing Thongchai, who'd recently gotten an OUI and could be counted on to do something stupid at least once a week. It might be a little fun to stir up the pot on this summer morning, get all the yahoos yammering away on the VHF, but then the whole afternoon would be gone. And there were bills to pay.

It was an old superstition that if a summer started out rocky it would not smooth out, yet every season seemed to start off with some damn thing or another, and he'd been doing this since he was 12. The summers never flowed, not in the way people seemed to imagine was the carefree life of the proud lobsterman out on the lone sea. The year before started with broken gear and then there was the summer no one could get his hands on good bait before it went soft. And there were always territory problems—long-held grudges over the winter spanning into the first real week of summer, where arguments at the docks and disputes over bottom had to be sorted out all over again. Every summer since he was a kid, there always seemed to be some crotchety hassle with one of the Fogertys over boundaries. And right now he could see the signs of another winning season about to start.

A half-mile separated the Eugley fishing grounds from the Fogertys' like masking tape down the middle of a warring roommates' room, and everyone knew that past Seal Rock was Eugley territory, yet as his boat skimmed up to the borderline, there he could see his strings tangled up with the alien colors of someone else's buoys. As a boy, out on the water with his grandfather Maynard, Jamie saw old Dale Fogerty out on his boat every day and it wasn't hard to recognize Fogerty's red-striped buoys trespassing near his grandfather's gear where the island coves and kelp beds were better for lobsters.

"Pappy, would you look at that?" Jamie would squeak. "They're over the line again!"

If Maynard were ever angry over this blatant pushing of lines, he managed to always maintain his temper. "Just relax, the tide could've carried them over." Maynard had no love for the Fogertys, but he had respect for genuine mistakes. Too much gear in the water and too many people lobstering—there'd always be some sloppiness. Except the Fogertys relied on murky intent to further their careers—it was a known fact—they pushed everyone.

Jamie stood planted on his boat, counter-balancing the swells until he got close enough and cranked the wheel, cutting the engine to peer down at the mess. These definitely weren't the Fogertys' buoys. These were quadruple-striped with fluorescent pink, lime green, black, and Day-Glo orange. The old guys, the highliners, all had one color—yellow, red, or orange. A solid color meant seniority, a long time in the business, but the more licenses that were granted, the more guys had to stripe up their buoys just to identify them. Jamie used the gaff to hook one of the fruity-looking buoys, working at the knots to untangle to see if he could identify it by number or name. He didn't recognize the small etched numbers. They belonged to someone very new to the business, someone with no skills in trap placement, for the experienced fishermen knew how the tides worked. He counted how many strings were snarled. His were yellow with one jagged stripe—his Charlie Browns, Maynard's original colors. He stared at his Charlie Browns, now all cozy with the crazy-colored buoys. It would take all afternoon to untangle them.

Jamie snatched the VHF mike off its clip. "Hey, *Delores* here, whaddaya know, some hammerhead's been over here by Seal Rock. What I'm looking at here has more friggin' colors than a Jamaican prom."

A few moments went by as the boat lurched against waves. A voice answered.

"Oh yeah, yeah, down there on the western bottom? I see that's jammed right full."

His salt-cracked fingers reached for the volume knob on the VHF. "I can't pull a trap nowhere—everything's all snarled up."

"Just cut 'em then." His father's voice over the radio—as if that were obvious.

"I'm not gonna cut them," Jamie said, irritated. "I don't know whose they are—they could be some kid's."

"Stop being all sensitive and tell me where they are—I'll cut them myself," James Senior said. He was showing off for anyone who was listening—though that kind of talk over an open channel was dangerous.

Soon enough, Thongchai joined in. "If they're that friggin' stupid to dump their gear all over yours, Eugley—you know what to do."

"I've got it *handled*," Jamie retorted. Though it would've been easier to cut them, he didn't want to start trouble with someone he didn't know.

Big Steve's voice came on. "Eugley, you'd better not be out there 'til nine tonight, untying them by hand there, guy."

It was a slow morning, now everyone had an opinion. Thongchai's high voice returned.

"Want me to come over? I'll rip 'em right out of the water. I'll wrap 'em round the neck of the guy who put 'em there. Tell ya what, I'll. . . ."

"I can *handle* it."

Jamie was about to turn the radio off when Anja's voice floated up amid the harsh static.

"Jamie? Do we knows where the cheese grater is?"

Jamie put down one of the knots and wearily picked the mike up. "I don't know, can you just figure it out? Check in the drawer by the stove."

"It not there!" He could hear the scrambling clink of metal utensils.

"And Jamie—this is the problem. I am trying to makes a sandwich and the problem is the cheese is not cut and I'm not using no knife and you can't makes a *fucking* sandwich without the *cheese*, Jamie and . . . oh wait." She paused.

He sighed. "Where was it?"

"In the drawer."

"By the stove?"

"Yes. . . ."

"Anja—remember what we talked about, easy on the cheese."

"Puh."

Jamie put the mike back on the clip and stared at the twisted buoys. He was tired, not feeling particularly generous, but he threw the gears in reverse, backing up to the first string. It could be some high school kid. The young ones coming up, the ones who made honest mistakes—they got a little leniency. If these buoys belonged to a teenager, Jamie had to let them alone—that was the code. As a 16-year-old, Jamie had been green himself, had overshot the distance a few times, tangling up a few of the experienced fishermen's strings. But now that he was a highliner, he had a responsibility to teach kids the right way. He didn't do things like his father, a known hothead who would've just cut them straight off and started the season wrangling with an enemy just for something to look forward to.

He set about untangling his Charlie Browns from the striped buoys. For each striped buoy he pulled away, Jamie wrapped two half-hitches of warp round the shaft so that it lay queer against the tide. This was the *back tie*, the first warning to read the tides properly and to stay away from Jamie's strings. Whoever it was, if the guy didn't get the message with the back tie, the next time he would get cut.

He could hear a large boat in the distance, his ears trained to recognize the engine. Out of habit, he dropped the buoys; it sounded like Marine Patrol. A spark off the water caught his eye—a glint of white. *Now what?* he thought.

It appeared to be a cruising yacht, spit-shine clean, slamming against the swells. He stood, his cap low on his brow, and took his binoculars hanging off a nail to get a look. Figured. *The Wet Dream* out of Fort Myers. Stories had already spread throughout the dockside pubs about this particular picnic boat. Dozens of toggles had recently gotten sheared off, ruining hundreds of dollars worth of gear in the harbor. And people argued over whether it was typical early-season mischief or if *The Wet Dream* had something to do with it.

The Wet Dream slowed, settling a half-mile away, coming to a stop among a plume of yellow and green buoys—Thongchai's—and Jamie laughed. They couldn't have settled in a worse place. Thongchai was a crazy-ass Thai, more cracker than the reddest of the rednecks in the Point. He'd been one of the guys hollering about the yachties and the cut traps these last few days. If he had any idea that *The Wet Dream* now sat in his territory, his golden face would've turned the color of brick.

Jamie turned a bait bucket over on its end and sat down. His stomach told him it was 9 in the morning. He opened his dinner pail, unscrewing the plastic cap off his liter of Pepsi, and set to work unwrapping the tinfoil off last night's sausage, bacon, and ham pizza. It was the best pizza in the Point, made by Colleen at the Beach Store, who advertised it as "The Vegan." Jamie crammed it, folding the triangular point like ribbon candy into his mouth, and checked to make sure the rest of his dinner, two chocolate puddings, a Ring Ding, and a Hostess fruit pie, were safe from salt water.

Jamie ate, squinting against the glare of the waves. A piece of sausage fell to the knee of his yellow oilskins and he flicked it away.

15

He had work to do, yet he stayed rooted to the deck, watching. Thongchai could handle his own business. Already the morning was wasted over the snarled traps—so he might as well chalk it up.

Suddenly, two men emerged on the top deck of *The Wet Dream*. Jamie put his pizza down and held up the binoculars. They were middle aged, deeply suntanned, with furred gray chests and curved bellies plunging over their madras shorts. They looked like the kind of dickhead yachties who still went by their college nicknames, like Smitty and Jonesy. Guys who liked to spread both arms across the backs of booths, talk and laugh too loud in restaurants. The ones overly familiar with waitresses. "Hey honey, what's yer name?" The wrist wavers: "Hey—sweet thing, get yer bucket over here and get us another round."

Smitty and Jonesy leaned upon the steel cabled rail of their yacht holding rocks glasses as a third man emerged from below deck with a beer in his hand. Jamie had to squint through binoculars to read the guy's T-shirt:

DIP ME IN CHOCOLATE AND THROW ME TO THE LESBIANS

This one with the cool T-shirt had wraparound sunglasses—he looked like a Cooper. Cooper had corralled what meager hair he had left on his head into a thinning ponytail.

Now a woman emerged, joining them. A blonde. The binoculars stayed on her for a moment. Her breasts protruded past the top and sides of her white tank top—her very own personal flotation devices. Jamie zeroed in on her face. Long nose with sun-furrowed lines. Hair deep-fried blonde. She was about as old as her companions, a yacht wife maybe, but certainly no one's trophy. What was a good name for her? Brandi with an i. Brandi began thrusting her finger at them about something. And he could see by the slight way the men turned away from her that she was bitching about their drinking so early.

Cooper then did something interesting. He produced a nine-iron from somewhere and began swinging it on deck, arcing it high above his head, the sun glinting off metal, shooting a flash of light across the light, choppy waves. The crack of a golf ball conducted instantly across the water. Jamie's binoculars followed four or five golf balls high into the blue morning sky. Each time a faint hurrah could be heard from the picnic boat.

The swells swept along with a loose height and fetch. The yachties soon tired of their game and continued to hang over the rail, drinking and staring at the buoys in the water like babies fascinated by tub toys. Jamie watched them with a tortuous blue squint. Nine generations of lobstermen watched along with him.

He saw Cooper lower his golf club into the water and look around, as if: *Do you see anybody?*

Come on you guys just do it, said Brandi, squealing, as she stumbled backward, licked her thumb, and wiped her drenched chest.

Jonesy: *Just pull it up.*

Cooper reached overboard, attempted to gaff the yellow and green buoy. It took two tries with a golf club and he began pulling up the buoy and toggle.

Jamie stood up, brushed his blond whiskers. He turned over the engine and swung the wheel of *Delores* hard left. He began hauling toward *The Wet Dreams'* starboard as the bow slapped against waves, coming down hard on the swells. On full throttle, *Delores* could sound like a bear in heat, diesel engine disgorging smoke. It took him less than two minutes to get to the yacht, but by then they'd let the trap fall back into the water.

The smooth and gleaming curves of *The Wet Dream* bounced light from the sun. The yachties stood on the top deck doing their best to straighten their expressions as Jamie banked his boat skillfully right up against the yacht. Up close, *Delores* was less than half *The Wet Dream*'s size.

"Hey there!" Smitty called down. He had one foot up on the lower cable rail, and from the lower vantage point Jamie could see straight up his madras leg into a naked tangle. "We just wanted to see if you used wire or wood. We had a bet going that in Maine, you guys still used wooden pots."

Jamie shut off his engine so that the sound between them was clear, wonderfully absent, just the slosh of two boats grinding up against each other and the high squalls of far-off gulls.

"Are these your pots?" Smitty asked. His face was saturated with high color as if from a deep, bad burn.

"They're my friend's *traps*," Jamie said, emphasizing the distinction in terms. His arms gravitated to the roof of the wheelhouse, his fingers locking onto the edge of the canopy, his favorite stance when stopping for a chat.

"Ah, well, we weren't planning on doing anything," Smitty said, shaking his rocks glass so the ice tinkled. Jonesy had one finger in his ear, rooting around. Cooper's golf clubs lay at his feet. Jamie noticed that Cooper's boat shoes were monogrammed.

"Fort Myers—that's a ways from here," Jamie observed, examining the picnic boat up close. She was all smooth white fiberglass, a calla lily with crisp curves and shadows by the upper decks.

"Sanibel Island, ever hear of it?"

"Nope." Wherever it was, it sounded nice and sanitized, not like the islands in Maine such as Herring Gut, Cold Arse Island, and Drunkard's Rock. He imagined what it would be like to bring Thongchai and Big Steve and The Kid down to Fort Myers where Smitty worked. He imagined Smitty at his job, an executive at a glass-encased luxury boat showroom perhaps. Just what would Smitty would do if Jamie and his pals plunked themselves down in his territory and broke out the scotch? Of course, not scotch—more like 30-packs of Coors Lite. Sitting in reclining lawn chairs knocking back beers watching Smitty trying to work a customer into buying tackle and fishing rods.

"Have you lived here all your life?" Brandi asked, shyly.

Jamie gave them the old back road reply. "Not yet." A roll of the high-hat. *Ta-dum.* It took them a moment to get it and they smiled. It emboldened them, now that they had a real conversation going.

"How many lobsters would you say you catch a day?" Cooper leaned forward, resting his arms on the rail.

"Depends on the day," Jamie said, truthfully. Here it was, question and answer time. Tourists did this every day—as if he were a fucking information kiosk.

"I heard," Smitty said, "that a lobsterman up here can pull over 300 pounds a day . . . if you're good." In saying this, Smitty's chin tucked down, spreading his unshaven jowls against his neck.

"I guess," Jamie said. "If you're good."

"Are you good?" Smitty asked.

"You want to trade places?"

They liked that and laughed. Smitty and Jonesy craned their gaze around Jamie's boat, taking in the various dials and instruments.

"Do lobsters really have sex through their feelers?" Brandi asked, with a little giggle. Immediately the men turned on her—it was the damnedest thing. Smitty scoffed as if he'd never heard anything so stupid. Cooper's head turned swiftly, his ponytail jerking across his shoulder. "Jesus—" Cooper snorted and shook his head, looking to Jamie. Brandi seemed hurt over this, her hawkish face crumpling. He'd seen a lot of broken bar girls like her, and it was probably safe to assume it wasn't the first time they'd turned on her. The problem with women like her was that no matter how many times somebody made her feel like a worthless turd in a bucket, she'd still emerge smiling up on deck the next day.

"You wanna see some lobster?" Jamie said, more to distract the men from Brandi. "Why don't you haul that trap up again—let's see what we got."

Smitty eyed him. "Really?"

"Yeah, my gaff'll do it, but that nine iron's just as good," he said, and once again the men laughed.

"Go ahead—haul her up. I want to see how many are in there."

Cooper used his golf club to pull the toggle up to the yacht rail, where Jonesy helped to raise the wire trap to the surface. Water poured from the green mesh rectangle choked with kelp. Cooper wrestled with it, trying to get ahold of the unwieldy cage. It was kind of funny to see how awkward a trap was in someone else's hands.

"Don't scratch my boat, asshole," Smitty growled to Cooper. Jamie didn't offer to help, watching as they tried to latch onto it.

"Relax," Cooper said. "Have another drink."

Jonesy and Cooper managed to pull the trap up over the steel cable rail of the yacht and set it down on the teak deck. Jamie could see five or six lobsters inching around inside along with kelp, along with some useless cunner and cod.

"Why aren't they red?" Brandi asked, peering at them.

"How do I open this thing?" Cooper said, grunting to unhook the bungee cord keeping it shut. He got it open and stood up, triumphantly.

"You ever fish for lobster before?" Jamie asked.

Cooper smiled at him. "No."

"Oh. You're a natural."

Cooper thrust his hand into the trap. "Careful," Jamie said, casually. "They ain't banded."

Cooper grinned at him sideways. "Will they take my finger off?"

Jamie loved these guys—they kept setting him up for the classic vaudeville answers. "They'll take off your whole pecker—with your fingers attached," he said. This time they roared. Smitty kept pointing at him as if to say, *"Oh you . . . you. . . ."*

The lobster that Cooper gingerly pulled out was easily over three pounds, a gorilla. It was green and black, mottled as a calico kitten. Its tail muscles convulsed, flapping violently in Cooper's hand, startling him to the point of almost dropping it. Brandi shrieked and tried to hide behind Jonesy. They all stood over it, trying to touch it. It was a throwback, Jamie could tell without even putting a gauge to it—too big, too long to be a legal catch.

"Oh my God, I have to take a picture of this!" Brandi gasped and whirled behind her. She dug around in a bag and produced a small silver and black digital camera.

"You want me to take one of all of ya?" Jamie asked. His meaty knuckles stayed fast to the canopy.

"Oh yes!" Brandi said, delighted. Smitty's smile faltered for a moment as she leaned ponderously across the rail to hand her camera to Jamie. "Careful," he said as Jamie reached out for it.

"Don't worry, it's a piece of shit," Jonesy said. "She's already dropped it twice."

Jamie held the tiny silver electronic in his rough palms. No bigger than a credit card, it weighed as much as a pack of gum. He turned it over and heard Brandi instruct him to press the top button to the left.

"Does this thing take good pictures?" Jamie asked.

"Only if you've got $400 to spare," Smitty said, and coughed sharply into his hand. "It's got two integrated lenses and eight-point-zero megapixels. . . ." He continued describing its features, but the terms he used had no meaning for Jamie. He'd only ever had a regular camera with film; his parents had one of these digital things, but he'd never used it.

Jamie stared into the glowing viewfinder and snapped a few pictures while they stood for him, smiling.

"So what do you give for Maine lobsters down in Florida?" Jamie said.

They had no idea what he'd just said. Smitty cupped his hand to his ear. "What's that?"

"If you go to a restaurant down there," Jamie said slowly, trying to keep his syllables relatively clear, "how much would you typically pay for a Maine lobster?"

"Aw, well, if you're talking a good restaurant," Smitty said, rocking back on his heels, "not one of those lobster shacks where you have to take it apart yourself, oh, I'd say, easily a buck and change for two people."

"You can get 'em at the Sanibel Inn for a decent price," Jonesy added.

"Yeah, but those aren't Maine lobsters, those are the Bahamian kind," Cooper said. "They have those same ones down in St. Kitt's, remember? It's the. . . . What is it? The spiny lobsters—no claws. No good."

"Oh, they're good," Jonesy argued. "I mean, divers have to hand pick each one—they don't put 'em in traps."

"They're trash," Smitty said, as if the subject were closed. "I had a waitress who didn't know shit try to pass some lobster chowder off as if it was from Maine, and I could tell right away. You can always tell."

While they were talking, Jamie's ears picked up the sound of a far-off approaching boat. It was the *Maisie May*, Thongchai's boat.

"Why don't you hold that one up," Jamie said. And they grinned, holding the lobster up like big game fisherman posing with the bloodied remains of a great white. The lobster continued to protest furiously, assailing their faces and eyes with flailing saltwater.

In the distance, Thongchai's lobster boat plowed toward them, and soon everyone's attention turned as it slowed, closing in on *Delores*. As his boat came up, Thongchai cut the engine and drifted. The boats all staggered against the waves—two snub-nose boats like pit bulls growling down a groomed show dog. It was as if all the tracing paper of the yachties' smiles had been lifted up, leaving only their charcoal expressions. Behind the wheel stood Thongchai. He had an evil look on his face, his crazy broom-straw bangs stuck at angles under his cap. He saw his trap upon *The Wet Dream*'s deck, the warp and toggle hanging like a string off the side.

Thongchai threw down his cap and jumped up on the gunwale of his lobster boat, his lithe body balancing against the waves. He placed a hand on the railing of *The Wet Dream*, his even white teeth showing.

"Permission to board?" he said, sarcastically.

"Okay, okay," Jamie said, looking into the viewfinder, snapping some more pictures. "Easy there, guy." Brandi huddled behind Smitty. Jamie could see the anxiety shifting across their faces.

"Thongchai—just hold up a sec." Jamie looked at the camera, then to Smitty. "Look here—you've got six of them lobsters in that trap there, but you'll have to throw back that one in your hands cause it's illegal. Still, I'd say that was a pretty fair trade for a camera like this." Jamie held it out to Thongchai. "It's got eight megapixels—your mom could use one of these."

"You can't keep getting in the middle, Eugley," Thongchai said, stepping down off the gunwale. His cut-off flannel shirt exposed his brown, muscular arms.

"Well you can't keep banging heads, neither."

Thongchai became exasperated. "What the hell am I supposed to do?"

Jamie shrugged. "Tell them."

Only a sliver of Thongchai's white teeth showed through his

lips. He pointed at Smitty. "I'm fishing for my family—my father needs some help. And here you are taking lobsters from my trap like it's no big deal. How would you like me coming to your house and taking your car just cause it was sitting there?"

Jamie knew it would be a good, fine day out on the water. Plenty of time to just set for a while, soak up the sun. Jamie held fast to the canopy, turning his wrist to see the last image on the bitty camera. It was a good one of their faces the moment Thongchai began to board their boat. He leaned over the wash rail to hand the little camera to Thongchai. They looked at each other. There was nothing but bottle-green water for miles. The yachties were way out of their territory, a long way from the rules of civilization, where bribes, charm, an offered scotch on the rocks had no currency. They didn't like where this was going. No one did the full head turn to check with the others—it was more like pairs of eyes sliding left, sliding right, to figure out what to say next.

"Well," Smitty said after a bit. "See now, that's a really good camera."

Jamie regarded Smitty, dismayed. He had it all worked out peacefully, and now this yachtie wasn't smart enough to cut a deal. *This* was why he could never get a full day of work in. *This* was why he couldn't allow himself to mind his own business. Everyone always expected him to deal with these things. Jamie lost his good mood then, framing the flat edge of his palm over his face, shielding his eyes from the sun. He seemed to be looking long into the distance.

"You know how you had your golf club all wrapped up around that toggle when I came along?" Jamie said. "Just figure if I'd been Marine Patrol, you'd be looking at a $2,000 fine just for touching that trap."

"Feck that, you're lucky I didn't get here first," Thongchai said, low.

"Or you might want to consider that." Jamie stretched his hand out to his friend.

Smitty drew up, his jowls hunched back into his neck. "Well, we didn't know."

Thongchai snorted. "You didn't know. I'll tell ya what you didn't *know*. Now I'm gonna take that monogrammed boat shoe you're wearing and jam it up your ass sideways."

"Okay," Jamie said, his hand out. The last of Thongchai's patience was gone. His face had become as splotchy as Smitty's sunburn.

Brandi emerged behind the men, then. With tentative steps against the gentle rocking of the boat, she reached both hands out to grip the stainless cable rail, her furrowed, tanned face upon Thongchai. "We're really sorry," she said. "We would've never done this if we thought we were taking anything from your family."

Smitty had nothing to add to that—the other men couldn't look at anything but the deck or out to sea. It was clear from Thongchai's expression that Brandi had said what needed to be said—that today wasn't going to start off with a good old-fashioned ass bashing.

Jamie looked at Thongchai. "You good with that?"

"Sure enough." Thongchai pulled the camera back out of his pocket and stepped back up on the gunwale to hand it to Brandi. "I don't need this." She took it back, tentatively.

"And look—it ain't like something for nothin'," Jamie told Smitty, once Thongchai was back behind the wheel of his boat. "Keep the lobsters. That's six good-sized Maine lobsters out of this—none of that Florida lobster shack shit."

Pretty soon, it all made sense. The yachties didn't go out of their way to thank Jamie for sparing them, but it was a grudging few steps to get back to some civil smiles. And it warmed Jamie to think that later, when they served up some steamed lobsters and made makeshift bibs out of linen napkins, they'd be thinking about what that camera was worth as they captured the moment with nothing but their five senses. Still, with a little Glenfiddich, the camera incident would eventually turn into a raucous story for the boys down in the yacht showroom one night after work when Smitty finally got the chance to yank loose his sweaty tie.

TWO

On Sunday, no one could work. The whole community eased into an old-time dream; the men stayed at home, rolled the knots out of their shoulders, and drank a beer; the women corralled the family together to throw a supper on. Jamie was grateful for the Sunday law. He needed it badly, just one pretty sunshiny day at home, holed up not doing anything.

But Anja was staring at him hard. She was 160 pounds, a hellcat in the lotus position, sitting cross-legged on the floor in her white tank top, watching him. Her head tipped back and her siren wail rose up and over the room.

"AWWWWWWWWW. . . ."

"Anja."

"YOU LIE TO ME!"

"Come on, stop it. I told you yesterday we weren't going."

Her narrow almond eyes turned to slits. "You don't tell me that."

She still had problems with memory, insisting that he failed to give her the right information, when clearly, yesterday, he remembered saying to her he needed a day off.

She wrenched out of her sitting position and labored to stand, her hand bracing against a chair. "But you tolds us we could! You said!"

"Anja, I don't want to go to the beach. Christ, I friggin' spend my life on the water—can't we just do something else?"

"But Jamie. . . ." She began to hyperventilate. Her breathing hitched, turned to hiccups—and her plump child's face seemed impassioned with only one anguished thought. "You always go everywhere and I go nowhere."

The elephantine rocks at the beach cut a sharp relief against the ocean. All the families on the beach sat up by the meager patch of weed-choked sand under umbrellas. Anja stood by the lazy curling water, her blocky form in a sunflower two-piece. Her limbs were fluid as she wrung her hands. The sun warmed her peach face and tiny, stubby ponytail. She was doing some kind of interpretive dance with the waves that tumbled up on the beach; she lunged forward as they receded and jumped back as they surged. She whirled and glanced upward, discombobulated.

A nearby family on the beach stared at her. The children forgot to eat their sandwiches. The mother was arrested in the process of slathering what looked like Crisco on her bare arms.

Jamie found them a good spot on the giant smooth rocks away from the families and put down a ratty old towel. "Anja," Jamie called. She turned, lips apart, and looked toward his voice.

"Come up here."

A faded blue-jean sky met the straight line of the horizon as the hard, hot sun burned deeper into his reddened neck and arms. In the distance, islands off the coast looked like breaching whales. He gave a big, over-impatient wave. She began trotting toward him, pausing carefully in her sandals to step up the rocks. Her blocky form lumbered closer. Her pageboy cut was like a kindergartner's depiction of crayon hair, a straight horizontal line across her head framed by two vertical straight lines, one on each side. As she got closer, Jamie could see a strand of her blond hair stuck in the corner of her mouth. Her face opened into a grin, exposing her fine white teeth.

Anja squatted then and began to rinse her hands in a shallow pool of salt water in the rocks. A roll of belly fat pooched over her bikini bottom. She immediately discovered dead crabs on the rocks dropped by seagulls and sniffed one. Jamie watched next, as she put the dead crab legs too close to her mouth.

"Anja!" he called sharply. Startled, she dropped the crab and looked at him.

"What the hell are you doing?"

"Nothing."

"Come here, ding-ding."

She sniffed her fingers and shuffled over to him, trying to stick them under his nose. She wheezed out a laugh as the wind whipped her short blond bangs sideways across her forehead.

"Cut it out now, come on," Jamie said, pulling a square of tin foil from the boat bag. "Want your sandwich?"

"No."

"Yeah you do."

"You eat it."

"No, it's for you."

She eyed his beer. "Gimme that." She clutched the can, white foam spilling down her chin. "Gosh," she said, breathing hard. She blinked as if she'd just scared herself.

There was a summer night when they'd first been dating under a moon on this very beach. They'd been sitting on an old driftwood log, sharing a beer. He could not get over how much he loved the combination of her brown eyes and her blond hair; it was as if he'd never before considered how warm and inviting that particular match of coloring could be. And from that moment forward, he would never be attracted to a black-haired, blue-eyed girl again. There she'd been, this elfin face with dimples, radiant with good health and . . . happy. Who had he known in his life who was ever effortlessly happy?

"So, what are your folks like?" he'd asked. His folks had been together for twenty-five years, woven into the community like dog hair into a sweater, everything seamless, as natural as a simple in-nocent question like "So, what are your folks like?" But in her eyes, it looked as if a wind had come through and snuffed out a lantern. And it was the first indication he'd had that Anja wasn't all that happy. She'd had a life that didn't include Sunday bean suppers, multi-family cribbage parties, lazy days with cousins stirring lakes with sticks. Her mother, whom he would later meet, was one of

27

those unmemorable mothers who seemed to have given birth without thought, as if it was just the thing people did, like celebrate Christmas or vote. Unlike his own blustery childhood always fishing, battering around in the snow or waves, fighting at the supper table, Anja's had been one of passive moments, card games of Solitude and hours of TV. Nothing horrible—no skeleton-in-the-closet alcoholism (no more than in his own family), nothing sexual, no beatings. But when he'd asked her about her folks and saw the light in her eyes snuffed out, he began to ask more questions.

He learned that she'd grown up outside of Boston, flung to one school, back to another, where she made no friends and spent her lunchtime by herself rather than face a cafeteria of kids who all had grown up together. Her mother was depressed, had literally locked herself in her bedroom for two years when Anja was 13. Her father had done the paternity two-step. In their life. Out. Back in, then out for good.

The night he'd asked about her family as she handed him back the beer, Jamie put an arm around her and said nothing. But looking up at the sky, he squeezed her slight body to his ribs. He didn't know how long they were going to last, or what other circumstances might change their lives. If he ended up being a complete fuckhead and ruined everything in one unforeseen moment (which, truthfully, could've happened; for all his best intentions, he knew he wasn't that together) he still knew that if she stayed with him, he could keep her happy.

Later, very much in love with her, that initial feeling of protectiveness surged. The ever-present arm on her back or around her waist wasn't just a demonstration to the world that this was his girl. He realized he was lucky to hold onto someone as good and beautiful and exceptional as Anja. He felt even more determined to make up for the desolate childhood and threw her into experiences that would prick her senses: camping under huge stars, climbing trees, four-wheeling up mountains, rope swinging into deep, cold quarries. He loved to see that giddy look on her face, and he took her canoeing for the first time in her life. Made her dig for clams. All the stuff Maynard had done for him, he tried to do for her. And it had been an awakening. After several years, the lonely Boston girl had become the Maine girl, and she actually enjoyed wearing rolled-up jeans and getting grubby, standing on his boat, the salt spray in her hair and eyelashes. The only thing he kept her away from was lobstering; he didn't care if women like Susie Q. had grown up doing it. It was dangerous, no place for women.

"Bleah," Anja said, handing him back his beer. There was foam on her chin.

"Told ya," Jamie said. He regarded her stomach, the way it ballooned against the thin fabric of her bathing suit. She'd been eating too much, it looked as if she'd been on a steady diet of donuts and Yoo-hoo for months.

"I think you're getting a little on-front there sweet-ay," Jamie said.

"What?"

"A little. . . ." He patted her belly. "You know." She didn't get what he was driving at. She had a hard time inferring meanings now.

"I haven't been buying junk food. What have you been eating?"

She looked at the rocks. "The cheese-orange things and um, chippy topatos, and I likes the nuts. The curly ones."

"Cashews?"

"Yeah."

"Who's giving you this stuff?"

"Carolyn," she said and he nodded, realizing he'd have to have a talk with her caretaker.

"What about carrots?"

Anja squinted at him. "Carrots?"

"Yeah, carrots. What if I pack your lunch with carrots?"

"I won't eat him," she said.

"Why not?" Jamie persisted.

"They not curly." She became impatient with this talk and declared, "I'm going now." Anja left the rocks and went whirling and scampering off into the sand. The family who'd been staring at her sat under an umbrella surrounded by a hamper of food and sodas like stuffed dolls in a crib. They followed Anja with dull, stupid expressions. The mother, with the Crisco all over her arms, observed her with her aggravating lips hanging open. He ignored them and walked down to the shore where the sand became dark and damp. Anja stood by the edge as the froth inched toward her toes. She backed up, avoiding the water as it seeped into the gray sand.

"Go ahead," he encouraged.

"COLD."

"Just put your toes in."

Anja began to trot in place as the surf ran over the tops of her feet. She began to wring her hands, her face a contortion of pain and excitement. It was silly, he thought. She'd been in water before; she took a bath every day. It was almost crazy what new phobias emerged; every day was something.

The water reached her ankles and this undid her. For no apparent reason Anja threw her arms around his neck, one leg trying to scooch up on his hip. "Holy," Jamie said, thrown off balance. "Christ, Anja, what are. . . ?" She'd managed to heave herself halfway up onto his back, her arms clamped around his windpipe.

Her weight forced him into an awkward canter. Jamie began to sidestep into the water as Anja muckled on, her arms choking his neck.

"Jamie get out!" she screeched, her voice piercing his ear. "GET OUT OF THE WATER!"

He actually saw her voice in color right then—as shrill as it had been, he saw the words in bright pink and orange. He continued to shamble involuntarily sideways, deeper into the water. This was not where either of them had intended to go. He felt it happening, could not stop it. He felt they were both about to fall, and rocky Maine beaches were no fun to fall on. The water was up to his shins, his feet painfully hobbling over the sharp rocks. At the last second, he hurled Anja into the deeper water, dumping her off like a heavy bag of grain so she wouldn't be hurt. Years ago, this would've been funny, both of them popping out of the freezing water momentarily astonished, then cackling.

Anja stood up, seawater to her waist, her dark blond hair melded to her head. Her eyes looked like she'd just found a murdered child in a patch of weeds. She opened her throat and screamed.

Jamie scrambled to stand. "Hey, it's okay."

Anja screamed in ragged waves, hands wringing, eyes wild. Now the entire beach was watching. She was behaving as if she were drowning in waist-high water.

"Anja, I'm right here," Jamie said, sloshing toward her. "Put your arms around me." But she would not move, and in his ear he continued to see pink and orange sound waves, wavering blasts of high-pitched fusillade.

"Goddammit."

Jamie had to drag her out of the water, her body weirdly both stiff and limp. Once he'd gotten her back on cold, pebbled sand, Anja began to sob. She was dripping, her body hunched. Her little-kid brown eyes were anguished and he could see she blamed him. *Why did you do that to me?*

"Okay," Jamie said, rubbing her shoulders vigorously. "It was just a little water. All right."

Of course, everyone judged him as he led Anja back to the blanket on the rocks. The small-town court of appeals. Families with their brows rutted with misunderstanding over what just happened. He'd done something to make her cry. And the whispers. *She ain't right, you know.* They all watched him with the steel mouth, the steel eye, as Jamie trudged with Anja up the sand beach back to the rocks. The Crisco mom and her fat family judged him too. The two kids with their entire mouths stained Kool-Aid red. The mother closed her parted lips, holding them in a priggish line as they passed.

All he wanted to do was get away, get back in his truck, the dust from his back wheels kicking up and obliterating all the twisted gossip that would follow him home, to the breakfast counter, to the wharf, to his family. *Jesus, did you see Jamie Eugley with his girl last Sunday? I heard he tried to hold her under. After everything she's been through? No shit.* Classic. Classic day at the beach.

The high-pitched squall of a gull careened overhead. Jamie

walked to the parking lot, past the white fence buried in the sand, his cap low, his mouth working with curses. At once he turned to tell Anja to keep up but she wasn't there. She had dawdled, hanging back at the gray smooth rocks, and now she was hunched down over something. Jamie grimaced and turned, his feet trying to stomp through sand. He found a jagged path down to her and was about to snap at her. Anja looked up at him, her finger touching something. In the indentation of a rock, there was a small pool shaped roughly like a kid's drawing of a heart, weird as that was. A heart of seawater. "Look Jamie." She was smiling bright. "I found for you!"

THREE

Driving by shacks, past tilty barns literally buckling over, this was the way to see the real Maine, not the side the Chamber of Commerce served up in the glossy guidebooks. Of course there were also crab apple trees and white churches. A stand of dark pine in front of a pale green field next to a half-moon little beach. But where they lived was still the Maine of the Depression years, the derelict trailers made of faux wood stained by rust, large rocks painted lavender with the family name, piles of garbage in the dooryard next to truck caps, plows. Broken trampolines punctuated by a fat guy sitting bare-chested on the bowed deck of his tarpaper shack giving the hairy eyeball to anyone who drove by.

And truthfully, Jamie still preferred this look. In the last decade, the waterfront near his neighborhood had transformed into a sprawl of architectural design. "Cottages" took the place of century-old saltboxes—new mini-mansions were being built every season and none of them could make up their minds: columns, dormers, colonnades, double cedar decks, trapezoid windows, nothing less than two and a half stories. It worried him to see this erosion of the TV dinner–looking trailers, as nasty as they were. He got the impression that the mini-mansions were playing a game of "Stop and Go" with the shit shacks all along the coast. When people's backs were turned, the smiling, nice houses were creeping closer and closer.

To get his mother on this topic was to invite a litany of outrage.

K. Stephens

Someone bought the old Parker Snow house in his parents' neighborhood—a stark harborfront property with the kind of deepwater access a fisherman could rarely find anymore. The house had been on the market a single day when a man drove up to the realtor's office and wrote a personal check on the spot.

"A check!" Donna railed to Jamie and Anja, her hair in a ponytail, a cigarette on her lips. She stood over the stove. "You buy friggin' eggs and milk with a check. Not a friggin' house!" Jamie was beginning to regret stopping over with Anja after the beach. "Yeah—that's what we need," she seethed, "a bunch of check-writing dipshits moving into the neighborhood—"

Her prejudice against check writers went a long way back. She was the daughter of a lobsterman, married a lobsterman, and lobstermen did not write checks. They paid in cash and most certainly kept their cash in shoeboxes, not a bank. She had grown up without a credit card either and refused to use one. His parents owned a brand-new vinyl-sided Cape overlooking one of the most spectacular views of Penobscot Bay. His mother didn't care that the house looked as if it had been pre-assembled in a Midwestern factory like every other new house in Maine —the fact was, it had been paid for in cash. And growing up in the post-Depression years, his mother had had enough of the type of house that was poorly heated, with rotted floors and blackened walls. This one wasn't a hundred years old, it didn't break every six months, and it contained not one goddamn antique.

From the kitchen, Jamie could see the back deck where his father stood, smoke curling up from the grill. Old metal traps lined the side yard. Beyond the lawn, the ocean laid out like a thick blue spread. It was late in the day, the sun hidden behind the trees, warming silky waves in tangerine. Inside the kitchen, his mother and Anja kept watch over two pots of boiling lobsters on the stove. It was the warm, claustrophobic smell of a thousand family get-togethers, those boiling lobsters, familiar as the smell of his own pillow.

Jamie wandered into the living room, found his brother-in-law Jeff on the sofa by himself, watching the game. Jeff made no move to get up.

"How's yer bug?" Jeff said, lifting his beer by way of greeting. The glare of the TV refracted blue off Jeff's big, misshapen head, which his skimpy blond fringe did little to cover. Jamie felt a little sorry for Jeff, who always seemed to be the last one to get the sly finger-against-the-nose gesture—the "not-It" signal—and by the time Jeff had knocked up Jamie's sister, Amanda, with their first child while they were still in high school, it was too late to call *Not It*.

"It's the bottom of the ninth. The Sox are up four runs," Jeff said, eyes on the game.

"Yup." Jamie stood, staring at the TV with Jeff for a few moments, to be polite. For Jeff, that was heartfelt communication. Usually, they covered the predictable round of topics: Jeff's drywall job, the weather, the Sox, fly fishing, the latest job over on the island, and how bad the deer flies were. Jamie waited to see if Jeff would say anything else, knowing, of course, he wouldn't, but he stood there more to delay having to go out to the back deck and greet his father. Jeff brought his beer to his lips every few seconds.

There was no sense in hiding out with Jeff, whose eyes did not leave the TV. The time had come. Jamie left the living room and opened the sliding screen door to the back deck.

"There he is—Jesus Christ," James Senior said, as if he'd been waiting for hours. He stood at the grill with a Camel in his clamped lips.

"Hey, Dad."

Senior's square head, rubbery nose and close-cropped gray hair gave the impression he'd been in the military, though he hadn't. The spatula and grill scraper were like extensions of his arms. He made an exaggerated show of glancing at his watch. "Jesus, thought that truck of yours shit the bed. Told your mother I'd probably have to go lookin' for ya, probably find you on the road hitchhiking or something."

"Nope," Jamie forced a smile. "We were just at the beach."

"So," Senior said with a slow, lazy smile. "What did you pull yesterday?" Standard question regarding lobster catch. What did he pull? Jamie always wanted to say, *My groin*.

"A little under a hundred pounds," Jamie said. "How about you?"

Senior's grin remained fixed. "Wouldn't you like to know?" That was his typical answer, which Jamie always found ridiculous. Talking about catch was typically guarded among strangers, but not among family.

"I was the first one out of the harbor yesterday morning. Last one in, too," Senior said, spatula prodding at the grill. "Three weeks now, me and Doug Kane been the only ones out there at three-thirty a.m., while the rest of you was still snuggled up in your footy pajamas." He gave Jamie a sharp wink.

Really? Jamie wanted to say. Up at three-thirty a.m., *OUT-STAND-ING.* He wanted to pound his fist against his palm. That is *FAN-TASTIC.* Last one in the harbor, too? That is *STUPENDOUS.* Holy shit, where's the phone? Does Channel 6 know?

Donna and Anja pushed the slide door open. "Anja, help me clear the table," Donna said, laying down a platter of burgers, brats, steamed lobster. Placed in the middle of the table like a center-piece were plastic and glass bottles of two kinds of ketchup and mustard, A-1, relish, and Louisiana hot sauce.

"So how 'bout you, Ma?" Jamie asked.

"How 'bout me, what?"

"What did you pull this week?" Anja sat down next to him.

Donna pondered that question, sipping her beer. "A rabbit out of my ass, basically." A variation on *My groin.* He loved it. Ma was quick on the uptake. He loved that she wasn't one of those dull, free-spending, gossipy highliner's wives with nothing to do. She had a sharp mind and wit, and a job as a town selectman in Owls Head. She also had a Scotch-Irish temper that could peel wallpaper and turn an ordinary town meeting on dump fees or boat ordi-nances into a screaming match.

Donna sat down next to Jamie at the picnic table and picked up a fork. "See this tomato?" She stabbed a little round cherry tomato in the salad bowl, causing the seeds to squirt out. "That's Barbara Dunner's eyeball."

Whenever the night started on a Barbara Dunner story, Jamie

was all for it. To get his mother on any host of topics was fun, especially when her wrath was directed at someone else—but to get her on a Barbara Dunner story was to practically sit back with a bowl of popcorn.

The feud had begun in grade school, carried through middle school, and simmered into a hot rage through high school. Known then as Barbie Dunner, she wore good dresses and pink makeup, whereas Donna, comfortable in her chunky Levi's and a ponytail, wore the same standard rural attire every day, a plaid long-sleeve over a rock concert T-shirt. Barbie wanted to be school president and homecoming queen and bragged in the school newspaper that someday a woman was going to be president of the United States, and the name of that woman would be Barbara Dunner. To which Donna responded loudly in class, No one would ever elect a woman whose name was synonymous with a dumb blond doll. To which Barbie declared in the cafeteria in front of Donna's friends that she shouldn't eat so many corn dogs, for they weren't doing her figure any favor. During marching practice for graduation, they'd finally had it out in the parking lot, where the words "cheap slut" and "fat troll" had been bandied through the air like a marcher's baton.

It only got worse. Three years ago Barbara Dunner had moved smack into Donna's territory, running for the vacant seat on the Owls Head town select board. Jamie remembered a distinct moment when his mother had thrown an entire pot of spaghetti off the porch after she'd gotten the phone call that Barbara had been voted in.

Since then, Barbara Dunner had become known for trying to revolutionize the town. She tried to get a national coffee chain a special permit to build a little store next to the gas station. The town went ballistic. At a special meeting that filled every seat, the vote was widely defeated, at which point Barbara Dunner was heard to exclaim, "I didn't move from Camden to Owls Head to drink trucker's coffee." It was a statement that would become a local catchphrase for years, morphing into other variations: *Jee-zus, I didn't move here to get woken up by lobster boats at 4:30 in the morning* or *Christ almighty, I certainly didn't move here to have to smell bait next to my condo.*

"What's Barbie doing now?" Jamie asked.

"You don't want to know," Senior said, stabbing at a sausage and flipping it.

"Really?" Donna said, staring at Senior. "Maybe he does want to hear about it."

"Maybe I don't want to hear about it."

"Gee Jim." Donna laid her arm across the picnic table. "I'm glad you know everything. Too bad the position of God is already taken." She rolled her eyes. She was the only one who got away with that kind of back talk to Senior. He was more afraid of her temper than she was of his.

"Get this," Donna said. "*Now* she wants to bring an international film festival here. She thinks we're not doing enough to 'put ourselves on the map.' "

"Are you kidding?" Jamie said. "Why do we even want to be on the friggin' map?"

"Exactly—Anja, darlin', do you want a lobster?"

Beside him Anja picked at her food, wordless. She was in that lethargic fog when she got overstimulated. Jamie bumped her knee with his own, trying to snap her out of it. Behind that blank stare of hers, he wondered if there were deeper thoughts processing in that secluded mind.

Anja's hand tentatively reached to the middle of the table to drag a lobster by its walking leg to her plate.

"You just had chicken," Jamie said, trying to put it back.

"Nooo—nooooooo," she said, her breath hitching.

"It's got no cholesterol," Donna offered.

"She doesn't need it."

Donna patted Anja's hand. "Just let her have the tail."

"Ma—she doesn't. . . ."

The front door slammed then—they could hear it reverberate all the way to the back of the house. The kids came storming through the kitchen, followed by Amanda, who barked after them. "I said TAKE THAT OUT OF YOUR MOUTH!"

His sister's voice had a way of making Jamie's teeth hurt. Amanda shoved through the open screen door, her beamy hips barely clearing the doorjamb. "They didn't have no red-top—I had to get *two percent.*" She made a flat frog-like expression of her mouth and stood out on the deck, tugging at her oversized Bugs Bunny T-shirt over black leggings. She had the classic hogger body—a kangaroo pouch of flesh below the belt line and a rear-end waggling like the transom of an old boat. Her two oldest boys pushed past her and began to tumble into the back lawn.

"Hey, quit shoving, *IDIOTS!*" she yelled. They stopped, frozen.

"Don't talk to the boys like that," Donna snapped.

"They ran right into me, Ma!" Amanda rarely spoke in a normal voice. Even at 25, with three kids, she still sounded like she was moments from slamming her bedroom door and throwing herself onto her pink-canopied bed.

"Maybe they just had a hard time getting around you," Jamie said.

"WHAT? *WHAT?*"

Behind her, Jeff walked out to the deck carrying the baby, with a beaten-down look upon his face.

"Um," he said, holding out the baby to Amanda. "It's wet."

"Well CHANGE IT!" she said, pushing past him back through the screen door. Inside they could hear her pounding the refrigerator door. "Ma, where'd ya put the brandy?"

Everyone tried not to stare at Jeff, with the leaking baby held in his outstretched arms and his shiny pink prematurely bald head. But then it was hard to know which was ultimately worse, to be ugly and not that bright or to be married to Amanda.

At 19, Jeff still had a full head of blond hair and big dreams of owning a Camaro with a spoiler. Back then, Jeff and Amanda's courting ritual consisted of drunken fights, drunken make-up sex, and jealous rages. Cheating on each other preceded vindictive sex with each other's friends, followed by make-up sex, followed by brief reconciliations. Amanda dropped out of high school six weeks shy of graduation, four months along.

By the time she was 17, Amanda was sneaking shots of Allen's Coffee Brandy from the bottle in the kitchen before breakfast and hanging out with frazzled divorced women in their fifties at the Tide Out Pub. Her weeknight outfit wasn't complete without a tube top, a pair of skin-tight Spandex pants, and three toe rings. She'd squeeze into her clothes, tease her rotini bangs, and trowel on the makeup.

One time, following the birth of the first baby, Jamie had stumbled upon Amanda as she nursed the child at their parents' house, with a rocks glass of coffee brandy in one hand, the baby in the other. Holding her big breast, she squirted a few streams of milk into her coffee brandy, stirred it with her finger, and drank her own home-made version of the Rockland Martini while cooing to the baby.

By the time the child had turned one, Amanda had broken up with Jeff and moved in with a new boyfriend, a coke dealer from Rockland who owned a billiards room. Word got around that Amanda was bragging to numerous people that he "did" her on the pool tables late at night after everyone left. For a fishing family's reputation, particularly one that Grandfather Maynard had taken sixty years to build as a respected highliner, she'd done enough in one year to drive the good, respected name of Eugley straight to the gutter. Following the month the coke dealer was busted, she announced she was pregnant again. This time, the father was a sailor in the Coast Guard and the night had been a hogger dream. She couldn't even remember his name to put on the birth certificate.

There was almost a community-wide sigh of relief when Amanda and Jeff got back together. The only one who'd felt uneasy was Jamie, who never really disliked Jeff or his big misshapen head. He'd always felt guilty he hadn't done more to dissuade Jeff from marrying his sister—he always felt he should've slipped him fifty bucks and helped him map out a sled trail to Canada.

The night before the wedding, Jeff had gotten obliterated at his own bachelor party. The genital warts the stripper had given him that night (he would later discover) had been humiliating enough, but that was secondary to a moment during the ceremony the next day when he was sweating, barely standing, during the Kahlil Gibran two-strings-of-a-lute passage. Finally he couldn't help it and regurgitated into his hand, which, unfortunately, several people in the front row didn't see coming.

FOUR

To be fair, Amanda hadn't been the only one to tank the Eugley name at an early age. Back in the days when a kid could still pose with a shotgun braced against his thigh for his high school yearbook picture, Jamie Eugley was NOTED FOR: *Burnouts in the parking lot and lobstering.* CRAZY ABOUT: *Novas and burnouts.* BEST MEMORIES: *quarry parties w/Thongchai and S.B.* PET PEEVE: *Chevys.* SECRET IDOL: *Grandfather.* FUTURE PLANS: *To own a Beals boat and party with every member of Metallica.* WILL: *To leave the high school one big burnout in the parking lot.*

In his senior year, wearing cut-off shorts and no shoes or helmet, Jamie jumped on a motorcycle at a house party and tore down the dark street at 60, then 70 miles an hour. He bombed across lawns, up and over hill backs, tearing up turf and flower beds. He ripped back toward the house, past friends who yelled at him with hands cupped around their mouths to stop. Sirens in the distance. Someone had called the cops, and in Jamie's dim perception, he decided it would be a fantastic idea to open up the throttle and zip back toward all the people from the party now standing at the edge of the lawn screaming at him. He'd tear by them one last time and, to make it even more spectacular, the moment he went by he'd execute a perfect wheelie, the kind he'd seen Evel Knievel do. Just a quick-thrust downward bounce and then one-wheel up in a resplendent, camera-ready pose.

It took a full week after that spring evening before they let him out of the hospital. And another week after that before they allowed him to go back to school. With two broken legs, Jamie had mastered a stiff, unbending waddle—two crutches out, swing, two casts out, swing. He returned to school a legend. Girls came up to him wanting to know how it happened, wanting to write on his casts. Even the toughest rednecks, the kind who went to school during the week and spent time in jail on the weekends, even these guys had to slap him on the back and convey in their own way that what he'd done was *frickin' awesome.* And so it had been a decent trade: excruciating pain for some all-out glory.

When the yearbook came out, and most seniors' FUTURE PLANS included *Sleeping 'til noon,* the yearbook committee voted Jamie "Most Likely to Get Out of a Cast When He's 40." That was no joke. Besides the motorcycle crash, he'd also suffered a broken clavicle, a broken ankle from jumping off a roof, and a collapsed lung from another drunk-driving incident involving a ride-on lawnmower.

His family got tired of visiting him in the hospital. His father told him if he didn't get his shit together, he was going to buy him a drawer in the morgue. And it *was* eerie. Why did some people cheat death over and over while others only got one chance? Statistically he should have died at ten different times in his young life, what with the motorcycle accident, the fights, the drinking and driving, the firearms, the time he and The Kid rolled the VW, and of course the close call when Frank Healey blew off two fingers with a bottle rocket. ("Is it going?" "I don't know, I can't tell.") Ten seconds earlier, it would've been Jamie's right ear.

He'd gotten his dual casts off two weeks after graduation and was not sorry to see the magic-marker graffiti-covered plaster split in half and fall away. There, greenish, puckered, and nearly translucent, like the thick fleshy stems of Indian Pipe, were his stunted legs. Standing up he felt cartoonish, like a newborn foal wobbling. He thought he'd immediately start running, leaping, playing baseball again, but the two sweaty wool socks that cushioned the armpits of his crutches were not ready to be thrown away. The stupid crutches were still necessary. Jamie continued to sit around the house, exercising his frail legs in the hot, listless days of summer. His friends were all out lobstering, making money. It was shaping up to be a mad summer of making money.

In August, he could no longer take the pent-up feeling of boredom and restlessness bashing around inside him. He announced to his family he was leaving Maine. He wanted to get in his Ford and keep driving, restless to see something other than shags and waves, traps and local girls. He began to pore over maps and routes, with no real destination in mind. Later in his life, when he'd become more hemmed in and superstitious in ways even he couldn't have predicted, he'd envy the days when he was open to all possibility and danger. But back then he was restless. He was reckless.

When the day had finally come, Jamie was anxious to leave. He'd woken at three and, too excited to sleep, walked down the road until the sun came up and then came back home for breakfast. He said goodbye to his family, thanked his mother for the pancakes, steak and beans, shook his father's hand, and took the envelope of money slipped to him.

The Ford took him across the northern part of the United States through the long, yawning midday hours, past flat, uninspiring landscapes, places he'd never in a million years live. He only stopped in Ely, Minnesota, because he liked the way it looked on the map—a town surrounded by shards of boundary waters with their endless mysterious channels. He ended up staying for a few weeks when a crew of canoe outfitters talked him into a playing a pool tournament four nights in a row. The town's only pub sold Leinenkugel beer for 75 cents. The cold nights reminded him a little of home, along with the touristy log cabin gift shops and the stuffed moose dolls.

Eventually Jamie moved north, into Portland, Oregon, and used his savings to stay at a youth hostel. He left his truck and walked everywhere, finding a city full of people his age, kids who seemed smart, fast, moody, in a hurry. He watched one kid on a skateboard soar up on concrete steps, ride a long metal railing, and smash back down. He watched a young black man cross-legged by the subway pounding a set of homemade drums. A dirty, disheveled woman with fetid breath harassed him for money, squinting up her right eye at him.

"You got a quarter?"

"No," Jamie said.

"Bullshit. Gimme a dollar."

"Um . . . no."

"All right, wait here," the woman said, walking off. "I'm gonna go get my man to stab you."

His third night in Portland, he sat stupefied in the lobby of the hostel, unable to watch any more people do any more things. But there they were anyway, a gaggle of outdoorsy women with loud voices and backpacks, barking at one another in loud camaraderie, holding hands and badgering the hostel clerks to make more green tea. His roommates on the boys' side of the hostel came in and out of the room twenty times a night, all night. Everybody seemed to have a purpose. More than that, a confidence, a sense of absolute assurance of his or her place. In Portland. In the country. Maybe that was the way everybody felt outside of Maine. Sitting there in the lobby, Jamie wondered what the fuck he was doing. Here he was clearly in the minority, a hick kid from the sticks. He wondered if he'd made a big mistake. The faces at the hostel ranged from pearly to mahogany; the languages a crazy mix of southern drawls, clipped British, a gobbledygook of German, French, and Arabic. He wrote The Kid a postcard that night. *Lots of people here,* he wrote. *It's hard to even know what to do.* And since his insecurity seemed so revealing, Jamie tried to lighten the mood before signing off. *Smoke one for me.*

That night it rained. The next day it rained. The following three weeks it rained, and a restless cloak began to tighten at Jamie's neck. He could take the crazies at the hostel for only so long, and their incessant chatter about where they were from, where they were so assuredly going, as he forded the street rivers at the curbs with his soaked and falling-apart boots. He walked into a dark-walled café with hurricane lamps on the six tiny tables. He didn't know if he wanted coffee or not; in fact, he had no goddamned interest in anything other than getting out of the rain and into someplace quiet. He missed Maine, the long stretches of woods, with no sound, no people.

When he walked in, it was four in the afternoon, as gloomy outside as if it had been evening. The tables each had a lit lamp; the room was done in red velvet chairs and red wallpaper. He sat and took a black coffee from the waitress and fixed his gaze on a piece of art on the far wall. A kid's yellow Tonka truck had been attached to the canvas and surrounded by charcoal words: "Remember," "Remiss," and "Recreate."

The waitress caught him staring at it. "Do you like it?" she said, refilling his cup. And she stood back, one hand holding the coffee pot, the other on her hip, to gaze at it. "I think it sucks," she said. She had long black hair parted into two messy buns like Princess Leia and a cotton blouse with silver threads.

"I don't know," Jamie said, staring harder at it. "I don't know if I get it." He sipped his coffee. He noticed she was still standing there. There was a slight burr in her tone. "What don't you get?"

"I don't know." He tilted his head. "What does it mean?"

"Oh my Christ," she snorted and left the table, brushing past the hanging red beads into the kitchen. Jamie stared at the red beads, then at the Tonka truck. He looked at his watch. The waitress came back out a moment later and yanked a chair to sit down with him. "It's about lost *youth*," she said, her black thin brows in an angry scowl. "Don't you know never to ask what a piece of art *means*? It means what it means. It's *art*."

Jamie blinked. "Holy crap."

"What?" she accused.

"Didn't you just tell me you thought it sucked?"

"That was my opinion—what's yours?"

"I . . . I really don't have one."

She put her hand on her chest. "That is my piece. Do you really think it sucks?"

He didn't know what to say. Something in her expression softened. "You're probably not from here."

45

"No." Jamie eyed her warily. "I'm from Maine."

"Oh," she sniffed. "That's why. You don't know crap about crap yet."

He'd never had a girlfriend before, but "weren't no ver-gin nei-ther," he was quick to point out to Pia the first night they slept together. She was the most intense person he'd ever met, and her love, as he would soon discover, was sharp and pointy. She was a mixed-media artist with a chip on her shoulder, a girl who'd never been to art college, who *didn't have the goddamned time or money to sit around all day drinking espresso and talking about Cézanne,* she once told him. She was determined to break into the Portland art scene and her plan, he discovered, was not so much to seduce the critics but rather to hunt them down and stab them in the neck. Jamie never met somebody so angry about her passion and found her fas-cinating. She had dark eyes that were always darting, thinking, and a large nose out of proportion to her face, which in quieter mo-ments almost made her vulnerable. She was a girl who didn't care about boys, who didn't glom onto him the way Maine girls did. Pia had a path of her own, and the more time he spent around her, the more he was happy to listen and learn. What did he know? When it came to artistic ability, he was little more than a slab of spiral ham.

In a month, he was living with Pia and meeting her friends, the kind of groovy people his friends back home would not understand. Part of him wanted to laugh at them too; God, some of them were so fancy and uptight. But he felt like an ambassador of redneck as he went with them to gallery openings. Jamie was determined to be open, to give everything a try at least once, and he found he actu-ally enjoyed listening to them complain and gossip bitterly about the artists who'd made it yet had the talent of a doorknob.

He allowed Pia to buy him a pair of city shoes; they were thick-soled, dull black, the kind that worked well with black chinos, a satiny cuffed and collared shirt. Pia tried to buy him a velvet-col-lared smoking jacket—*It's retro,* she insisted—but it was the equiva-lent of asking him to wear a dress in public. He made her take it back. The shoes, however, were shitkickers made in England with translucent soles the color of rubber glue. He liked the way they looked and chucked his ever-present Timberlands in the closet. One night before they went out, he spent thirty minutes battling his past with his outfit in the mirror. *I won't get away with this,* he thought. *I'm gonna get my ass kicked.* He'd never actually before owned an ensemble of color-coordinated clothes, much less anything referred to as *an outfit.*

At the party, when it was clear no one gave a rat's ass about what he was wearing, it jolted him to realize that he'd always cared too much what people thought. From his family name to the lobster code, he was reared under the tight scrutiny of others, who ironically considered themselves fiercely independent thinkers. Yet no one could wear anything but jeans and cords, and they couldn't be any fruity color like red, and music had to be country or hard core, it couldn't be alternative or new. No one could talk about death or dying or where souls went when they died, or if people even had souls to begin with. These were the kinds of conversations Pia and her friends had regularly over coffee, in cab rides. Whereas in his family, to mention death was to court it. When his grandfather or father talked about a bad day on the ocean, they deliberately avoided using the words "ocean" and "sea" and "waves," but instead used code words, like "the old girl" and "across the bay," so the ocean wouldn't take offense and retaliate. Everything was buried code and even his words had to follow a certain line; they had to be corralled like a trailer-park dog behind a tightly enclosed fence. To use new words or words with larger meanings basically invited derision. *What? Did you just say con-vo-lu-ted? What are ya, a fuckin' dictionary?*

Jamie wore the shoes everywhere. He tried Japanese food for the first time and suffered through Middle Eastern food. Hey, it wasn't all fabulous. He bought a mountain bike and began biking on the winding public concrete trails every day after work, building his legs back up to their former strength. In doing so, he lost 20 pounds and forgot to drink as much. Every day there was something new to explore. He had enough money to keep him going and a girlfriend.

Pia came home one afternoon and jumped on the bed. "I'm gonna have my portrait done!" she yelled, and banged the pillows. "It's gonna be part of a collection at The Jury!" She'd taught him enough to know that the gallery four blocks away called The Jury was a rundown little place for beginning artists. It wasn't earth-shattering news. "Why are you posing for a painting?" Jamie said, not matching her enthusiasm. "Why aren't you getting your own stuff at The Jury?"

"Because I'm getting my portrait done," she said coldly. "That's why."

"Well, who is this guy? Do you have to take off your clothes?"

She stood over him. "Yeah. It's a nude, Jamie. You generally have to take off your clothes when it's a nude portrait."

"Bullshit," he said.

She was like a force wind hauling up and backing around. "He's a real painter! And he challenges my mind!" She threw her hand at him. "What do you know about real art? Do you fucking do anything? No—you just sit around watching the Animal Channel."

That wasn't true—he'd tried to read the books she'd assigned. He'd pulled out a child's set of watercolors one night and tried to remember the dazzling colors of the sea through the cheap plastic brush, but the grinding memories of dark gray sea against dark gray rock, the fish oil smell of his babyhood, these images didn't come out in happy, primary colors.

True, he did like his TV a little too much. But he wasn't an artist. And he never claimed to be. The more Pia hounded him to be like her and take a maniacal interest in the things she found interesting, the less enthusiastic he was to try it. Weeks later, Jamie came back to the apartment one night to find her spreading a viscous fluid onto a canvas. It was threaded with blood. "Good God," he said. "What the hell is *that?*"

Pia didn't bother to look up but continued to knead the clear slime across the canvas. "It's my new piece."

"But what is *it?*" He kept pointing. He'd never seen something so disgusting in his life. And her hands were completely in it.

"It's Jodie's placenta. She gave it to me. I'm going to tack it up and let it dry on this canvas. Then I'm gonna glue-gun pictures of dead fetuses onto Lucite and make them the centerpiece."

"Uh huh."

She raised her sticky hands to him. "It's about women, you know? The way that the world oppresses them, all right? And it's about babies, and . . . I don't know . . . I just got the placenta today."

"Wow, that's wow . . . that's. . . ." No words for this. He scratched his chin as she spread her hands in a concentric motion across the canvas. "So, do you really think anyone's gonna want to put that up on their wall when it's done?" he asked.

She scowled, displeased.

That same burst of energy Jamie had felt the previous summer just to go out and explore every new day turned into a tangle of emotional knots, until he found himself embroiled in way too much of whatever was up or down in Pia's world. Her friends were constantly over, staying the night when they couldn't walk home or pay rent. They weren't the fun kind of stay-over guests. Everyone in Pia's life had a sky-falling-down dramatic crisis. Jamie began to believe it was what got people through the week. The highs, the lows, so they could have something to talk about Monday. He began to look forward to the nights when she was off posing for the portrait so he could be by himself. Just sit and think, look out at the city and sip on tin cans of local beer.

When he finally began to run out of money, Jamie took a job as a furniture mover, carting gargantuan armoires up and down stairs, moving office equipment, and hauling away estate antiques. One day, he bent to pick up a dolly and his back convulsed. Even moving a fraction of an inch produced white-hot pain. He had to rely on strangers to bring him back to the apartment, where he lay just as prostrate as he had been six months earlier in his casts. A depression sunk him for weeks afterward, and Pia seemed disgusted. She railed about money, how she couldn't pay her rent with him out of work, and as he lay on his side, saying nothing, he wondered how she'd done it all by herself before they met.

Within time, Pia had made it clear she was done. She said nothing to him at first, but paced the rooms. Finally, as if mustering herself into battle, she charged into their bedroom and stood, her thin body like a spindly, wintry tree.

"You didn't scrape the burnt cheese off the pan," she accused. In bitchiness, Pia was truly more herself than in any other facet of her personality. She was bland in her job; bland in bed. Only when provoked to angry passion was she the girl he fell for. She was, he realized, black and white. White thin body, black brows. White face, black mood.

"I'll do it tomorrow." Jamie rolled over.

"How much longer do you think you'll be lying around?"

"I'M NOT LYING AROUND."

"Well," she said briskly, picking up some clothes off the floor, "You're not lying around, cause I'm not sticking around."

And that was it—like a threadbare deerskin bladder, its last threads split at the seams, it all slopped out with a disgustingly predictable finality. She didn't want him around anymore cramping her style. As he lay there spangling with pain, her admission leapt out, coming at him like sparks off a bonfire, burning through his sleeve and skin before he even registered what was happening. She admitted that the painter of her portrait had become her lover.

Jamie spent the rest of that month in a rented-out room lying in a lopsided bed, his back like a hot poker. He chatted occasionally with the other roomers, Jeremy, an affable ex-con, Nadine, a recovering methadone addict, and Rill, the landlady, who had a restraining order against her brother. Occasionally Rill checked on him, brought him leftovers. But mostly Jamie ate little to nothing, cold soup out of the can, not wanting to bother anybody. Every night, lying in a room with cracks in the ceiling and a heater that sounded as if it was being repeatedly bashed with a lead pipe, he thought of Pia snuggled in with the lousy painter, of the sweet smile she could muster when she was content. He thought of all the places he had forfeited seeing in America when he'd had the money and could have kept on going. Of all the girls he could have met. All the friends in Portland he did not have.

At age 19, Jamie came home to Maine. He asked Maynard if he could stay a while. His grandfather gave him the spare room in his house until Jamie could find a place. And for a while it felt like sleeping after weeks of being forced to stand guard, half awake. In the spring, he fell back into his old role as sternman for his grandfather, and the routine was good. His muscles were fluid; his back felt good. The money was slowly coming in. One morning he came down to the kitchen, excited to get on the water.

"We goin' out hauling today?"

"Nope." Maynard was at the kitchen table, eating bacon.

"Why not?"

Maynard didn't look up from the marine catalogue he was poring over. "It's the first Monday in April."

"So?"

"So, that's Cain's birthday." Maynard flipped a page. The bacon in his back molars sounded like gravel.

Getting back into Maynard's routine took an eye on the calendar and a little adjustment. Fridays were unlucky days to set out on the water, for the Crucifixion took place on a Friday. It also drove Jamie nuts that they never went out on the thirteenth of a month, even if it was a glorious day. If there was an eclipse the day before, Maynard would not go out hauling, but if there were reports of a meteor in the sky, Maynard set off the moment the sun rose.

Another day. "We goin' out or *what* today?"

"Nope."

"Why?"

"Had me a dispute with Ruthie this morning."

It was bad luck to have a fight with one's woman before starting out the day.

Jamie stood, his body at an angle as if the house were heeling. "What are you talking 'bout? Grandma's dead."

Maynard cast a look at him. "That don't stop her from bitching at me. Believe me."

That was it. They weren't going out on one of the most beautiful days of spring. Jamie turned back into the house as his grandfather took another sip of coffee and turned the newspaper page.

It took awhile to absorb, but it was simple seafaring theology. A smart fisherman believed in signs—God's warnings of a coming storm or an impending shipwreck. Jamie came to realize that the information was all there if a person had enough sense to read it. Even if he looked ridiculous, he needed to stick his nose right down to the ground and smell and lick everything. He had to notice the patterns of light, the moon, the direction the rain slanted. He had to put his senses right into what the tides were doing, the swells, if cattle stood or lay down. He needed to look to the dew on the grass, the droop of a poplar's leaves. Smell the fog, listen to the hum of telephone wires, heed if a spider spun more than one web. Maynard had been doing this for nearly fifty years, working off his nerves, listening to his arthritis. Being smart where others had not, living when others perished. They lobstered on Maynard's thirty-two-foot boat, approximately five miles offshore, talking all day long. He taught Jamie to trust a hauling wind, but if it had trouble making up its mind, to come in for the day. God and Fate didn't usually strike without warning, Maynard said. He'd had ten friends in a lifetime, from grade school on, who'd died on the water, and for every friend who died, human error was the reason. Fog caused Maynard's best man at his wedding to run aground and sink the boat. Others got themselves unwittingly tangled in gear and pulled overboard, their boats found later turning lazy circles. "You just pay attention to the signs, watch and learn, you'll be fine," he'd say.

At age 10, Jamie leafed through a loose-bound book on Maynard's oak desk. The pages were brittle and the illustrations were reprints of wood carvings. But they were irresistible images of a sailor's nightmare. On one page was a crude wood etching of a masted ship upon rolling seas. In front of the ship, an enormous goblin's head arose from the sea, dripping, its horns visible, its long, taloned fingers reaching for the ship. This so inflamed his imagination, it gave Jamie nightmares. When he went to sleep, he thought of his uncles, his father, his grandfather on boats little more than specks in a vast, watery universe.

"If all the dead rose up from the sea," Maynard casually told him several days later. "You'd have an army of tens of thousands stomping across the swells." He came out with things like this all the time, and it chilled Jamie the way he blended fact and fiction. The mermaid had stuck deep in the rivets of his memory, the goddamn mermaid, who still slithered up from the beaches in his dreams and showed him her kelp-heavy hair and barracuda teeth.

Maynard told him about a mermaid he'd seen all of his life on Criehaven, where he'd grown up. Jamie put up with the tales, and the ribbing his smirking grandfather gave him—just to see how much he'd believe. This mermaid had crawled up to the isle of Criehaven in the latter century. She'd arrived by herself—no boat, no relative to anyone on this remote Maine island that took two days to reach. She just appeared one day to a small community of 200 people, Maynard said. She fell in love and abandoned her scales for a land husband. Back when no one wrote anything down, they just told it to the neighbors, they spoke of this woman. They whispered and gossiped about her, but no one ever got close to her. In public, she was a sweet, childlike creature. He remembered people talking about her, but not much else. She'd made a home with the man, producing children, until a few years later when she'd learned of her husband's infidelity with a neighbor's daughter. Then, Maynard said, eyes blue and serious (and this is when Jamie had no idea whether to frown or smile), then the mermaid took her children down to the gray, rocky edge. The sheep and oxen of their farm followed. The tables and chairs, through her spell, suddenly picked up on their own legs and followed, soon joined by the pots and pans and trunks. The slaughtered pigs, hung up on hooks for winter's store, cleaved their severed limbs together and came down from the hooks to follow. And the mermaid, clutching hands with the children, entered the waves of the sea, her legs and the children's legs bubbling into scales. Everything followed her in.

Story after story on rainy days, knitting trap heads out of sisal with

Maynard in his shack, plastic hog rings hanging from the rafters, a bottle of peach schnapps on the small card table, Jamie watched the woodstove, absorbing Maynard's supernatural talk. There was *The Hascall*, a fishing vessel, which had broken from her anchorage in George's Banks a century before. All hands aboard drowned, and for many years the ghosts of the drowned sailors would come back to *The Hascall* and go through the motions of fishing. "Everyone saw them," Maynard said. "Don't think they didn't. People talked about *The Haskell* for years. I remember in the war, my friend wrote me that the ghosts had come back. He'd first seen them working in the mist, which changed form, and the next thing he knew it was a man working beside him, but no man he'd ever signed up with. The ghosts never did anything bad; they just worked, as if no one ever told them they had to stop. Oh, Jee-zus, did it scare my friend, let me tell you. He wasn't the only one—they all saw them, and it frightened the crew so much the owner of *The Haskell* could never find a full crew after that. It had to be dismantled."

The fall days were good, his grandfather beside him with his cigar and his great barrel chest in a Buffalo plaid wool shirt. A black navy watch cap over his white hair. Dark green wool pants and white socks. The gorgeous feeling of coming home led to familiar routines. The evenings lulled with the same sirens of friends and old patterns, and after not drinking for six months, Jamie thought the time had come to start again. After hosing down the boat for the day, Jamie pulled on his old cords, a nappy sweatshirt. He went looking for his friends afterwards, so they could go to Churchie's or the Tide Out Pub. He let his shaven cheeks grow out and began to eat junk food again, the kind of fat-ass, grease-laden pizza at the beach store that was made with sauce out of a jar and pepperoni out of a package—none of this sun-dried artichoke and goat cheese slop that passed for West Coast pizza. Jamie spent comfortable, numbing days on the water and nights with old friends, ragging on school chums who'd gotten knocked up or roped into marriages over the knocking up. Oh, it was good to be home.

When he puked over the rails once, then two days later, Maynard abruptly motored back to the dock without a word. The sun hadn't come out yet and the morning was indigo blue and cold. "What are you doing?" Jamie kept asking him. There was nothing recognizable in his grandfather's expression. "Why are we going back? Did you forget something?"

He knew by the way Maynard ignored him that he'd angered him over something. With Senior, it was always obvious—"Ya fuckup! Stop fucking up, fuck-up!"— whereas the few times Jamie had displeased his grandfather, he knew it by the silence. Maynard dropped Jamie off at the dock the moment the horizon began peaching right up, making Maynard's gray face falsely cheery with light. The boat's outboard continued to growl and spit in the water. Jamie's grandfather nodded at him curtly to go, his apple cheeks flattened down, eyes dull and dark. "We'll go out again when you start having respect for me and my boat," he said. Jamie stepped over the washboard onto the dock with his hands in his sweatshirt pockets as Maynard whistled a tune and cast off again.

Jamie watched him go, feeling hurt like a little kid, feeling wretchedly hungover. He knew how he looked to his grandfather, like a stinkin' dub, like a drunk with no future, no pride. The grand adventure of the West was long over. Everything he'd expected for his future was turning to shit and, after Pia, there was no more luxuriating in self-pity. This was just a nasty bath of shame. He felt like a spoiled brat who'd had everything handed to him and he still couldn't get it right.

When he thought about how Maynard had come up from nothing in the '30s, sometimes eighteen-hour skin-flaking days with his own father, lobstering off Criehaven, he felt worse. Nobody screwed around then, getting drunk, when it was survival just to eat. There was a reason the lobstering community held Maynard in such high esteem. Maynard worked hard every day of his life. He never fouled another man's lines on purpose, or dumped gear or scabbed during strikes, or acted like a pompous ass in town. Even his known disputes with the Fogertys were always held aboveboard. He set up private fish shack forums for men to talk to one another rather than get all hot and wage war. When telephones were first installed in people's cottages all along the coast, Maynard was the first one to start the trend of picking up the phone rather than a shotgun. "Listen here," he'd say in his affable way. "I ain't looking for trouble, but you keep pushing over my lines, I'm gonna have to take care of you. Simple as that, bud-day."

For a few days, they lived together with a little more silence than usual. Jamie couldn't look directly at Maynard when they spoke. It didn't make him quit drinking altogether (for the pain of shame still needed the same salve as the other pains in his life), but living with Maynard, the change happened gradually. "I've stopped drinking," Jamie announced to his grandfather at 4:00 one morning while they were getting breakfast at the beach store.

"Oh yeah? Since when?"

"Since before six o'clock every night."

A joke, but not a joke. It felt good to wake up without a knife through his forehead or a queasy stomach. For once he could even handle Maynard's nasty old reeking bait. Every day they'd fish from o-dark thirty in the morning to o-dark thirty at night. The hard work felt good, and instead of looking at it as a fuck-off job while he tried to figure out what else he was going to do with his life, Jamie began to fine-tune all the tricks he'd learned.

"See that peninsula?" Maynard asked.

"Yeah?"

"That's the eastern border of our territory."

"Yeah, I know that, Pappy," Jamie said, baiting bags.

"You don't know a wart bean from your ass. See that overhanging spruce at the edge by that small beach? It looks like it's trying to take a drink of water?"

"Yeah?" Jamie squinted.

"That's the cut-off. You look down to the beach, down there to the praying spruce, and that's your marker. You don't need the plotter. Just use your eyes. Beach—hanging spruce. Got it?"

"What's beyond the spruce? I thought that was ours."

"Nope, beyond that is just a bunch of mixed fishing. That's Fogerty area, don't even bother. You go over and they'll take it from you anyway."

"But what if it's on our side of the peninsula?"

"Don't matter." Maynard scrubbed his light cheeks.

Maynard, for all his talk, had a radar, a fish finder, and charts. But he worked by old signposts, rarely using the Loran-C. He worked by ridges, holes, ledges and kept his daily findings in a small black book. His black book was a lifelong map of trial and error. Men always tried to offer Maynard money for the book. One time at a card game, a guy had offered to give him $10,000 for it.

"Here." He gave Jamie the black book. It was thin, pocket-sized. "Copy all of my headings down. But don't show anyone and keep it off the boat. You keep that on you at all times, along with your knife."

Maynard took him around, refined him in a school that only existed with relatives, taught him to scout the bottom of an area and gauge the depths, dropping traps at the correct fathoms. He made Jamie move an endless amount of traps, shifting them like chess pieces on the sea floor.

"Pappy?"

"Yeah?"

"Why are we moving them so much? Why don't we just let them soak?"

"We're just changing out the water in the traps," Maynard said, shaking out a match after his cigar. "In Arnhem, we didn't stick around in one area waiting to find out what was gonna happen. We kept moving when no one else did."

Jamie moved a trap up onto the rail, disgruntled about the extra work. "It seems pointless. It's not like we're at war. "

"Oh you think I'm just talking about bugs," Maynard said, his apple cheeks smiling. "When you get exhausted and lose your taste for this, someone else will come in and take your place. Just you watch. And then it'll be war." Maynard leaned over the washboard and spit, simultaneously snatching up a toggle. A pint of cold rum swung from it. He unswiveled the cap, gave the first sip to Jamie.

"Let's go home soon," Jamie said, tipping back the pint.

"Oh yeah? Why? Ya fagging out on me already?"

Jamie handed the bottle to Maynard. "I got a date."

Maynard's cheeks swelled. "Ooooh."

"Yeah, a third date actually. She's pretty nice."

"That girl, Anyer?"

"Yeah. It's been a few weeks."

"Hee hee," Maynard said, taking the rum. "Jimmy Boy's in love."

"Naw."

"Yeaaaahhh."

Jamie's own warmed cheeks found the light. He smiled. "Did I tell you she's a teacher over at the McClean School?"

"Yeah, ya did, yeah. She's some smart, that girl."

"She teaches messed-up kids."

Maynard was loving this. He took a nip. "How messed up?"

Jamie made a grotesque face and staggered around the boat. "You know."

"Hmm."

"What?"

"Now I get what she sees in you." Maynard hitched his waffled sleeves up. "Bring her over for suppah."

"Not yet. I don't want you scaring her off."

"I ain't gonna scare her off, just bring her over."

Jamie scowled, leaned his palms against the rail. "All right, maybe just you. I don't want her to meet anyone else yet."

"Aw kid, don't get all shit-tay, just cause you're in love."

"I'm not."

Maynard paused. "Y'aint in love."

When Jamie had nothing to say to that, Maynard's cheeks became pinker than the babiest pink. "*BAWW.*"

FIVE

Anja stared out giant windows as tall as barn doors. They were the factory windows of an old tannery, streaked with dirt, splattered carelessly with white paint spray at the top where no one could ever clean. She was watching two men in their white naval uniforms and sailor caps walk down the sidewalk opposite from the window where she stood. The way they bounced when they walked, their faces open and animated, elbowing each other as if expecting the night to unleash fantastic possibility, captured her attention. She watched them intently, wondering what they were so excited about. Was the traveling fair in town? Did they want to ride the Tilt-A-Whirl?

"You see this?" Arlo bellowed behind her, causing Anja to flinch. One of these days, Arlo was going to get a backhand across the face. He was perpetually underfoot. Though he was 36, everything was adolescent about him, even his sparse, patchy chin whiskers. Arlo showed Anja a flattened coin, stamped with an angel. "See this? I foun . . . I found it on the floor, I FOUND it."

Unlike Jamie's territory, the great expanse of the sea, Anja's territory had definitive boundaries: tall white walls, closed and locked doors. And people like Arlo, who had an epiphany over something every single day, trampled those boundaries regularly like the wacky neighbor always barging in. Right now it might be some crap piece of stamped coin he found outside of a Wal-Mart, but the day before it had been a perfectly dead stiff baby mole,

59

and the day before, an empty can of Moxie. There wasn't enough time in the day to simply sit without someone bugging her, prodding her, imploring her to work on her skills or make lists or make a sculpture out of oatmeal canisters.

Anja sighed. She was a big-time sigher, especially with the Coasties. She knew she should've been much more patient with their haphazard interruptions of her time, but all she wanted to do this afternoon as she looked out at the sun-supple trees was sit out on the steps and wait for Jamie.

"So?" she said, unimpressed.

"I'll be all right," Arlo smiled. "You'll be all right. I'll . . . I goin' baseball, I goin' baseball game tonight." Arlo beamed. His family usually came to get him around four.

"Fun." Anja gazed at the doorway. She wanted Jamie to come there, now.

"You'll be all right."

Arlo wore a Red Sox cap, a bright blue warm-up jacket, and jeans. That was his daily outfit; he'd worn this same combination for the last three years. He stood with his hands in his jacket, bouncing on his heels, as if still trying to think of things to say.

He'd gotten his by hootenannying around in the back of a pickup driven by his uncle. He and his cousins had been on their way to the Union Fair with a goat in the back of the truck. His uncle and two cousins had taken up all the room in the cab, so Arlo offered to stay in the back with Elvira. When his uncle veered off the shoulder to pass a slower car, he hit a rock and torpedoed the truck's equilibrium. They never made it to the fair. Elvira's neck snapped the moment she flew from the truck, and she hit a stand of hackmatack like a horseshoe clanging around a stake. Arlo, 14 years old, straight-A math student, junior member of the 4-H club, hurtled into the woods after her.

Anja pointed to his Red Sox cap. "You wear that in the shower?"

Arlo's hands flew to his prized possession; his sunny smile whisked behind a cloud. "No, my hat . . . this is . . . this is *my* hat. I goin' baseball tonight."

"Let me see it."

"You can't take it," Arlo said, his eyes darting.

"I won't take it."

He lifted the cap off his black shag of hair, now matted down into an upside down bowl, and warily handed it to her. "It'll be all right; you'll be all right."

Anja put on the cap and tapped the brim. "It sure is *nice*."

Arlo's smile came out, wavered, tucked back in.

"Yeh, yeh." Olive watched them and banged her walker. Her mongoloid eyes and small, shrunken apple face lit up. "Yeh, yeh, yeh, yeh, yeh."

When Anja had arrived three years ago, Olive was the only female patient. She was, in the rehabilitative vernacular, pretty much fucked. Her brain injury had been in addition to a mild case of Down syndrome. She'd been there the longest. Carolyn told Anja that at age 9, Olive's sister convinced her to climb up a tree so they could talk to the birds. Olive got up to a high branch, spread out both arms, and joyously flew. With thinning brown hair in a bowl cut, she looked like a little man. Recently, Anja had gotten her to carry a little pink purse with her walker.

"Your purse is pretty, Olive," Anja noted. It was important to praise Olive often.

"Yeh, yeh, yeh." Pause. "Yeh, yeh, yeah, yeh."

Low light slung across the Coastal Center's wide laminate tables. The tall room used to be part of a leather tannery and had been converted into a rehabilitative center. Overhead, an elaborate grid of pipes, air ducts, and hanging fluorescent lights had been painted eggshell white. When the afternoon light hit the far windows, it was always time to go home, and Anja wanted to go home now. The longer she sat there watching the light move down farther on the windows, the more anxious she became. Manny stood at the other window, watching as well. He was the oldest, with a white crew cut and no teeth, so his sunken cheeks curled in a grimace. He knew a few rudimentary signs—a fist to his chest, a fingertip to his forehead—so he could communicate he was hungry or needed the bathroom.

It was Friday afternoon. Everyone wanted to go, including Carolyn, who was on the phone in her office making arrangements to pick up her daughter from the babysitter. Anja sat grumpily with her elbow propped up and her chin in her hand. Arlo and Olive had formed a tight circle around her as they always did—neither one of them could understand personal space. As soon as Anja turned, there was Arlo right at her elbow, smiling maniacally.

Anja pushed him. "Move."

"It'll be all right."

"Heh, yeh, yeh, yeh."

"Arlo and Anyer gonna do the naaaaaassssttty!" Bruce called from the other side of the room. He was eating a banana, which was getting mashed in his mustache.

Arlo whirled around. "No!"

Bruce was the only one at the Center she couldn't stand, and he made himself so repulsive that no one liked him. He was a new patient, 270 pounds, with an overgrown black mustache. Everything he ate seemed to clump to it, like the dingleberries off a long-haired cat. She couldn't stand much of what came out of his mouth either. Bruce talked about nothing but sex, day and night.

"HAAAA HAAAA HAAA, Arlo and Anyer gonna sex it up, sex it up, do sixty-nine, licky, yum yum. . . ."

Anja stood and turned. "Stop it."

"Arlo probably can't get it up, huh Arlo, huh guy?"

Arlo stood, dazed, unable to defend himself, while Olive grinned fiercely. This happened many times in a day. Manny continued to look out the window.

It was always up to Anja to say what needed to be said. "Bruce, you are rude and mean and fat and rude."

Bruce responded with depraved laughter. "Why don't you come sit on my pole?"

"What?" Anja said, irritated. "What pole?"

"BAHHHH." He slapped his leg repeatedly, then cupped his hands around his crotch. "This pole, baby, this fat flagpole—why don't ya run your undies up this pole. HAAAA HAAAA."

Anja frowned. She still didn't understand. "This is bad talk. Bad, Bruce. You are bad and mean and fat."

"I'm not fat."

It had been a long day in a long week of Bruce's bullying and deliberate provocation. And when Bruce talked about nothing but the ugliest things two people could do to each other, what he was going to do to his wife, to hookers, to nuns, to Carolyn even, Anja's reserve of control broke. She walked over and stopped within four feet. The smell hit her immediately. "You just shit yourself," she accused.

Bruce blinked as if that were news to him and scooted slightly to the left on the couch. Then it occurred to him that yes, there was definitely something not right in his pants. The banana still stuck to his mustache.

"Anja," Carolyn said, coming out of her glass office. She stood outside the doorway, her heavy arms folded. "Come in here." She turned back to her office. From the back she looked like a stack of griddlecakes. Her legs were white-pale, even in the dead of summer, and on her left leg she had an enormous tattoo from ankle to calf of a scaly purple and green dragon.

Anja's tiny nose and her blond eyebrows were in a conspiracy, huddled all together, mounting a mutinous attack. She followed Carolyn *like a bad girl* into the office while everyone stared after her.

"Jamie is coming when?" she pouted. "He said he be here."

"He'll get here when he gets here," Carolyn said, tired of the same questions.

"Carolyn," Anja suddenly burst out. "Bruce said me and Arlo was having sex and we're not!! Carolyn, we are not. Jamie is my boyfriend!!"

"Pull the bullhorn out of your mouth—I'm right here," Carolyn said, settling down into her leather chair. She clasped both hands on her desk and glanced at the photo of her daughter next to the framed inscription *Every day is a gift*. Her fingers drummed the desktop. "He can't help what he's saying right now. You used to have the same problem, so don't take it personally."

"But he—"

"AND—" Carolyn raised her voice in the deft and dominant way she had with the Coasties. "And," she continued, now softer, "you're only here to work on you—not everybody else."

Anja stood, her arms crossed over her thick waist. "I try."

"Yeah, you try," Carolyn said. "That's what your journal's for. Have you been writing in it?"

"The windowshades—" Anja pointed to the windows behind Carolyn's desk. "They not hanging down even; one is higher than the other."

Carolyn looked over her shoulder at the shades. Her whole body turned back to Anja. "So they are."

"Can you fix them?"

Carolyn straight-armed her desk and stood up to pull the other shade down slightly to match the first one.

Arlo knocked on the door, his hand fumbling with his Red Sox cap, his fingers jabbing nervously at his lips.

"Arlo, what is it?" Carolyn said. Arlo pointed to where Bruce had been sitting at the long table and jabbed harder at his lips. "I says it's all right, it's gonna be all right." Carolyn looked around, not finding Bruce, but she could smell it. Everyone in the room could smell it.

The direct sun had disappeared from the frosted hopper windows. And when the daylight dimmed, the place faded back to its shabby existence. The floor tiles were cracked; the lights were yellow and frazzled, some permanently out.

Anja sat at the laminate worktable watching Steve, the physical therapist, say goodbye to Carolyn. None of the employees wore actual uniforms. Jolanda, the occupational therapist, had red balloon pants and an extra-large purple T-shirt. She wasn't that friendly; always wore earphones. She, too, was leaving for the day—and unlike Steve, who always made a point of saying goodbye, Jolanda would just leave. Olive's and Arlo's families had already picked them up. Bruce walked home, three blocks, to his assisted-living apartment. Manny stood by a window. His sister would be along later. Just watching Manny stare that way made Anja feel even more pent-up. She wanted to be out on the porch, in the sun.

"I'm going out waiting," she told Carolyn.

"Fine, I'm right behind you," Carolyn said.

On the gray, paint-curled porch, it was better. Anja rested her chin on her knees, sitting on the top stair, her high-water corduroys revealing duck-patterned socks. The summer air was cool and salty, with a deep breath of spruce and the smell of decaying hay from the next lawn over. Summertime. Friday summer nights when Jamie got out of work, they'd grab a drink at the Landings with Donna and Senior, or ride across the bay on the boat with Thongchai and the boys. Picnics on islands, backyard barbeques. She wondered if Jamie's parents were down at the Landings now with all their friends. Friday nights were always hopping. Donna liked the seats by the railing, always got there early. Donna liked rum and Coke. The middle school teachers at Anja's old job, the ones Anja used to have wine with on summer nights, they might be there too. Then, of course, there were the college girls, the dorm room sisters from the Boston days. The late-night Letterman-watching, pizza-chowing best pals who used to visit her in Maine every summer. She hadn't seen any of them in years. Now she watched a man in a wheelchair make his slow way up the weed-choked sidewalk next to the Coastal Center, his arms thrown out with each push of the wheels.

Finally, finally, she heard Jamie's truck coming down the road, Metallica blaring out the window. She bolted to her feet and stepped lightly down the stairs. He parked, got out of his truck in his shambling way. He'd gone home first and cleaned up, was now in a clean white shirt and jeans, his dark green cap framing his tanned face. Anja's eyes blazed to see him.

Anja clattered down the rest of the stairs and jumped on him. "Let's go to Landing, let's go, Jamie."

He stumbled, trying to push down her leg, which tried to lock onto his waist. "Okay, hold on, hold on."

Anja rubbed her face into his sleeve. The salt, the maple smell of him. She put her cheek against his muscled arm.

Carolyn came out to the porch and locked the door behind her. "Hey, Jamie."

"How ya doin?"

"Oh, you know," Carolyn said, swinging her keys. "Typical week. I'm just gonna lie myself down behind the wheels of your truck. All you gotta do is start it up and reverse hard."

He smiled. "Has Anja been giving you any trouble?"

"Naw!" Carolyn said, exaggerating. She walked up to them. "This one here—she's great. They're all perfect *angels*." She ran her fingers through Anja's limp bangs, untangling them. "It's funding, staff. Everything. It's Friday. Usually I have to clamp down on my urge to kill everyone on Friday."

"Guess what?" Anja said, with the kind of hand-clasping glee that precedes good gossip. "Bruce crapped himself today."

Carolyn snorted. "I wouldn't be so happy about it, kid. There was a time you did too."

This was unexpected, and Anja's face became rigid, bright pink. She looked at Jamie, embarrassed. "I did NOT." She walked toward Jamie's truck, arms at her sides.

Jamie still continued to talk with Carolyn; they spoke in low voices, and she knew it was about her. This was about all she could handle. She'd been waiting all day and wasn't about to wait anymore. Anja wanted him to follow her and get in the truck so they could go away from that place, but Jamie stayed where he was. Anja climbed into the cab of the truck and glared out the window. They were still talking, always about her, how much better or worse she'd gotten each week, what skills she had learned. The thing that Carolyn just said was mean. She'd said it in front of Jamie, and boyfriends did not like girlfriends who did that. Anja simmered, hating Carolyn just then. Hating that stupid Center. This was her third summer there. She wanted to be free from it.

After a bit, Jamie got into the driver's side. He seemed in a great mood, slightly out of breath. "You ready to go home?"

Anja turned to him. She yearned for this moment to be like the sort of Fridays that she once remembered, away from places that were gray and peeling. "Am I still cute?"

He patted her knee. "Of course, sweetie."

"You still love me?"

He reached in the glove compartment for a cigarette. "I tell ya all the time, don't I?"

She turned, her narrow eyes on the dirty windshield. "I wanna go Landings. I want a lobster and to see if Donna got a rum and Coke. Jamie, can we go to the ocean? Can we go on the boat like we used to do? It's summer now and I been waiting a long time to do everything and I want to go to the Landings and do some fun."

Jamie seemed to think about it, and turned the engine over. "I know where we can go," he said.

There was absolutely nothing extravagant about the Black Seal. The booths were wooden, torn up. The curtains on the window were calico and heavy with dust. There were only two waitresses on duty any night, busy or not. The young one was sweet but completely inept. The old one was a horror but quick with the beers. Her name was Elaina. A British couple stood in front of them, trying to make sense of the hand-scrawled menu on the blackboard. The blond British woman put on her reading glasses and leaned in close to the board. "What is that? Shod? Scrod?"

Elaina, in her tan and white blouse, waved Anja and Jamie ahead of the British couple, who soon realized the inequity and looked at each other before they began to protest. "But, excuse me, I'm sorry, but we were. . . ."

"She's frickin' handicapped!" Elaina snapped. "We got a booth just for handicapped—you want that booth? Or do you wanna wait for a real table?"

The British couple stood mute and Elaina snatched the menus—black marker written on cardboard. The look that smeared off her face said *I thought so.* She sat them down at a booth by the kitchen.

"How you doing, dear?" Elaina said to Anja. "Ain't seen you in awhile. I heard you're getting betta." To Jamie: "I'll set you up real nice where I can see you."

"Thanks," Jamie said. "You got a busy night I guess, huh?"

He got a big sigh with a flutter of the whites of her eyes. "Be happy when summah's over."

Anja watched the people waiting in line at the door. It occurred to her then. "Why not we go to the Landings?"

"We will when you're ready. You've got to warm up to this kind of stuff."

"But I'm ready!"

"Just trust me. You're gonna have a good time here, too."

Elaina came back with Jamie's beer and Anja's soda. "Okay," Elaina said. She never wrote anything down. "All set?"

"Pizza," Anja said. She smiled at Jamie.

"What do you want on your pizza, dear?" Elaina looked toward the door, where more people began to gather without a clear understanding of who was in charge. "Be right there!" she shouted.

"Pepperoni."

Jamie leaned in. "You don't need the pepperoni. How about mushroom?"

Elaina scowled. "All right, pepperoni for the lady. And what do you want, Slim Jim?" she asked Jamie, her mouth crouched all the way to the side.

"Let me have a half a chicken over pasta."

"All right then." Elaina walked away.

Anja slathered butter on the bread that Elaina brought and started eating it. He sipped his beer, watching her. After her fourth roll, Jamie put up his hand and she put up her defiant face.

"I'm hungry!" she said.

"Supper's coming."

"I just wants it."

He looked away. "I swear to God, you are like the kid we never had."

"What do you mean?"

Jamie returned his gaze. "You wouldn't know if I told you."

Anja slammed the bread down, attracting the attention of others. "I am not stupid, you don't not talk to me like I don't understand."

"All right. *All right*, Anja. No, you're not stupid—I never said that." His voice was low. "I just said there are some things you are still trying to understand, that's all."

"I *do* understand."

He leaned back in the booth, frustrated, looking around.

"I'm getting better," she persisted.

"I know."

"Every day, Jamie, just a little."

By the time they left the restaurant, the heat of the day had drained away. Anja held onto the grease-stained takeout box holding the last of her pizza. Jamie turned right, past the Salvation Army and the Dairy Queen, taking back streets to avoid the summer traffic. The radio was on, some song from high school days. Anja had the passenger's side window down; the wind flipped through her pale bangs. As they drove past the sanitation plant, the air smelled like shrimp shells boiling in urine. That was the smell of summer for many people in this part of town.

Anja stared at the sky over the ocean, the orangish red light warm and deeply inviting. As they drove by the Landings, she craned to see if Donna and Senior were there. The sounds on the harbor were of boats coming back in, drinks and laughter up on the deck.

They drove silently back home to Porter's Cove, to a crabby-looking Cape at the ocean's edge with cedar shingles weathered to the color of beef jerky. Saltwater spray had pickled the house over the last seventy years. It was a house handed down to Jamie by his grandfather.

The phone was ringing the moment they stepped into the mud room. Jamie set the leftover pizza on the counter and picked up the wall phone in the kitchen.

"What's up there, Natural Born?" Jamie said as soon as he realized it was Thongchai. Anja looked at the box with its alluring damp oily patch. She knew she shouldn't be hungry already.

Anja flicked on a light while Jamie was on the phone. She pushed back the white lid of the pizza box and stared at the last two pieces as Jamie leaned against the wall, the cord wrapped around him. "Naw, I don't think so. I told you." He looked at Anja. "She can't."

"I can't what?" She slipped her fingers under a cold crust.

"I really don't care," Jamie said, his fingers on the stretched-out yellow cord. "It's the same old people, same deal. All right— 'ee ya later." Jamie hung up. He pulled a Bud out of the refrigerator, and a green apple soda for Anja.

"I guess there's a party tonight," Jamie said.

Anja perked up. "At the Landings?"

"No, the Ogdens. I guess they're having a bonfire."

"OH MY GOD LET'S GO!"

"Naw. . . ."

"Why can't I, Jamie?"

"It's not going to be all that fun." Jamie picked up the remote from the chicken coop coffee table. "I think you're probably going to need to go to bed early tonight."

She snorted. "Why?"

"Cause it's been a long week and you're cranky."

Anja found that to be ridiculous. "You can't tell me what to do. If I am tired, I am go to bed myself." She settled on the plaid hunter's couch facing the TV with an irritated glance at the dingy things they had: bachelor furniture, a floral La-Z-Boy, a wooden chicken coop for a coffee table, a TV, and a telescope. The walls were made of horsehair plaster and had permanent cracks from the settling of the foundation. The floorboards, made of old heart pine, foot-wide planks, were blackened with scars. The dark ceiling beams that ran the length of the house were made from rail ties, which Maynard had methodically tonked into place with mortise and tenon. When it rained, they gave off a deep smell of black oil. In the center of the living room stood a flagstone fireplace so inefficient it barely heated the room in the winter. Next to it, Jamie installed a small Vermont castings woodstove. The only light this house got came from two enormous picture-frame windows in the living room.

The only things of value that had been left on the walls were paintings by Winslow Homer and Andrew Wyeth. One of the Wyeths was an original, a sketch Andy had given to Maynard as a casual gift, never to be framed or, God forbid, sold.

Anja had tried years ago to add things—curtains, wildflowers in vases, some of her own art on the walls. But every time she added something, they both looked at the change and realized it was hopeless. The house had its own personality. It liked being dusty, blackened, and old. So Anja gave up, took down everything she'd added, and let the house have its own way again.

Jamie flicked through the channels. "Oh, look, a vampire movie."

"Oooh," Anja said, her mood passing. Jamie took the end of his lighter and levered it under the soda cap, *fffft*, and handed her the soda. "Here."

The phone rang again, which annoyed Jamie as he shoved his weight off the couch. "What?" he snapped, picking up the wall phone. There was shouting and music on the other end. "I told ya I'm not going."

"I can go," Anja said from the couch.

"Hey assbag," Jamie said. "Speak up. How's that tequila treating ya? Yeah, I'll bet."

"WHO IS IT?" Anja yelled from the couch.

"You better not be driving." He paused. "All right." And hung up.

She eyed the last piece of pizza, her attention wavering between Jamie and the box. "I don't want you to go," Anja said.

Jamie pulled the phone off the hook and let it dangle to the floor. "I said I wasn't," he muttered.

"But you wanna."

"I really don't care."

"You want to though."

"Yeah?"

"Then LET'S GO!" she said and jumped off the couch.

He took a breath. "Anja, just let it be."

Jamie settled back down on the couch and looked at the pizza box. The only things left were hardened globules of cheese and stains of sauce. "You ate it all?"

"Uh huh." She had sauce around the edge of her mouth. Anja snuggled in right next to him. She reached up to tug the matted mess of brown curls beneath his ball cap. "Jamie, I love you more than anything in the world."

He sighed and flipped the remote end over end in his hand. Anja tugged at him, trying to shake him out of his thoughts by poking and prodding. He called it *nerdling* when she did that. She couldn't help it. On the TV, an older man in white makeup with dark circles under his eyes roamed a dark castle.

"Do you love me more than anything in the world?"

His eyes flicked at her briefly, then at the TV. "Yes."

"You do?"

"I said yes. Now come on, are you going to watch this?"

Anja paid no attention to the man in the white makeup. Her eyes were only for Jamie. "More than . . . beer?"

He lowered his neck against the back of the couch, his eyes on the ceiling. The images of the small TV in the dark played against his white shirt.

"Jamie?" She tugged at his ball cap. "You love me more than beer?"

He turned the remote in his hand. "Well ya know, darlin', I'd have to say it really depends tonight. Are we talking just one? Or the whole six-pack?"

SIX

At one time, they shared the master bedroom, which faced the sea, but then she drowned. And came back to life. And then it became necessary to set Anja up in the spare room, where she'd be up at odd hours, like a kitten skittering across the floor, batting curios off the dresser, keeping him awake all night. He'd nailed up a couple of Anja's watercolor paintings in the little bare room to cheer it, but the paintings looked back like a dog left behind on a country road. Still, she moved into it without protest. In the early days, she accepted everything with passive resignation; heard him say *That's your bed now* and nodded *Yes, that's my bed.*

She slept in a red tent designed to fit over the corners of the twin bed. It was shaped like a Volkswagen Beetle, with a plastic window for a windshield and a zip-up door. Several years ago, he'd stopped at Reny's on his way back from Portland to find some duct tape and saw the Beetle tent on display. Anja had always said that on her thirtieth birthday she was going to trade in her battered Chevette for a brand-new red Volkswagen Beetle. "I'm owed," she said. "I've driven this shit-box thing for far too long."

Jamie stood, staring at the display. At the checkout counter, he had two rolls of duct tape and the brightly colored box with the red car tent inside. The checkout girl smiled when she rang it through. "Your kids are gonna love this. I got one and my kid *lives* in it."

When Anja saw the red dome and its zip-out door, she gave a funny, ecstatic squeal. Her brain, so dormant, had become fitful—

it was the first spontaneous reaction he'd gotten out of her in months. He'd take a squeal over that slack-jawed gaze, anything to get those almond eyes back to their former sparkly, spangled state. She unzipped the door and climbed in, and Jamie tried to follow. Trying to squeeze two full-grown people into a space made for a 10-year-old kid wasn't easy. Through the window of her room, the velvet night came into her plastic windshield with stars bright as nickels. It made the tent feel as though it was really pitched out-side—no one else around for miles. She never took the tent down, and it became their ritual for Jamie to unzip her car door at night, give her a kiss goodnight, and zip it back up again.

The sun had gone down, bloodied the water, snapping crystals of light in a single path before dropping away. He'd watched the whole thing in a plastic chair by the pebbled shore, the light turn-ing a deep, drowsy blue. It was Friday night, the old anticipation of the weekend calling him. There was a staver happening at the Ogdens, a bunch of the lobstermen hanging around by a bonfire, sipping on PBRs, telling jokes, ripping on each other. The Kid told him about it, Big Steve, Thongchai. Thongchai would bring his guitar, butcher a Pink Floyd song—someone would throw up. Just a stupid party, where everybody would stand around a fire, listen to a band, drink. Nothing much. Tell hilarious stories.

The minutes ticked, the harbor water darkened. Had he known about it before, he would've planned to have someone watch Anja, but now it was too late to call his mother and see if she'd come over. His parents were probably out with friends at the Landings having drinks and dinner as they always did on Friday nights. Jamie sat still in a plastic chair, restless, the toe of his boot kicking stones into the water. He couldn't leave her here; couldn't take her with him. Af-ter the accident, he'd been like a new father, completely sleep-de-prived. Once, he'd awakened to the smell of burning, jolted awake at 1 a.m. to find the ironing board set up in the living room, the iron searing its shape into one of his shirts. Anja, on the outside deck, oblivious, stared at the moon. Another time that year he'd come back from the Stop N' Go, gone only minutes to find Anja hysterical in the kitchen, a pot of water boiling on the stove. A note left on the counter gave insight into her murky state of mind: *Stove on, find off, Jamy gone—HELPME.* She bawled when he walked in the door and sobbed some incomprehensible words indicating she thought she was in trouble and didn't know how anything worked in the house anymore. It had only been 15 minutes.

There was some whiskey by his plastic chair, not his, a partial bottle one of his friends had left. He didn't like whiskey, but bit it back in neat nips anyway. House lights across the bay winked. He felt both nauseated and exhilarated by its taste. Felt sorry for himself on a clear, sharp summer night when other people were enjoying their lives. He was 27, getting older, soon to be 30, and then what? Guilt, like a hand on his shoulder. It wasn't her fault. She was alive, each year getting better (*but how much better?*). The migraines, the fatigue, the confusion not going away as each summer ticked by. *If it'd been you, she would've taken care of you.* And truly, had it been the other way around, Anja would've never left him.

He fell in love with the obvious things first, those almond eyes, how easily she laughed, her willingness to put on a pair of boots and bibs and shove her hands into a bucket of maggoty herring. He didn't realize until he'd been living with her for a year that what he really loved was her kindness. It made her stand out from any other "nice" girls he'd known. She was a girl who hadn't been given much in life and who could've spent all of her time trying to fill that hole as an adult, but in turn she just gave her time back to everybody who needed it. That particular quality had no definition, no flash, but it made her easily the most beautiful girl he'd ever known.

A lobster boat burbled through the quiet bay. It didn't take long for the whiskey to calm the gnawing inside. With that dullness, he gazed out on the black glass of the ocean. Moonlight dug a narrow row on the water. With not a ripple, it gave one dark, impertinent smile. He never liked being out on the water at night, didn't like thinking about what was there. Far beneath the surface, the sea's heart was as black as space, where light couldn't penetrate, where life disappeared and the pressure became intolerable. At its pebbly bottom, ghost-white crabs and fish edged along. In perpetual darkness, a solitary hell, those eyeless things crept. Traps, long severed, lay in permanent disrepair, hulls of dead whitish lobsters floating in the parlors—the ones that didn't get away. That's where the old Anja lived. That's where the sea kept its greedy little prize, chaining her ghost to the sandy floor, where she sat in perpetuity, playing with the albino crabs.

A gray sea with gray skies bodes ill.

She wore cotton jeans, two wool sweaters, a slicker, and sneakers. *Jamie, I've been on the boat a hundred times. I can haul the traps myself.* His stinkin' back felt like hot knitting needles sliding in and out of his spine. She used the gaff, pulled in the warp, switching on the hydraulic winch. That warp came into the hull of the boat, cold and slimy and curled around her ankles like some slick fat snake. *Get your feet out of that warp, dammit,* he snapped, because she knew better than that. She'd jumped back, less confident. The first trap they wrangled together, his teeth clenched. The pain made him want to punch something. They balanced it on the rails, took several lobsters out of the parlors. Showed her how to measure it from the eye socket to the carapace.

By the second and third trap, Anja was hauling up the traps on her own, doing well. He didn't praise her; that would make her ask to join him all the time. To have a woman on a boat was bad enough without making it a habit. If it weren't for the truck payment coming up, he would've told her to forget it. Bolts of pain shot through his lower back, the kind that kept his teeth grinding even after the spasm passed. He heard the last trap splash into the water and dug his knuckle into the sorest spot on his right side, hoping to massage it. *All right Anja,* he said, *when we come up to this one—*

For as many years as he'd been smacked around by his grandfather, yelled at by his father, trained to watch his step, Jamie stood dumb and mute. His eyes took in the stern: the lobster tank, the gearbox, the bait bin. A zag to the left and right and . . . nothing.

Anja was gone. The engine kept running. *Delores* kept propelling merrily along.

The boat hit a thudding wave the moment he yanked the wheel to the right, spinning *Delores,* and the crunch of turning force brought white heat to his eyes. *Oh Jesus, oh Jesus.* He knew exactly what had happened. He slowed the boat down with a fast reverse and churned a sputum of wave and froth from the engine. Then hobbled over the side—and dove.

In October, the Maine ocean is a painful, stinging, unholy cold. The shock alone panicked him into wanting to clutch for the ladder and get out of the water. His legs kicked, his hands jerkily searched, grabbing in the dark, finding nothing. He groped, found the slick warp. After only 40 seconds under black dark water, diving deeper in his insulated jacket, the cold became unbearable. He couldn't feel his hands. His lungs began to pump—that panicky sensation, sickening; he couldn't stay down there. His legs thrashed, felt like they were burning as he came back up and broke the surface.

He had trouble climbing back up the ladder; his hands felt hot and raw. Jamie bent, hands to his knees, staring at the agonizing water. She was dead. She was down there, no way he would find her in time. He began to wheeze; was afraid to go back down. He could see no one on the horizon. He had no survival suit. No time to call anyone—and he was wasting time. He tried to think—had it been seconds, not yet a minute? She could hold her breath that long— after that she'd start to lose consciousness. He pawed at the hauler valve with curled stumps for hands. There was only one chance, if she was still anywhere near the trap. He punched it and screamed at the motherfucker to *move.* Shaking violently, the warp began to pull up, sixteen, ten, four feet. Burbling up from the gray ice-black color, the yellow slicker appeared and Anja's face appeared. Her mouth hung in an O.

Jamie's back screamed as he grabbed her slack arms and pulled them out of the water. The cuff of her cotton sweater (*Never wear cotton; never, Anja!*) was snarled in the wire trap. His breath pillowed in the air. He pulled her body up over the rail and onto the deck hyperventilating, everything in front of him going black. Her hair was dark gold, slicked off her face. When he pushed at her stomach, seawater spilled out. He pumped her heart roughly (too roughly) and blew his breath into her blue lips. When he kept giving her breath and the moments continued to hurl by with no change, he stood outside of himself, from the top of the canopy, and looked down at the two of them on the boat floor, eyes swarming. What if he kept doing this, pumping and blowing, and nothing happened? Would there actually be a moment when he'd have to stop? If he stopped, he'd have to accept that that cold, blue face of hers would never change.

He pumped and blew, two long breaths; straddled her chest, found the sternum and palmed her chest. One two, three, four, five. Back to the breaths—when the blue lips began to sputter, frothy pink sputum dribbled out. He ripped off his wet wool sweater and draped it over her, fixing his mouth to hers to blow once more, but she coughed at his attempt. He stumbled to the VHF.

"MAYDAY, MAYDAY. This is F/V *Delores*. I'm about 3.5 miles north of Petit Point Harbor, just west of Wolf Rock." He tumbled over to lie on top of her and massage her arms. Listened to her breath again; felt warmth on his cheek.

When he heard the Coast Guard's horn coming in the distance, he stroked her cold face, sweet-talked her until they got there. *Anja, listen to me baby, it's gonna be okay, you just keep breathing; I'm right here, I'm right here.*

A rescue team climbed over the rail. Jamie crawled off Anja, let them take over.

Jamie shook, watching them work on her. The trembling had turned into a full-on quaking and he supposed that even if he were in a hot bath, the quaking wouldn't stop. An oxygen mask went over her face while the head paramedic scissored off her sweater and wrapped her in a metallic bag. They communicated in muted, practical commands and just that—just having someone in charge take over—lessened his anxiety in a way that made him feel that it would all be better now. She'd warm up and wake in the hospital and it would be all right. He already had some news for her when she woke up: never, *never* would she work with him on the god-damned boat again.

This is the beginning of what Jamie will remember as the stomach drop, the sick, overwhelming free fall. At nearly ten at night, they are able to move her into intensive care and they allow him to see her. She is still intubated, on a ventilator, with electrode wires and plastic tubes coming out of her head and body like puppet strings. She is waxy, pale, her limp blond hair on a cheap white pillowcase. The sound of the ventilator takes up the room with its staccato whoosh, like the tide coming in. He isn't sure if it's the morphine in the pills they gave him for his back, but this is the most surreal, out-of-control feeling he's ever had.

The days staying at the hospital are intolerably, deathly slow and hollow, wandering the featureless hallways, reading stupid women's magazines for anything to do. He's been home twice in three days and falls into an exhausted sleep on their bed, waking up at two in the morning with a panicky feeling that she's dead. And he goes right back to the hospital. His parents have been frequent visitors by this time, and Senior slips him an envelope of cash to make up for the time Jamie's missed lobstering. Anja's mother is the only one on Anja's side of the family to show up but is hardly a help; she blends into the grayness of the room, offering no words of comfort, just sits there oppressively hunched as if she, too, will need a hospital bed in a matter of days.

It takes nine days for Anja to come out of the coma. He's in the snack lounge at nine in the evening when one of the nurses runs in to tell him. He's in the middle of gnawing on a Baby Ruth bar, having forgotten to eat anything earlier.

"Jamie, she's awake—"

He walk-runs, the kind of stiff, super-extended walk that kids try to get away with in the hallways before school lets out. His heart yammering, he forgets to chew and still has Baby Ruth bar cement-ed in his back teeth when he rounds the corner to her room.

Anja's eyes are open, with Dr. Nayar standing over her, asking her questions. Jamie enters the room almost at a full run and swivels to a standstill at the foot of her metal bed just as the doctor asks, "Anja, do you know where you are?"

His heart is an open window with a gale blowing through it. He sees her waxy face alive and looking at him.

"Who the fuck are all these people?" she asks.

Jamie almost laughs, because Anja almost never uses that word. He kneels down next to her and takes her hand. "Babykid."

Anja looks strangely offended. "Why is the phone on your pants?"

The rest of the doctor's normal questions are met with bizarre, disjointed answers. He can't think, because her entire face has changed. The pert face with snappy eyes he's used to is completely gone. Someone else is behind those vacant eyes and her thick, slow speech. Her head movements lumber. Just blinking seems to happen in slow motion for her. Jamie continues to kneel right next to her and he holds up one of her hands to his mouth. Her brown eyes narrow at him:

"Stop looking at me," she snaps. "I didn't do it!"

In quieter moments when no one else is visiting, Jamie sits by her bed and asks her if she wants to go home soon. She nods, her brow a thunderstorm. Words are like ping-pong balls in a jackpot machine, dropped out of her mouth in random order.

"Is drive hungry fish."

"Are you hungry?" he asks.

She blinks as if he's the one not making sense.

"You want fish?" he says, knowing that she doesn't even like fish.

As Jamie drives, he thinks about how this abandonment of her family has made her especially clingy as an adult. How once, when Anja was 20, she and her then-boyfriend made a spur-of-the-moment road trip to California. They'd gotten in a fight and the stupid ass boyfriend told her to get out of the car on the side of a highway, whereupon he spit gravel and sped off. She had no money and walked to the nearest gas station, four miles down the road, enduring truckers honking at her and creepy men stopping to pick her up, until she persuaded the gas station clerk to let her call her roommate in Boston.

Jamie knows that under no circumstance would he be angry enough to put a woman out of the car in the middle of nowhere and take off. Driving around, he wishes he knew where the sonofabitch lived so that he could drive up to his house, introduce himself as Anja's current boyfriend, and knock the shit right out of him. Abandonment is the last thing that will ever happen to Anja, as long as he lives.

Later Dr. Nayar tells him, "At this point, we can put her where she can be maximally stimulated, like a brain injury center; we'll get you some names. They'll work with her, move her arms and legs, have loud music playing to stimulate her various senses. With a lot of hard work, she'll get back a lot of this."

"Is she going to walk?"

"I honestly don't know. With someone there to love her and help her and with an awful lot of hard work, she will get better than without all that."

"What about all the weird things she's saying? Is it going to stay like that?"

"She's not conscious she's doing it. Her brain is scrambled. It may be a year or two before you see some of the old Anja come back."

Oh my God, he thinks. *A year?* "Will she ever be the same?"

Dr. Nayar hesitates. He looks up at Jamie with dark eyes. He looks like a child who is hiding a guilty secret.

"Be honest with me. Be honest. I need to know this."

"Maybe not in the same way that you knew her before."

There are moments in that second week that make him so depressed, the only place he feels safe crying is in his truck, driving. One evening, after a frustrating interaction with a nurse, he storms out of the hospital. He kicks over the first solid object he sees, which happens to be a federal mailbox, breaking the last two toes on his left foot. The buddy splints on his toes keep him on crutches and out of work for yet another month. The accident and her three weeks in intensive care, plus her ongoing rehabilitation, work out to be just under a million dollars. He doesn't have insurance himself because he's young and self-employed (who thinks of this stuff when you're 24?) and he struggles to understand all the nuances of co-insurance and deductibles. Thongchai organizes a group of lobstermen to donate a portion of the lobsters they catch each day to the "Jamie and Anja Fund," and when he finds out about it he weeps again, this time, embarrassingly, in front of them.

The question of what to do with Anja is smacked like a volleyball over a net, and no one on Anja's side of the family is lunging for the ball. Anja's mother is a helpless, faltering woman who keeps asking how long they need her there in the hospital. She stays with Jamie and during that time, everything that comes out of her mouth is stupendously inane. She offers a running commentary on everything but her daughter; chooses to always sit in the farthest-away chair. Anja's stepfather, Joe, calls and yells at Anja's mother. After she hangs up she announces she needs to cut short her visit to get back to Boston. As if this is just a *visit* to Maine, a regular clambake.

She needs full-time supervision for the next month. Therapists come to help her improve her daily life skills, from walking by herself to the bathroom to picking out her own clothes each day. Anja's mother is, not surprisingly, reticent about the role she plans to play when Anja is released from the hospital. Jamie's father is all for suggesting that Anja's mother take her back to Boston for therapy. "Think about it," he says one night over the phone. "You're way over your head. You weren't married to her, and legally you're not responsible for her."

Jamie slams down the hospital pay phone. The next call he makes is to Anja's mother in Boston.

"Listen, no one's making a plan and I need to have one. By the end of the week she'll be coming home with me. I just have one question for you. She's going to need full-time supervision for the next couple of months. Do you think you'd be able to come up and help me with the day-to-day stuff? Cause I gotta make some money and I need someone there for her." He listens to Anja's mother for a long time, and before he hangs up the phone it's understood that as much as she would like to come up and take care of Anja, Joe wouldn't want her to be gone that long.

The last call he makes from the hospital is to his mother. "Ma, I need you."

Donna is already poised to be out the door. "I'll be right there."

The first year of Anja's recovery is by far the hardest year of Jamie's entire life. In those first few weeks after coming home, she sleeps up to eighteen hours in a fetal position. When she is awake, she stays rooted to one spot. Her brown eyes have a faraway, unconnected expression and her slack mouth hangs open, often with a little thread of drool hanging off her bottom lip. It kills Jamie to look at her. Donna severely cuts back her own work hours to watch Anja during the day, helps her to bathe, feeds her until Jamie gets home to take over.

Anja goes through more linguistic phases in the first six months after her accident than there are actually names for the phases. She gets excited when Donna comes through the door each morning and cries, "Bonkers! Bonkers!" This is the Eugley family dog, a chocolate Lab. The first time she does this, Donna comes over to her. "Do you want me to bring Bonkers over, Anja?" Anja grabs Donna's face and rubs her cheek against Donna's cheek. She then starts scratching Donna's head and croons, "Bonkers," until Donna steps away and stares at Jamie.

"Well, Ma?" he says. "Sit. There's a good girl, now roll over."

Then there's what they call "the sitcom phase" that precedes real communication and lasts almost a month. It starts one morning when Anja wakes up and calls out to Jamie and Donna, "Smiles, everyone, smiles," while grandly gesturing about the room. When she speaks during this phase, she cannot convey any of her needs, thoughts, or emotions unless it is through the characters of a sit-com. It is if she has become stuck within a nebulous Technicolor world of 22-minute shows, and each door she walks through as the wacky neighbor only opens into the living room of yet another set, with yet another laugh track.

She speaks in Laverne and Shirley, quoting dialogue from the California episodes; ruminating on Welcome Back Kotterisms. She thinks Jamie is Dwayne Schneider for reasons only she understands. She can't stop giggling and talking about his thick mustache, den-im vest, and tool belt.

Nobody can believe she can remember this much inane detail, but when she says "Boo Boo Kitty" over and over, it becomes clear, finally, that this means she wants comfort—an extra blanket. On the phone, her parents become Donnie and Marie. Mostly Marie is talking, randomly, about Boston. When her stepfather asks how she is, Anja hears, "Cute, Marie, real cute," and hangs up the phone angrily.

Within six months, Anja's brain has been jump-started; her memo-ry has improved, her muscle coordination is mostly back, and she is taking care of her own needs. She continues to make progress; her language skills improve and she remembers up to sixty, then eighty, then a hundred words. Jamie comes back home one afternoon to find Donna terribly excited. He tenses, thinking something bad has happened. "Jamie, she went to the bathroom by HERSELF today!"

"Jesus, no kidding?"

They have both been working on toilet training Anja and, as the months go by, notice a sharper, more aware air to Anja's behaviors. Parts of her brain begin waking up and taking over the damaged areas. After the success of the toilet training, Jamie and his mother cheer over Anja's every accomplishment (she dressed herself; she learned to dial a phone number; she pushed the tape into the VCR and pressed play) as if they are the proud parents of a toddler. It'll be no time before she cruises right back up to her normal self. He becomes buoyed up with incredible hopes, getting his traps ready for the season. He sits out in the sun, repairing his bait bags as his mind lingers on old times, and on new dreams. He envisions proposing to her when she's back to normal, and in his mind plans a boat wedding like Billy Mack and Sheri had last year. All the lobster boats in the harbor decorated with flowers, horns going off wildly. Everyone watching Anja walking up the narrow aisle of the ferry in her wedding gown, cheering and clapping for all that she's been through. Even for a hard-ass like him, he knows he will be wiping away tears (just as he is now, thinking about it). Their wedding day will more than make up for all this lost time—that one moment when they get to turn to everyone and raise their hands together as if to say, "See?" He is dead set on this idea, wondering when he should get the ring, after more rehabilitation maybe. The reception could be held up in the Fish House, the whole town turning out for it, 200, maybe 250 people. He knows the time will be right when he sees that old smile of hers again, that quick, flirty flash of her eye.

He could duck out for one hour, just be back by eleven. He stands looking at the hump of the red Volkswagen car tent in the dark. Inside, Anja snores like a dog—he imagines her lips curling in her sleep as her breath clutches in, sputters back out. Was she chasing cars? His cousin The Kid calling moments ago didn't even wake her up.

"*Ah Jamie, I'm telling ya, this one's a rager— Dewie's setting up the band. Just for an hour, guy.*"

"Yup."

"*What's that mean—yup, you're coming?*"

"Nope, just saying yup."

As he stares at the red car tent and smells the summer air through the house, cool and salty with deep undertones of spruce, a sound comes up through his guts. It's involuntary, like retching, he can't help it. It rides on the memory of cruising across the bay on the boat with Thongchai and the boys. Friday nights when his back always hurt, guys were fighting on the water, money was tight, but nothing was terrible, nothing that interfered with knocking off work and going to find Anja. Everyone knew that the summers were short—that's why the colors at dusk were so rich and the tang of the shoreline smelled so rude and hearty. He wanted to rip into it with his teeth, cram it all in—in those days, every morning opened with that lustful, infinite possibility.

The sound rushed out of him, he couldn't help it. It came out strangled and brutal, loud enough to stop the snoring.

"What?" Anja called, alarmed. He could see the outline of her, sitting up within the darkened red tent. Her sleepy voice repeated, "Jamie?"

He dragged his shoulder past her doorframe, to the opposite side of the hall, to the master bedroom. His words were lethargic, underwater. "Go back to sleep."

SEVEN

At the blue-black hour of dawn, the sun was a slitted eye across the water. It warmed the only store that stood on the edge of the harbor. The beach store used to be a decent place, with creaky, bloated floors and bowed shelves of canned goods, until miniature traps and hand-carved buoys, as well as books on "How to Tawk Like a Mainah" began surfacing on the shelves for the influx of summer visitors. The fishermen were the only ones up that early, lording over the breakfast counter out back, dressed in sweatshirts and canvas jackets, giving the lurched eye to anyone unfamiliar.

Jamie pushed the screen door with his hands crammed into his blue hooded sweatshirt and headed for the back porch. Every morning between 3:30 and 4:00, he started hard, like the tin woodsman, his back and shoulders aching, his neck refusing to turn. Under the sweatshirt he wore a stiff T-shirt, a pair of pungent, zesty long johns. He topped his head every day with a *Sea Lure* ball cap, all sauvvy and salt-rimmed, which had taken six years to break in.

He sat down next to Dan Moran, who was reading the *Gazette*. Jessi, the morning waitress, slid a chipped cup of coffee in front of Jamie. "Farmer's breakfast," she mumbled, just as tired as he was.

Dan didn't look up from his paper. "How ya doing there, Ugly?"

"Staying alive."

"Them guys ain't killed you yet?"

"No, not yet."

Dan raised both arms, yawned and stretched. He shook his head like a dog flapping its jowls.

Jamie knew that look. "Rough one, huh?"

"I guess." Dan opened his eyes real wide then squinted. Then tapped the paper. "Check this out."

The headline read "Woman Caught Stealing Over 100 Lobsters."

Jamie peered at the first two sentences of the article.

"Some real bright chick out celebrating her birthday," Dan said, "drove out with her boyfriend over to Quinn's. They managed to break in and get into the holding tanks and take about 120 lobsters back with them."

"Nuh."

"Looks like they brought a dozen into the house, boiled 'em up, left the rest in the car. And then get this. Apparently when they ran out of the *brandy*, this girl jumped right back in her car to get to the store. And that's when the cops nailed her for speeding." Dan picked up a piece of bacon and chewed it. "Imagine being that cop, shining his flashlight in back of her car to see a hundred of 'em all crawling over each other."

"Did Quinn get them back?"

"Oh yeah, most of 'em."

"That's just foolish."

"It's going on the board," Dan said, his large stomach in plaid bumping against the Formica counter as he stood to tack the article on the bulletin board above the lunch counter. This was the local board, crammed with pictures, articles busting on locals, and the latest joke going around ("How does a Mainer know when his trailer is level? His wife drools out of both sides of her mouth").

Jamie got up to see what else was new on the board while he waited for breakfast. He noticed two new police logs had been posted up. He squinted. "You see that Chuck Yeager's mother got a new OUI?"

Dan sat back down to his coffee. "Oh, that was sometime last week. Guess she didn't realize she hit someone 'til about an hour later."

Jamie read the details. "Says here it was eight in the morning."

"She was on her way to the dentist."

Jamie searched the board for other news. He held his ceramic coffee cup loosely.

"I thought my sister would be up on the board this week."

Dan looked up. "Not there?"

"It's been a whole month since the cops have been around."

"Hey—that's something."

Jamie's eyes wandered to an ad that had been pinned to the board: a glossy color magazine ad of two lobstermen in yellow hip waders on the deck of a lobster boat. Only these guys were dark-haired models with a noticeable absence of body hair. They were lifting lobster traps bare-chested in bibs and boots with their waxed, muscled chests and not a gelled hair out of place. Next to them were three cute women in short shorts and high heels sitting on the gunwales. It was an ad for some shoe company. Jamie took a pen out of his pocket and wrote "The Kid" next to the one of the male models. That was a well-known joke, for his cousin had been blessed with unusually good, strong looks for a Eugley. What made this worse was that The Kid had posed for the "Lobstermen of Maine" calendar a few years back, and people would never let him live it down. At every Christmas party in the Fish House, The Kid got facial masks and bath beads, scented candles and pretty-girl stuff. Jamie considered crossing it out, as his cousin already got enough shit for being too good-looking, but this was too perfect. He drew a cartoon bubble over The Kid's name, linking it to one of the male models, and wrote *Scrote Waxer*.

By 5:00, he was on his way, walking down to the wharf to a forlorn bait shack, which stood at the very end of the dock with its untreated pine boards beginning to curl off the nails. The air around it had the kind of rank, sour smell like the shithouse door of a tuna boat. Next to the bait shack, the floating dock humped up and down. At this hour, the sun was a pat of melting butter on the horizon and the water in the harbor was calm and slippery.

Nearby, hundreds of green and yellow wire traps sat on the stationary dock, stacked six-seven traps high, the warp stuffed inside. Behind the shack was a mess of old planking, disheveled pallets, a rusted gas tank, broken window panes, a bald tire, and a crumpled no parking sign. It all needed to go to the dump, which Everett never got around to. That's where Jamie found Everett, pouring the cuttings from the bait truck into 55-gallon oil drums. Everett had a cross-hatched face from years of harsh weather, with deep bags under his eyes, but he had a good disposition, particularly for a co-op manager, and Jamie preferred working with Everett over some of the other buyers.

"Help me with this," Everett said, grunting to steer the rim of the oil drum under the chute. Jamie shouldered the weight as the cuttings came out in a slippery, nasty gush. Sour herring billowed into their nostrils. "Suzy Q is coming to get this, told her I'd get it ready for her," Everett said.

"Oh that'll go over well," Jamie said, knowing that Suzy could get her own bait. But Everett was full of the old days when women didn't come near boats and found checkbooks impossible to balance. Done with the task, they walked inside the dirty little shack. The plank floors were black with the rage of boot marks. The morning had cheered the small room slightly, the sun orange across the counter and cash register. Suzy came in first, followed by Big Steve. She'd seen what had been done for her.

"What the fuck, Everett? I can pour my own bait." Her strapping body loomed over Everett, her long brown hair in her customary fishtail French braid. There were a few other girls who'd grown up lobstering with their dads, but she was considered a highliner in Petit Point.

Everett chuckled. "I just do it to give you a little extra time in the morning to curl your hair there, darlin'."

Suzy leveled a look at him. "You're looking to get a friggin' beating, I swear."

Big Steve lumbered up to the counter beside her with a hidden bearded smile. "Promise?" he said. "Can I have one too?"

Suzy slapped the counter to get Everett's attention. "I just ran through my last pair of gloves. Got a box of dunkers?" She reached into her back pocket.

"For you I might." Everett tipped back on his metal stool and plunked a package of gloves off the peg board. "You bring your truck round back and I'll load it up for ya," he said.

"The hell you will."

"Quit flirting, Everett," Jamie said, leaning on the counter.

"Yeah, old man," Big Steve said, "why don't you load up my truck too, while you're at it."

"Cause you ain't Suzy Q," Everett said. "And you ain't got the gams."

Big Steve turned around and pointed to the back of his pants. "I've got clammer's crack. . . ."

"Not good enough," Everett said.

A newcomer ducked into the bait shack then and it jolted everyone, like a stranger wandering inadvertently into the stall of a bathroom. The man looked around the shack in a breathless way, as if he'd just stumbled onto a hot cocoa stand on a wintry day. Reddish hair and a schoolboy face. He had on a red nylon puffy ski jacket with the expired ski tags still clipped to the zipper. Jamie had never seen him before but could tell instantly that he was from away and had money, and neither of these observations made Jamie feel very friendly.

The stranger nodded to Big Steve and Everett. "It's going to be a beauty day out there, huh? Man, you guys got it made year round." He jerked a thumb toward the water. "You just don't see this where I come from."

The flattery he put out there hung awkwardly. No one spoke for a moment.

"And where is it you come from?" Suzy said, cleaning her nails with the tip of her Red Ripper knife.

"Massachusetts. North Quincy—you know where that is?"

Suzy folded her lip, shook her head.

"You know who I got into the other day?" Big Steve said to Everett, as though the stranger had never walked in. "I've seen him, what's his name, over in Wheeler's Bay, he had that big dragger 'bout four, five, six years old, he used to lobster fish all through there—he had a big pink boat. . . ."

"Martin Bragg?"

"Yeah, I had a trawl out there that got hooked down on me and got mangled up. I was ready to cut the whole length off. Anyway, he'd come along, and all the rest of my gear in the area was fine, he just came along, got tangled up in my trawl, ended up cutting my rope in a hundred places."

"That right?" Everett said.

"And then I had a pair of wire cutters and I was cutting pieces of wire trying to get the thing out—I had a whole boatload of cut-up rope."

"That's a bitch."

"Yeah, it is."

Suzy broke in absently. "You guys hear about Churchie's going smoke-free Friday night?"

"No," Jamie said. "What for?"

"Some new thing they want to try—they want to get a DJ in the corner."

"That ain't gonna work," Jamie said. "I can see that whole area by Jeannie clearing out. By eight, no one will be there."

"Yeah, that's a mistake," Big Steve agreed. The stranger had been standing patiently, listening, but now made a move forward to the small counter with a smile on his face. Everett wasn't looking at him. He was leaning back on his old chair watching Suzy, who was buffing out her knife on the cuff of her flannel shirt. "You know what, though?" Suzy continued. "Think about it—just something different—anything. On a Friday night? I can see people sticking it out if the music's all right."

"Naw," Big Steve groaned. "The DJ will be chewing on glass."

"Can I buy eighty bags of salt from you?" the man asked Everett, clicking his nails on the counter. He looked to Big Steve. "Sorry—were you done?"

Big Steve's shoulders hunched into a careless shrug. Jamie frowned at the stranger.

"What do you need eighty bags of salt for?" Jamie asked, not gently.

The big smile emerged, dimples under the freckles. "Don't worry, I have a license."

Everett reached under the counter for a ledger. "What was that . . . eighty bags?"

"Yes sir."

Jamie examined the stranger, his eyes wandering up from the man's boat shoes to his brand-name red jacket. "You ain't got a Maine license if you're from North Quincy."

"Excuse me," the man said, politely. "But I own waterfront property in the area and yes, I have a Maine license." He smiled at Suzy apologetically.

"A recreational license," Jamie corrected. "You get five traps if you live on the water, that's it. So I don't know what you need all them bags of salt for."

The stranger's reddish hair and sunburned ears made him look as tough as an altar boy, but in an instant his pleasant, business-like tone turned authoritative. "I've got a lobstering license recognized by the law, and according to the law I can put my traps anywhere," the man replied coolly.

Big Steve smiled and drank his coffee.

"Really?" Jamie said. Staring him up and down. "What are your colors?" The sun from the dirty window fell across his eyes. "They wouldn't happen to be pink, green, black, and orange?"

The stranger glanced at him, hesitating. "What do you know about that?"

Jamie scratched his chin. "Cause those happen to be the colors that got all snarled up with my gear the other day, and I didn't cut you cause I didn't know who you were. But now that I know, I might just have to go back out there this morning and do it right."

The man squinted at him. He turned back to the counter and paid Everett in cash. "Can I just grab the salt outside?"

Everett didn't answer, but pointed his thumb toward the back to indicate that the man could get them himself.

Jamie kept his hands in his sweatshirt pocket. The stranger turned to leave. As he walked by Suzy, he touched the brim of his cap: "Ma'am."

The bait shack door slammed. Steve cast a look at Jamie.

Suzy's face contorted. "*Ma'am?*"

It was June, early in the season still. The lobsters were migrating inland, traveling huddled on the canyon floor, like wartorn refugees, clustered and secretive in their long underwater trek toward the warmth.

Beyond the Point, the waters became clearer, turning from gray to the dark green of a beer bottle. The boat bounced against the chop. Along the 10-mile radius of his family's fishing grounds, his orange and yellow buoys jostled against the whitecaps. Jamie shifted *Delores* a few degrees, checking the tidal currents. He knew exactly where those little refugees hid. They traveled the hills and gullies, the canyons and ledges of the ocean bottom, hiding in kelp beds. Half of his traps were in shoal water on short warps. The other half were positioned in the places they liked to hide, in deeper waters, along rocky outcrops.

High above the boat, the gulls crawled and crouched for bait, always with their fretful, bellyaching cries.

The scene with the redheaded stranger still had not left him; he could not let it go. This was his father in him, that mean miserable side to his nature that growled at people for being in his territory. And that part was just getting old. Half the time he was out to haul he wasn't enjoying it, not in the way he used to love it as a teenager. Now his thoughts always seemed to be on some bullshit thing like the stranger and why he needed so many bags of salt. The bullshit things were piling up. Maybe a couple of years ago he had a closetful of them; now he needed to rent a warehouse in his mind for them—and that nerve-jangling adrenaline turned his stomach, keeping him awake nights. Over what, some stupid jerk from Massachusetts? Only it wasn't just that guy, it was a thousand guys over a thousand days. It was his father coming out in him the older he got. All of it, getting very old.

Jamie made slow time over the shoals and through the lap of ocean at five knots. Salt spray spattered against the bow and cuddy. Every once in a while, a cold snap of spray hit his face. He worked in layers: two pairs of white cotton socks on his feet, a pair of Carhartts under oilskins, and a dark blue sweatshirt, which reeked so miserably it could not be brought into the house. He still had a young body, the stocky build of a Maine boy, all Popeye arms and cannons for thighs. But after eighteen years of lobstering, he had an old man's aches and creaks. On the water he worked with an economy of movement, a small smile.

Delores was a good, solid working boat, a thirty-four-foot Beals design, which he kept all nasty-neat with the deck scrubbed clear and everything in its place. He didn't throw wrappers or beer cans around like Thongchai. All she had on her were the electronics she came with, the instruments and dials on the bulkhead, a depth finder, a compass, a GPS plotter. He had a stove for warmth and a bait bucket for a chair. Hanging by a shoelace off the VHF radio was a shark's tooth to ward off shipwrecks. Unlike a lot of fishermen, he made a deliberate choice not to own a cell phone or a beeper. As for the Internet, he could've given two craps in a corned beef tin. At home, no call waiting, no caller ID. If someone called him and he was already on the phone, the caller got a busy signal and hung up.

There were a few lobstermen out that morning. He waved to a few of his dad's friends as he came up on his first strings. Jamie backed off the throttle, circling the boat a quarter. His left hand nudged the wheel, maneuvering *Delores* up into the wind and close to the first buoy. He pushed his hands into cotton gloves and used the gaff to hook the buoy, pulling up the warp's slack to the snatch block until it was positioned between the sheaves of the hydraulic trap hauler. As the spinning wheel of the hauler pulled the trap up 16 fathoms, the line tightened and a spray of water and kelp gunk doused his orange bibs. The wire trap broke the surface, and he hauled the twisting, dripping hulk onto the wash rail.

Only four lobsters. He didn't know why he was dreading this haul, but each trap he gaffed expecting it to be Christmas, and it was a pile of junk. Everyone he'd been talking to was itching to get on the water to pay off a heap of winter bills. It made people greedy and unethical, the way the strong trampled the weak to get to the exits in a burning building. Already in the season there'd been the usual smattering of trap molestation, stealing, "mysterious" boat propeller cuts. The Kid had hauled up a trap last week to find some jerk had taken out all the legal-size lobsters and replaced the trap with urchins.

Jamie pulled the lobsters out, their tails flipping. The first was a berried female, full of eggs. Jamie took out his Leatherman and punched her tail before tossing her back. Two were shorts, undersized. The fourth was a male, legal—but just barely. He held up a brass gauge to it and banded its claws with bright yellow rubber bands. With the kelp yanked out of the trap, all that was left were sand crabs. He threw them back. He shoved his fist into the bait bin, rebaited the mesh bags with herring, and closed its drawstrings. The trap eased off the rail and fell back into the water. He watched it disappear, where it would settle down to the bottom and soak for another two days before he checked it again.

The parking lot of Churchie's was glutted with trucks and motorcycles. The crushed-shell path to the door was flanked by barrels, traps, and a hulking rusty anchor. This was the only bar in Petit Point, the only home for fishermen, lobstermen, quahoggers, and draggermen. Some tourists had heard about it and tried to make it their hangout too, but Randy Church never did encourage the hokey dragger nets and fake plastic lobsters hanging on the wall. Instead he allowed every lobsterman in the area to hang their family buoy off a rafter or outside on the lamppost. Jamie walked into the ghastly light of the bar, which smelled of oil, leather, Jägermeister, and Lysol. He found Chuck, Bill, and Jimbo hunched over on the wooden stools, no surprise. They were there every day.

"Ugly!" they called out cheerfully.

"How's yer rug?" Chuck said, patting the stool next to him.

"Not bad," Jamie answered. He took the stool next to Chuck. This was the meeting place of beards and plaid shirts, off-the-shoulder rayon tops and tiger tattoos. Of missing teeth and missing legs. Of the whitest bastards the whitest state had ever seen. He looked around to see if anyone else was there as Jeannie put a PBR in front of him. Behind her, the sign by the cash register read: *Don't Like the Service? Suck A Fart Out Of My Ass.*

"I'll tell you *what*," Chuck was saying, his face blotched with rosacea. "I'll tell ya the best feckin' bumper sticker I ever saw. You know what it said?" His head bobbed slightly, his lips shiny. "It said, 'First, use your goddamned turn signal. *Then* go save Tibet.'"

The entire bar broke up. Jeannie shook her cigarette at him. "That's good," she said.

"I had this guy in front of me yesterday." Now Chuck had the whole bar. "Swear to God, we're doing sixty on Route One and he just slams on his brakes, soon as he gets a view of the ocean. Not fucking kidding. Dead stops so he can get his view. I had to veer completely over to the other lane, and I was lucky no one was coming that way. Can you believe that?"

"That's nothing. One time," Phil countered, "I'm in Bristol doing sixty, seventy, whatever, coming up over a hill and there's this feckin' station wagon right smack in the middle of the road. Completely parked. The friggin' ya-yas are on the side of the road taking a picture of a moose!"

"Oh, I hope you let 'em have it," Rufus said.

"Coss I did."

"Take a picture of this," Rufus said, opening up his pants.

"Oh Jesus," Jeannie said, rolling her eyes. "You know the rules. No balls on the bar."

"Put that shit away," Chuck growled.

The bar reeked of its usual—cigarette smoke and Lysol. The floor was worn down into grooves, the ocean visible from the chunky holes in the floor. When the rollers came in, the comforting sound

of the tide could be heard bashing against the pilings. A couple of small mismatched tables crouched under a mullioned window. In the corner, the jukebox played Stevie Ray Vaughan, and at the bar, Rufus and Pete were slapping down dog-eared cards. A guy at the end of the bar slept on his arm, his fleshy lips slack and open.

Jamie looked into his beer as Chuck and the guys continued their comforting drone of conversation. By the time Jeannie had set down his second beer in front of him, Big Steve had come in.

"Steve!"

"Steve-o."

The bar opened to him, faces turning. "Ladies." He hefted himself onto a bar stool next to Jamie. He was trying to keep it light, but Jamie could tell by Steve's colorless expression that he'd had the same kind of day out on the water.

Big Steve scratched an ear and swiveled to the side to show his enormous stomach. "What a joke."

"I know it," Jamie said.

"You?"

Jamie shrugged. "Not even a hundred pounds."

"I ain't even getting my bait back yet," Steve said, reaching for the beer Jeannie had poured.

"Yup," Jamie agreed.

"Can't blame it on the weather," Steve said, his bottom lip grasping at the foam of his beer. "We've had perfect sunny days, flat-ass calm out there." A slop of beer fell onto his dark green wool pants. He used the cuff of his plaid shirt to wipe it off and took another sip from his mug. "Ain't my traps, not the bait, so who the hell knows? I don't know, maybe my goddamn fish finder is off."

Jamie sympathized, but only for a moment, for this was a common refrain every night at Churchie's. Anytime a lobsterman came into Churchie's after work, the bitching started. He'd gotten adept at ignoring it, for it was out of everyone's control. The annual landings of lobsters hadn't changed in the last few years. The lobsters were always there, they were always going to come in, but everyone expected the landings to be like a vending machine:

put your quarter in, get your lobster out. In reality, lobstering had the same kind of unpredictable ups and downs as the stock market. Maynard even had to turn to cod fishing for a couple of years in the fifties when the lobster larvae dropped. His father experienced it in the seventies. But memories were short. The last seven or eight years had seen nothing but steady growth, and that's what people expected every year—everyone except the lobster scientists, the "fishcrats" who faithfully predicted there'd be a major collapse of lobster stock any year now. And though most lobstermen were tired of the sky perpetually falling, almost every summer, when the season was just beginning to start, someone always got edgy, wondering if this would be the year.

"They'll come," Jamie said. He was sick of hearing himself say this over and over. "They're just late this year."

"Yeah," Big Steve said. "By the time I pull my boat out for the season, they'll come in." Jamie was sick of hearing that one too.

"Goddamn right!" Rufus thundered from down the bar, banging his mug. A wave of gold splashed out. "I think someone's stealing from your traps, Steve-o, and we're gonna root 'em out!" He let forth a peal of chunky smoker's hack. Big Steve looked in no mood to be joking. He didn't even turn around.

"Let it go," Jamie said. "Or else you'll be thinking about it all night."

Steve swiped at his hair. "I need to friggin' relax."

"That's right," Jamie said. Jeannie put out some hot, saucy buffalo wings for the guys; fingers crawled across the mahogany bar toward the crock. Set around the side of the building were several coolers holding lobsters, quahogs, littlenecks, and crabs, which were hauled in daily and sold at the bar. She put out a homemade tureen of lobster chowder too. No one even looked at it.

"Oh, I meant to tell you," Steve said, brightening. "I found out who your new friend is."

"Who?"

"Cap'n Cheesehead this morning."

Jamie groaned. It took him all day to forget the redheaded man from the bait shack. "Who is he? Somebody connected?"

"Naw. His name is Neal Ames, a restaurant guy."

"You sure he didn't come up with anyone around here?"

"No, but he's got himself a lobster boat."

Jamie frowned. "What boat?"

"He's got himself a brand-new Novi."

Jamie snorted. It figured. "You can't get a license that way anymore."

"Well, he's obviously got money, so I'm sure he figured out a way."

Jamie set down his beer a little too hard. "Well, that's clever, don't you think? That's just some smart thinking. It don't matter if you've never done it before. Just come up to Maine, buy the best Nova Scotia boat around, and start lobstering. It's easy!"

"Hey, that's the American dream," Steve said.

Jamie chewed the inside of his cheek, glad for the numbing golden goodness of PBR. "He said he's got property around here. Do you know where?"

"Oh yes," Steve smiled. "The best part. I checked around on the VHF today. He's the one who bought the Parker Snow house on the point."

It felt like a whack across the head. "The one who wrote the friggin' check?"

"That's the one."

Air escaped Jamie's nostrils. Better his mother didn't hear of this; if she knew she'd sink her teeth into this guy's carotid.

"It's got a slip and a boathouse. And he's getting some gear together to fish this summer."

This was the mallet that knocked the croquet ball even farther up Jamie's ass. This guy had no earthly idea that he couldn't just walk into lobstering, that centuries of families had already determined fishing rights on the water—apart from what the laws said.

"Ah, don't worry," Steve said watching him. "He's just wasting his money."

Jamie sighed. He braced both arms against the bar. He wanted to get home to Anja. "All right." He cleared his throat. "I'm gonna head out."

"Yeah. . . ," Steve said, glancing at the back of the room. He put up an arm across Jamie to stop him. "Hold up a sec. Look who just walked in."

The Fogerty boys had ducked inside, standing there in flannel and wool, waffled long johns beneath spattered T-shirts, appearing ill at ease. Ev was the older one, in his mid-thirties, with a deeply lined face and scarred eyes. He had a bulkier build than his brother, Russell, who was thin and twitchy, his eyes and body always jerking to peripheral stimuli. Russell was known for coke, whereas Ev, rumor had it, had diversified the family business, selling Oxy to fishermen the moment they got off a monthlong stint.

They were from Courage, the next town over, a rival fishing town. They were not welcome at Churchie's and knew it. Did not care. Like crickets in the grass, everyone in the bar grew quiet as the rollers pounded the granite below. The Fogerty brothers began to make their way through the room. Rufus and Pete acknowledged them half-heartedly. Jamie turned back to his beer. Three-beer limit—that was his rule. Here he was at the end of his fourth.

Jamie looked straight ahead, dead-eyed. The last time he'd seen Russell Fogerty, he was 19. Sure enough, on a hunch Jamie had come around the Point to find Russell hauling up Jamie's traps and stealing lobsters from them. Just like a thieving Fogerty—it didn't matter what generation. And so Jamie did what Maynard and his father had done before him—he boarded Russell's boat and punched him four times in the neck and face until Russell dropped to the deck. Even though that was the code and Russell couldn't technically retaliate, there were murmurings around the harbor for up to a year after that incident that the Fogertys had better not find Jamie alone anywhere or they'd beat him until he was unrecognizable.

He didn't feel like getting into a fight, which was a problem, because now he had to psych himself up for one. The Fogertys were the type to look for the weakest guy, a wrong glance, a whisper. Any signal would do. Now this was going to be on the agenda tonight, when all he wanted to do was go home, eat some supper with

Anja, and fall into bed. They were moving his way, scanning, scouring, prickling up the room. It wouldn't take much more to start the room going, just a variation on one of three phrases:

"What are you looking at?"

"What did you say?"

"What are you, some kind of faggot?"

He'd seen guys who didn't fight often try to dance around these phrases, as if they could be dealt with logically. Jamie had been in enough of these situations to know it was just best at this point to square off. His body trembled, his hand wrapped around his beer. Once, in his early twenties, Jamie had gotten kicked in the head by the steel toe of someone's boot, and after the initial shock he remembered his temple throbbing with a sickening looseness, as his vision spangled with shots of light. The thin skin by his temple had broken, and the contusion had swollen up to the size of a purple Cadbury egg. The spangles, triggered by headaches, didn't go away for a year.

And now they were walking toward the end of the bar. Jamie could feel the breeze of their approach on his neck and slid casually around. He wasn't about to keep his back to either of them.

"What's up, Eugley?" Ev said. Russell had a faint smile, but his eyes had the same look as a dead coyote lolling in the back of a pickup truck. The eyes moved to Jeannie. "Two Jack and Cokes."

She mixed them up expertly and slid them across, taking their money. Every person at the bar tried to appear as if he weren't watching the Fogertys as they sat down. Jamie caught the flash glances of Steve, Chuck, Rufus, and Pete, regulars of the harbor, but not exactly the fighting kind. Which was why everyone liked Churchie's rather than the Tide Out Pub; Churchie's wasn't a brawler's bar. Jeannie went back into the kitchen and said something to the fry cook. She came back and wiped down the taps, murmuring to Jamie, "The back of the line knows what's up."

Minutes ago, the place had been full of lighthearted conversation, glasses clinking, the mild foolishness of a dart game in the corner. Russell appeared to be hopped up on something. The moment he sat down, his leg began jimmying, as if pressing a sewing pedal. He cracked his knuckles and arched his neck side to side.

For the moment, they both seemed to be keeping to themselves. Jamie finished his beer, and with his dirty fingers pinched two bills out of his hip pocket and laid them on the bar. Steve watched him do this. "You ain't goin' nowhere, guy."

Jamie's foot accidentally kicked the bar. "I'm not sticking around to find out what their problem is."

Steve's big hand covered Jamie's money as he slid it back to him.

Jamie pressed his lips into a line. "What are we waiting around for?"

Steve looked down the line of men at the bar. He caught Jeannie's eye and told her, "Pibbah for Jamie on me."

Anja was waiting, had no concept of time, probably was sitting at the kitchen table as the moments ticked by, continuing to get more confused. He could hear the old Anja now. *Get up and leave. So what if they have a problem.*

Oh sure. I get up and leave and all of a sudden at the beach store tomorrow, it's all about yeah, big fight last night, but Eugley had a touch of it and left before all the action.

Action—like this is a battle. Bunch of numbnuts sitting around a bar.

What if I leave and something happens? Next time, if I'm out at sea and my boat takes on water, who am I gonna call, the guys I left tonight?

Look around. Nothing's happening. The Fogertys are just checking out a new place for a drink.

That was the thing. No matter how innocent it looked, they would all have to wait; no one could leave. It was all a matter of time. They were all going to sit around the bar feeling squirmy and on edge until something happened or one of the phrases popped out. Ev and Russell were just like their old man; everybody in the bar was, until it went back nine, ten generations, the faces getting craggier and hairier, the noses broadening and flattening out; foreheads becoming prehistoric. Bunch of ass-scratching apes, that's what it was all about, this sitting around waiting for the inevitable. Someone would eventually stand up to take a piss. "Whaddaya getting up for—ya going somewhere?" someone would say, standing up, the bar hushing. The aggressor would advance with his chest all thrust out. The tucked-in chin, the two-handed shove. The grunts of excitable apes on the sidelines.

Jamie stayed. People sipped beers, warily eyeing one another as the Fogertys sat by themselves, unconcerned.

So is this gonna happen soon so we can go home?

You are home, shut up, get out of my head.

This was moronic. He finished the beer Steve bought him. His fifth. He was starting to feel drunk and irritable. Not good. Jamie purposefully looked at his watch. "So?"

"You just wait."

"I got a girl at home with a head injury. Right now, my fuckin' house could be on fire."

A look came over Steve's face. He'd forgotten and was momentarily sympathetic. "Just call her." He pulled his cell phone off his large belt. Jamie shook his head.

"Nothin's gonna happen, Steve. Know why?"

"Why?"

"Cause it ain't up to them. You can just walk out right now and not have to be part of what may or may not happen tonight."

"Then the Fogertys know they can drive us out. No way."

"Oh, people will stay, believe me. Not everybody in here is that smart."

Big Steve drew in a deep breath. He looked around to Rufus, Chuck, and Pete, who began murmuring again; the crickets had begun to tentatively chirp. He wanted confirmation. "You gonna head out?"

"Yeah, so are you."

"Yeah, all right, I'm behind ya in about one minute."

Jamie clasped Steve's big paw. And, pausing, looked at Jeannie and pulled out a twenty from his pocket, the last of what he'd made that day. "Two more Jack and Cokes—bring it over to them." Jamie slid off his stool. The front door was closer. Nice and easy.

"Where you going, Eugley?" The thin, high voice of Russell. Naturally. It couldn't have been aboveboard, neat. Jamie paused by the door as Jeannie came over and set down the drinks in front of the Fogertys. "Compliments of him," she mumbled.

"Who?" Ev said.

"Jamie," she said, louder. "No one wants you starting trouble here, you understand me? This is my bar."

They ignored her.

"Why don't you sit down and have a drink, Eugley?" Ev said to Jamie. There was something in his face that was miserable. Not ugly miserable, but *sad.* Same with Russell's dead eyes. Russell and his jimmying leg looked as if he was trying to run from something. Ev seemed mired in it. "Get him a Jack and Coke," Ev told Jeannie, which pissed her off, because he'd spoken to her not like the owner, but like the help.

Jamie hesitated. Part of him wanted to, but Anja was all alone, and that wasn't something they knew about or would understand. He could tell they'd be offended if he didn't. Maybe a fight would generate from *not* taking up his offer.

"I can't tonight," Jamie finally said. "Another time."

Ev and Russell said nothing to that, and Jamie reached for the door handle, comfortable with the end of that exchange. Nobody won or lost anything. Nobody got the upper hand or lost face—it was all real, no queer one-liners; it had even been a little *sensitive,* though he could live with that.

He wasn't looking where he was going and collided with someone coming in, the two of them bouncing chests.

"What the FUCK is going on?" James Eugley Senior said, shoving Jamie out of the way. Ev and Russell stood abruptly. The raw sound of wooden stools backed sharply off the pickled dark wood floors.

"I just heard you two were here," James snarled. He stood a head over Jamie, red-jowled, his shoulders curved. He was slightly taller than Ev. "This sure ain't your fuckin' bar."

Ev's mouth tucked in, lips over teeth that were sharp and small. Russell had lost all his jittery movement; he was now rigid.

Being shoved like that by his father for no reason—in front of the Fogertys and everybody—drove a spike of adrenaline through Jamie's chest.

"Everything's fine," Jamie said, disgusted. "They're not doing nothing, just having a drink."

James turned his square head toward Jamie, his face a web of lines. The red wall sconce colored his tight military cut completely red. "What?" He didn't allow his glance to remain on Jamie long and turned back to the Fogertys. "If I fuckin' find out that you fuckin' come back to this bar. I'll fuckin'. . . ."

Anja: *Jeez Jamie, do you think your fuckin' dad could learn a few new fuckin' adjectives?*

Ev grimaced. Russell looked around wild-eyed. But it was Ev who naturally took the lead and decided the course of things. He had his father's scroungy thin face, his measured appraisal of a situation. That miserable look was still there with the same malevolence Jamie had seen at the age of 12. Ev Fogerty had no fear of Senior, which everyone could see. Ev stared at James, chest out, as he picked up his sweatshirt off the back of the chair, Russell beside him.

"Can't wait to tell my dad how *cool* you all are over here in the Point," Ev said. Everyone watched them leave, listening to their boot heels crunch all the way down the mussel-shell walkway.

The turgid room contracted. The stiff stalks of bodies all upright in the center of the room drooped as the fry cooks headed back to the kitchen and the regulars swung back around on their stools. The dart game resumed, glasses clinked at side tables. Below the floorboards, the water pounded at the pilings.

James Senior, like a prom king now, sat down on a stool and let others congratulate him. "You see them haul outta here, Eugley?" Rufus said. "'Bout time they got the message."

Jamie stood at the door, watching the same people who, moments before, had a dump in their diapers over the Fogertys. Now they couldn't get enough of the back slap, the command to Jeannie that they were buying the next round.

"See ya later, Ugly," Chuck called merrily as Jamie stepped out the back door. He didn't bother to say goodbye.

EIGHT

Real stellar move on Senior's part to start it up with the Fogertys. Real smart, like the time The Kid battered a fallen hornets nest with a shovel just to see what would come out. While his father was perched on that stool basking in the sycophantic praise of his fellow idiots, Ev and Russell were probably sitting with their father, Dale, in some scorched-out fish shack, covered in bait and effluvia, teeth black, plotting the next move. For that was what fueled that Fogerty family. Not food, not territory—pure calculated revenge.

The blood had turned bad between Maynard Eugley and Claire Fogerty in the 1930s. A lot of old lobstering families had generational enemies like that, like the hillbilly wars of West Virginia, and every season there was always some suspicion—a few traps nipped here, nickel and dimed there—that the Fogertys had done it. Or they'd hear the Fogertys suspected them. No one ever used the telephone to verify, so retaliation was taken out on random strings. Maynard made sure Jamie knew how far back it went and Jamie listened to every scrap of information on that family, true or not. In a weird way, because of that Jamie had grown up knowing more about what went on in the Fogertys' family than in his own.

Nelson Fogerty hadn't started off lobstering—he'd been a bootlegger and a logger. Stories circulating along the wharves in the 1920s told of Nelson creeping down the coast to the barely inhabited township of Courage to make the booze that Maine had staunchly prohibited. Nelson had come to the wildest tangle of oceanfront woods he could find where no one would come looking, found a girl, married her, and produced a son, Claire, who kept up the fine family tradition in the manufacture and sale of illegal whiskey. It was a thriving era for the Fogertys, while other families in town were on the brink of starvation wearing bleached-out grain sacks for clothes. Jamie's grandmother Ruth told a bitter story of childhood friends dying with no money for a doctor or proper medicine while the Fogertys tooled around in a brand-new Model T. Men worked only a certain number of traps and could spend only a certain amount of time and energy each day hand hauling. Lobsters were 30 cents a pound and even the best lobster fishermen were starving.

Claire and Maynard were the same age, and though they had never been chummy, they were cordial. At that time, Petit Point had a better reputation for lobstering, with the Eugleys, the Thatchers, the Santerres, and a few other families running the line. One day, watching the Eugleys bring in wooden totes filled with lobsters, Claire Fogerty got the idea to try it himself. He saw the proud way they carried themselves, the respect they got from the communities and, more than anything, Maynard recalled, Claire wanted *that*. Claire didn't know what *that* was, had never grown up with *that*. "He brought me over a bottle of whiskey one afternoon," Maynard said. "It was a bribe, but then again, those were bad, miserable days, and sometimes you just wanted to forget. He told me his father had kicked him out of the business, out of the house. He sold me this line that he didn't want to be a bootlegger like his father. He wanted someone to teach him a real trade so he could provide for his family and have something he could teach his son."

Maynard had one rule: that Claire restrict his territory to the other side of the Point and remain in Courage. In those days, few lobstermen clogged the waters and could make only a couple hundred traps by hand, so there was no need for territory wars, but the Eugleys hadn't gotten as far as they did by being unnecessarily stupid. Claire agreed and signed a handwritten letter. Soon after, Maynard started teaching him the basics: how to build oak traps by hand, construct the parlors, how to knit the heads, how to navigate the waters, read the bottom, determine what bait to use, and how to set traps. Each day Maynard pulled a dirty black waterproof notebook from his oilskins and scrawled a few notes. Maynard caught Claire eyeing that little black book, where he could see penciled charts in there, landmarks and notations where the fishing was best.

After a month, Claire set off on his own, as agreed, in Courage waters. Each day, he baited the bags with herring or menhaden, just like Maynard had showed him. He worked alongside other lobstermen, feeling the pride of making an honest living with his hands. He felt the wind on his wet finger, pored over charts, used the sextant, and set his traps up by the rocks, just as Maynard did. And each day, while the Eugleys continued to haul in wooden traps teeming with lobsters, Claire's traps produced little to nothing. *I'm just learning; they'll come in*, Claire said to Maynard. But after a month of hand-hauling yet another trap filled only with horseshoe crab, snorts, and whelks, Claire began to stew on the same thought all green lobstermen had. What if Courage's harbor was barren? What if the area on the other side of Petit Point with its long finger of ledgy shoals was just naturally better bottom? What if Eugley was saving the best spots for himself, only pretending to show Claire how to lobster in exchange for all that free whiskey?

He waited until the Eugleys left home for Sunday services and stole through the side porch door, which was unlocked, like everyone's house in the neighborhood. It took him thirty minutes carefully leafing through the closets, under beds, in the rafters, before he found Maynard Eugley's little black book tucked inside a heavy rubber boot. The black book was every lobsterman's secret weapon—a treasure map detailing where the lobsters could be found, based on years of trial and error.

Within months, Claire's catch tripled while Maynard Eugley began to have a peculiar dry spell. Maynard never said anything about the missing book, and Claire watched him even more carefully, as each day Maynard went out to sea and fished by memory, even without the notes. One afternoon, when the Eugleys had all gone home to their wives and corn and cod chowder, Claire took his boat back out in the late day and found a particularly good piece of bottom beyond the border, in Petit Point territory, where the nutrient-rich waters flowed. Maynard's traps were everywhere and Claire began hauling them gleefully, poaching all the lobsters he could find and transferring them to his own traps. He'd been doing this for several months, careful not to take all of them. Instead, skimming a little off the top proved to be the best strategy, so that Eugley would just think he was having a bad season.

The sun had set that night, the sky dark blue, sticking with stars. The sucking sound of a dory right up against his boat caught Claire by surprise. Maynard Eugley lit a gas lamp, with a dreadful smile.

"We both pretty much knew at that moment we were always going to be enemies," Maynard said.

After that, a never-ending onslaught of shifty events plagued both families. A heap of newly built traps in Claire's side yard caught fire. Then, Maynard's father discovered his boat had been cut from its pennant and found damaged up on the rocks. A month later, Nelson's whiskey business was sabotaged by a tip-off to the sheriff, who found stockpiles of grain alcohol in a false floor in Claire's attic. Nelson and Claire served a two-year jail sentence, which silenced troubles for a time. Then a coincidence in the timing of the Fogertys' release from jail in late spring and fifty of Maynard's traps found cut one morning renewed the clash. "It's like dealing with sharks," Maynard explained. "A shark will swim by you and bump you once to see what you'll do. If you don't fight back the first time—that's when they come back."

And so it went down the line. Maynard had a couple of sons; Claire had a couple of sons. Unlike Claire, Dale turned out to be one of the most prolific lobstermen in Courage. The difference between James Senior and Dale Fogerty was that Dale inherited an enormous amount of gear and capital from his father at an early age, while James had to earn up his traps one by one. And, with illegal vices part of Dale Fogerty's blood, that would not be all he inherited. Booze and a little pot on boats were benign, as prevalent as the shags in the harbor, but by the late 1980s, around the time when the coast was experiencing an unprecedented surge in lobster landings, Dale Fogerty had developed himself a rocking cocaine habit.

A month out at a time on those boats in close quarters, Maynard had warned Jamie, it could happen to anyone. The signs were obvious: if a young man had too much time, too much money, and spent time with self-destructive friends, drugs would find him. Dale got sucked into it as a young fisherman. At the Tide Out Pub, the eighties saw a lot of men like Fogerty with a stack of twenties on the bar and neat white lines next to their beers. Maynard didn't know how much Dale had spent each day, but told Jamie, "When a guy comes off a boat with three thousand dollars in his pocket and three days later you hear he's trying to borrow twenty-five bucks from someone, you know that ain't good."

The real shame was Fogerty's wife, Alissa. They had five kids: Kenny, the oldest, Ev, Russell, Robby, and a baby girl, Peggy. A fisherman's wife was used to the long stretches of time her husband was out to sea, but the moment Fogerty stepped back on land, he rarely came home. The common opinion held that Alissa wasn't exactly all that bright or high-bred to begin with. Leaving the kids at home alone or, oftentimes, dragging them along, she began to spend more time at Tide Out to keep their marriage together. People remembered the kids crawling around the pool table while Dale and Alissa went off somewhere. Sometimes they didn't come back and the bartender's girlfriend had to bring all the kids back home at closing and put them to bed. And they were out of money. The bank had threatened to foreclose their cottage on the ocean.

Whatever Dale made on the water was gone, and he was already borrowing money before his next trip out. Alissa began to work the pool halls to make some quick side cash. Those were some seedy days, with family services coming to take the kids away after they lost their house. The public shame of this didn't touch Dale; he was either too far gone or too disinterested to care. They'd become one of those low-rent, always-in-jail harbor families that the community turned against. After the second time Alissa Fogerty was jailed for prostituting herself in front of a drug store in Rockland, she cleaned up. She took the baby girl with her and moved away, leaving her sons alone in a cramped southside apartment with Dale.

"Well, what do you expect when you raise your kids in shit!" his grandmother Ruth used to say in exasperation. She hated Dale and Alissa with a passion, but she was the only one who ever felt sorry for the Fogerty kids when they were young. "They're gonna grow up to be shit!"

Ruth had been right. They'd all grown up in shit, like twisted white mushrooms, poisonous and emotionally malformed. It wasn't just Ev and Russell. The entire family of Fogertys—brothers, cousins, and uncles—carried on the bad name. They were shape-shifters who stole through the waters at night. As many of the Fogertys self-destructed, lost their licenses, and went to jail, there always seemed to be a new weed of Fogerty cropping up as they cross-pollinated with other bad families.

There had been one ugly day in particular.

Jamie was 12; his muscles were just beginning to form on his sinewy little frame. Maynard alongside cut a rugged figure, his barrel chest in a tan Dickies button-up shirt. He had one uniform on the ocean in the summertime: a tan Dickies cap and a pair of tan Dickies pants tucked into rubber boots. "Captain Khaki" Jamie and The Kid called him.

As they approached the Point, Maynard's genial expression darkened, spying a boat that wasn't supposed to be so far over the territorial line. It was Ev and Russell Fogerty—they couldn't have been older than 17 or 18, but they were trespassing on Seal Rock—just standing there on a gang of slick black rocks.

As his grandfather steamed over, Jamie saw what the Fogerty boys were up to. They'd cornered a baby seal, which was aggressively protecting itself—croaking at them, its whiskers electrified.

He saw Russell raise a baseball bat. The contact of that bat on the seal's head sounded like a dodge ball smacking against the school-yard wall. Jamie had no recollection of the brief, antagonistic in-terchange between Maynard and the Fogerty boys before they charged off. All he saw was blood. The skull of that baby seal was caved in and blood floated like a distorted halo around its head. One eye had rolled upward in its socket, white, death-clamped. Its body floated, unmoving, and the sound—he was horrified by the sound. Instantly, the other seals on the rocks, in the water, began wailing and keening like baritone opera singers with hoarse throats. They raised their heads and wailed at once, in all direc-tions, at the sky, at the boat. A huffy, lung-collapsing feeling envel-oped Jamie as Maynard cursed and throttled forward, away from the cluster of rocks, back toward shore. His grandfather said not a word the rest of the trip back. In bed that night, Jamie thought of the way a skull was meant to be round, intact, how limpid pup-py eyes were supposed to be frisky, not rolled heavenward in slack death. The anger of it exhausted him, and the lung-collapsing feeling returned until he was hyperventilating. Jamie cried his eyes out over that baby seal that night, over a stupid animal that everyone thought was a pain in the ass just because it stole bait from traps.

It was the next day, quiet, in his grandfather's fish house, Ja-mie mending trap heads while Maynard smoked, watching the news. Maynard reached down, tugged up on his white socks. "You know the selkies have their own kind of revenge. . . ," he said.

Jamie looked up, the pink bags under his eyes making him look overtired, irrational. He'd not slept all night. Maynard called the seals "selkies," as the Irish and Scottish did. Jamie heard his soft inhale on the cigar.

"I've heard stories about them all my life. My dad knew this hunter who lived in Criehaven. It was a misty day this fella went out on the rocks. He came up against a bull—raised his rifle and heard it squeak out, 'Don't shoot!' or so he thought. It troubled him for a second, but he raised the gun again and heard 'Don't shoot' again. He thought he was hearing things and shot it anyway.

When he walked over to inspect it, there weren't no seal there at all, but a dead man with his skin all peeled off."

Jamie squinted, unwilling to get sucked into that tale. He was too old to think the story was true, but the day was subdued enough, the fire in the woodstove a hollow roar.

"They ain't mean, they don't do no harm, but you treat them the wrong way and. . . ." Maynard gave a curt nod and a *tsk*. "Let's just say there's a price to pay if you kill one. . . ." Maynard said this with a slow nod, which was just enough to keep Jamie going, having forgotten about being sucked in.

"What?"

"Accidents happen."

"Like what?"

"Like that hunter in Criehaven. He went stark ravin' out of his head and shot himself in the face that year. Right through the cheek and jaw."

"Did he live?"

"Barely. The islanders stayed away from him after that. That's what my dad told me. The hunter died alone, not long after, maybe three years. Horrible life." Maynard gazed at the greasy window. "The Fogertys killing that seal ain't the worst thing they've ever done. But they just brought some bad luck on them for this one, I'll tell you. Those crying selkies are going to stop crying real soon. It's gonna get real quiet over on that rock tonight. Some skins are gonna come off in the moonlight, and then some of them are gonna stand right up. I wouldn't want to be Ev or Russell lying all defenseless in their beds tonight, no sir."

For a while, at least, it eased the hurt. It made Jamie want to believe that bad people got what was coming to them, and not by a human court or after a lifetime in some nebulous place of hell. It gave him comfort that night to think that the sea had her own justice and that he'd wake up the next morning to hear that Ev and Russell Fogerty died mysteriously in the night, choked on their own tongues, their eyes inexplicably bulged with terror.

Of course they hadn't. Instead Ev and Russell continued to wake up every bright and cheery morning. Ev eventually went to jail for heroin trafficking; Russell, for taking a baseball bat to a neighbor's windshield; and Kenny, for shooting off an M16 at the Coast Guard off Nipple Rock. Only Robby, the youngest, stayed clean, and not even really that clean. Robert grew up just as strangled in the face as his father, with a body like a piece of stretched taffy. He had a raging, hidden habit of his own the last Jamie'd heard.

"To truly know your enemy," Maynard would say, tapping the side of his head, "know what drags him out of bed in the morning and keeps him going."

"More drugs?" Jamie guessed.

"Greed."

Later that summer, Jamie had seen firsthand what his grandfather meant by greed, and what it did to a man's face.

As soon as Maynard approached Dale's traps, Dale came blasting on over in his boat. When the two lobster boats were three or four fathoms apart, Jamie got his first ever glimpse of Dale Fogerty's face. He stared down Maynard with deep holes for blue eyes. His face was sun-shrunk, deeply creased—as if something clutched the skin beneath his eyes, dragging it down.

Over a hive of graying goatee, Fogerty aimed his long deliberate stare, while Maynard rolled his cigar to the other side of his pink cheek. "Hey Fogerty," Maynard said, both hands reaching up to casually grip the roof of the wheelhouse. "You're gonna want to move these soon. That is, if you still want them—"

Fogerty's mean, hard expression didn't change. "They're just fine where they are."

But Maynard just smiled, his chummy demeanor cooling. "No, I think they'll be moving along shortly, back over to your side— where they belong."

"I don't think so," answered Fogerty.

"Oh, I do," Maynard continued. "Next time I come back here, we ain't gonna be having this little talk." The parts not said were said very loud. Jamie remembered watching Fogerty, feeling scared but terribly proud of the way his grandfather spoke. At that, Fogerty grimaced and nosed his boat back toward Courage, but not before drawing a knife-straight line in the air with the flat of his hand.

Maynard chuckled as they watched Fogerty drive back over to his side of Seal Rock.

"What was that he did with his hand?" Jamie asked.

"That's what they call the old *fuck-you wave*. You're never sure if he's actually waving at ya or telling you he's gonna cut ya."

NINE

July had gone by too fast, the way summers did. Rounding into August was the depressing part, for in no time it would be September, and it seemed immediately after that—January. As summer rounded the hump, he felt he deserved a little something to look forward to—nothing obscene like the Ogdens' party, something small, the guys over for cribbage. *Whaddaya gonna be, a friggin' invalid all your life?* Thongchai drawled the night before at Churchie's. Thongchai was right, he was living as if he'd just shut down, marking the seasons as they passed.

On Saturday night, when Jamie answered the door, the only thing visible about Thongchai were his teeth. It took a second to register the rest of him beyond his broad grin. Thongchai stepped into the house carrying a paper bag. "Ugly!" he brayed. "You matha facka."

Jamie stepped back to let him in. He noticed Thongchai's bandaged hand. "What happened to you?"

"What? Oh, nothing."

"What did you do, idiot?"

"I jumped on the Ogdens' pig and wrestled her down."

"No, you did not."

"Yeah, she bit me."

"Is it bad?"

Thongchai looked at his tightly wrapped bandage. "Yeah, it hurts."

"Let me see." Jamie unraveled the bandage to see an angry crescent of torn skin. "Jesus, guy, did you get a shot or something?"

"Naw. It'll be all right."

"You oughta get a shot," Jamie said, leading him into the living room.

"We gave her beer all night long—that was *supposed* to make her quiet and nice, that's what they told me. Anyway, it don't matter. I got the cure." Thongchai pulled out a six-pack of Moxie soda from the paper bag and a bottle of yellow tequila. "New drink I made last night. Call it 'Toxie.' Hah!"

The Kid came through the door next. In his right hand, he held the family cribbage board, fashioned out of pine. In his left, he held the remainder of a cardboard suitcase of Narragansett.

"Hey, The Kid." Thongchai said.

"How ya doing." The Kid took off his jean jacket and whipped it across the back of a living room chair. He paused to give them both the handshake—the interlaced finger grasp. "Where's Anja?" he asked.

"Sleeping."

"Should we be quiet?"

"Naw, she's out for the night, don't worry."

Last one to come in was Cary, dressed in a raggy sweater with a large hole in the shoulder and muddy boots. Wiry and lean, Cary kicked out his legs in a goofy dance as he entered the living room. "Oh yes it's Ugly's night, and we're feelin' right, oh yes it's Ugly's night, oh what a night."

Cary was the only one of his friends who wasn't a fisherman. Cary, whose FAVORITE PASTIMES in the high school yearbook included *Painting* and whose FUTURE PLANS were to *Live happy,* was on the other side of Jamie's color wheel, the one non-redneck friend he had. In high school, Cary had woolly blond hair like a frayed Q-tip. Naturally, because he wasn't interested in hunting and wearing plaid, the rednecks called him a fag.

Jamie had noticed Cary's dry sense of humor in a math class they shared junior year taught by Mr. Johnson, who was known for his pair of overly tight khaki pants, a pair he'd probably had

118

for ten years and wore literally four out of five days of the week. They were stained, with one tell-tale grease stain on the knee and several faded ketchup or coffee stains on the thigh. "When they come off at night, them pants just stand up on their own in the corner," Cary whispered one day. Jamie found that funny, and then every day after that became a commentary on "The Pants," which Jamie began to look forward to. One day, Mr. Johnson turned from the blackboard with chalk dust smeared across his crotch. Cary coughed the word "*Pants.*" He covered his mouth and coughed again. "I want to nuzzle your *Pants.*"

There had been a suppressed bubble in Jamie waiting to burst. Thinking back on it, it was the word "nuzzle" that did him in. Nuzzle was something kids did to bunny rabbits or moms did to their babies' faces. Just the image of Cary lightly petting and rubbing Mr. Johnson's pants made him emit a sound he'd never in class made before. It was sort of like the sound of a gym sneaker squeaking across an indoor court. But it was enough to disrupt the class and make others laugh. Beside him, the dirty bastard Cary managed to laugh silently—only his shoulders shook. Then Jamie found himself wandering up to the principal's office for a detention.

After that, they became friends. Cary introduced Jamie to the art of listening to the entire album of *The Wall* with his eyes closed and to movies like "Fritz the Cat" and Monty Python shows. And because he was so verbally adroit, Cary was forever making up dirty puns, dirty limericks, and dirty dialogue as they listened to the TV with the volume low. Unlike other kids' rooms with posters of the Patriots and rally race cars on the wall, Cary's room was a warren of easels and canvases. His shelves were cluttered with brushes, sponges, books, totems, and talismans. Oil paints were dried up like crusted egg. The paintings that were hung up were dark, always in blues, blacks, and purples of Maine landscapes in the Apocalypse. Not only was Cary funny and low-key (good enough requirements for a friend), but he was talented.

Jamie opened the refrigerator, took out several beer bottles, and placed them on the counter. "What's up there, monkey spank?" Thongchai drawled, hand out to Cary.

"Not much. How's things been since the OUI?"

"Ah, you know," Thongchai smiled, digging into the pretzels as The Kid set up the cribbage board. "I gotta take a few classes now."

"What happened to your hand?" Cary asked.

"He tried to get some off a pig," Jamie said.

"You should've seen him last night," The Kid said gleefully. "He jumped off the porch and took her out. He was like one of those guys in westerns that jumps off a roof onto a horse. Then she reared up—I never seen anything like it—and she turned around and took a bite out of him. Jamie, you missed such a good party last night."

"Yeah, so you keep saying." Jamie brought a tray of snacks to the coffee table.

The Kid sat down on the leather recliner. "I mean it. Why didn't you go?"

"Because you guys are stupid and everything you do is either moronic, retarded, or stupid."

Thongchai's teeth came out in a taunting smile. "Just cause you lost your zest for life there, numbnuts, don't make me necess . . . nessarily . . . is it ne-cess or nessarily?"

Jamie looked at Cary. "Are you *trying* to say necessarily?" Jamie asked.

"Ne-cessally stupid," Thongchai finished and jutted out his chin.

"Way to nail it," Cary said.

Cary's fuzzy blond hair had been shaved down to his skull for the summer like a dog's fur. "Hey," he said, knocking his fist into Jamie's shoulder. "You want to go to a real party this weekend? One of my clients is throwing a big deal at a castle in Camden."

"*Clients*," The Kid sniggered. "Cary's got clients."

"Yeah, your mother's got clients," Cary said.

Jamie scratched his arm. "I don't know . . . Camden."

"Fuck Camden," said The Kid.

"Yeah, fuck Camden," blustered Thongchai from the kitchen. "Hey, why aren't you asking us to go?"

"Cause you're idiots," Jamie said.

"Cause Jamie needs to get his ass out there and stop sitting around feeling sorry for himself." Cary smacked him again. "It's about time, you gotta get out there."

"What am I gonna do with Anja? I can't leave her here, I can't take her with us."

"Get your mom to babysit," Cary said. "Donna will keep her company."

Jamie found himself getting frustrated—everybody always thought they had an easy solution. "What's the point? I hang out with you while you talk to a bunch of art fags?"

Cary smacked him. "You're coming."

Jamie smacked him back, a good whale across the face. Cary smiled and belted him across the head. "Fucker."

"Cock knocker."

"All right," said Thongchai, coming back into the living room stirring a glass of dark viscous liquid with his finger. "Let's play."

Cribbage was never, ever, *ever* to be taken lightly. It was invented by English poet Sir John Suckling (a name not lost on Jamie as a kid) in the 1630s, and the only way to play cribbage was to play to kill. They always played on the Eugley family board—a long board like the ones used in fraternities to paddle pledges, punctured with 121 holes in tracks running in 180-degree curves. Anyone who took too long to make a decision and held everyone up was known as a "Suckling." Any move in which a player was down 20 points and managed through great luck to leap ahead of everyone else was known as a "royal squamping." And the kiss of death, failing to reach peg number 91 when one's opponent had already zipped forward to the last peg, 121, was known as a "skunking." Cribbage in the entire Eugley clan was played year-round at family gatherings, weddings, funerals, in lake camp tournaments, lasting all day into the night. It was played in the car, on the boat, on the bus, at school, at lunch,

and long after the supper plates had been cleaned. It determined who had to take out the garbage, who had to wash the
car, and who had to stand on his head and sing the Oscar Meyer
weiner theme song. It leveled all arguments, settled all bets. As
a kid, Jamie took to cribbage the way Bobby Fischer had taken to
chess, single-mindedly and with unchecked arrogance. He'd
memorized strategies for three-handed cribbage and Captain's
cribbage, as well as low-ball cribbage. And many a board had
been broken over the years when the loser of an all-weekend
game finally snapped and hucked it against a tree. This was the
fourth or fifth family board in ten years.

They all sat down to play, arranging themselves around the
low coffee table. Jamie and Cary hunched forward on the couch,
Thongchai on a stool, and The Kid crammed onto the La-Z-Boy.
The Kid fiddled with arranging the pegs. Jamie cut the deck,
came up with the lowest card, and set out as dealer to shuffle
the cards once more. "I call the Muggins Rule," he stated. Cary
balked; the worst player, he'd only gotten into the game three
years ago. "No Muggins," Cary said.

"My house," Jamie said. "My board."

"Eat tuppy."

Jamie threw out six cards to each and they snatched them up.
The white-lined creases of Jamie's dog-eared deck fanned a little
fortress in each person's hands.

"Ooh," The Kid sang. "I see a major drubbin' coming on."

"Liar," said Thongchai automatically.

The Kid stared at Thongchai. "You're gonna be wailing for
your mama after this match."

Thongchai shuddered. "You talk tough for someone who likes
to experiment with corncobs." He fell to the side, laughing at his
own joke.

Cary sipped from his beer; it came off his lip with a wet pop.
"Just play."

Jamie leaned forward on the couch as cards slapped around.
"So what else happened last night, besides the Chief's sweaty hog
hump?"

"Oooh," The Kid said. "Rose Davis took out her boyfriend with a hockey stick around midnight."

"The cop?"

Thongchai cackled, because Rose had been his girlfriend eight years ago. "She friggin' housed him. That's the last thing I remember before passing out."

"Were you and the pig spooning by then?" Jamie asked.

"Shut up."

Jamie kept going. "Did they find you in the pasture, by the trough, all curled up and warm next to the pig, rubbing her eight nipples?"

That got them all going, particularly The Kid, whose laugh was still adolescent. "Fifteen two and the rest won't do," called Jamie, moving a peg.

"What was the problem with Rose?" Cary asked.

The Kid sighed. "I guess earlier in the night she'd found an email he sent to Rachel Wichenbach."

"Nooo," Cary said. "Jesus Christ. Is that who it was?"

"That's who it was."

"Well shit, do you blame her?" Thongchai said. "Dumb ass. Thinking that Rose wouldn't find out."

"That's where his mistake was," Jamie said. "Rose'd friggin' pummel her own grandmother for less."

"Like I didn't go out with her for two years," Thongchai said. "Jesus Christ, you don't have to tell me."

"Okay ladies," Cary said. "Stop spanking and get cranking, let's go." He laid down a card and announced his move. "Foe-ah."

Thongchai leaned forward, laying the next card, a seven. "Eleven . . . aahhh crap, my back just tweaked." He'd been having muscle spasms since his last car accident.

"That's what happens when you drink and drive," Cary said.

"Ah, shut up and go paint a patch of lupine, you stinkin' hippie."

Cary reached for the peg. "I'll go paint ya ma in the nude."

"Aw yeah," said Jamie, clapping. "Now we've got some GAME going!"

When he grinned, Thongchai's teeth could render ships off course. In his hot sweaty hands, he found himself holding a classic run of cards. "Twenty-five for six," he announced.

"Go," said Jamie.

"One for the go," Thongchai added, jumping his peg once more, putting him dangerously ahead.

Jamie scrutinized the board. "Oh, I don't like the looks of this."

Thongchai laced his fingers and turned them inside out. "By the time I finish my drink, I'll skunk all of ya." This was met with rude sounds.

"Chief," Jamie said cheerfully, "if you played the game half as good as you do gonnareahin' all them Rockland one-toofed scuppahs, then I'd be truly scared. . . ."

Thongchai waited until the guys stopped laughing before he said, "Ugly, the only thing keeping your sister out of that category is that she ain't got no biscuit ripper."

"Ahhhhhh. . . ." None of the guys wanted to picture Amanda getting it on, least of all Jamie.

"I just saw her last week at the Tide Out too. Aw Christ, ain't she some wicked gamey. . . ," Thongchai said, almost unable to get that out without a grin.

The Kid hopped in his seat and threw his cards down, he was laughing so hard, as Thongchai leaned in, contorted his face, and continued. "She was all hogged up in an off-the-shoulder top, all sweaty under the pits dancing to Madonna. . . ."

Jamie covered his ears. "Stop, don't do this."

Thongchai stood up and began to sway his hips. He licked his finger and touched his nipple. "Like a veeeergin—ewwww, touched for the very first time."

They all lost it, their laughter pounding through the small living room. Jamie slapped the pillows on the couch. "Stop . . . stop!"

A door opened in the hall, almost tentatively. Anja stumbled out of her room, her eyes bright as a bunny's, and stood before them. Her blond bangs were bent at slept-on angles.

Thongchai, still singing, leapt up from the stool to dance with Anja. The sudden movement startled her. He picked her up in his arms, stumbling slightly, her weight and his intoxication knocking them both against the wall.

"Thongchai, put her down," Jamie said, sobering. He got up at the same time as Cary, who put out a hand to steady Thongchai. The Kid, figuring now that Anja was awake, decided it was a good time to crank up the stereo and annihilate the living room with Metallica. Thongchai put Anja down and raised his fists in victory. Inexplicably, he leapt up on the stool, thrashed his fists to the jackhammer metal music, and attempted a belly flop onto the couch. Jamie wondered if the caveman part of Thongchai's brain was trying to recreate the scene of the previous night.

Instead, Thongchai did not anticipate that the force of landing on the couch's springy cushions would create an equally opposite force. It was like watching a little kid hurl himself onto the ground. You knew there would be consequences—you knew it would hurt and the crying was moments away. But you really itched to see it happen. Thongchai hit the couch in a fetal position. There was a momentary grunt of old springs before the couch pitched him off. As he flew off the couch in the same fetal position, his body slammed into the coffee table, collapsing it to broken spindles, spraying bottles, cards, and pretzels everywhere. Upon his face remained a vacant expression of joy.

TEN

Driving up a hidden dirt road with the windows open in Cary's little Escort, the moon illuminating the clean, night sky, Jamie immediately regretted his decision to follow Cary to some heathen castle in Camden, imagining he might have to suffer through New Agers prostrating themselves before a fire. "These people better not be all friggin' special and groovy," he said grumpily. "Nobody better be sitting around a room full of candles, wearing black and talking about painters of the Renaissance, Cary, or I'm gone."

Jamie's arm rested on the passenger door, where the window used to be. It was sticky. Cary still hadn't replaced the window that had been knocked out. All summer he used plastic adhered with duct tape.

"You've been in the Point too long and it shows," Cary said cheerfully. "You stink of small town."

"Just hand me a beer and don't shake it up none."

Cary reached under his seat and handed Jamie a Pibber. "And so you know," Jamie said, "I did that big-town thing already, remember? I leased my nuts out to Pia in Oregon and it took me more than two years to get them back."

Cary squinted in the moonlight to see the road. "Don't stop being open to new stuff or you're gonna end up like Thongchai, who thinks rodeo riding the Ogdens' pig is the highlight of the summer."

Jamie lifted his arm, gummy with duct tape residue, and rubbed it to get the stickiness off. "I'm gonna have to help him haul some of his traps now while he heals."

"Now he's got a sprained arm from your couch and a hand all maimed up by a pig. Maybe you should've let him sit around and think about it some."

"Oh, what's that gonna do? Teach him a lesson? Besides, don't forget he hauled my traps when Anja was in the hospital."

"Mm hmm."

"He and The Kid both helped me out. So it's only right I help him. That's the good part of the small town, don't forget." Jamie looked out the window. He could see a glimpse of a tall, gray-stoned castle through the pines. He sighed. "Are we really doing this?"

"Oh, stop crying, you'll have fun."

Cary hadn't exaggerated anything about this castle on the ride up. For all the times Jamie explored the midcoast as a teen, trespassing across the groomed lawns of oceanfront houses, he'd never seen this nineteenth-century fieldstone castle with giant mullioned windows. Cary turned in to the private driveway, past thick stands of dark pine.

At the great cathedral door, they could hear the muffle of thumping bass music. They pushed the solid eight-foot wooden door open. The great hallway was cool with a slate floor and, above, ceiling ribs of iron. Inside, two women floated by in black cocktail dresses and red lipstick. Close to the entrance stood a small cluster of yachtie types in pressed pleated khakis and white open-necked shirts. Jamie looked at Cary. He wasn't going to stay five minutes here, even if the worst threat these guys could pose were their $75 haircuts and docksiders.

Of course he could always turn back, find solace in the local tavern. There was always the option of staying home on familiar turf, going to the same places, enduring the same four or five topics of conversation from the same friends he'd known since grade school. He looked around some more, thinking he'd give this place ten minutes.

Farther in, the castle was done up in flowing sheets of downy red silk and other colors—purple, green, lavender, and canary yellow—billowing from the stone archways. Candles everywhere, white, dripping wax on floors, mantles, hearths, tables. Crazy liquid music echoed from hidden speakers, stuff they never heard in Petit Point. In the corner, by the granite spiral staircase, they saw a more familiar sight—long-haired boys in flannel, army pants cut off at the shins, threads dangling. These weren't hippies but another type altogether—outdoor boys, rock climbers, surfers, skaters, bikers. And soon, mutual recognition of their non-khaki uniforms prompted the longhairs to offer Cary and Jamie a hit of the good stuff. "Check out the food," one said, his voice squeezed with smoke.

Cary and Jamie drifted through another archway to find an industrial kitchen with three fireplaces and a dull-shiny stainless island in its center. The stainless steel was a theme, as it covered everything: the refrigerator, the stove, the dishwasher, the cupboards. Another smaller entrance through the kitchen led them to the dining room, where a massive oak table dominated the room. Easily twelve feet long, the table held the remains of a banquet. They circled the table. A spiral ham, a twenty-pound turkey, a roast beef, and a silver platter of lobster and gulf shrimp had been put out. Most of it had been picked over, but there were plenty of crackers, cheese, grapes, tapenades, and other dips. The end of the table was messy with empty champagne bottles, a few cocked to their side, dripping from the table.

"Who the hell throws a party like this?" Jamie said, pouring champagne into a plastic cup. "What is it, a wedding reception, somebody's birthday?"

"Nope. Just a 'dad's out of town' party."

Jamie picked up a piece of fruit he'd actually never seen before, holding the misshapen peach-colored thing in his hand. "Seems like such a waste of money to me."

"Hey, for some folks this is just a regular old Saturday night," Cary said. "That's why I dragged you out here, so you can get some class."

Jamie took a haul off a glass of champagne. "Gawd." His nostrils flared as it backed up his nose.

They wandered to where the music was the loudest, in the great room, where the party had concentrated with a full DJ set-up in one corner. A few girls were dancing by themselves in the center of the room. They both focused their attention on a girl with glasses who was dancing in a pirate hat and chain-mail halter top. While she was out there with two other beautiful girls, everyone's attention remained affixed to this girl and her goofy dancing. She laughed, head thrown back, completely unaware, her body unabashedly sturdy. Tiny feathers flew from her pink feather boa. All the rest of the people in the library followed her with their eyes like toddlers at suppertime watching the airplane of a spoon come swooping in. She danced not with the self-conscious posturing of a girl trying to be sexy, but with stupid abandonment. More people joined her on the dance floor. Cary nudged Jamie to come with him. "Come on."

Horror flashback to the hometown bar—a giant dance floor of parquet surrounded by bar stools and booths in a horseshoe shape—where everyone went to dance on a Friday night. This was Jamie's worst social nightmare, to have to dance in front of girls. Some of the most capable fishermen he knew could get on a dance floor and gyrate like a bunch of uncoordinated Rhesus monkeys. Only excessive alcohol could make a redneck get out on a dance floor and flail around. For Jamie, it'd have to be excessive alcohol and a cattle prod. Nothing else would make him succumb to the siren song of willing nubites and bad music.

Jamie stood there in an uncomfortable slouch, hands shoved in his pockets, over-sipping his bottled beer for something to do, sliding the occasional furtive glance around the room. He was swaying on a taut line between appearing disinterestedly interested and looking like a complete loser. Cary went over to dance with the girl in the pirate hat and her girlfriends as a disco song began to fill the room. Cary beckoned Jamie to join him. Suddenly everyone took to the floor like a wave of paramecia. Hands grabbed at him to pull him in. But he could not do it. Could not.

Especially not with Cary out there dancing in that horse-doing-math stomping kind of way.

Cary the goddamn artist. No matter what anyone in Petit Point thought, he had girls down to an art all right. The pirate girl laughed, wrapping her feathery boa around Cary's sweaty neck as he clomped along to the music next to her. Jamie watched this all happening, barely conscious he was grinding his back molars. Goddamn Cary could have any girl he wanted.

When the music died, people drifted off, fanning their shirts, and Cary came back over to Jamie with the pirate girl. "This is my friend," Cary said, introducing Jamie.

"Hey," said the girl with a wide grin. "What—ya got a wooden leg? You can't dance?" She tipped her black hat, revealing a face full of freckles.

Jamie clutched his beer with two fingers; his other hand stayed jammed in his pocket. "I'm actually better at standing than I am at dancing."

"Yeah," Cary butted in. "He's actually better at breathing than dancing."

Her eyes rewarded Jamie with a crazy spark of light. "Right," she said. She had a smile like an invitation to jump out of a plane.

Jamie followed her to the private bar. "Tequila sunrise, please," she said to the bartender, and looked at Jamie. "What do you want?"

"Uh . . . I'll get it, just a Bacardi and Coke." Regaining a small measure of self-confidence (now that Cary was elsewhere, chatting up yet another girl), Jamie fully intended to pay for the drinks. But before he could get out his wallet, the girl had already handed money to the bartender for both of them. "No, no, no," Jamie said, trying to push her money away. "Let me get this." She shifted, put her hand on her hip, and gave him a withering smirk.

"Come on now," Jamie said, hand on his back pocket. "I'm not going to let a woman pay for drinks." His fingers felt knobby and uncoordinated trying to wrench his wallet out of the lining of his pocket, so he didn't notice her nod to the bartender. By the time Jamie looked up, the bartender was handing back her change.

"Maybe you oughta let a broad take care of you," she said, patting his arm.

He was a Rottweiler's chew toy, deflated, watching her go back to her friends. He should've just let her buy the drink, now seeing it from her perspective; he was just another guy who couldn't let a woman control a simple situation with her own money. She'd gone back to her crowd in the corner, to a bunch of boys with tans and scruffy beards. He surveyed them, not yachtie types. They looked like working boys, like painters or boat boys, and she was awfully familiar with them.

"Let's go upstairs, I want to find this girl I know." Cary stood with his chambray shirt wide open to his nipples. All that was missing was the gold medallion. He ran his hands through his blond sweaty hair so that it stood in a sort of duck's ass homage to the 1950s.

Jamie craned his neck, looking again for the pirate girl. "Hey, did she tell you her name?"

"Nope. Maybe you should've danced with her."

"I would've, but I was afraid you were gonna friggin' knock me out with your disco moves."

Jamie reluctantly followed Cary up the granite staircase to the upstairs apartments. The second floor had a warmer feeling as they walked across English rugs cushioning hardwood floors. The Gothic windows over the stairs rose to a twenty-foot ceiling, and the faint cast of moon through the mullioned windows showed how close the castle was to the water.

They peeked into almost every bedroom, finding four-poster beds, frou-frou wallpaper, strawberry-scented potpourri. Other rooms were strident, masculine, with massive stone fireplaces and iron balconies overlooking the harbor. Cary followed the noise of a small party to a room where a group of women were sitting on the window seat, smoking, sipping red wine. A few of the girls were discussing the places in Europe where they'd spent semesters studying. Cary found the girl he was looking for. "Jamie, this is. . . ," Cary said, introducing her with a name Jamie'd already forgotten once he said it.

It was exactly the last place he wanted to be. He was back in Portland, Oregon, in a smoky room full of girls like Pia, cold, superior girls in black who flicked dismissive looks at him and went back to smoking.

The girl Cary introduced him to thought she was something special. She had black hair, ruler-straight, an inch higher than her eyebrows, and a limp handshake. If it's possible for two people to fall in love with each other at first glance, it's equally plausible for two people to hate each other at first sight. She gave him the once over, her mouth indicating by the way it forced itself into the tiniest line that Jamie would have nothing interesting to offer. And Jamie returned the look with the expression of someone who'd just witnessed a homeless man soil himself.

"I'll be downstairs," Jamie mumbled, backing out of the room.

"Oh, come on," Cary said. "I want you to meet some people."

"I think you can handle this all by yourself." Jamie smiled, backing out, and gently closed the door.

Yachtie World waited at the bottom of the staircase. The long-haired stoners had left, replaced by a tight group of five guys discussing the races they'd recently been in. He heard one of them actually refer to a dinghy as a "dink." Jamie stood at the top, looking down upon them. All five of them stood in a huddle, blocking the last stair, so that he'd have to squeeze past them to get by. His boot casually dropped to the first stair, determined not to get all wormy with them. So what if they were different and wore polo shirts with the Hinckley monogram?

"How's it goin'?" Jamie said, coming slowly down the stairs. It was okay that they all wore their hair parted on the side, with frosted highlights.

"Goin' great. Having a good time?" one of the guys said, friendly enough. The group parted to let Jamie through.

"I guess."

"Well, there's food in the dining room and plenty of drinks. Have whatever you want," the guy said, and went back to talking to his friends. The instinct to be at the ready and start shoving never left Jamie the entire time as he smiled. But to be let by without a problem—that was interesting. Had he been in the Point encountering these guys, it wouldn't have been as friendly.

It was mighty generous of everyone to offer him hash in the kitchen, as well. In the bathroom, two guys snorted rails. Silver platters went by with test tubes of alcohol, tiny tabs of acid, pills of Ecstasy upon velvet pillows. Champagne by the case. Jamie went to the kitchen refrigerator, pried open its dull metallic jaw, and dug around in the vegetable bin before he found a Heineken. Heineken was what they called quee-ah beer, but it would have to do. After seven of them, his face felt numb. He'd been there for maybe two hours in this fun house, mingling with a hash-mash of people who'd never, ever wander down to his neck of the woods. Cary was still nowhere to be found; he'd obviously ditched Jamie for that severe-looking Vulcan girl with thoroughfares for nostrils. Music still pounded, bass clouting the hallways, silk drapes billowing under fans and smoke machines. Two guys walked into the library holding hands.

Only forty miles down the road there was a whole other world.

As a kid, his father had dragged him to a few of Bin Ogden's parties. Binford Ogden, a sandy-haired hulk of a man, did a little of this and that, fishing, farming, landscaping, and painting to keep the family afloat. Jamie didn't remember much of his wife, but they had a sprawling farm of some thirty acres with horses, sheep, goats, and chickens. A dirt driveway was always clogged with some crapped-out car up on blocks. The lawn was always littered with kids' bikes, baling wire, tires, car parts, old rusted oil barrels. The inside of their three-story farmhouse smelled like cat piss and feet. The kitchen table was always filthy with last night's supper plates and the garbage pail in the hall was rank before someone thought to take it out.

At Bin Ogden parties, everyone got shithoused within the first fifteen minutes. On a sunny afternoon, the women sat around in vinyl lawn chairs with jugs of Allen's Coffee Brandy by their swollen ankles, while babies with diapers half off stumbled around the dirt yard barefoot. The Ogdens' dogs were feral, slept in the dirt, and barked at everything. On one particular Saturday afternoon, Bin Ogden and a few boys put together a pig roast. James Senior was already off hammered somewhere; reports of .22 rifles and shotguns could be heard in back of the barn. It took three men to string up the 200-pound pig, hoisting it over a tree branch with pulleys, while the crowd drank their beers and cheered. Bin Ogden made no ceremony about it; he took his knife and slit its throat, which made a sound like a rusty zipper. Giant crimson arcs of blood poured forth into the dirt and the air filled with a sour warmth, gave off a heavy smell of iron and sulfur. After the pig was drained, Bin stuck the knife in the belly and gutted it, while all the kids watched. The viscera dumped into the dirt, muted coils piled nearly two feet high. Jamie remembered looking around for his dad, while the Ogdens' dogs came out from their hiding place and attacked the pile of entrails.

Different worlds—they had no idea. These were Camden people—almost unreal the way they thought they were all starring in some hidden-camera movie, but it was surprising to find they were sociable and accepting, even of him in his blue work shirt, jeans, and boots. Wouldn't be the other way around. Forget two guys holding hands—if any of the people in this castle ventured into a harbor party forty minutes down the road, they'd have to know a lot more than how to raise a sail.

Jamie kept moving and wandered toward the back of the castle, to a quieter area. He discovered a converted indoor room of horse stalls and grooms' quarters. All the stalls had been outfitted with overstuffed chairs, tables, candles, and more shimmery curtains, so each one looked like an intimate train compartment, with several people in each, talking closely, clinking wine glasses. The dancing queen, the one with the pirate hat, sat alone. Jamie looked around, trying to sense if she was with anyone else.

He held his beer close and sat down on the cushioned bench

opposite her. Without a word, she smiled and held up a deck of index cards and began reading from them.

"Name, please. . . ."

"Jamie," he said.

Her head tilted.

"Age."

"Twenty-seven."

"Occupation."

He leaned back in the compartment; with his finger, he traced the beaded fringe of the curtain. "So, if I'm not a trust fund kid like everyone else here, what will that get me?"

"Not much off me."

"All right. . . ," he said slowly.

"Come on," she said. "Do you really think I care? I live on a boat. I have other ways of judging you." She examined his hands, which were winter white—the rest of his arms were browned.

"That's my glove tan," Jamie smiled.

"You're a lobsterman?" she said.

"Yeah."

"Do you ever take people out on your boat?"

"Mmm, it's not that I wouldn't want to take you on it, but I just can't."

"Why?"

"I just can't."

"Why? You gonna tell me that women are bad luck on boats?"

"Well, on mine they are."

"Oh *come on.*" She frowned. She continued reading from the cards. "Worst place you ever woke up."

Jamie thought for a moment. "On an island with seaweed down my shorts."

She looked at him. The smile was back. "A story for another time."

"Definitely for another time."

"Favorite color."

"Sunset . . . whatever color that happens to be." Just as Jamie was starting to catch onto the rhythm of this game, she snorted and said, "That's a bunch of sap. Do you like puppies and walks on the beach too?"

"Uh. . . ." He hesitated. "Wow, you're mean."

She shuffled the cards, clacking the neat stack onto the table. "I told you. I'm a sailor."

"Oh *really*."

"Yeah, the sea doesn't like anything soft."

"No shit."

"Married?" she asked.

"No."

"Girlfriend?"

Jamie hesitated again. "Not really."

She slapped down another card and said plainly. "Well which is it, yes or no?"

"Too complicated to get into right now."

She tipped her pirate hat and stared. He could see blue eyes behind her black glasses, a smart girl. Her mouth squinched to the side, evaluating him.

"How about you tell me *your* name," Jamie said.

She clacked the cards on the table. "I'm running the show here, mister."

He reached over and gently took the cards from her hands "What's your name?"

She relented, head tipped to the side. "Happy."

He laughed. "Happy?"

"What—you don't like the name Happy?"

He put up his hands. "Okay there."

"Would you feel more comfortable if I was a Mary-Ann or Sally Jane? "

"Okay, *Happy*." He let out an exaggerated breath. "Jesus. Y'ain't exactly *cuddly*, are ya?" He looked down at the homemade index card in his hand and squinted at the words *Where is the most embarrassing place you've ever been caught having sex?*

"Aww, that's not right. I am not asking you that question, sorry."

"What is it?" Happy pulled at the corner of the card to read the question. Suddenly capricious, she leaned her elbows on the table and clasped her hands. "Do you like stories? I'll tell you a story." She threw her head back and took off the pirate hat, ruffling her hair. Her look was tomboyish, with no-fuss straight brown hair, no makeup. She was a little too masculine for his taste, but there was no denying she had spark. Her freckles and the blue eyes behind her glasses were an unnerving mix of dorky and attractive.

"The most embarrassing place I've ever been caught having sex was in the closet with my high-school boyfriend," Happy said. "By his *father*."

"Jesus."

She nodded. "Yeah, okay? Embarrassing? No kidding. We were fooling around on his parents' bed while his parents were out, and by the time we heard them come home, it was too late to get out of their bedroom. So we hid, completely butt-naked, in his parents' closet. You can only guess what happened next."

"They found you."

"Worse. *They* started getting it on, right then and there in the bedroom."

"No."

She leaned closer. "Oh, yeah. Picture lying naked all scrunched up in a dark closet terrified you're going to get caught while his parents start going at it—I mean think of your parents—"

"I'd rather not—"

"Grunting and groaning. I mean, beyond embarrassing. I was this close to passing out from trying not to laugh with my boyfriend's hands clamped over my mouth. Then afterwards, it got worse. They turned on the light and found my bra on the other side of the bed. His dad opened up the closet stark naked. I thought we were all going to have heart attacks. Especially since we knew that *they* knew we'd heard everything."

"What happened then?"

"Oh." Happy shook her head as if the memory was still painfully fresh. "I don't know. I just ran out of the room and ran downstairs, still naked, got into my car and drove home. My boyfriend was left to deal with the whole thing. It was beyond nightmarish."

"You're blushing!" he said.

She fanned her face. "I know."

Jamie liked seeing her face turn red; he put the index cards down. "Okay, how many years have you been a sailor?"

"Nine. I'm the first mate for the *Sea Hair*, one of the schooners that's in the bay right now."

"I know that one. Where did you come up from, Key West?"

"Sure did," Happy said proudly. "That's my hometown."

"So you're a Floridian, huh?"

"Oooh," she whispered, "don't say that too loud. I don't call myself from the state—that's Heaven's waiting room. No, I'm a purebred conch from the Conch Republic."

"What's that—like being Estonian?"

Happy let out a high ring of laughter and he was surprised, for he hadn't meant it to be funny. "No, that's what we call Key West. Although I've spent a lot of time sailing in the Caribbean. This is my first time in Maine."

"Really? Well, I could show you around. Christ, I've lived here all of my life."

"Well Kee-rist, that'd be great," Happy said with a broad smile.

"Hey. You making fun of me?"

"No, I just love your accent."

Jamie made a face. "What accent?"

"Oh no," she laughed. "No accent at all. Thick as a chow-dah, I'd say."

"Mm—" Jamie shook his head. "That was bad. Don't even try."

"Chow-dah," she tried again.

He pronounced it for her. "Chowder."

"Chow-d'uh."

"Nope, too much emphasis on the 'd'uh.' That's how everybody says it, or tries to, drives me crazy. I hate the way people think we say 'ayuh' too."

"Ayuh, me too," Happy said deliberately, to taunt him. Jamie felt compelled to set her straight on the Maine "ayuh."

"Listen here, Happy, you're saying it like you're some friggin' yahoo in bare feet on a dirt road. Now listen closely—ee—," he said with a sharp intake of breath.

"What?" she said. "What was that?"

"Listen now, I'm telling you a Maine secret. That's the way you say it—as if you're just breathing and a little hitch gets caught in your throat. That says 'yep, I hear ya.' "

"I see."

"Point is, don't put so much effort into it." He abandoned the cards. "So, are you up here for the whole summer?"

"Pretty much, and then we sail back down either late October or early November, depending on how bad the captain wants to get back to the Keys."

"And then what?"

"I don't know." She shrugged. "See what happens."

"What do you do on the schooner?"

"Everything, from scrubbing the heads to raising the sails to entertaining the crowds."

"How many knots can you tie?" Jamie asked.

"Over twenty. Drunk even."

"Hmm."

"Hmm, what?"

"I don't know. Nothing. You're just having a good time, then."

"Yeah, of course!"

"What else do you want?" Jamie asked.

Happy's head tilted. "What do you mean?"

"I don't know." And he didn't even know why he was asking her this. "I guess I mean beyond sailing, what else do you want?"

"You mean, out of life?"

"Sure."

She sighed and messed up her hair again, slumping back in the horse-stall booth. "Oh God, I want it all, man. This time of year always makes me feel absurdly happy. I want to live more than one lifetime in my lifetime. I want to sail around the world. I want to try every drug known to man, but yet I want to live a good, aesthetic life. I want to grow gardens and live in a peaceful country cabin, but I also want to party my ass off at Mardi Gras. I want to give it all I got. This is it—my one free pass."

There's an old sea saying applied to a harbor obscured by gales and storms and to the tired sailor who yearns to go in: "When in doubt, stay out." The way she talked, the fierceness of her words, even the crazy glint in her eyes when she sat back and laughed, drove straight to his nerve endings. He looked down to his brown arms, found them goose pimpled. More superstitious than anyone, he saw her animated face, heard her siren call, *knew* this was going to be a problem.

ELEVEN

By seven in the morning, very few cars clogged the acre-wide parking lot. Bright sun bounced off windshields; asphalt rainbows made halos around the cart return. Anja stared at the chipped letters on the store sign from inside Carolyn's car. She ran her tongue back and forth along the front of her teeth. "What if I doesn't have enough money?"

"You got sixty bucks, that's more than enough," Carolyn said in her languid way. "Just budget as you go. Now step on it—clock's ticking."

Anja got out of the car and slung her green courier bag across her hip. She continued to assess the grocery store with a worried squint. "What if. . . ?"

"You'll do fine," Carolyn said, applying ChapStick. Anja got out of the car and walked haltingly toward the front doors. She gave one look back at the car. Carolyn was writing something in a notebook.

The sliding doors gave rubbery way and forced cool air onto Anja's face. She felt like a child who'd just wet her pants in public and didn't want to move. She blinked rapidly, shielding her eyes as the store's harsh lighting spangled everything in sight. All at once there were unfamiliar smells, determined people scurrying, grabbing at items. Resounding easy-listening music, some violin and drum machine samba, seemed to come from the ceiling, startling her. Before her, a display of apples ran twenty feet long: green Grannies next to Red Delicious, then a paler row of Macoun next to rows of Cortland, Gala, Braeburn, Empire. The rest of the produce section screamed bright colors—okra, kale, snap beans, assorted mushrooms—all waiting to be selected. The quantity of decisions alone made her heart yammer. She hadn't yet moved.

"Excuse me, dear." Behind her, an elderly woman stood with a sweet, patient smile, waiting for Anja to move out of the store's entrance.

"Oh, sorry." Anja stepped aside as the glass doors closed behind the old woman. "Oh, uh, where you get those?"

"Carts? Outside."

"Oh."

Anja tried to go back out, stomping on the black rubber mat that activated the sliding glass doors. It didn't work; the door she'd entered wasn't two-way.

"How I go back outside?" Anja hesitated in asking the old woman, who by now had already started inching her cart toward the produce section. The old woman's finger shook as she pointed. "Well, I suppose you could go all the way to the other side of the store. At the checkout, there's always a door."

Anja checked her watch, which said 7:07, and panicked. Had she really been futzing around here for half an hour, trying to figure out how to get in and out of a grocery store? She whipped the flap of her bag open. Inside was a small handheld walkie-talkie. She thumbed the dial to "on."

"Carolyn, help me."

A static click. "Right here. What's up?"

Anja's voice crept toward a whining note. "I can't find a cart and it's been a half an hour."

"No it hasn't. It's only been six minutes."

"But I can't find a cart."

"Use a basket."

"Where are they?"

"They're usually inside."

"Oh."

"Keep going." Carolyn clicked off.

Anja swallowed and pushed through the sliding glass entrance doors. Little tricks to stay on track, little tricks to stay on track, she remembered. *Close your eyes, count to ten.* Little tricks. Anja opened her eyes and pushed her way past the apples.

Her bag, an old pea-soup-green courier bag of Jamie's, held the tools to keep her on track. Anja opened it to check her grocery list. The list had been painstakingly rewritten four times in black pen with *DAIRY, MEAT, PRODUCE, GRAINS,* and *MISC.* fastidiously grouped and highlighted with different pale colors. She had a map of the store's layout. Carolyn had drawn in a route, starting with the farthest aisle. ("That's where the staple items are; see, they design each store so that you get sucked into buying all the crap first before you get to the staple items.") As if Anja needed any more complications in this task, she had someone deliberately trying to mark her path through a store. She looked at Carolyn's map and arrows with fierce concentration. Her bag also contained a calculator, a small dictionary (for words she had trouble accessing), and a day planner. The day planner's notes on this day said: "Buy grosheries at eight." And, as always, she wrote to remind herself "See your notes!" A tweet sounded from her digital wristwatch, alerting her to the fifteen-minute on-the-hour prompt. "Shut it," Anja hissed.

Sometimes it hurt to think. The reasoning, the processing, the mental zigs and zags of weighing decisions, figuring and analyzing, left her depleted in a state she called the Wash-Out. Too much thought brought on a sort of light-spangled shower like a severed electrical cable throwing sparks, obliterating everything in her brain and making it impossible for her to even think for nearly a whole day, sometimes two. After the Wash-Out came either the Monster Truck Headache or the Fog, whichever felt like seizing her head. Her daily life depended upon little tricks to stay on track.

At the hour mark, her watch beeped. She peered down aisle 7, which she'd already been up and down four times. Her basket was heavy and she looked around. There was a cart in aisle 7 that

143

no one seemed to be using. She peered into the baby seat, which contained a loaf of bread and a bag of oranges. If someone was using this cart, he or she wasn't using it *now*. Anja removed both items and put them on the shelf and took the cart. Little tricks to stay on track.

"Excuse me," said a woman coming back to the aisle with an arm full of cereal boxes. "That's my cart."

"Oh," Anja said. "It was just sitting here."

"Yeah," the woman pointed to the items Anja had placed on a shelf. "It was obviously being used—you took my stuff out and put it on the shelf."

Anja frowned and rubbed the side of her ear with her knuckle. "Can I have this cart?"

The woman uttered a harsh laugh. "No!"

Anja walked over to her, intending to whisper that she was having a hard time. But the woman misinterpreted her approach and stepped back, alarmed, as Anja tried to put a hand on her arm. "I just. . . ."

"What are you doing?" the woman demanded. She looked around to see if anyone was witnessing this.

"Can you find me a cart? I can't find none and I don't want Carolyn to know."

"What?"

Anja looked back at the cart. "That's a nice one. Good wheels on it."

The woman appraised her, did the up-and-down survey. She brushed past Anja and took her bread and bag of oranges off the shelf and walked off.

"Thank you!" Anja called. She turned the cart around, pleased. After twenty minutes, her cart held the trophies of a million decisions. Milk (a gallon? a quart? light-blocked? one percent? two percent? whole? skim?). Potatoes (Maine or Idaho? white, yellow, or red? russet? small or large? by the bag or loose by the pound?). Corn was easier. It was just a can. It said *Corn*. She ignored the other cans of corn with their siren-like pictures of white corn, shoe peg corn, yellow corn, packed in water or vacuum-packed—it was all a ploy to steer her away from her main goal. To the other cans of corn, which had taken the last of her patience, she muttered, "I'm not listening to you," as she placed the can of basic yellow corn in her cart.

A child stood in her way in the bread aisle, his big head in a direct line with the focaccia. He was standing idly, waiting for his mother, oblivious, his fingers pressing into the soft packages. "Move," she said. Her hand pushed his small head aside and he glared at her. "There you go."

She still had wine to pick up and a six-pack of PBR—that was down an aisle she'd already passed. Anja sighed and maneuvered the cart back around. She had a cross-reference schematic set up in the baby seat of her cart and without looking she continued to push the cart, which had twice already collided with other people's carts. Anja referred to her flip pad of notes to accompany the highlighted grocery list. Her notes:

Chicken—not boney, flat
Peppers—red or green? (Green was crossed out.)
Hot sauce—Jamie likes kind from Nu Orlens.
Bisquits—frozen
Salad—Which lettuce—green fluffy kind
Tomatos—big
Cellry—1
Cumumbers—1
Mushrooms—box. DO NOT FORGET DRESSING.
PBR—SAME!

Her head was killing her. Anja stood by the fish department and flicked the walkie-talkie back on. "Carolyn?"

Click. "Right here."

"I'm tired."

"You've been going for more than an hour, I'll bet you are. So you have everything?"

Anja sighed. The unnatural light over the fish department and the mother wheeling a lumbering, overfilled cart with a crying baby in the baby seat were starting to bring it on. Anja didn't even want to keep her eyes open and she rubbed her temple with her knuckle.

"Anja?" It was Carolyn. "You there?"

"Yes."

"Can you make it?"

"Hmm."

"All right. Leave your cart and find a place to sit for a couple of minutes. Do the Block Out practice."

"Okay," Anja said wearily. In an aluminum sunglasses display, Anja saw her own smeary face as she looked for a safe haven. Shoulders rolled, she trundled to the quietest part of the store she could find, the whole foods aisle, which was labeled "NEW AGE." A rubber stepstool at the end of the aisle beckoned. Lavender smells filled the aisle. Anja sat down on the stool and buried her face in her arms.

Dark and muffled—a place that didn't allow people or talking or any sort of visual input. Thoughts trickled, dew drops of manageable brainwork. "It's okay, rest. Rest." Her watch beeped once and then again, fifteen minutes later. It was okay, Carolyn taught her not to get annoyed. It was part of the outside world; control meant not responding to distraction. The pressure in her head killed, the sound of people talking was too much. She hated this; it had been like this all the time three years ago, a flash of images and sound from people she knew but couldn't place from where.

Children, it's time to go to school.

Nooooo. Uncle Beee-yoll.

Come on, let's go. Cissy, get your books. French, please bring the car around.

A man in a green smock approached her.

"Miss . . . are you okay?"

She nodded, her head still buried in her arms.

"Do you need help?"

Anja looked up, sighed. She was startled to see Tom Corbett from "The Courtship of Eddie's Father" there wearing a green smock with the image of a cornucopia of food upon it. Beside him stood his young son, Eddie. "Is she okay?" Eddie asked, looking up at his father.

Mr. Corbett ruffled his son's dark hair. "She's okay, sport, she's just tired."

Anja blinked. "I didn't know you worked at the Shop N' Save."

"Sure—" Mr. Corbett's friendly smile encouraged her.

"So did you quit magazine publishing?"

"Oh no—still do that too." He rocked on his heels.

Anja's brow contracted. "Well, I don't understand how you got two jobs and still always spend all your time walking with Eddie in the park."

The walkie-talkie spat. "Anja—"

"Excuse me," she said to Mr. Corbett and flipped the button. "Carolyn, guess what! The Courtship of Eddie's Father is here and they talking to me about how many jobs Mr. Corbett has."

"Uh huh," Carolyn said. "I'm coming in."

"Why?" Anja protested. "I'm fine now!"

"Yeah, right. You're talking in 'sitcom' again and that ain't good. This little exercise is over, kiddo."

"No, no, no," Anja said, looking up at Eddie, who seemed not to mind having his hair continuously ruffled by his father. "Carolyn, I got it. I'm going to check out now."

"You'd better be out in five minutes or I'm coming in." She clicked off.

"I can bring your cart to the checkout for you," Mr. Corbett said.

"Okay." Anja brightened. "Thanks!"

At the checkout, she looked around. Mr. Corbett and Eddie were no longer there. A clean-cut teenage boy with the knuckles of his hands inked with the letters READ and BOOKS dragged her items through the scanner. He held up the wine. "Can I see your ID?"

"Oh." Anja snapped out of the draggy fog and fumbled around in her wallet. "Yes. Okay, I don't drive, but I am old." Her mouth scooted to the side as she tried to think of a better word than "old" to describe that she was, in fact, too old to be trying to scam a bottle of wine past a teenager. "Here, my ID."

The boy gave her the cranked eyebrow before looking at her driver's license. "Uh. . . ." He looked over his shoulder, signaling the manager.

"What?" Anja laid both hands on the conveyer belt. "What's wrong?"

"It's just that your license is expired a few years ago. . . ."

The manager, a woman whose glasses were perched on her forehead, swept in, took the card from the teenager. "It's expired," she said curtly, as if Anja had been making trouble. Anja stared at the woman's eyebrows, which had been drawn in with a brown pencil. "We can't take it. Do you have any other ID?"

The Wash-Out, despite her best intentions, began to creep over her. Naturally her license was expired; she hadn't driven in three years. Anja felt exhausted and looked through her wallet: library card, movie rental card—remnants of her old life, nothing useful.

"But I need wine for the chicken sauce," she said.

The teenage boy removed himself from the discussion and went to help another cashier bag groceries. The manager, with her mouth set, looked like the mother of teenagers, as if she'd heard every excuse ever invented.

An older, mustached man behind Anja offered to help. "I'll buy the wine if it'll move this line along."

"I'm sorry. I can't allow you to do that," the manager said. "We can't sell you alcohol for her if she has an invalid ID."

"Why not?" Anja protested.

"I'm *sorry*."

"But I needs this wine to make the chicken sauce—"

A wave of groans in the back of the line galvanized her stress. "Ma'am," the manager said. "You're going to have to purchase the rest of these groceries. These people are waiting."

Anja fumbled through her bag and whipped out the walkie-talkie. Because the move was so sudden and herky-jerky, the manager flinched.

"MAYDAY—MAYDAY!" Anja yelled.

Click. "What's wrong?"

"The . . . the . . . she won't take it cause it's expired!"

"Calm down, Anja. . . ."

"I CAN'T MAKE NO FUCKING CHICKEN WITH NO COCK-KNOCKING WINE!"

Static. "I'm comin' in."

By ten, Carolyn and Anja were allowed to leave the manager's office after giving a full explanation to security. They worked it out that Anja wasn't actually *banned* from the store, but in the future, it was understood, she would need an escort. Anja followed Carolyn back to the car in silence. They loaded the paper bags into the hatchback.

"Well," Carolyn said once they were both back in the car. "I'd call this an interesting morning."

Anja slumped, the back of her wrist to her forehead. Her words came out hoarse. "Suck this."

"Actually, apart from some minor things, you completed your goal. You bought all the ingredients for under sixty bucks."

Anja looked out the window.

"You want a bacon cheeseburger?" Carolyn held up a fast-food bag. "It's a little cold."

Anja turned her crumpled face to Carolyn. "Where that come from?"

"What do you think I've been doing for the last three hours, sitting in the parking lot waiting for you? Here, you want it? I got some fries, too."

Anja continued to stare out the window, but her hand reached for the bag.

TWELVE

On Wednesday evening, he didn't have any plans. Felt himself propelled back to Camden, he didn't know why. Yes, he knew why, he was simply trying to pretend that he didn't know why, as if it were some sort of lark to go on a drive, to head down to the wharf, to take a look at the boats. As if he did this all the time.

As Jamie drove in, he looked for the flags of the *Sea Hair*, an eighty-six-foot rigged schooner. Unlike the other visiting ships, the *Sea Hair* was a working vessel, five trips a day and she'd be docked right at the wharf. She was a dinosaur-sized moth in Camden's harbor, with a topsail and a tree trunk for a mast. In the wind her giant sails looked like velvety ripples of muscles under taut Dacron skin, now lowering for the evening. He could see the last of the passengers stepping off and moving down the gangplank.

"Hey there, mister friendly neighborhood lobsterman," Happy called. He looked around the empty deck, his gaze drifting up. She was cowboying up on the boom, sitting astraddle, tucking and adjusting the sails that had been lowered.

"Hello," he said. He didn't know why, but he felt foolish saying her name aloud.

"Did you come to see me?"

"You wanna go for a drive?" Jamie blurted. He realized that was something a guy would say to his dog, not a girl. He'd never been suave enough to come up with something offhand and clever.

He'd actually worked himself up to be completely indifferent, and what came out of his mouth just now—pure poetry.

"Sure!" Happy said as she tugged and pushed the sail into neat folds. "Just gotta flake and furl this throat—one sec." He realized that her upper arms were incredibly muscled for a girl. He supposed they'd have to be if she was the first mate, hoisting the mainsail and the staysail with the rest of the crew.

She wore a chocolate bikini, and a baseball cap over her ponytail, working with no awareness of her body, her belly rumpling as she bent over. Jamie watched her roll off the boom nimbly, her bare feet touching the deck. "Cap'n—," she called to a young man by the quarterdeck. "Gonna head out for a bit, all right?"

The captain looked no older than Happy. He nodded, busy scribbling into a notebook, then said, "Are all the coolers stocked for tomorrow?"

"All set and ready to roll."

He waved at her and turned his attention back to his notebook.

Happy stood in front of Jamie, her hands on her hips. "Where we going?"

"I don't know. I thought we'd go inland. I'll show you a little bit of the back country."

"Give me five minutes, okay?" she said, and stepped down a ladder into the fo'c'sle.

After a few moments, Happy returned up on deck in jeans and a loose white shirt tied at her waist. Her feet were clad in flip-flops.

"Who's your captain?" Jamie asked as they walked toward the parking lot.

"Oh, he's great. His name is Nick, and he's really cool to work with. And the crew loves him." Jamie wanted to know more about the clean-cut captain, Nick, a good-looking kid, a guy who looked dashing and in command (never covered with herring guts), someone who might look mighty attractive to a brassy first mate, but luckily there was an inner voice that kept repeating *Play it cool, dipshit.* A voice that sounded very much like Cary's.

151

"Nice truck," she said, as he opened up the passenger's side of the Ford for her.

"It starts kinda hard," Jamie said and got in on his side. Before he turned over the ignition, he stared over the wheel for a moment. "By the way, before we go anywhere, I've got to ask you something." Jamie turned to her.

"Okay," Happy said slowly. She put her hands primly in her lap.

"What are your feelings on Metallica?"

Happy laughed. "I . . . I don't really have any."

Jamie stared straight ahead. "That's too bad." He reached across her lap and opened the passenger's side door. "I'll guess I'll be seeing ya then."

Happy remained where she was. "You're kidding, right?"

"Listen, I've got a tape of Metallica's 1984 concert here in the tape deck and I'm going to play it for you." Jamie pressed Play and the tinny sounds of metal guitar filled the cab. She nodded, listening. "Okay, in order to go for a ride, you must be dead honest about Metallica. What do you feel when you hear this song?"

She tried to follow. "I feel like. . . ."

"Like. . . ?" He prompted.

The guitar and bass sawed through the speakers. "I feel like . . . dropping a sack of kittens off a bridge into traffic." She turned to him, mimicking his expression.

"Wow," Jamie said, his eyebrows lifting slightly. "You're nuts." He seemed pleased and turned the engine over.

One of the best memories of Maine, Happy tells him later, is riding in the passenger's seat of a dirty, beat-up truck that takes her through miles of forested back roads, with a beer in her lap. She has been in cars that took her across expansive bridges over turquoise water in Florida, and this is different from the hilly, majestic coastline of California and definitely far superior than the highways, thoroughfares, and interstates that connect one Burger King to another. Maine back roads offer her flash glimpses of the dark gray-green ocean in between a million trees that bend the light of the sun so that her arm shimmers as it rests on the passenger's side window.

And there, as Jamie points out, is Ragged Mountain to the left. He names just about every mountain they drive by and ticks off a half dozen islands. He is like a tour guide, and informs her that there are around 3,000 islands in Maine. In return, she tells him that in Key West the best meal to have after a day of working on a boat is Drunken Shrimp, that is, about a pound of Key West shrimp boiled in beer and spices with a frosty colada that costs only a buck. This discussion leads to the best Maine comfort foods and why baked beans are the only thing some fishermen will eat when they come home for the day. In Key West, there is a place that has the best hushpuppies and Johnny bread anywhere in the land. "The owner is fourth-generation Conch," she says.

When Jamie asks her, "What are some of the best things you've ever seen out on the water?" she very much likes this question. It makes her realize that she had him all wrong at the party at the castle, pegging him as a simple lobsterman when, in fact, she recalls, that night he happened to ask her a very interesting question: what did she want to do with her life. What guy ever asks that? Usually, it's the same old uninspired thing. *Where do you work? Where did you go to school? Do you know so-and-so?* He asked what she wanted to do with her life.

So she answers his latest question regarding some of the best things she's ever seen on the water after cracking another Budweiser out of the built-in cooler in the cab and handing him a fresh one. The wind is breezing through her hair, the air pine-sweet for a change, not salty.

"One time, I was up on the bow," she says, "and I saw this pilot whale and I was so excited to be that close to a pilot whale—I could see his eyes and his mouth. And just as I was having this awesome moment, the two of us face to face, the whale sneezed and blew snot all over me. It was disgusting. I was completely covered in it. I looked like I was trying to fight my way out of a placenta."

Jamie really likes that story. They discover by bashing away the niceties that they share the same sort of juvenile sense of humor, and it prompts Jamie to tangent off on a really foul joke with a punch line about sodomizing a leprechaun, which makes her laugh.

"So one morning," Happy continues, "I got up super early for my watch, it was just bluish out, about to see dawn, when these dolphins, I swear to God, these dolphins are running alongside the schooner, phosphorescent with this crazy neon bluish green light to them, and they were jumping, leaving trails of floating blue-green *in the air.*"

"And you made fun of me for liking sunsets," Jamie says.

"Oh . . . oh, I did do that, didn't I? Wow, that *was* kind of mean, wasn't it."

"Yes, and you *really* hurt my feelings."

"Oh, right," she says and giggles. "I made you cry like a little girl."

"You ever been four-wheelin'?" Jamie asks.

"Uh. . . ."

At this moment, the whole world changed from light jokey talk and elbows hanging out the window. Jamie veered off the paved road and onto a dirt road that caused the Ford to jounce Happy hard up out of the passenger's seat. "Make sure that belt's on good," he said, his hand reaching over to tug on it.

The dirt road going up the mountain looked wide enough for a baby carriage. Elms and poplars crowded the sides with choking branches that made horrible scraping sounds against the hood and truck doors. Happy yelped, "Won't this ruin your truck?"

The shrug said it all: too many years of banging on the vehicle. In less than two minutes, the Ford went nearly vertical; they looked like astronauts getting set for takeoff, except for the violent rocking side to side. Happy stopped laughing. "Jamie!! Holy shit!"

"You just hang on." He wrestled the wheel as branches smacked the windows on both sides. The engine gunned and smoked. Despite the seat belt, Happy's shoulder battered against the side door. "I've been driving up this road since I was 16," Jamie yelled. "Wait 'til you see the top!"

At last, the crowding trees gave way to the bright blue of the sky and the angle of the truck leveled out. Happy rubbed her shoulder where some nice bruises would appear the next day. They came to a bald spot on a mountain, through patchy islands of blueberry maroon, as the truck rolled to a stop. "Wow," whispered Happy. She got out.

They were the only people on the top of the mountain. The cornflower blue of the sky went forever, grading down to the darker blue of the ocean. Other mountains in the distance shared the landscape, with rich valleys of pine trees, knobby like a carpet of abaca, not a multimillion-dollar house in sight. Farther to the right, they could see a lake with a dark sheen to it, patchy shadows on which a triangle of a sailboat moved undetectably slowly. The kayakers were like yellow and pink water bugs. Happy looked back to the ocean, which could have been wild with waves, but from up on the mountain it was motionless, pewter gray with layers of light blue. The coastline looked like a piece of fabric that had been violently ripped in half, all the shredded edges formed into peninsulas and coves.

"Look at those islands over there," Jamie said. He pointed to a cluster of mossy mounds in the far distance that looked like the humps of a giant sea serpent. "That's LaSalle and Thousand Acre Island. And see, you can just make out the Camden harbor."

"Oh, yeah, look, there it is! There's the *Sea Hair*!"

The harbor was a tiny little divot in the coastline with miniscule schooners, the little town laid out like a department store Christmas scene. Almost twenty feet off the side of the mountain, turkey buzzards played in the thermals, flying like kites with their ragged brown wings and razored curved beaks. They climbed and dipped, never once flapping their wings, before falling into lazy spirals down the face of the mountain.

"So," Happy said, hoisting herself up on a large rock. "How does this work? Are you dating somebody at the same time you've got me up here on a date?"

"Who said we're on a date?" Jamie said, his back to her. "I just took you for a drive."

"Oh really," Happy said, adjusting her tone. "Well, why don't you just tell me about your girlfriend who isn't your girlfriend, or however you said it."

Jamie scratched the back of his neck. "See that island over there? The one next to the one with the lighthouse?"

"Yeah?"

"That used to be owned by a sea captain out of Searsport, who willed it to his wife. When she died, they had no relatives, no kids, so she left it to her parrot. A whole island left to a parrot. The town scrambled to figure that one out. Now I think it's been donated to the public."

"Uh huh," Happy said. "So, do you still love her?"

Jamie gave a short sigh. "Do we really have to talk about this right now?"

"Oh yeah, we do."

"Why?"

"Cause I just want people to be straight-up with me."

Jamie stared at the rocky clearings on the mountain, where drooping sac-like flowers fought the wind. Silence up here but for the birds and crickets, the occasional dog barking down in the valley. "Her name's Anja." Jamie took his cigarettes out of his shirt pocket. He offered Happy one. She shook her head. "We met at the high school. Not as in we went to high school together—it was later, when I was teaching."

"Hold on—you're a teacher?"

"Not really, I was just a sub in the winters for a couple of years when I was first starting out. I taught biology just to hold me 'til spring. Anyway, she was an art teacher there—she'd just come up from Boston."

"How long ago?"

"That was six years ago."

"Mmm hmm. So, when did you break up?"

The answer to that question should've come immediately, but it didn't. Happy waited.

"Yeah, okay." He turned from the horizon and came over to the rock; hitched himself up right next to her. "I'll tell you everything, but just let me talk. Nothin's gonna be in the right order."

It had been a long time since he told "The Story," beginning with the days they lived together before the accident, then the day on the boat, the coma, the years of rehabilitation. He told it without emotion in chronological order, figuring it was a story that needed to be abbreviated. People weren't that much interested in the details unless they directly affected their own lives.

"And her kind of head injury didn't just happen in one spot, the way a car wreck hits you right in the front of the head," Jamie said. "Hers was from a lack of oxygen, so it was everywhere, affecting everything, the way she talks, walks, thinks. She can't drive, can't work, sometimes she can't even have a full day without problems. And it's been three years. In some ways she's like a six-year-old—" He looked at Happy and found her nodding. "So she still lives with me, to answer your question. She may or not get better."

"Wow." Happy bit her thumbnail.

"That wasn't what you expected, huh?"

"No, it wasn't. I thought you were going to tell me you were still in love with someone who wasn't in love with you anymore. I'm really sorry."

Jamie shrugged, threw his cigarette on the ground. He looked at Happy, who was staring at him, and he didn't want that. None of this pity, the way people always looked at him after they knew the full story.

"You gonna pick that up?" she asked. He looked down at the cigarette butt by his boot, realizing that was why was staring.

"Oh," he said. "Sorry." He picked it up. "So what kind of last name goes with Happy?"

"Klein."

"What is that, Jewish?"

She snorted, "No, Lithuanian."

He stared at her.

"You're not really staring at me thinking I'm Lithuanian, are you?"

"No. . . ," Jamie said, startled by her splintery humor. "Never mind. So where is your family, where are your folks?"

"Oh, my mom's still in upstate New York; my dad just jumped into his third marriage in Philly." She swung her legs, her chin jutting out toward the sea. "Yeah, right before I came up to Maine, my brother and I had the good fortune to attend the wedding. It was a blast, really. He picked a Christian gal this time. Not only that, he told us two days before the wedding he was *converting* to Christianity too."

"Wow."

"My dad, he's got more money than he knows what to do with—he sets us both up in this flea-bitten dump downtown, but in different rooms on different floors. I think it was a crack house. The bedspread had stains on it—it smelled like dirty socks—and the toilet overflowed the first time I flushed it. So I just went to my brother's room and we huddled on a single bed all night long, while sirens went off outside, dogs barking. I heard someone scream at one point." Happy's expression curled into a smile. "That morning our two brand-new stepbrothers picked us up at the hotel to take us to the church.

"My brother and I, we're both sitting in the back seat, while my new stepbrothers are up in front, and they haven't said a word to us. We're all complete strangers—so I say, 'Hey guys, how much fun is this, huh?' I mean, I figure, someone's got to break the tension. We're all going to be this one big happy mixed Jew-Christian family now. They didn't even look back or say anything. You could tell that they couldn't stand this situation and they couldn't stand us."

"Oh, man."

"Oh yeah, it just gets better. So we get to the church on this gray rainy morning. Richie and I walk in and sit down in one of the pews. There's all this confusion—people on the bride's side, standing up, talking—all I can do is find a pew and sit down. So Richie leans over to me and says, 'Happy, whatever you do, don't look up.' And I almost do, but he puts a hand over my eyes and makes me promise not to look up. At this point, we just start giggling.

What can you do? So I don't know what he's talking about until the organ music starts and my dad and his new wife start walking down the aisle. That's when Richie says, 'Okay, look up.' That's when I see the far wall behind the priest: there is a gigantic effigy of Jesus Christ up on the cross—I mean he is like fifty feet high— made of this realistic-looking plaster, blood is literally running in rivulets out of his hands and feet into this pool, which is then re- directing the red water back up through these little pipes. . . ."

"No," Jamie said. "Like one of those cherubs peeing in a fountain?"

"Oh, yeah! So I start laughing—I mean I get really going. I can't believe what I'm seeing. Richie's trying so hard to keep me quiet. So the entire ceremony stops and our dad turns around and glares at us and all these people start grumbling at once and someone tells us to get out. So we got up and left. We were kicked out of our own dad's wedding! We went back to that shitbag ho- tel and stayed for two more days, just hanging around until our plane took off. Our dad hasn't spoken to us since."

"Jeez, what a great story."

"Some of the crappiest ones are." She rubbed her nose, not in the least upset by the retelling.

"So you don't really get along with your dad, I take it."

"No, not so much. We're just two completely opposite people, but my mom and I are tight."

"Yeah, same with me. I'm really only close to my mom, " Jamie said. Talking with her, he liked how she was completely open, unguarded. She was easy to be around.

"What's your dad's deal?"

"He's just one of these guys who thinks he owns the harbor and everyone in it. He's uh . . . I don't know how to explain it. I mean, he's a good person, I probably shouldn't talk about him like this."

"It's not like we're gonna run into each other."

Jamie sighed. "Yeah, I know."

"What are you going to do about it?"

He looked at her. "What do you mean?"

159

Happy jumped off the rock and stood in front of him, her fists clenched. She had the largest biceps he'd ever seen on a girl. "Ya gonna give it to him? The old smackaroo?" She bobbed and threw a slow-motion punch, which Jamie fended off with his palm.

"My God, woman. You've got bigger arms than me." Happy continued to box at him, her features screwed down, her tongue between her teeth. She was very cute, in a weird and unsettling way. Women he knew didn't act this way; she was acting like one of his friends, goofin' and play-fighting.

"How hard can you hit?" Jamie said, raising his right hand out in front of her.

"I won't really hit you," she said, her arms now settling demurely at her sides.

"Have you ever been in a fight?" Jamie asked. "A real one, none of this girly pushing and hair pulling stuff?"

"No, not really, I'm from a hippie family. You ever see a hippie in a fight?" She pretended to be tracing the sky with a finger, her expression slack.

"Uh huh."

"But you, mister lobsterman, you live for fighting, I'm sure."

"I don't *live* for it, but I've had to do it."

"I should've been taught to fight when I was young," she said, and went at him again, her fist jabbing at his outheld palm. "Nine is a little too young to be opening up a rape kit." She continued to bat away, but Jamie lowered the hand she'd been using as a target.

Happy seemed to realize the impact of what she'd said. "I'm sorry, I forget how it sounds when I just blurt it out like that. It's something I have to tell people right away when I meet them. Sort of like sitting in a wheelchair when you first meet someone—the big elephant in the room. I just have to get it out of the way and then I can be myself."

"What happened?" Jamie asked.

Happy shrugged. "Silvia and Jack—my parents—before they divorced, they had these friends who had this teenage son, Frank.

160

He was sort of this floppy-haired, shy, bucktoothed Jon Voight. He was my babysitter and I adored him, which, of course, made it worse. We were making popcorn and he let me stay up with him to watch "The Twilight Zone." He started chasing me around the house one night; it was this game we played—if he didn't find me, I didn't have to go to bed. I just remember the sound of the air popper spitting out exploding corn kernels. Well, I was too young to know that when he pinned me down on my parents' bed, the game was not quite over." Happy's mouth flattened into a grim line. "In and out, just like that, probably not more than ten seconds. But it hurt. It did *hurt*."

She smiled, and for all of her tough-guy stance, it was a broken smile, a betrayal to her face. "I didn't tell my folks 'til I was 16, and by that time they were divorced. They tried to hunt down Frank, but the lawyers said the statute of limitations had run out."

Jamie put his hand on her shoulder, nothing more, as they sat side by side looking out at the blue patches on a gray ocean. "I'm really good at telling that story, you know?" Happy said. "I've been telling it forever, so no big deal, okay?"

"Okay."

"That's why I have to tell the story quickly, get it over with— move on."

"Is that why you're a sailor? You gotta always move on?"

Happy smiled. "You've got an awfully lovely town here, but I don't think I could ever stay."

It was beginning to get dark, the sun already down below the trees in the west, the clouds a warm marmalade color. Happy didn't like the silence, made a face. "Can we just forget all this? Just go back to being stupid and silly, okay?"

He let his hand remain where it was. "Hey, I'm already stupid, so . . . you can just be silly."

"Fair enough."

THIRTEEN

A snowmobile accident in high school had wrenched his collarbone out of place and the injury had never properly healed, which turned out to be fortunate, for it gave his sensory perception an uncanny boost. Jamie trusted his collarbone more than he ever trusted a weather report. Some meteorologist could sit at his desk, analyze computer data, read printouts until he went blind. Jamie felt any slight shift of weather in those beveled bones every time.

Winds, freshening, came off the southeast. It was a cloudy day, the swells were dark gray and oily. Grim stuff, not helping his case, as he'd been off the beam the last few days, more interested in playing than lobstering. Happy Klein had worked herself hard into his thoughts at night when he tried to go to sleep, in the morning when he woke. In tandem came the familiar warm damp guilt thinking of Anja. A sou'easter coming on, that was the root cause of the ache in his collarbone. The other ache was harder to identify, disembodied but sharp—coming from things he shouldn't have been thinking.

Weather was beginning to churn. He needed to get out there and bang out some traps, needed to make some money. He gunned the throttle against the lunging waves, bracing his boots against the chop. No one else was out there today. It was going to be a hard day with this weather, a backbreaker, as it took energy just to withstand the jerky momentum of the boat.

Shortly before Seal Rock, he slowed *Delores* to an idle and looked around. After all the warnings, the obvious back-tie, what he saw in front of him was truly dumbfounding. They were there again, the orange, green, black, and pink buoys in his territory, bobbing a healthy distance from his strings. Jamie blinked rapidly for several seconds. He looked about as if someone might be putting him on. Was it truly possible that Captain Numbnuts really didn't have a clue how all this worked? Was it fair to say that a businessman who obviously had a college degree would loosen all the back-ties Jamie had put upon his buoys, wipe his hands, and think, "Yep, time to put them all back in the same place"? Jamie had heard from several other people how Neal Ames was already parading the Point in his brand-new forty-two-foot Nova Scotia boat, hanging around the bait shack as if his boat, his summer cottage, and his class 1 license gave him a VIP pass into the world of highliner fishermen.

"Oh, you poor, sorry bastard," Jamie said, throwing the motor in reverse.

Maynard Eugley: You have two ways to go about it. Confront the guy, or take your time, cool yourself. Talk reasonable.
Jamie: Which is the best way?
Maynard: Depends who the asshole is.
Jamie gunned *Delores* all the way back to the dock, black smoke chugging from the exhaust pipe. Everett McAdoo was there waiting at the dock. "Watch my boat," Jamie told him, throwing fenders over the side. He tied up to a cleat. "I'll be right back."

His parents' house was empty, with cold overcast light darkening the old caramel colored floors. The grandfather clock in the living room clicked away, the only sound in the house. He took the carpeted steps to the second floor and headed straight for Amanda's room.

The whole room had been decorated in buttercup yellow when Amanda was a teenager, from the frilly canopied bed ("Ma—I just *have* to have a canopy bed") to the lacy country curtains. Posters of faggy-looking musicians in makeup with guitars still adorned her walls even though she was 25 and long past adolescence, long past even living here. ("Ma—don't take down my posters, it's like taking down a part of me!") Her dressing table mirror with vanity lights still remained plastered with concert ticket stubs, dried prom corsages, wallet-sized school pictures of every moronic girlfriend she ever had and every guy she ever banged. Amanda's room remained exactly the same as it was in high school because of a teary fight she'd had with Donna years ago not to turn it into a guest bedroom. With tears and an ability to always get her way, Amanda was allowed to let her room remain a shrine, while Jamie's old room across the hall became the guest bedroom and workout room. If he ever wanted to find one of his old yearbooks or baseball trophies, all he had to do was spend forty minutes pawing through a water-stained box in the attic marked *Jamie's Crap*.

He gripped a net bag firmly in his hand. Lined neatly across Amanda's bed and all along the bench seat under the bay window lay every doll she had ever owned from the day she could pop the thumb out of her mouth and scream "Mine!"

Jamie started with the ones on the bed. Betsy Wetsy, Baby Long Hair, and the obscene Cabbage Patch collection. He proceeded down to the army of Barbie dolls she had in every size, shape, era, outfit, and color. He plucked each doll's head off its body like a ripe raspberry off a bush, until he had a heavy net sack of decapitated smiling faces. Before Jamie strode out of Amanda's yellow shrine, he took one last look at the denuded forest of beheaded dolls, all sitting upright on her bed.

By 10:30, Jamie's collarbone gave out a steady signal of pain and the sky had finally turned. Darts of rain began to hit his windshield on his way back to Petit Point. A good froth of his earlier anger worked up as he drove back under the slap of rain and the drone of whiny windshield wipers. He goosed that anger thinking of the cottage owner. He'd seen him once in town with a red brand-name jacket on, that well-fed face, the kind that didn't so much smile as smirk, as if now that he lived in town, *everyone* was his best friend.

"Channel 7 says it's gonna get nasty," Everett McAdoo said, poking halfway out the bait shop, trying to keep out of the rain. "Thanks—" Jamie jumped into his boat and opened the door to the bunk. He checked how many shells were in the shotgun. By now the gray chunky clouds looked tethered to the ocean with silver cords of rain.

Back on the water, he sawed the wheel against the waves, the wipers on his Plexiglas windows fogging up with condensation. The gulls did their usual thing swooping overhead, following him, and Jamie hoped they wouldn't telegraph his presence before he got out there.

As he came back up to Neal Ames's buoys, he took out his binoculars, surveying the area. No one would be out in this weather, which was good. The rain came down so hard it bounced off the water pelting Jamie under the chin.

Every one of Jamie's family and fishing friends had had poachers, encroachers—territory pushers who violated boundaries, pushed the lines. A lobsterman had two choices: allow it or fight it. Those who allowed it woke up one day to discover their territory whittled down to a square inch of nothing.

Delores moved up right alongside Ames's buoys. With the gaff, Jamie hooked the warp of the striped buoy and looped it into the wheel of the trap hauler. He watched as the wire trap broke the surface. Jamie spun the trap around and settled it onto the rail. Inside were a few lobsters, which he confiscated. He took his time examining the trap. Its aluminum wire was galvanized and brand new, not a dent on it, not a sign of weathering. The parlor head nets were white and crisp. He stuck his fingers into the racks and sniffed them. Neal Ames was using bluefish brim, expensive stuff if he didn't catch the bluefish himself, which Jamie doubted he did. This guy had more money than brains. The brim also revealed Ames was overcompensating for his inexperience (like the guy who goes out on a camping trip with the latest in brand-name hiking boots, a backpack, and a GPS compass, but inadvertently wipes his ass with poison sumac).

Jamie uncinched his net bag of baby doll heads, picking up the fat, dimpled one of a Cabbage Patch doll. Classic era—he remembered a time in the 1980s when Amanda shrieked and wheedled until she'd received this doll for Christmas and ended up getting three of them. He shoved a penny nail into the soft plastic of each lamblike eye of the doll. He became almost serene, whistling an old sea chantey, as he hefted the trap down onto the deck of the boat and opened it up, shoving the doll head into the parlor. Jamie surveyed the horizon, looking for Marine Patrol, or anyone else who might be near—saw no one in the hard rain—no one would be out there. Carefully he picked up a 4 x 4 piece of wood from his deck and placed it on top of the trap. Then he stood on the gunwale of *Delores* and jumped on top of the trap, bringing all of his weight down onto it until it began to sag. For the rest of the afternoon Jamie pulled up every trap out of Ames's strings but one, sweating in the rain as he pummeled the ever-lovin' shit out of them. He left the triple-striped buoys of the destroyed traps alone, unhitched, so that when Neal Ames came out the next time to blithely pull his traps, the toy prize inside each one would be a gaggle of doll heads, each nail-stabbed eye winking as if to say, *Howdy neighbor!* Maybe then it might occur to Ames he was fishing in the wrong place.

Creamy, hot peppery smells drifted from the kitchen the moment he stepped inside the house. Sounds of light classical music on the stereo. A stew pot simmered on the stove, its glass lid clattering lightly. On the counter a single can of PBR stood with a crayon message underneath: DRINK ME. Jamie flipped the tab with one finger, noting the spotlessness of the house, which smelled like lemon and yeasty bread baking in the oven.

"Anja?"

She emerged from her room without her usual running, jumping, tackling entrance. She deliberately walked slowly, dressed in a light pink summer dress. Her hand flew to her mouth, trying to suppress a giggle. She drifted to him in a sweet cloud of freesia, her old perfume, and wrapped her arms around his waist. Her fingers fluffed his wet plastered hair, springing up his curls.

"You look . . . nice," he said, bewildered. That freesia perfume shifted his senses in such a strange way.

"You like it?"

He nodded and moved toward the stove, out of her grasp. He lifted the lid on the burbling pot. "What's this?"

"Corn chowder, but oh, oh . . . it got little peppers in it and some hot sauce in it. It's Southwestern," she said proudly. "Oh, and the biscuits." She moved to slip on oven mitts and pulled out a cookie sheet with a dozen perfectly browned biscuits. Stuck to the kitchen cabinets were varying sizes of Post-it notes with reminders like *Oven 450 degrees!* and *Peel potatos!* Next to the stove, her notebook lay open with extensive notes on ingredients, the order in which to combine them, even estimating the time he'd be home. *DON'T FORGET THE PBR!* she'd written.

Jamie's eyes lingered on the dining table by the giant windows, set with chipped plates, knives and forks, almost in the right order. On each plate lay a white paper towel folded to form a pocket—limp dandelions poking out of the pockets. "Anja," Jamie said. "Did you do all of this yourself?"

When she was embarrassed to receive a compliment, she rubbed her nose rapidly and shook her head, but this time she lifted up on her toes and bounced, pleased with herself. After the day he'd had in the driving rain, the anachronism of dinner on the table and the perfume made him forget his earlier anger. In the center of the dining table was a large wooden bowl of dark greens and tomatoes, sprinkled with edible flowers. She'd even gotten new white tapered candles and stuck them in ceramic candle holders, which he forgot they even owned.

"How long have you been planning this?"

She looked troubled for a moment. "A week?"

"I can't believe it."

"It's true!" she said vehemently.

"No, I meant, it's just good, that's all." Jamie sat down and untucked his little paper napkin pocket of dandelions. She ladled soup into two bowls for them.

Anja lifted her spoon, blowing on the hot chowder. She then

tucked her fine blond hair behind her ear and reached for a biscuit. Those familiar gestures were disconcerting. She had the same radio station on, the music they used to put on every Sunday night, their one night to have supper together, what with their schedules back in those days. She was going for an advanced degree, taking classes at night, and he was exhausted, in bed by 8 p.m.

Are you sure you're not gonna want some guy with a college degree? Some big framed certificate on the wall? A joke wrapped in insecurity then.

Her arms around him. *No, I want you. You're my family.*

Cause it'll kill me after all this, when you graduate and some guy with a ton of money and six cell phones on his belt takes you away.

Why would I want some guy with six cell phones hanging off his belt if he doesn't know how to talk to me?

Well, what if he does—and what if he's good looking to boot?

Well hell, Jamie, what are you waiting for, introduce this guy to me.

Aw, see? Now that's not helping.

Quit worrying—I'm not going anywhere.

Anja smiled at him as the windows mutated with the bluer light of dusk and the candles warmed her face. "Good, Jamie?"

"It's great. . . ." He laughed, shaking his head.

"What?"

Jamie bent to sip at the chowder, his clunky, fish-smelling fingers on a biscuit, pulling it apart. "Nothin'—it's just good, that's all."

She put her elbows on the table, her eyes on a place beyond the ceiling. Thinking, wherever she was, thinking, the flickering light on her cheeks. She tried to make it look as though this was just a dinner she threw together in a night, but he knew better. Carolyn had been teaching her how to shop at the grocery store for more than a month—every week, he was privy to each step of her accomplishments. While other girls could make supper effortlessly in a few hours, this was momentous, a huge undertaking. He should've felt elated, watching her sip on her soup so happily. After all this enormous effort she'd made, he should've been complimenting her up and down—she was searching for it. "Is this right, Jamie?" she asked. "Do you like the bread?"

"It's great, it really is." That was all he could come up with. He felt lousier by the second. Where was all that energy and praise he used to have for things like this? She wanted so much for this moment to make him feel that nothing had changed.

The candlelight warmed her sweet face. If only those dull brown eyes would snap to focus and her words would come out normally again, words that were sharp and capable, keeping him slightly off step. If that was there, the wanting would be there— no doubt about it. But the last few years had ground him down, and she couldn't see it. It was as if she'd bypassed all of it and now expected things to be the way they once were. As the candlelight wavered and Anja noticed he was watching her, the dopey smile came back. She wiped her mouth with her napkin. "I got more, Jamie," she said, standing up.

"No, no—" He stood up with her. "I can get it."

"But I want to." She tilted her head to the side and looked at him with such love, he felt something bottom out. He took her shoulders and pulled her in, kissing her sweet-smelling hair. Her face was somewhere in time, on a parallel Sunday night he'd never know, her brown eyes snapping with light. And on jumped tracks, he saw her cold slack face, lips blue on a slab in a drawer. It was a thought that suffocated him, for in a horrible way it might've been better to mourn the death of the greatest love in his life than to look down here—now—and see the facial bones, the tawny skin, the brown eyes of what used to be Anja.

FOURTEEN

The back entrance to Churchie's was classic Maine architecture—
little forethought, scant design, just slapped together in an afternoon so that the builders could get down to more important business like drinking a beer in the back of the pickup. So instead of
coming through the front door and entering Churchie's straight-
away, a person had to imitate a lab rat by first turning right, hitting a wall, then turning left, hitting a wall, and eventually making
it through the next two doors, which opened to the dim grotto
of the bar. Inside, clusters of faded buoys hung from every rafter.
The windows were propped open with sticks to give the small-
ish room some breeze, letting in the scent of beach roses, letting
out cigar smoke. Behind the bar, a service window opened to the
kitchen, where a hairy forearm bounced breaded clams in a fryo-
lator basket before lowering them into grease.

The afternoon was warm, glasses of light beer on the chess
tables to the side, where two couples, thick-waisted, mouths furrowed from forty years of smoking, sat and chewed the rag. At the
bar, no surprise, were Chuck Allen, Bill Erskine, and Phil Elliott,
whose low-hanging jeans offered an unappetizing view of clammer's crack. When Jamie veered inside, the elder couples smiled
at him. One of the couples was Thongchai's parents, who were
wearing the exact same blue chambray shirt. His father had the
same wide face and gleaming teeth as his son. To Jamie he ex-
tended a comfortable grasp. "How you doing?"

"Gaining," Jamie said.

"Ah, we're all gaining." Jamie let Thongchai's mother hug him. She wore her long, glossy hair in a single braid. "When are you coming over for supper again?"

Thongchai's father talked over her. "Sold my boat," he told Jamie.

"No kidding? When?"

"Last week, to a guy in Portland."

"Really," Jamie said. "You're really retiring?"

"That's right—gotta quit sometime."

"Wow," Jamie said, rubbing his chin thoughtfully. He was surprised to realize he felt envious.

"I've got some clothes to give your mother," Thongchai's mother said, holding onto Jamie's sleeve. "When can you come by and get 'em?"

"If you don't want 'em, Donna won't either," his father said.

"I'll come by next week," Jamie said, and she smiled.

He took his place at the bar while Jeannie poured off a PBR for him. In front of each of the regulars were a stack of twenties, a pack of cigarettes, a sweaty beer, and an ashtray. He sat next to Chuck, who smelled like bait. Last Jamie knew, he was part-timing as a soda vendor for high schools.

"So, anything happening?" Jamie asked.

Phil nearly spewed his beer. He was a big boy with tufts of black hair creeping out his T-shirt collar.

"So check it out." Chuck leaned next to Jamie, his cracked fingers tapping ash into a bent tin tray. "Pete rolled his truck three times last night. It landed upright and he managed to drive it home."

"No shit."

"Cops got him in the morning. Found some glass and his wallet in the road." Chuck, with his weary eyes, found joy in this. All three of them grinned as if waiting for Jamie to get the punch line.

"Oh, I think he'll pay some fines, but that's probably it," Bill said. His tuber fingers adjusted the brim of his Dip Net cap. Never without that cap. "Friggin' lucky, if you ask me."

Phil smoked rapidly, his breath cut short when he put in his opinion. "That's nothing. One time I totaled my Jeep, missed the corner, went down over a bank. Flipped it end over end three times. The third time, it ricocheted itself right up, hit a telephone pole seventeen feet in the air, snappin' it right in half. Chopped the transformer right off." Phil's shoulders jiggled up and down. "Not a scratch. I crawled out of the Jeep and stumbled home."

"Yeah, but they got you," Chuck reminded.

"Well, yeah," Phil said. "I went to jail for it. The cops came and got me outta bed."

"Tell him what you said," Bill said, as if hearing a favorite bedtime story.

"Said, 'Can't you come back in the morning? I'm *tired.*' They took me down there anyway, booked me."

"You bounced the friggin' thing seventeen feet in the air!" Bill said.

"Weren't wearing no seat belt neither," Phil said sheepishly, tapping his cigarette ash. Jamie stared at the hairy forearm in the service window, at clams flipping into a cardboard bowl. "Hope Pete's all right," Jamie said.

"He's fine," Chuck said. "His first OUI."

"Awww," the boys echoed

"Wait 'til he's up to number four." Phil nodded.

Bill tilted his head forward to look at Chuck. "So that reminds me—how's your ma doing?" Common knowledge in the harbor: Chuck's mother, Renata, had just gotten busted the week before, blasted on "box o' wine"—her second offense. She hadn't been aware that she'd torn the back bumper off a car trying to pass it on the right.

Chuck ignored him and said, "When Pete comes in tonight, I'm gonna buy him a beer." Jamie didn't say anything as he sipped his Pibber. He'd gotten his first OUI at 18. Harbor rite of passage.

When the barn board door to Churchie's opened, everyone turned reflexively to see who it was. Jamie's eyes slid away first.

"Hey, how's it goin', Chuck?" Neal Ames said, brightly. He stood there in his red skier's jacket, but now he was wearing a hat with a

bait shop logo on it. "Phil, how we doin'?" His cheeks were wind-
blown, rusty as his hair. "And lovely Miss Jean Churchill," Ames
said ceremoniously. "Would you be so kind? Bushmills, neat."

As Jeannie put down her cigarette to make his drink, Neal
Ames stretched his laced fingers, cracking the knuckles. "Hell of
a day out there, huh, Phil?" His genial tone evoked an odd an-
tipathy in the room. The merrier he was, the colder they grew,
although he was either the last to notice or determined to not
care. "Yes suh," Ames said, winking at Jeannie as she pushed his
drink across the bar. "Some wicked good fishing down by that
outer ridge."

Jamie's face spindled. He turned on his bar stool, hand on his
knee. "Guess you didn't get my message yet, did ya, pal? You might
wanna go check on your traps this afternoon," Jamie said. "You
know what? Better yet, I'll give it to you straight. Don't bother
taking your boat out no more. You're all done lobstering around
here."

At that, the five other bar stools nudged around so that everyone faced Neal Ames square. Even the older couples at the chess
tables watched him. It was rarely done in the open to make a pro-
nouncement like that—these decisions were made by the harbor
godfather, Don Thatcher, behind closed doors, not like this, for
everyone to hear. But at this point he wasn't going to back down.
Ames's hearty hey-ho, 'nother round on me demeanor now flittered
away, and one had to wonder how many times Ames had brought
this kind of situation on himself. For a moment, the little redheaded kid in him shone through; he looked stricken. Ames's lips
parted, he was about to say something. They wanted him to say
something, but as he looked around he saw nothing to encourage
him. Ames swallowed the rest of his whiskey and dabbed a bar
napkin to his lips. He carefully placed a twenty on the bar, favoring Jeannie with a warm smile. "Buy that man a drink," he said,
indicating Jamie. "He needs it." And turned to leave.

When the back door closed, the hush in the room exploded.
Thongchai's parents were grinning; all the regulars had something to chatter about. Jamie sat there in a muted cloud while the

back slappers came around to extol him. The mood was exuberant, same as the time when Senior kicked the Fogertys out. This was going to be big news around the harbor.

FIFTEEN

How many things did he hide from people? With the guys it was emotion, which they'd only find weak or use to eviscerate him with nonstop jokes. With Anja, the things he hid were typically for her own good, like candy bars, or bills, or his day-to-day problems (she had enough of her own). In the entire time they'd been together, he never cheated on her or did anything behind her back. Which is what all the guys—all of them—*said* when confronted by their women, but none of them—*none*—could ever claim as complete truth. Not when the cold long winters and randy summers offered nonstop temptations of topless donut shops, skank strip clubs down in Westbrook, endless bachelor parties that inevitably ended up in "fuck-for-alls," and the incessant boredom-induced swap meets of husbands and wives. As if life was too mundane to be with one person; as if the Vegas lifestyle people watched on cable was nirvana; and somehow in the most beautiful place in the country they all thought they were missing out. It seemed all of his friends needed a diversion—alcohol, drugs, swapping—to keep from feeling useless, discarded, lost amongst the desolate pine forests. Until now, the things he hid from Anja had never been these things.

"Hey Mumma, you got tomorrow night free?"

"Maybe, why?"

Jamie leaned against the wall, phone to his ear. "I was just wondering if you could come by and keep an eye on Anja. I've got some stuff to do."

"This is the third time this week, what's up?"

"Nothin'."

"Well, either you got a new girlfriend or a new Oxy habit. Which is it?"

His mother. Nothing lost on her. "Jesus. It's not a big deal, I just need somebody to keep Anja company for a few hours."

Silence.

"Ma!"

Silence.

"Ma, would ya come on?"

"Why don't you just tell me?"

"Because I'm friggin' twenty-seven and don't need your friggin' permission! I'm just asking a favor!"

She was all smooth dulcet tones. "I didn't say I was giving my permission, sweet-tay. I just want to know the truth."

Jamie sighed, cranked the phone to the other ear. "I'm hanging out with this girl. She's works on the *Sea Hair*."

"Uh huh, what's her name?"

Jamie sighed. "It's Happy."

"Happy?" Donna snorted.

"Yeah, her name is Happy, all right?"

"Happy," Donna repeated. "God. And she's a Camden girl?"

"She's not *from* there. She's from Florida. She's just up here for the summer. She's the first mate."

"How long has this been going on?"

His knuckles turned white gripping the cord. "What are you, my mother? I don't know. A couple of weeks."

"Mm, and she knows about Anja, *obviously.*"

"I told her."

"And how did she react?"

"She was cool."

"Cool," Donna mused. "Does Anja know about her?"

"No, it's not the right time yet. Fuckin' A. Do you want her social security number too?"

There's a moment before a fiery explosion blows the doors out; it's the silent, sucking retreat of smoke. That was what lurked behind his mother's tone. "James, did you just say the eff word to me?"

"Uh. . . ." Jamie stared out the living room window. "No Ma, it wasn't, like, *to* you."

"Cause let me tell you something you little *tick*. No one in the family, not even your friggin' father, gets away with saying the eff word to me." Even though she herself sprinkled the word like Mrs. Dash in her everyday vocabulary.

"Mumma, listen. I really wasn't saying it to you, okay?"

"All right," Donna said finally. "Tomorrow night. I'll be over after work."

When Donna arrived the next evening, Anja didn't come out of her room, didn't come out to greet her with her usual Tasmanian knock-down drag-out hug. Donna handed Jamie a six-pack of homebrew in mismatched bottles, wrapped in a plastic grocery bag, and hung up her coat. She had on her dark brown business suit. Her hair, which was customarily in a ponytail, was up in a neat bun.

"Did you have a selectman's meeting today?" Jamie said, gathering his keys.

"More like an afternoon at Chuck E. Cheese with a bunch of screaming brats," she said, levering the cap off one of the beers. She gave him one, which he stuck in his jacket pocket for the road.

Jamie called down the hall. "Hey! I'm taking off! I'll be home late—so you and Donna have a good time, okay sweetie?" He found his wallet on the TV. "I think there's a good vampire movie on at ten. She likes those now."

Donna's mouth went slack. "That is *not* the way to say goodbye."

"What? Oh, come on. She's fine." He stared at her. "Really, she's fine; she's just in a mood."

Donna held off on drinking the beer. Her brown eyes were all depleted of warm mother-love. "Oh, you figure? Go back there and say goodbye the right way."

"It's okay, Ma. She'll be fine."

"Do it."

"Oh, for friggin' . . . all right!" Jamie stamped and turned back down the hallway.

"Sweet-tay?" He rapped on Anja's door lightly with his knuckles. "I'm going now. I just need to go out for a little bit. I'll see you when I get home, okay?" He peered in her dark room. Anja was in her car bed, lying on her back, with the door flap hanging open. She looked like an Indian widow preparing to immolate herself on the funeral pyre. "Did you hear me, sweetie?" he asked. Without a word, her fingers found the little pull tab and she zipped the half-moon arc of her car door closed. The sound was like the drone of crickets on a lazy hot day.

"She's fine," Jamie announced, coming back to the kitchen. "Make anything you want from the fridge." He leaned in to kiss his mother on the cheek. Donna's fingers clutched his elbow, her voice low. "I'm just going to say one thing."

He stared across the room. "What?"

She moved in closer and whispered, "Maybe you don't feel the same way about her anymore—and maybe you feel a need to hang out with this . . . new girl—but Anja needs to know you care."

"Ma, just stop. You don't know how I am with Anja."

Donna whipped her fingers from his arm. Appraised him up and down. "You better."

A fleet of schooners had sailed into Camden the night before. When he was 12, he looked forward to seeing them every summer: the square-riggers, topsail schooners, ketches, smacks, cutters, yawls that came up from the Caribbean. They sailed in with creamy smooth sails, beaming brightwork, oiled teak decks. And that was truly the sad, disappointing part of being an adult, for after the third or fourth year, no matter how massive and dramatic the masts were or how the wind in the giant sails looked, the ships ceased to be awe-inspiring. Now they were functional art, water buses for tourists. Jamie hadn't been back to see the tall ships in more than fifteen years.

The top masts and stays were visible above the town's tallest buildings. Families and tourists thronged the harbor, spilling out to the parking lots. A Celtic trio played on a raised platform: a fiddle, a flute, and Uilleann pipes. A costume party raged down on the docks, with deck hands and sailors and women dressed as figureheads. Steel drum music bounced through the town. The congestion forced residents to put "No Parking" signs on their lawns, reinforced with lawn chairs. Jamie had to circle the main strip three times before he finally found parking on a side street. The bars were cranking, doors wide open with sea chantey music. The lobster shack by the wharf had every table filled, folks chin-deep in claws and tails. Every ten minutes, a camera flash went off as a table full of diners photographed themselves wearing lobster bibs.

Every time Jamie saw the frenzy surrounding lobster shacks, he thought, *Keep it coming.* The future of the lobster industry hinged on regular folks like these. When people wanted to feel special or celebrate an important event, they didn't order a can of Spam. The masses took their cue from the rich, who demanded their lobsters come from Maine, their caviar from Beluga, and their champagne from Champagne. *Keep it coming.* He loved a tourist with a plastic bib and a chin smeared in tomalley.

Jamie edged his way carefully through a crowd of people blocking the south end of the dock amid the blurred zag of halyards and rat lines. He saw a green bottle flip high in the air, end over end, and caught a glimpse of a blue flannel overcoat with brass buttons.

"You gonna try that with knives?" a male voice in the crowd called.

Jamie heard Happy's voice ring up from the center of the crowd. "Yeah. I'm gonna try that with knives. What are you, *funny?*" He couldn't see her, but from the crowd's reaction, they loved it.

He moved in far enough to see Happy standing barefoot on the wharf, whipping three bottles in concentric circles five feet over her head. What she was wearing was comical: a white blousy shirt, black pantaloons tied at the ankles, and a regal velvet vest. Her face was bronze, eyes upturned to watch the bottles, her brown hair tied in a long braid under a black head scarf. She looked fantastic and silly, her broad smile enticing the crowd. "As you . . . can . . . see," she breathed irregularly, timing her movements to coincide with catching the bottles, ". . . you can really hurt yourself if you're trying this for the first time. Unless it's with corn muffins. . . ." She mixed it up, passing one of the bottles behind her back before tossing it. "Which is how I learned to juggle."

The crowd burst into applause. Happy finished her act, set down her bottles in a brightly painted toy box, and took a deep bow. The audience cheered, giving her whistles, and some people moved forward to place a few dollars in the toy box. A deck hand untied the rope down to the gangplank and announced that the sunset sail was leaving. As the crowd began to file down the gangplank, Happy saw him standing there. Jamie was trying not to smile. He covered his mouth with his hand.

"What?" she said, coming over to him. "What's so hilarious?"

"I just. . . ." He shook his head. "You juggle. You're a *juggling* act."

"I can walk on a tightrope too, bet ya didn't know that either."

"I just thought we were going on a sail, and then I come round the corner to find you juggling . . . in your little pirate outfit."

Happy gathered her stuff and slung a net bag of bottles and balls over her shoulder. "Get yourself on that boat. You haven't even begun to see the show."

Once aboard, Jamie sat alone on a wooden bench as the crew prepared to leave. The *Sea Hair's* massive rigging and disjointed lines of tackle, stays, and fairleads all worked together once they were under way, like the way a torso and legs move on the command of thousands of interlocked nerves and muscles. As the deck hands pulled in fenders, adjusting the schooner's lines, the captain lined up the gaff, judging the tack out of the harbor. The lumbering awkwardness turned graceful once the vessel broke the confines of the harbor. Its heavy sails became a laundry line of caught wind—the fore and aft sails cracking with such unexpect-ed force, some kids became startled and yelped. Jamie felt pres-sure to help, not used to being a passenger, but this ship already had a captain and he knew well the old adage: *Lead, follow, or get out of the way.* He watched Happy. The moment they were under way, she knelt down by an ornate, gold-leafed chest that looked as if it had once contained doubloons. She flipped open the lid, revealing various alcohols and mixers within. The sun was like a warm hand on the back of his neck. Happy poured a rum on the rocks and thrust it at him. She jumped up on the rail so she could be heard.

"Folks! All right, folks, there are a few things that the Coast Guard requires of you and a few things that you might actually be interested in. First of all, let's talk life vests. Down in Key West, we do a real nice snorkel trip; down in Key West you wanna go in the water. Take my word for it—up here in Maine, you *do not.* But should you happen to see somebody in the water, don't keep it a secret. Please—let us know. Shout out—make a racket. But most importantly, don't take your eyes off the person in the water 'til we have a hand on that person." She swung her sword in an elaborate arc.

What a ham she was; what a blast to watch. She turned fore and aft so everyone could hear her. It was a mellow group, lots of parents and kids, older people in sweatshirts and visors. Happy spoke in a huskily loud voice, a girl used to commanding atten-tion and respect. The confidence she possessed was incredible, possibly more than he had himself. She hopped down onto the deck and began pacing the length of the ship so everyone could hear her. She held up the life jacket.

"Now, should you find yourself in the water somehow, if you see the captain or any of the rest of the crew edging toward the rail and putting on a life jacket, you *may* want to put one on your-self. It's not particularly comfortable or fashionable, but we do have plenty of them located in these boxes here. Now, should things really get ugly and we need to part company with the lovely *Sea Hair,* we have this nice, hydrostatically controlled self-deploying life raft. This has everything you need to keep a dozen people alive for a month on the open ocean—it's got your fresh water, your canopy, your life raft, Nintendo, wet bar—wait, sorry,"—she made a chagrined face—"that's for the crew."

A wave of laughter came from the passengers, which was no surprise, as she'd had them entranced at the gangplank. Jamie sipped on his rum, liking the way the amber liquid looked in the short glass with the slick ice, liking the oily swells at dusk, all around the boat. It made him want to plunge his hands in it. He was a tourist, along with the rest of them, watching the sun tuck behind layered clouds, splitting the sky into tangerine and melon. Every moment, the colors of the sea fluctuated, and how had he not noticed this before? The smart snap of the mizzen and staysails melding with the sharp air, the dark green of the sea, the bronze on Happy's cheeks, the amber in his glass, and back to the sun (which he had to watch every second, that tricky thing), gazing through near-closed eyes at colors that burned into his eyelids. The people by the foresails, clinking glasses of champagne, telling stories about Pennsylvania, had only moments to see the colors turn before the sun was gone behind the mountains. They were oblivious—missing it. Fat thing, that lolling red sun—it rolled the red carpet of diamonds back down into the dark blue water. He suddenly felt ridiculously happy. It might've been the rum that made him chuckle for no apparent reason, and Jamie clamped his mouth shut, turning to face the horizon again, hoping he didn't look foolish. His eyes went from the velvety liquid of rum in the glass to the warm reds on the edge of the ocean. He was alive. He was alive and feeling euphoria over what—a sunset sail? He'd seen a million of them.

He watched Happy bend over to play with kids on the ship, teaching them how to juggle with bean bags. With another person, it might have looked contrived, a calculated move to butter up the parents for tips. But her joy seemed real. When her eyes locked onto theirs, they were brazen. This is what she did for a living; she lived to entertain people, even for only two hours.

As they came about and the sun set, the sky turned to faded

denim and made silhouetted humps of the mountains. From the sea, the hills looked like a curvy size 16 woman, like a Sophia Loren or a Marilyn Monroe, lying on her side. One of the deck hands introduced himself as Gabe, took out a fiddle from a small case and lifted it to his chin. He began fiddling, rendering old Celtic tunes. The crowd had gone silent, even the kids, listening to the sweet notes against the whip of the wind on the sails. As he played, Happy climbed up on the boom and stood like a woman about to jump from a burning building. She inched out farther and farther, holding the strings of the baggy wrinkles to steady her until she was hanging way out over the edge. Her white pirate blouse flapped crazily; behind her was a blend of blue-green sky and green-blue sea. Had the wind suddenly fluctuated, she would've been flicked off the boom like a crumb off a shirt. And she knew it. The tourists snapped pictures of her and not once did she look at them. She wasn't doing this for attention or pictures—she was up there, smiling in the wind, completely at home.

The night sky had become navy; the tips of waves had turned black as the schooner slowed into the harbor. There was thin light coming from the marina—from a few lit windows and a string of Christmas lights on the masts of sailboats. The schooners were huddled, sleeping giants. By this time, the families with young children had gone home and the wharf celebrations had died down, leaving only the harborside restaurants brisk with activity. After two hours, Jamie had gotten to know Captain Nick, whom Happy had talked about a lot. Nick was equally at ease talking to the passengers as he was maneuvering a 64-ton vessel into a harbor crowded with sailboats. Nick slowed the *Sea Hair*, the engines deep below rumbling as the schooner reversed alongside the dock. It was a difficult accomplishment, and Jamie was impressed. While the passengers filed off the boat, Jamie heard one of them telling Happy, "That was THE best sailing trip I've ever been on—and let me tell you sweetie, I live for these things."

"Thank you very much."

"We'll be down in Key West this winter. I'll get all my friends to sail with you."

"Remind me when you're down there, I'll hook you up with a Maine discount."

Jamie waited until he was almost the last passenger to leave. Happy was deep in conversation with Nick and another passenger. He didn't know if he should stay on the schooner, or if that was overstaying his welcome. She had work to do and they hadn't discussed any plans afterward. If he continued to stand around aimlessly, he'd look foolish. He lifted his hand to get her attention with a quick succession of jerky gestures that conveyed, "Hey thanks for the sail and the drink. You're obviously busy—I'll be on my way!"

Happy held up a finger to indicate he should wait. When she finished talking, she trotted over to him. "Hey, don't go anywhere. We've got a party to go to after I clean up around here."

He brightened. "Okay."

"Give me your glass—I'll freshen you up."

Jamie glanced at Captain Nick and Gabe and the rest of the male crew, who were hard at work, cleaning the deck. He didn't want to stand there while everyone else was working, drinking their rum for free.

"I'll just wait at the bar 'til you're done."

"You sure? You can hang out while I'm working."

Jamie looked beyond her. "You tell the captain to come over when you're done and I'll buy you both a drink."

He made himself at home at the local wharf bar, which, unlike Churchie's, effected a phony nautical look with dip nets and hanging lobster traps on the ceiling. If he closed his eyes the sounds were still the same: the drone of a sports game on a mounted TV, the low murmurs of talking, and the soft thwack of cues against pool balls.

When Happy found him half an hour later, she'd changed out of her pirate gear into cargo shorts and a dusky blue T-shirt. An army green flop hat covered her loose pigtails. Captain Nick waited for them outside the wharf bar. Off the water, Nick could've been anyone, an unremarkable skinny guy in torn cotton shorts and sandals. He was a handsome guy, not Ivy League handsome but shaggy-haired, like someone's little brother. Jamie guessed he was several years younger.

"I hear you lobster out of Petit Point. You work year round?" Nick asked Jamie as they all walked off the wharf and up the street.

"Just up 'til Christmas if the fishing is still good. But yeah, no matter what, I'm still working year round."

"I'll bet your winters are great. I love skiing more than sailing."

"So what are you doing on a boat?"

"Yeah, well, I tried the ski instructor route," Nick said. The night was warm as they walked by crowds of people dressed up to go to dinner. "But that just about paid for my ski pass, that's it. My girlfriend and I are looking into buying our own charter boat next year."

"Yeah, where to?" Jamie said, glad to hear that Nick already had a girlfriend.

"Jamaica, or Belize."

"I hate to tell you this, Nick. But . . . there's no snow there," Jamie said.

"Goddammit," Nick said. "Nobody told me that." Jamie smiled, liking him. He liked him even more as they walked, talking about regular stuff. Nick didn't immediately launch into a treatise about his expert skills as a captain, as so many yachties did when they encountered another boater. He was all right.

"I need a sandwich," Happy said, yawning and stretching her arms above her head, which caused her neck to crack. She looked alarmed. "Did you hear that?"

"If we get to that store up the street, they've got BLTs, but they're closing soon," Nick said, looking at his watch.

"Jamie, what the hell is with this town at night?" Happy said as they walked up the hill from the wharf. "It's not even eight p.m. in the middle of August and they're rolling up the sidewalks."

"What do you think, I make up the rules?"

"If I don't eat something right now, I'm going to make both of your lives miserable," Happy said, walking faster. Gone was the fun, adventurous, juggling pirate. Nick flashed a look at Jamie that intimated that not all of Happy's moods were uproarious and jovial. "At least it was a great trip tonight," she said, unearthing crumpled dollar bills from her shorts pocket. "Tip money."

"You had them on fire tonight," Jamie told her.

"She's always great," Nick agreed.

"I'm glad you had a good time," she told Jamie, linking arms with him. "Not every trip goes that well—tonight was a good one."

"Yeah, some trips are just miserable, no matter what you do," Nick said. "People will just sit there like they've been forced to go on a sunset sail. Happy'll throw everything at them—recite a ballad, give them drinks, juggle—nothin'."

"Yeah, and then some sails, we get *the questions*." Happy nudged Jamie.

"What are those?"

She blew her hair out of her eyes. "You know, the questions. What are those fuzzy things up there on the sail?"

"You mean the baggy wrinkles?" Jamie said.

Happy nodded. Nick joined in. "Here's my favorite: Are we gonna see whales?" Nick pretended to look down at a clipboard and check off a line item. "By my calculations, at 5:34 p.m. we should see a whale, yes."

"What do you *do* in the winter?" Happy said with an exaggerated drawl.

"Oh Jesus, I get that all the time," Jamie said. "My friend Thongchai hates when people come up to him when he's working and ask him questions. My cousin Ben, we call him The Kid, he's like this giant, overstuffed Disney mascot, you know, a real ambassador of the harbor—I'm surprised he doesn't wear a lobster uniform to work, because he lets people take his picture all the time. He'll hold up lobsters for them, pose with them. But Thongchai—he hates it. One time, we were finishing up for the day and this guy comes up to us on the wharf. He had a pink visor on, this friggin' moose on his sweatshirt, so you know it's going to be good. And he looks out to the islands and says to us, 'How do you keep the islands from floating away?' And we're thinking, 'Huh? Is this a joke?' But no, he was dead serious, wanted to know how the islands didn't just float away by themselves."

Happy cracked up, her hands flying to her mouth.

"What did you tell him?" Nick asked.

"I didn't know what to think. But Thongchai, he just stands there looking out at the harbor with the guy and puts his hand on his chin and starts making up this story that the harbor had this elaborate underwater pulley system that worked with the tide and that's what kept them anchored. And the guy apparently thought that was a rational explanation. Oh, he killed me—I had to walk away."

"I believe it," Happy said. They'd reached the doors of the small grocery store and now pushed the glass doors open.

"Here's another one people ask us all the time," Nick said as they squeezed down a narrow aisle. "Do *you* raise the sails? As if my crew is just there for decoration, you know, like we've got this special squad of qualified sailors below deck just waiting to come up and raise them."

Happy squinted at Jamie. "Here's one I got recently: How *long* is your two-hour tour?"

Jamie: "You did not get that question."

Happy: "I did."

Nick picked up a sandwich from the cooler. "One time I had a woman ask me, 'What time of year do the deer turn into moose?' "

Jamie paused to regard Nick and shook his head.

"I told her they usually completed their transformation by November," Nick said. He sifted through sandwiches in the cooler. "All they have left is salami?"

"Get tuna fish," Happy suggested.

"No, it's been sitting there for eight hours."

"And are these *kids* asking the questions?" Jamie asked.

"Oh, no," Happy said. "These are all adults."

The checkout girl rang their items through. "Just in time," she said. She was a cute high school girl, thin and blond. "We're closing."

Happy checked the clock above the door. "Eight o'clock," she said triumphantly. "What did I tell you? Rolling up the sidewalks."

"I know, right?" acknowledged the checkout girl, with the bored tone of someone who'd clearly been forced to live in this small town all her life.

Happy and Nick led Jamie down a sidewalk by the bay into a waterfront apartment full of sloppy, buoyant boat people, more yachtie than deck hand, and for Jamie, this was beginning to be less and less strange. They watched Captain Nick blend right into the friendly crowd, where small groups of people clumped to-gether on the threadbare sofa or stood in football huddles with red plastic beer cups held loosely in their hands. The girls were all thin, tan, in the latest fashion, showing skin. The guys were similar to the clean-cut, prosperous crowd at the castle party.

"It's kind of crowded in here," Happy said.

"Yeah."

"At every party I always have to check out the roof."

"Okay." Jamie followed Happy up the stairs until they reached a ship's ladder that led to the roof's cupola. Outside, back in the night, Jamie felt more at ease, where they could see the masts and rigging peeking over the rooftops. They sat down on a gentle slope of asphalt shingles. Below the roof, someone had positioned a bubble-making machine by an open window so that a cascade of bubbles floated up past the roof into the dark sky. Happy and Jamie watched a man and a woman stop in the crosswalk of the main street and jump, trying to catch the bubbles. They seemed not to notice they were stopped in the middle of a road.

"Watch—a car will come along and run them down while they're trying to catch bubbles," Jamie said.

"Aw, and here I was thinking, 'Look at that cute older couple, having fun.' "

"Oh."

"You're mean."

She leaned back on her hands, looking at the sharp cinema of stars in the sky. "The sky gets so black at night here. The other night we saw some northern lights. No place I've ever lived has been dark enough to see the northern lights." Happy rubbed her nose on her sleeve. "I try not to fall too in love with the places I've been, because at the end of each season, I've got to go."

"You're sure you have to go? You wouldn't want a regular year-round job here? Come on, canning lobster, picking crab? Those are great jobs. Pay pretty good." He nudged her.

She humped forward, her back a C curve. "Yeah, that's my dream," she said. "But to work most places you need a driver's license. And I don't have one."

"Really? You don't know how to drive?"

"Nope."

"Why, did you get in trouble?" The typical reason his friends had no licenses.

Happy's slender arm slid back, propping her up. "No, I just never learned—I grew up in weird places: Canada, Nicaragua, upstate New York . . . on a houseboat. My parents met at Wood-stock—and yes, I am *that* cliché."

"Wow, a true natural born hippie."

She gave him a sidelong glance. "For years they told people they conceived my brother there, but neither of us have birth certificates, so I don't know. It's strange. Then I guess they decided to get married after that, once my brother was born. Then a lot of it is a blur—we moved to Waterloo after they divorced—my dad remarried and moved to Philly. I had my bat mitzvah on his wedding day—I think my mother scheduled it on purpose. So in high school, I didn't have to drive, not when you're home schooled on a houseboat. After that, I started working on boats, so I never had a car. I'd just find the nearest schooner and sail away." Her hand made a rolling wave.

Jamie tried to comprehend the unordered path of her life, compared to his own. "Now I get why they named you Happy."

"Sunshine and Rainbow were already taken. I'm one Jewish funk princess of two raging hippies, yup."

"Do you shave your armpits?"

"Yeah—but not my legs." She held one up for him to feel. He'd already seen her hairy legs when she was in her bathing suit; he didn't need to feel them.

"Do you use a crystal instead of deodorant?"

"*No.*"

He sniffed her. "You sure?"

She twisted her hair up in a chignon. The ends fell lazily back to her shoulders. "You should talk. You smell like herring crotch. What did you do, take a bath in it before you came out?"

He exhaled. "Jee-*zus.*"

She wrinkled her nose. "Ugh. Listen, don't be offended. But I'll probably never eat one of those little bottom feeders that you so love to catch. They're not kosher and pretty much disgusting."

Jamie shrugged. "It doesn't bother me."

"Good, I thought you might be annoyed."

"I'd rather have a hamburger anyway."

She made another face.

"Oh, don't tell me you're a vegetarian too," Jamie said.

"There's nothing wrong with it."

"Wow," he said, reclining on his back. He looked up toward the rigging. "Wow, a vegetarian, too."

"Nothing wrong with it . . . unless you're a meat-eating, small-town head banger who smells like girls' underwear."

Jamie looked away. Shook his head a little. "I don't think you should meet my friends. You'd turn them all into little puddles of goo."

"Hey—I'm a sweetie!" she protested. "I'm a nice girl."

"With a heart like a bilge pump."

"It just takes getting used to." Happy sniffed and curled into a ball.

They were silent, looking up at the night. It seemed like a typical dumb move to say something about the stars. She probably expected him to comment on Orion or the Dogstar, maybe launch into some sage story about the maritime. After a while he couldn't help himself. He actually loved to look up at the stars. "It's pretty," he said. And checked himself. He just said *pretty* like a little girl.

"Yes. Yes it is," she said.

"And here you are, all alone with me."

"In your evil clutches," Happy said, rubbing her hands together.

"That's right."

"Except I haven't been clutched yet."

"Easy, woman, I can't be rushed." He sat up. "Let me see your wallet." Jamie picked up her Indian fringed bag.

"Why?"

"I just want to see if you're jerking me around or if you have any ID on you at all."

"Go ahead."

Jamie opened the wallet and thumbed through the cards. "No pictures. How do you buy alcohol?"

She shrugged. "I'm always with people who can buy it."

"And you don't drive?"

"Well, I can . . . a little."

"I'll take you driving. We'll take my truck to some quarry and you can pound the shit out of it."

"Really? You'd let me do that?"

"Yeah, it's just a truck."

"All right, let me see your wallet," Happy said. "I want to see what yours looks like."

Jamie pulled his wallet from his back pocket. Happy opened it and laughed. "Why does everyone's license look like a mug shot?"

"I was feeling a little rough that day."

She peered closer and rubbed the corner of it with her thumb. "That's what cracks me up about most people's pictures on licenses—they're either always hungover or pissed off. Hey, what's this?" Her fingers pulled out a tiny watercolor portrait the width of a library card from the wallet sleeve. It was a lake, framed by bluish mountains, a branch of leaves in the foreground and this haze of late-in-the-day color, a bruise of purple blue into yellow.

"This is fantastic, did you do this?"

"No, that was one of Anja's. She did a whole bunch of them at one time. That's looking off the side of Maidencliff onto Megunticook Lake."

Happy flicked a lighter and examined it closely. "This is really detailed. If you hold it back, it almost looks like a photograph."

"Yep." Jamie stared at it for a moment. Of the two artist girl-friends he'd had in his life, Anja had more talent than Pia ever did.

"Is she still painting?"

"Yeah." He took the watercolor gently back from her. "She's not at this level anymore, but yeah."

"Did she go to art school?"

"The Museum School in Boston."

"And you said she was an art teacher. Smart one, huh?"

Jamie shrugged and edged the tiny watercolor back into the sleeve of his wallet.

"You proud of her?"

He nodded. "Yeah, I guess."

She scrutinized him. "Do you guess, or are you really proud of her?"

"Yes. I mean, there's still a lot of work she needs to do, but, ah . . . what are we doing? Every time we go out, we end up talking about her."

"Your girlfriend?"

"I don't. . . ." Jamie rubbed the back of his head vigorously. "I don't call her that anymore."

Happy chewed on the edge of her thumbnail. "Does she know that?"

Downstairs, the party was hopping. Several college kids sat around the couch and played a game of quarters on the coffee table. That was a fundamental difference between college kids and fishermen: a game of cards, dice, or coins actually had to be used as a device in order to get drunk. Downstairs, Jamie waited for the bathroom off the kitchen, with its 1970s faux oak paneling and goldenrod backsplash. He stood against the kitchen counter, which was congested with bottles of vodka and rum, mixers, cigarette butts, the scrittles of corn chips and salsa left to die on a plastic plate. A guy slumping against a wall was on the phone, trying to order Chinese food. "What do you mean you don't deliver? We're right here IN TOWN."

It was nearly three in the morning. Jamie was tired. He stared into his beer, swishing it. Happy came around the corner with a fresh drink in her hand, high-spirited, as if it was still early evening. "There you are," she said. Using his shoulder to give herself a boost, she hopped up on the kitchen counter. "Are you waiting for the bathroom?"

"No. I don't know . . . I'm sorry if I seem all weird," Jamie said. "I'm not really sure what I'm doing hanging out with you. . . ."

"It's okay."

He lowered his voice so the two girls in front of them wouldn't hear—but they were already engrossed in their own conversation. "I'm not looking to just get into your pants, okay? I mean, they're *nice* pants. But . . . and I'm probably sounding like . . . I don't know . . . I'm just. . . ." *Jesus, when words fail.*

She rested her chin on his arm. "We'll be friends, okay?"

"Friends."

"I promise never to call you at home or do anything to upset Anja, okay?"

He nodded.

They walked through a silent town back to the wharf. The breeze was soft, with poor light coming off the opposite side of the harbor. The *Sea Hair*'s rigging looked like a twisted harp. He walked up the gangplank with her. "Come down with me a minute," Happy said, climbing down the narrow shaft.

"I should probably get going."

"Come on, just for a minute."

Jamie ducked so he wouldn't smack his skull on the low ceiling. Down in the aft cabins, it was dark and stuffy, smelling of varnish. He could hear the crew snoring. At the end of the ladder, he stood staring at possibly the narrowest mahogany door he'd ever seen. It was only eighteen inches wide. Happy opened it. They both had to turn sideways to enter the door.

"Where's the owner?" he whispered.

"Falling off a bar stool in Rockland," she whispered back. "This is where I sleep when he's gone." The bunk was wide enough for one person, but they both crammed onto it anyway, on top of the covers. The porthole window showed a tiny cluster of stars. Lying with her, every nerve ending in his body felt like it was glowing. There was no way in that tiny bunk he *couldn't* touch her, and he was deliberately trying to avoid putting his hands near her. Happy's shoulder dug into his chest, her hip to his hip. He was grateful she didn't wear patchouli. She smelled clean, like soap, her dark hair spread across the pillow.

"So, you're not a big fan of shaving your legs," Jamie said, trying to keep it all light. He was almost afraid of silence, the kind of silence that precedes the locked gaze. He wasn't ready for the locked gaze and what came after.

"So," she whispered, "maybe I shouldn't put up a fight if you try to get into my pants." She bumped him with her hip.

Instinctively he turned away. "Is that what just friends do? I don't know. I don't know these things. "

"Well, no need to get all choir boy on me *neither*," Happy said, in possibly the worst Maine accent he'd heard since the castle party.

"*Neither*. Stop using our words."

"You don't have a patent on 'neither,' I'm sorry to say."

"When you end a sentence with 'neither'—that's a Maine word."

"Oh . . . sorry." She cracked up. She had a hoarse laugh, which sounded even louder in the dark. They heard one of the crew groan in his sleep through the thin walls. "Shh," she said. "Shh." When she stopped giggling, she turned on her side to face Jamie, which in that tiny bunk was like two hot dogs on a convenience store roller. "Back to the business of you tackling me," she said with a sweet smile. "Are you?"

"Jay-sus. I didn't know you'd already turned it into a business."

That spurred another round of suppressed giggles. He was tempted to keep joking, to keep it light. Lying there with her, just elbows and hips touching and the smell of soap in her hair, felt odd and thrilling. Then another image, serene, Anja slow dancing, her sweet face tipped to the side. Happy kissed him and a power-ful repugnant flash of Anja with her slack expression and overea-ger mouth jolted him. He hadn't realized that he'd wiped his mouth.

"You okay?" Happy asked.

He didn't answer. "Yeah," he finally said.

"It's all right." She rested in the crook of his arm, her brown hair spilling over. From the peephole corner of the porthole window, he could see the dark black sky had already lightened a shade. After awhile, he could hear her slow breathing. She'd fallen asleep. His inner clock had already kicked into morning time and he was wired awake. He gently extracted himself from her arms. He thought about leaving her a note. He looked down at her. It was best to just go.

SIXTEEN

Anja appeared in Jamie's room, a ghostly block of white in her nightgown. She stood at his bed until he woke up.

"What is it?" His voice was croaky.

"I had a nightmare."

Jamie lifted the corner of his quilt, the signal to crawl in. It was 5:24; he'd only been asleep for an hour.

Anja's cheek lay next to his. "My dream I didn't have no friends and I was all alone," she whispered. "And by the shore there was two clams who was my friends, holding hands. They talked to me and we did everything together. Then I had to let them go back into the sea until I couldn't see them anymore."

A grunt of sleep escaped him. "You'll be all right." He rubbed her back. "Just shh, give me another hour."

The tea kettle on the stove sung faster than usual, pointing to a change in the air. Mare's tales high in the sky were thickening, signaling some weather coming in. Already it was quarter to nine, a shameful hour to start working. He was itching to check on his traps on the west side. She'd taken an hour and a half to get ready and Jamie tapped his knuckles on the kitchen counter, growing anxious. That and he felt like soured bait with a stavin' hangover. He struggled to be patient. Anja had the phone cord wrapped around her, talking to his mother.

"And Donna, I'm gonna make that dinner again. I did made it for Jamie and he really liked it."

"You got almost everything ready? I wanna get going," he interrupted.

Her thundercloud brow. "Jamie, I'm on the phone!"

No shit, he thought, and you're talking about a supper you made more than two weeks ago like anyone still cared. She'd been going on about that southwestern corn chowder for the last couple of weeks, rhapsodizing about it to anyone who'd listen, and he found himself annoyed with her every time she mentioned it. It was reaching the top of Mount Kilimanjaro for her but deathly friggin' boring for anyone else. She still couldn't gauge people, and after they'd been bludgeoned for twenty minutes with her stories on the merits of southwestern corn chowder as opposed to the standard New England kind, they'd get the thousand-mile stare. His mother was the only one who listened to the stories with patience. *It's a big deal to her Jamie, so let her talk. What does it take, twenty minutes of your life?*—his mother's retort to his complaints. Yet she didn't live with Anja, and everything about Anja took more than just twenty minutes.

He took a breath. It was bad luck to have a fight with a woman before starting out the day. "Anja, check the clock, okay? I really need to get out on the water soon."

"Okay!"

Anja sat in the passenger's seat in her red jumper with her lunch and her backpack. For some reason, her nightmare came back to Jamie as he drove. "Clams," he shook his head. "I can't believe you had a nightmare about clams."

"When?" she said.

"This morning? You came into my room?"

She wheeled to face him. "I remember that! That was this morning."

"Most people have nightmares about falling off a cliff or running from the bogeyman. You have nightmares about a couple of clams."

"They was my friends, Jamie! I was so sad when they went back into the sea."

"Yeah, okay. I'm going to get you a bumper sticker that says *I*

197

Brake For Bi-valves." He squeezed her knee. Checked to see if she got it. Of course not. She was smiling, staring straight ahead, her mind out somewhere.

The gray weathered front steps to the Coastal Center had already rotted and broken through in places. Jamie touched the slack, wet wood where part of the riser had collapsed, concerned that someone would fall through. He considered bartering with Carolyn to fix the front steps, then noticed the wooden wheelchair ramp was also a minefield of decay. Olive stood at the top of the porch in a prairie dress, with pink barrettes clasping her pitifully thin hair. She lifted her walker, happy to see them. "Yeah. Yeh. Yeh."

"Olive, this ain't no place for you," Jamie said, directing her walker toward the door. "Come on."

Olive pointed down the hall. "Yeh. Yeh. Yeah. Yeh."

"I'm gonna stay for a minute, talk to Carolyn," Jamie said. He patted Anja on the butt. "Go help Olive, all right?"

"Okay." Anja hugged him, her lunch bag with its pungent tuna fish sandwich pressing against his back. The smell of it was making him spin. "Bye, I love you," she said. Jamie kissed her goodbye. "Have fun at your job," he said.

"Okay, Jamie, you have fun at yours."

He rapped the back of his knuckles against Carolyn's door.

"Come in," Carolyn said, leaning back in her chair. One pale leg was sticking out from behind the desk, a purple and green dragon tattoo stretching all the way from her ankle up her calf. Her 5-year-old daughter, Casey, a solemn little blonde, eyed him from her perch in the corner chair.

"Hey, kiddo," he said to Casey, who squirmed and buried her chin into her doll's hair. Jamie handed Carolyn an envelope of cash. "Anyway, here's for the next two weeks."

"Thanks," Carolyn said, and stuck it in the top drawer.

"You need to do something about them front steps. Looks like the whole thing's rotting right out," he said.

She rolled her eyes. "I got an estimate back for three grand."

"Frig that. I know a ton of people who can help you for way

less than that."

"Well, you tell them to call me, maybe you and me can work something out."

Jamie sat down in the cracked black leather chair on the opposite side of the desk. He exhaled slowly. Nothing was going easy that morning. "That money ought to cover the food for next week, too. You've been awful good helping her buy all them groceries. I really appreciate it."

"That's part of the deal."

He dropped his head in his hand, his temple pulsating. "I know, but to come home, you know, exhausted, the last thing I want to deal with is buying food."

"No problem." Carolyn reached behind her to turn down the radio. Piles of papers and mismatched folders covered her desktop. From the bottom of one pile, she zeroed in on a manila folder and pulled it out, licking her thumb to open it. "Anja's been organizing menus these last couple of weeks, using calculators. Jamie, she's getting better at it." Carolyn jerked a thumb over at the craft table, where Anja was helping Olive with a sculpture of what looked like oatmeal canisters. "She needs to stay organized and not get so frustrated. I'm working on calendars and systems with her, daily reminders. Communication skills. . . ."

"Just keep doing what you do," he said. He stood up, unable to stay still for a progress report this morning when he was quite conceivably two seconds away from yorking all over her desk. His hand gripped the door trim. He nodded to her with a sickly smile. And slipped out, a wind-up toy in paroxysm.

Seventeen

When Anja got down to her tasks, she looked like a truck driver guarding a diner breakfast, her head bent in fierce concentration. She pressed the pencil too hard, breaking the lead, smearing lead and dust across the white page.

"FFFUUUUUUCCCKKK!" she yelled.

"YEAH!" Olive echoed from the opposite corner of the room. Arlo sniggered and reached for his baseball cap to reassure himself it was still there. Anja sat by herself under the windows at a green laminate table, blank paper within the circle of her arm. She brushed the smear away, erased it, backhanded it off the page. Again looked at Carolyn's instructions on the nearby index card: DESCRIBE THE ROOM.

Describe the room. On one level this was the most asinine exercise she'd been given yet, as if she were a 4-year old just discovering the world for the first time. She could see what was in the room, and it was obvious. There was the thing and that thing, and over there, that thing. She hated these exercises, feeling itchy and squirmy about anything that required her to sit for too long. In the past, she'd overreact to new challenges, clear the table with her arm—like the swoop of a dog's tail—knocking books, flash cards, calculators, rulers, and pencils to the floor. *Hey, you want to stay here forever, keep it up,* Carolyn had said in her unrelenting way, but the point had stuck. In order to get out of *here* and go back to work out *there,* Anja needed to rein in the tantrums. She needed to work on her attitude. She was always working on something; if it wasn't math and reading, it was how to be a normal, functioning human being. And here she was surrounded by two guys who lit each other's farts on fire when Carolyn wasn't around and Olive the one-word wonder. None of them had goals; they just lived cheerfully day to day, except for Bruce, who bashed about, terrorizing everyone and champing on his mustache. But The Big Picture, which she and Carolyn had been formulating of late, required work, starting with improving her words.

I WANT:

I want not to come here every day, though I like Carolyn and Casey a lot. I want a key and a car with my own keys. To Stop treating me like a baby. I want Jamie to feel love about me again. I want ice cream, but I want to be small. I want to writing and painting and reading and cooking and driveing and swiming—no swiming, okay maybe swiming. I nont want to be AFRAID of swiming. I want to teach and be a mom and have parties and remember everything.

She looked up, distracted by the TV that Arlo had turned on, her gaze drifting, thinking about things that happened just moments ago. That was another problem, her focus slipped away even when she was motivated. But at least the focus was there—it hadn't been six months ago. Just this summer, something had *changed* in her brain, she'd actually felt it, like stepping out of a misty shower into a clearing of cool, dry air. Early one morning upon waking, it began *processing*, organizing the day's itinerary with ease. Her brain began ticking, humming, as it planned in the right order to take a shower, what to wear, how to call the phone company after breakfast to ask about getting a new PIN number. She was aware of this smooth functioning all of a sudden, remembering the order of her plans five minutes later. There was no need suddenly to capture each thought on a pad of paper or a voice recorder for fear it would flitter away. The frustrating fog of each thought, separate as an island, had begun to form little communities of reason, intellect. And, amazingly, self-awareness. *I'm thinking about thinking!* She felt joyous. Her brain was processing and retaining. And walking into the kitchen, she felt like she was wearing a new pair of glasses. Those were *cabinets*; that was a *range*; those were *drawers, oven mitts*. The glass door open to the outside deck let in the malty scent of ocean. Words written in invisible ink appeared before her eyes in fully recognized sentences. *The air is cool today; maybe I'll put on a sweater. I have to call the phone company. The number is where? In the desk drawer, with the other bills.*

With increased awareness, she became giddy. She began to access more sections of closed-off rooms in her mind, whipping away the dust cloths. More tests at the rehabilitation center; a diagnosis that she'd had another breakthrough. With that came more confidence. She no longer became enraged with Carolyn's writing exercises. Now she had a goal, a big fat lofty one. By the end of the summer, she was going to get enough of her skills back to have a good job. She'd be writing cover letters that "knocked 'em dead," as the books promised. With the goal came fantasies: the first day at a new job. (The job itself still hadn't been defined—its sole purpose was to provide enough money to pay for a form-fitting charcoal power suit and smart gray sling-back heels.) In this dream, she'd also be thirty pounds lighter (this was another mental reminder to quit 'nackin on the sour-cream-and-chive chips). She projected ahead to what it would feel like to come home after that first day. She'd breeze through the front door, and the walkway lights would be backlighting her as she stood, arms draping the doorway. Jamie, of course, would be all nasty in his reeking blue sweatshirt, but he'd do a double-take with a pop-eyed expression at seeing her, which she'd laugh off with a husky chuckle. Twirling her car keys, she'd say, "Get showered, babe, I'm taking us out to dinner." And the chorus of angels would cue up as Jamie, smelling of herring, walked toward her, his face bathed in love. He'd take her face in his hands as if he hadn't actually seen her in a long time. And she'd allow it only for a moment, because his herring hands were getting too close to her brand-new suit. . . .

"ANJA!"

Her head whipped backward, overcompensating. Loud noises still rattled her to the point of pants-wetting.

Carolyn stood in her office doorway, holding a clipboard. "You've been staring off the last five minutes—are you having trouble with the assignment?"

Anja looked over her shoulder slowly. "No."

"What have you got so far?"

Anja stared down at the white page at letters that were funny little glyphs, hobbled together. "The room is too big," she read.

"That's it?"

"Yeah?"

"How 'bout more? How big? Colors, textures, shapes, sounds. Let's incorporate more of that."

"Okay."

What was the color of things? She looked up at a sixteen-foot tin ceiling snaked with ductwork, copper pipes, and peeling paint. The ductwork was gray and dull, like the back side of aluminum foil, but as soon as she tried to reach for the words "ductwork" and "aluminum foil" they faded into a black place. And this was the reality, breakthrough or not. Sometimes words played hide and seek and it hurt to find them. Not all of her days were filled with clarity as she'd expected. Sometimes the fog hung around for days and days. It was that frustrating "now why did I come in this room?" syndrome.

So instead she wrote, *The thing on the roof is gray and it is not sparky*. She couldn't remember "shiny" but associated it with the sparks of a match. That was the best she could do.

The texture of the room was difficult to describe. Texture. Texture. The word held spectral meaning—it could almost be seen through a dooryard window, but the harder she looked, the more atomized it became. She wrote about how she *felt* about the room. *I feel the big room have no friends. It is alone at night and when we go home. It like us here. It like the lights on.*

She snuck a peek over her shoulder to see what Carolyn was doing in her windowed office. She'd forgotten that Casey was still there, sitting in the big black leather chair, a flaccid doll hanging off her lap. She was wearing her pink tutu. The last three days she'd come in with Carolyn, in the same pink tutu and little red cowboy boots. Anja held her pencil to her teeth, preferring to watch Casey rather than deal with more descriptive detail on the room. She loved kids but they didn't seem to respond well to her anymore. They became shy, self-protective around her, but Casey had her mother's directness. She didn't pull any of that shy crap. For once, it was refreshing not to get a strange look from a child. She caught Casey's eye in the window and smiled, making a little "c'mere" gesture. Anja was pleased to see Casey come out of the office and allow herself to be pulled up onto Anja's lap. She slapped her wheat-colored baby hair from her face. "Know what?" Casey stared directly into Anja's eyes.

"No. What."

"I got this bracelet."

Anja peered at the candy pieces strung together with elastic upon a wrist no bigger across than a silver dollar.

"And Mommy hates it."

"Why?"

"Because Daddy's new friend gave it to me."

"Is Daddy's new friend a girl?"

"Yeah, but she ain't my mom's friend."

Anja stared for a moment at Carolyn as she paced in her glass office talking on the phone, realizing for the first time that Carolyn had problems outside of the Coastal Center. It was like a sharp slap on the cheek. Everyone had problems.

"Do you like that bracelet?" Anja asked.

"It's okay." Casey rubbed her nose on her wrist.

"Can I have it if you don't?"

Casey yanked her hand away. "No."

"Okay," Anja said, looking away.

"Know what else?" Casey said.

"No, what else?"

"I don't have to go to day care any more."

"Huh," Anja mused. "Is that why you be here all the time now? Cause the day care lady—her husband get arrested for touching kids?"

"I don't know," Casey said.

204

"Oh, that's what Jamie said was in the paper."

"Oh."

"ANJA!"

Anja jumped. Her focus snapped back as Casey crawled off her lap toward the big hazy form of Carolyn in the doorway. "Do you need me to come over and help you?" Carolyn said, hand on her hip.

"No I got it!" Anja yelled. "I can DO it. Don't come over!" She huddled protectively around her paper.

"Okay then, step to it. You've got ten more minutes."

The physical therapy room was in the opposite corner of the craft room, separated by a wall with windows, just like Carolyn's office. From where Anja sat she could see Steve, the physical therapist, guide Olive along the parallel bars. Anja checked the clock to see how much time she had left before Carolyn came back. The large digital clock in red numbers above the door displayed a minute before eleven and Anja slammed down her pencil. Everybody knew that was "Shining Star" time. Anja walked quickly toward the door of the PT room. Carolyn got up and stood in the doorway of her office. Olive and Steve stopped what they were doing.

"It's eleven!" Anja screamed. "Where's the fucky record?"

The way puppets are made to lightly, tentatively dance, the way their careful knees are raised and then brought down with a deliberateness, never quite getting the rhythm right—that was how all the head-injured people started dancing, once Anja put on "Shining Star." She began to dance in her own unique style that combined elements of the martial arts crane movements with whirling pirouettes. Olive's small, wizened face glowed as she raised her tiny arms in victory, and even Steve got down and funky in his awkward way. Anja grabbed Manny's hand, whispered into his ear. She brought him by the hand into the PT room with its heavy blue wrestling mats. Manny held the penny up high and gave his arthritic hips a waggle. Arlo shuffled onto the mats, held Steve's hand, and began his patented series of movements, which to the untrained eye almost *looked* like a seizure but for the fact that Arlo was smiling.

"Dance with us," Anja said to Bruce, who stood against the wall, glowering at them and combing his mustache with his bottom lip.

"No."

The song was half over. Anja tried to take his hand but he yanked it back and held it with the other as if it were injured. "Fine," she said and did a shimmy before him. She bent her knees and shook her hips, intending to straighten herself up, but the effort was erratic and for a moment she teetered, a girl rolling backward off a high-rise building. Anja fell prone onto the blue mat. The music was drowned by Bruce's booming laugh. It wasn't a laugh so much as a rumbling chortle that built up in his massive gut and came out as AHHHHHH HA HA HA HA HA HA. "You fall," Bruce said, his entire face lit up.

Anja lay there, squinty-eyed. She got up. "So? Least I'm dancing. You do it."

He shook his head, clearly pleased.

Anja said, "You can do it."

Bruce shoved her; she shoved him back. Each wore an aggressive smile.

EIGHTEEN

On Saturday, the lobstermen aboard their snub-nosed boats assembled in a large circle in the harbor, each slowly passing by the wharf dock, where a priest in vestments stood, waving a smoking lantern. The priest's colorless hand chopped the air in his blessing of the fleet. His breath fought to rise up in the rain. It was an annual toast to the ocean, a ritual to appease it, so it wouldn't take any fishermen or their boats. Jamie didn't believe in priests. He chose, instead, to ride on Thongchai's boat, the *Maisie May*, to keep him company.

"Hey, Ugly, pass me another, *guy.*" Even though Thongchai had been out until three the previous morning, drinking began promptly at 8:06 a.m. They had six cases of Coors Light stacked three-high next to the boat stove.

Jamie stood in the rain with his beer, two sweatshirts and a cap doing a poor job of keeping him dry. There were still fifteen or so boats idling in the water ahead of them in a semicircle, all waiting in the drizzle, which came down like a sneeze. The better boats had a closed-in wheelhouse, some got by with a well-protected canopy. *Maisie May*, of course, was a junk boat, looking the way Thongchai kept his apartment, a dirty, disheveled hulk with flat potato chip bags and empty Mountain Dew bottles scattered about the muddy deck. They were all cramped together; it was difficult to walk around, the deck further cluttered with a loose pile of rusted chain next to a couple of fish totes. Cigarette butts everywhere. Jamie wished he could've just ridden with Thongchai alone, but Thongchai could rarely be alone. Bud Brown and Tadpole Hollis were tagging along, two guys Jamie could do without, the kind of dimwits who Thongchai attracted. Drove Jamie crazy, and it was one of the reasons they rarely hung out anymore.

As it was, the *Maisie May* had turned into a sausage party, everyone well into his first six-pack before the vendors of the Lobster Weekend had even begun to set up. Thongchai had allowed a three-day-old beard to grow, like potting soil stuck to his face.

"Guess who I run into last night?" he said with a grin. "Seen your sister, James, last night at the Tide Out raising all kinds of hell."

Jamie rolled his eyes, as if this was news.

"Christ. Hair was a mess, wearing a tube top. Was looking pretty *on front* in them Spandex too, I'd say. She ain't pregnant again, is she?"

"Who knows? Was Jeff there?"

"Nope, just her. She was friggin' putting away vodkatinis too, like she only had one night to live. She kept trying to get me to dance with her. I told her I wasn't really in the mood so she called me a 'fucking fag-oid' and punched me right in the chest."

Jamie turned to face the wharf, not interested, but of course Thongchai had a crowd to entertain.

"Each time the song ended, she kept coming back and trying to pull me on the dance floor. Then like the third time I said no, she went back out onto the dance floor and puked her guts out."

Jamie watched the boats ahead inch along the semicircle. They were only six or seven boats away from the priest.

"You shoulda seen that room clear," Thongchai continued, one hand lazily on the wheel. He continued to scan the horizon. "But it don't matter to Amanda, 'cause she just kept dancing anyway, horse-stepping in her own puke and giving everyone the middle finger."

Next to them, Bud Brown's massive shoulders shook with fitful giggles. "I'm sorry, man," Bud said to Jamie, who shrugged. Bud's ponderous bulk and bullet-hole eyes made him look like a prison thug to everyone who didn't know him. But underneath a neatly shorn goatee, he had a baby face that gave him the semblance of a paper boy. Thongchai began to entertain the boys with another story, this time about a girl he took home the night before. Jamie, on his fourth beer, held his arms crossed and leaned against the wheelhouse. He decided to give it back to Thongchai.

"Oh yeah, what's her name? Becca? I know that girl," Jamie said. "She's got herself a tattoo, 'Dave Forever,' on her shoulder, right?"

Bud thought that was amusing. "Who the hell is Dave?"

Tadpole Hollis, shorter than everyone on board, chimed in, "I heard, I heard, check this out. I heard that she got that tattoo in eighth grade—but get this, it was the name of her *biology* teacher."

Tadpole was younger than the rest of them by about five years. He wasn't a fisherman himself, but aped the Carhartt look, the stubbled bleariness, to fit in. Jamie found him to be incredibly cocksure for a guy five-foot-seven who had never really been in a fight. Every working guy had his own signature cap he wore on the wharf, the shabbier the better. Usually the logo represented a type of boat engine, a well-known fishing camp, or a lobster co-op. Tadpole's grungy, canvas-flayed-off-the-brim CAT cap annoyed Jamie. Even though Tadpole drifted on the edge of the Churchie's crowd, Jamie had never really warmed up to the kid. Partially it was because Tadpole was a boat salesman and had perfect English for his customers, but with the boys he lapsed into the thick Maine pronunciation with a little too much zeal. When Jamie had first stepped onto the *Maisie May*, Tadpole had clapped him on the back. "How you do-in', bud-day?" he said generously, as if the *Maisie May* was his own. With a wide grin, Tadpole persisted. "Why doncha git yer friggin' *drunk* on with a tall boy. Here, I'll set you up," he said as he bent to yank a cold beer out of the cooler.

Now he was stuck with all of them, and it was taking an unearthly long time to get this ridiculous blessing of the fleet ritual over with.

The priest stood in front of a small crowd of people. A thoughtful woman was trying to hold a blue umbrella over the priest's head. Smoke churned up from the idling boats, skimming past the pilings that looked like compound fractures jutting out of the water. As the *Maisie May* approached the wharf, they spotted Russell and Ev Fogerty standing in the crowd to the right of the priest. Russell had his right arm in a blue hospital sling.

"Look at them assholes," Thongchai muttered.

"What the fuck are they doing here?" Tadpole said, lifting and resetting his cap in what was supposed to be an aggressive gesture. It only served to irritate Jamie.

"What are you gonna do about it?" Jamie scowled at Tadpole.

"I'll friggin, I'll feckin. . . ."

"Yeah you'll go sell them a boat, I'm sure." He turned to Thongchai. "What do you think Russell did to get that arm in a cast?"

"Don't know," Thongchai said. "Everybody, put your beers away."

The *Maisie May* churned forward, her low guttural pitch the language of the harbor. The boat slid slowly by as the priest's hand came down to bless the *Maisie May*, prompting a weak cheer from everyone on the wharf, everyone except, of course, the Fogertys, who wore perpetual strangled expressions. If that entire family had won the lottery and the cameras were in their faces, a reporter's breathless question under their noses, *What will you do with all the money?* Jamie imagined the Fogertys would still wear that disgusted-with-life look while holding the giant check.

For all the pomp, all the priest did was yammer some Latin and rain a few drops of holy water upon the bow, while boats ahead blared their horns. Now she was saved, the dear *Maisie May*, and for another year the sea would not plunge her into its heaving bosom.

Then Tadpole did something inordinately stupid. "Hey!" he yelled to the Fogertys as the *Maisie May* cruised out of distance. Tadpole gave them the elaborate forearm-over-forearm gesture that left no doubt for everyone on the wharf, the priest who was standing in the rain, and all the Fogertys that this was an altogether other kind of blessing.

Lack of space around the U-shaped wharf prompted Thongchai to moor his boat in his usual spot fifty feet away. "You guys are staying here," Thongchai told Tadpole and Bud, as he stepped down into the dinghy with Jamie.

"Why do we have to stay here?" Tadpole said, now a petulant little lamb.

"Cause you're fuckin' idiots," Jamie said, untying the warp off the cleat and cranking up the outboard. "Watch the boat." They headed toward the floating dock.

The drizzle began to let up and the Lobster Weekend, like a forlorn cow in the field, had begun to shake it off and stand up again.

On the coast, people talked about Lobster Weekend in the same giddy way that kids rhapsodized about Christmas. In other parts of the coast, there were a few outdoor charity-sponsored events— "Mentally Challenged Day" and the Crohn's and Colitis Foundation's "Heal and Wheel-a-thon"—but they didn't have the same turnout as Lobster Weekend, which summoned the entire community's resources like a baby tornado gathering energy. In three days, the town laid out the harvest of quahogs, chicken lobsters, mussels, steamers, fat-kernelled corn on the cob. They cheered on the hokey crowning of Miss Teen Blueberry and strained their vocal cords in support of the King of Neptune (under whose fake gray beard was really Bob Gagne from the town office's licensing department) as he gallantly glided up to the wharf on a lobster, one knee bent and scepter held high.

The sun finally turned out for the celebration late in the day, and the crowd, rammed right up to the dock railing, amassed three deep. Everywhere, people dangled their legs off the docks, off lobster boats. Teens ran by, the girls with their hair all in cornrows, the high school fashion that summer, the boys in baseball jackets.

Jamie and Thongchai staggered through the crowd amid smells of hot dogs and sauerkraut cooking in the side tents. The mildly pleasant reek of boiling lobsters wafted everywhere.

Every family in the area had staked out a place on the sloped grass of the wharf. It reminded him of the human litter at Woodstock from images he'd seen on TV. This made him think of Happy, and her hippie parents. He thought about her almost every day now, but there were a few things about her that weren't exactly perfect, like her masculine strength, her hairy legs, and her Indian fringe purse. He'd have to get beyond that. He wanted to be around her now, just to see what she would say about the kids running crate races and falling smack on their faces into the water. Or even a comment on the tired polka band on stage, where the guys worked at their instruments as if trying to do CPR on a dying body. Happy could make this fun. She could make the most everyday experience, even sitting in the dentist's chair, fun. She was happy, goddammit; he could even get past her goofy name.

A sliver wedging deeper. He was starting to think of her more and more as *his*, which was also beginning to be a problem. Because it had been made clear from the start, this would not work. But then he had to go and kiss her a few times, and whether or not that fit into the strict definition of "friends," it was becoming a problem in the same way that cocaine was seductive in the harbor, even though Jamie made a deliberate choice not to court that either. All the machinations of his mind, the little cubbies where he put Discipline and Loyalty, Conduct and Control, would not stay put. It was starting to hurt, and what he didn't know was that this hurt would breed like bacteria, uncontrolled, day after day, until it consumed him. He wouldn't leave Anja, but he might get to the point where he'd start a separate life—something he found repugnant and weak in his married friends. So maybe this was how it started. The meeting, the resistance, the wanting, the resistance, the pain, the dissolution, and the decision. He was moving toward dissolution, which in itself created a rationale he still found repugnant, but sadly, he realized, he could live with it. This tide was moving with a slumbering, wicked current and he found himself checking for her face in the crowd.

He could hear the lobster boats dragging the string of crates across the harbor, signaling that the crate races would soon start. The last of the kid champions, a 10-year-old boy with one black sock and one orange sock, prepared to scamper nimbly across the fifty wooden lobster crates tied together like a string of child's blocks between opposite sides of the wharf. On either side of the dock, adults with clipboards and mothers with warm clothing and towels stood at the ready. The 10-year-old in his swimming trunks was poised like an athlete waiting for the gun to go off. "Go!" the announcer called over the loudspeaker. The crowd of nearly a thousand people cheered him on. In his T-shirt, swimming trunks, and two different-colored socks, the kid sprinted swiftly across the wobbly wooden lobster crates.

"My mother is around here somewhere with Anja," Jamie said to Thongchai. They wound their way through the crowd, past strollers and beach chairs and trash cans already beginning to overflow with red and pink lobster carcasses. "If you see them, let me know. I think my sister's with them too."

Thongchai shuddered. "Amanda." Then he began to sing softly. "*Oh Mandy, you came and you puked without shaking. . . .* Hey, Eugely, what would you do if I married your sister?"

"Jesus Christ, I wouldn't even wish that on the Fogertys. What are you saying?"

"Think about it. I'd be your brother-in-law!"

"Yeah, but think about what you'd have to come home to every night." They both beheld the same image: Amanda, with sunken eyes and a deathly pallor betraying a hard-core hangover, in her classic elastic waistband black stirrup pants that prominently delineated her V-shaped mound. Three kids crying in the kitchen for supper and the ashy end of a Marlboro sticking out of her sour, downturned mouth.

"How does Jeff do it?" Thongchai asked.

"Jeff has got built-in numb, that's how."

"So you're saying he don't need drugs or alcohol to face Manda at night—"

"Oh yeah he does."

"Poor guy."

"Speaking of, how them OUI classes going?" Jamie asked.

"Ahhh. . . ." The noise guys make when the fun has ceased in a conversation. Thongchai wasn't like Cary, who took things in, and didn't analyze much. He was a stocky, square-built guy with solid, one-way thoughts. He was like something Happy once said,

"The sea doesn't like anything soft." Thongchai's grandfather had fished out of St. George since the turn of the last century. They fished the old way too, using the four-foot woodies, hauling everything by hand on long, windy, back-breaking days, using cheap bait to fish for bluefish, then grounding that down into brim. Like Jamie, he'd grown up doing everything by hand and having no one give him any more than he could do for himself. He was native, more native than most white kids. But he was not soft, never would be. And while this made him one of the better lobstermen in the harbor, it didn't make him very adept at the kind of conversations people needed to have every once in a while.

"Thongchai—you going to those classes or not?" Jamie demanded.

"Naw . . . I just . . . I don't know."

"You gotta go, bud-day—you gotta get your license back. You can't be one of them guys people have to drive around for the rest of your life. You don't want to depend on people, do you? Come on, you gotta be a man and get it done."

Thongchai's hand slicked across his stiff, black hair. "See, the thing is, you gotta get . . . I gotta go to a couple of these counseling things before I can get the license back."

"Well, fuck it—go!" Jamie said. They stopped walking and stood by a wooden railing overlooking the harbor. He looked at Thongchai directly. "You could use the counseling."

Thongchai shook his head.

"You asshole. Don't let that stop you from getting your license. So, it's a couple of counseling sessions—so what. You probably need it. I need some friggin' counseling. I'll go with you, just make the appointment."

"You'd go with me?"

"Yeah, maybe I'll sit outside the door and take notes. I'll just be respectful and leave when you want to bring up your masturbation problem."

A smile crept up; Thongchai's brilliant white smile seemed to threaten his entire face. "Cock knocker," he said. Then his expression turned thoughtful. "That would be awesome if you could come with me."

"I'll even drive you there. I'm your brother, man. You don't need to marry my sister for it to be like that."

Thongchai was silent, his smile like a sail quailing in slack wind. He couldn't say it back, not because he didn't feel it, but because the sea didn't like anything soft.

"So, where do you wanna go?" Thongchai asked.

"Hell if I know." Walking around was getting old. The crowd roared and they turned to look at the crate races in the harbor. A man in orange Grundens, one hand on the outboard, buzzed a short way across the harbor in a six-foot aluminum skiff to fish out the kid who'd fallen off the crates into the water. The crowd went nuts. "Let's get a beer." Thongchai said, his solution for anything. They made their way up the hill to where the Tide Out Pub sat. On the back porch, a better band was playing good-time rock-and-roll, Bob Seeger stuff, the kind of flavorless music that appeals to drinking crowds.

Coming down the hill, he saw her and all his quiet reserve got shoved rudely aside; now his stomach felt like a day on rough water. Happy was holding two paper cups and when she saw him, she winked and held out the two cups like an old gunman from the West, pretending to shoot him with both barrels. She had on a pair of cut-offs, a burgundy man's shirt tied in a knot that exposed her belly. A paisley kerchief held down her hair.

He felt himself begin to shake without knowing why.

"Hey, mister lobsterman," Happy said, handing him a coffee. "Want one? I was supposed to give it to my friend, but I can't find her."

The last thing Jamie wanted was coffee; he sipped it with a grin. "What are you doing?"

"I thought we'd come down and check out the scene," she said. "See where you live. See your people."

"This is my friend," Jamie said. "Thongchai." Who, naturally, could not stop staring.

"Thongchai—yeah—hi!" Happy said, sticking out her hand.

"Heard about you from Jamie. Not a big fan of the tourists." She laughed, one big *ha*.

Jamie looked down at her freckles, her sassy eyes behind her glasses, conscious of Thongchai beside him trying to figure her out. "Who'd you come with?" Jamie asked.

She pointed to a group of people up on the hill. Jamie recognized Captain Nick and a few of the scraggly-haired boat boys. "We're all sick of being together. I told them I was going fishing," she said and poked a knuckle into his side to tickle him. Thongchai's eyes widened at this suggestion and his smile began to reemerge.

"Well if you want, we could go," Jamie started to say, before a siren of laughter shot out, vaulting high and bottoming out like a horse canter. He could see Anja barreling toward them in her pink corduroy pants, running with her arms stretched out. "Jamie!"

"GO!" the announcer said over the PA. Another kid began running the crates.

Anja slammed into him and put her hands on either side of his face. Her clammy hands clutched his cheeks. "Jamie, I'm so happy," her bright, animated face shining up at him. She had pink plastic barrettes holding back her blond pageboy. "They got fried dough here!"

Jamie tried to position himself between Anja and Happy—to keep Anja's focus elsewhere. He glanced at Happy beside him. She sipped her coffee, smiling.

Thongchai was no help, nor did he even seem present. His smooth, caramel expression had become flat, in the way Jamie had seen on the water in a storm. His eyes were not on Jamie, but rather upon the three approaching figures coming down the hill. They came toward Jamie and Thongchai: a fat man and two scroungy thin men, in muted blues, drab fawn browns, and shuttered hats.

Kenny Fogerty led them. He was a huge oaf, his gut swinging in a pair of jeans too wide to stay on his hips. As the story went, back in the eighties, one afternoon when Kenny was sauced up, he stood on Nipple Ledge and fired off an illegal M16 rifle at the Coast Guard, which won him a year and a half in jail. Dumb, but not nearly as bad as his brothers beside him. Ev and Russell Fogerty bounced like underwater reeds, swaying. They were coming fast. Jamie pushed Anja behind him. And Thongchai moved into a stance. They were chess pieces dragging into place.

"Hey!" Anja said, her brows thundering. She bumped against Happy and did not alter her annoyed expression.

The Fogertys needed no introduction, no brief little verbal two-step. In fights, they had the reputation of coming in fast, without warning. They did not waste time with the crowd-pleasing "Ya wanna go, huh? Wanna go?" (chest smacking followed by vapid look). Russell straddled right up to Jamie with his left arm in a blue sling. He was messy drunk, eyes sliding. "Don't you fuckin'," he slurred, and the rest was indistinguishable, but it was safe to assume that Tadpole's gesture on the boat had worked them up.

Jamie's throat closed and he felt flashy, chromatic red all over—red in his eyes and in his muscles. Drunk Fogertys were unpredictable. Ev was giving off nothing—he was watching Russell, whose good arm came up to carve the air above Jamie's head. Russell's timing was off, his balance awkward, but Jamie was fluid. He blocked Russell's punch with the meat of his own ropy forearm and drove his fist into Russell's sling. It was nearly the same move Jamie'd made eight years ago, standing over Russell, his scabbed knuckles connecting with facial bones.

You thought you'd get away with stealing from me?

That same bone sting, that drill to the flesh. It felt sickening. His knuckles connected and slid, into what injury Jamie didn't know—a healing compound fracture? Whatever bones, nerves, ligaments were healing had now been split open. Jamie could feel what he'd done and began to tremble. *Who the hell comes at you with a broken arm?* Russell's face, a twisted snarl. He howled, dropping to one knee, his good arm gingerly cradling the sling.

Kenny was a useless fighter and his outsized presence did nothing to subdue Thongchai. Kenny made the plodding attempt to start a shoving match with Thongchai. There were only moments to watch.

Thongchai's small wiry chest, his thrust arms, knocked Kenny back a foot.

A crowd had gathered and Ev Fogerty began to twitch, his mouth sour. They were seconds from this turning into a free-for-all. Anja huffed, silently at first, then in great wheezes.

"You hit him," she said loudly. No one knew who she was referring to. She turned an anguished face to Jamie. "Why? He don't need his arm hurted. Oh my God, mister. I am so sorry. SO SORRY." She knelt down to pet Russell's hair, as if he were a mangy pup lost on a country road. A strange bubble separated the crowd from what was going on this moment. In this bubble were Anja, Jamie, Ev, and Russell. No one else's faces or voices. Anja tenderly petting a man's hair, stroking Russell. Her hand touching his face with a soothing caress where his tears from pain had trickled down. Ev staring, disbelieving. All of this a warped moment and a rushing in Jamie's ears where time was moments from running out. Where something very bad would happen to Anja if she kept her hand in the jaw of the injured tiger. She had no instincts, no perception, no background, no *history*. No history. She was horribly mistaken if she thought she could soothe Russell Fogerty.

"Get over here!" Jamie barked.

Her worried face lifted to his, her hand on a dark head that was turning now, turning to reveal glittery eyes. Touch was not soothing to a Fogerty; it was an invitation.

Jamie grabbed her arm roughly and brought her startled face to his. "Goddammit, you ever fucking listen to me? Get out of here—go home. Nobody wants you here."

The soap bubble had been pricked and now the crowd was vivid. Many had gathered in a tight circle to see the fight. The sounds rushed back in; he could hear gasps, murmurings, the jury of unseen faces, condemning him for mistreating a girl *like that*. He caught a short glance of Happy by the fence, her face recoiling. Thongchai, his lips tight, maintaining the garrison of his body against Kenny.

Anja began to cry the way she did when she was embarrassed or deeply hurt. No one else could read this, or see that she was experiencing the overload, the Great Wash-Out. Her senses like a deck of cards flittered into unordered pile at her feet. She cried, gathering momentum, in that jagged, head-injured crescendo that tore Jamie's insides from cell to cell.

It took the fight out of Ev, while Russell knelt helplessly on the ground. Ev scrutinized Anja; he could see what was at work here, that she was not right.

"You always thought you was so much better," Ev said carefully, his mean and drunken eyes strangely clear. He staggered back a step and stared long at Anja. His eyes back to Jamie, cut dead. "You got nothing."

NINETEEN

He woke early at three a.m. And in the darkness, all the problems he'd been shoving down loomed larger than the distorted remains of exhausted dreams.

Anja was asleep in her bed. She'd curled away from his touch on the way home. He imagined Happy for a moment—her face in the crowd when he told Anja to get away from him. He lay there, imagining the same sort of disgust.

Other than a quick snort at Churchie's, he didn't go to the bars, he didn't start fights. He kept to himself and to his business, and yet trouble managed to seek him out. He thought of Russell's mangled arm, of the rage that might follow over this. Once the incident got back to Dale Fogerty, there might be some late-night discussions in the burnt-out fish shack. He thought of Tadpole Hollis and his stupid, sycophantic need to belong. So many harbor disputes over so many years. Ev Fogerty hadn't touched Jamie, but he'd gotten to him. *You got nothing.*

As a child of 9 or 10, working alongside his father, he'd screwed up. Shoved a trap overboard, which had not been tied off to warp. It was a new thirty-dollar trap, brilliant galvanized coated steel, one second at the frothy, burbling gray surface— then gone to the ocean floor. Senior had roared the usual insults: *stupid . . . useless . . . idiot.* Jamie had to pay him back for the trap, which took him a month. He'd stood behind the laundry room door listening to an argument between Pappy and his father late night in the kitchen in Port Clyde.

Kids make mistakes. Lighten up.

Then he should pay for it. You don't teach him by letting him get away with it.

Help him pay for half of it, goddammit, you don't need the kid's money.

He's already fucked up my GPS this month, lost my bait iron—he's bad luck.

Jimmy, Jesus, don't say that.

I'm saying it. It's true.

Jamie stared at the ceiling. All his life, Maynard and James telling him that the Eugleys were a good family. *Better than most,* said with a highliner's pride. Jamie had stopped going out on the boat with his father after that night in the kitchen. No one knew why; Donna always assumed it was over the lost trap, but truthfully, after overhearing that conversation behind the laundry door, the joy of lobstering had been completely ground out. He would've gotten chastised for being too sensitive if he said why. It wasn't as though James had beaten him or abused him. Only because Maynard had coaxed him back into it at the age of 12 did the joy begin to bubble back. It took apprenticing alongside his grandfather rather than his father—an unusual move in the harbor—to motivate Jamie back into the daily routine. He spent his teen years and twenties heading out from the wharf at 5 a.m. with his father's boat always ahead of his, an awkward allowance, the five steps behind royalty. Always conceding to the better fisherman.

Ev and Russell, big stoner Kenny, always getting the same. Even worse, growing up strangled in the face, strangled in the heart.

I gotta get away from these people.

TWENTY

Low pressure had built fog all around the empty beach. It grayed the sand, darkened the slick rocks. The boats in the harbor were indistinct. Happy blew into her beer bottle, a low cool sound. It had been a week since he'd seen her, but a chill had settled in, and unlike their previous times together, he found himself with little to say. He stared obdurately ahead. They'd been sitting for long, uncomfortable minutes. The more the silence stretched, the harder it was to pretend it wasn't there. Happy blew into the bottle again.

"That's a groaner," Jamie said. "That's what they call the sound of a foghorn."

"Wow—a whole sentence out of you. Stunning."

He tried to find something to match her sarcasm, but the words forming in his mind were overbearing and unfunny. He slumped, giving up.

"Listen," Happy said. "If we're going to sit here and you're not going to talk to me, then I'll just go back to the boat and juggle some knives. At least that will be entertaining."

He threw a stone into the surf. "Dow."

She stared at him for a moment longer. "That's it? That's all I get? Fine, I'm going swimming." Happy whipped off her glasses and tossed them on a blanket. She took off her tank top as if it were nothing, revealing her brown bathing suit. Then, just as easily, she shimmied out of her shorts. She had a bit of a belly, yet she didn't care. "Wanna go in?" she said over her shoulder. She had a beautifully shaped butt from working on a boat.

"No I gotta keep my *shots* on, in case anybody I know goes by with binoculars."

"You're such a Puritan—just go in naked." She walked, a brown and white tan-lined vision with clunky black sandals, into the fog, disappearing.

"Naw."

He watched her wade in, feeling all of his Puritan New England upbringing push up against him. It would be *different*, it might even be fun to go swimming in the fog, if he could swim. It would change things considerably, lighten the damn pressure in his head, to romp with her in the surf, go back to being silly, as she liked to say. He sat in his long Carhartt shorts and work boots in the sand, unable to move, though he could hear her screech and splash in the water. *How do you manage to stay happy. . . . Happy?* Wouldn't that be nice, to feel that way once in a while. Just cast it all off and feel something different, be the kind of person he himself couldn't even recognize. Soon she came running back out and Jamie threw her his sweatshirt. She burrowed into him and he was glad for that, at least.

"That was FREEZING."

"I'll bet."

She shivered and threw her hair into a messy wet ponytail. "My toes went numb in like thirty seconds, I'm not kidding. Down in the Keys, you walk in the water and it feels like walking into a bath or hot springs." She shivered her way back into her clothes. "You know, grumpy, you really should visit me down in the Keys this fall. I could show you things you've never seen."

"I imagine."

"There's this huge event down there every year, it's like a gigantic Halloween party, Mardi Gras and an Electric Kool-Aid Acid Test all rolled into one. They've got these body painters and they literally spray-paint the person's whole body these surreal colors— whatever you want. We're talking a whole town crammed with lovely women nude and painted like something out of the Mists of

Avalon. Just streets filled with wacky, crazy fun people dressed like spirits, phantoms, Celtic gods, druids, high priestesses, sorcerers, sea nymphs, hobbits, and elves—all that kind of stuff."

The way she talked mesmerized him, as if her mouth were trying to catch up with her brain. The image of painted women was quite interesting. "Have you, uh . . . gotten spray-painted?" Jamie asked.

"Oh sure, many times. It's unbelievably powerful to walk the streets with no top on, a drink in your hand, and music of drums, cowbells, and kazoos in your ears. And you look like a blue alien, your body is literally a canvas, all these beautiful vivid colors swirling around. Everybody smiling—everybody having the time of their lives. I go to this pirate costume contest every year. We start in the morning, usually with some light and rowdy Jamaican or Cuban band and, of course, buckets o' rum. By mid-afternoon, you can just guess where it goes from there . . . I did get second prize two years ago for the swashbuckling contest, though."

"You know what I like about you?" Jamie said.

"What's that?"

"You make my drinking look like it's not a problem."

She snorted and put on her glasses. "Listen, why don't you come down on the boat with us? You don't even have to be gone from Anja all that long. Come on down for a couple of weeks."

He looked out at the dismal gray beach, his mind full of bright blue alien colors, sloshy, frosty rum punch thoughts. "What would that be like?"

"We'll wake up, go to Bahama Mama's and get some of the best cheese grits and hash cakes you've ever had in your life. Then we'll bypass all the typical tourist shit on Duval Street. I'll introduce you to my friends; we'll go sailing on a catamaran or a schooner. Or we can lounge on the beach, walk around, have lunch at this raw bar I know. They've got these fantastic Key Lime garlic oysters." She closed her eyes as if she could taste them.

"Keep talking." He felt himself drift.

"Somewhere in the afternoon we'd have to take a nap. And then after we freshen up, we'll go find a party. All you have to do is pass a house with a bunch of people hanging out on the porch, introduce yourself, and go in. You don't even have to really know the people who live there, as long as you're friendly. That's the way it is down there—people give you plenty of room to be yourself. I love it."

The barest grunt escaped him. He bit off what he was going to say, his lips clamped. This dream was all nice and seductive, and slightly more convenient for her, as all she had to do was throw her backpack on the nearest schooner.

"I wish I could."

"You can!"

His sandy fingernails scratched at his ear. "Yeah."

A short sigh escaped her. "Okay. Let's get this over with. Ever since you picked me up, there's been this black mood hanging over you. What's the problem?"

Jamie took a rock and hurled it into the ocean. It flew from his fingers with an angry jerk. "I've got things I've got to take care of. If you need to go—just go down there. It's not like you're not gonna have fun if I'm not there."

He was looking into the fog, not at Happy, but he could hear her tone shift, the click of a knob turning, dialing up sarcasm. "Hey, Hard Luck Harry," she said, "we've all had our share. Save the good times for someone else, wouldja?"

Jamie glowered at her. Happy briskly rubbed the sand off her palms. "Sorry, but that's crap. It's your life. You decide how you want to live it."

"I don't think you really know, so let's not get into it."

"Hey," she said, "it's not that I'm blind. You've got to keep taking care of somebody who needs all your time and energy. But you ever think about how much better your choices are than hers? You're an idiot if you don't give yourself a little release valve now and then."

He shook his head. "People are already talking. One of my mother's friends, this nosy"—he tried not to say the first word that came to mind—"*woman* came up to me at the beach store this morning and started lecturing me that she heard I'd yelled at

Anja in public and what a lousy person I was and all this stuff. And how she always thought I was better than that. That's the thing about this area. People can't mind their own business—they literally have to stop you on the damn street and tell you everything on their minds. You know? That woman wasn't there—she didn't see how Russell Fogerty was. I had to yell at Anja to go away because she was going to get herself hurt."

"I know. I saw it."

"You probably thought I was a jerk too."

Happy looked at him levelly. "No, I didn't. It's what you had to do."

"Yeah, so, just think what everyone is going to say if I take off with you for a couple of weeks. Great, what an asshole that Eugley guy is."

"Who cares what they think?"

Jamie exhaled. He stared out at the light gray line where the fog met the water. "Goddamn, all you have to do is take off on a boat. Of course it doesn't matter to you what people think. If there's a problem, don't even bother dealing with it, Happy—just fly away."

She was silent and he realized he'd just stabbed her with the same dull blade that she'd been using on him. He pulled on the loop of her belt to make her look at him. "If I told you how I really feel . . . you wouldn't like me."

Happy sat with her knees up, her arms protectively around them. She lowered her chin to the top of her knees. "What—that you're sick and tired? That you don't even know if you can help Anja anymore?"

"Yes."

"Gee, that's a shocker. I'd feel the same way. But at least you've stuck it out through the good and bad with this girl. I don't know what to tell you. Half of me is jealous—I don't know anyone who'd do that for me. Half of me is feeling awful that I'm even here with you."

Jamie listened to the stones tumbling with the surge of the tide. He wanted Happy to keep talking. He wanted to take her by the hand back to the Point, introduce her to his parents, settle her into a pipe-dream life that would only work played against the gray rim of fog of his imagination. After a moment, Happy stood up, wiped the sand from the back of her shorts.

"You said she's getting better every day, even if it's just a little bit."

"Yeah."

"Well, you've got to stop this sad-sack shit and look to the future, mister lobsterman." She tipped her bottle, blew the low foghorn sound.

"What are you talking about?"

"When you're feeling like this—like you're at the bottom and crushed on all sides—that's the time to do something completely unexpected and random." Happy whipped the green beer bottle up into the sky, white froth spewing in circles. She pirouetted, stuck out her tongue, and caught the bottle behind her back.

TWENTY ONE

The two enormous windows in the Captain's House kept the fog at bay. As the light of the day drained, the two spruce trees outside the windows softened, their hard, spiky needles disappearing against the glass. As the grandfather clock ticked, the light gray cigar smoke outside turned a darker flannel gray, then, with night, turned cornflower blue.

The fog seemed to follow him home, settle in his coat, come out his nostrils. Jamie opened the front door to find Anja at the other side of the living room. She stood before an easel he'd set up for her the week before. On the bright canvas, a corner of detail had been fleshed out, a pale delicate representation of Luce Beach. She was still in her pajamas.

"Hey," he said and dropped his jacket on the floor. After the afternoon with Happy, he just wanted to be by himself, go to his room and think.

Anja bent over her canvas and didn't look up. "Did you get the red kind paint?" she asked in a peevish tone. Jamie sighed and shook off his boots. "Sorry, I didn't get to it today."

She exploded. "I KNEW IT!" And furiously painted, dark blue slashes across the top of the canvas.

"Aw," Jamie said, slumping. "What the hell is it now? It's not like. . . ."

"Three days," she interrupted.

"What?"

"STUPID Jamie, only think of you."

What had started at Lobster Weekend only seemed to get worse. Lately, they'd been having these little wars.

"You mean like that brand-new easel you're painting on? I just bought that for you that last weekend—so that's how I never think of you."

She had no reply for that, which was not surprising. Of all the language skills she'd recovered, sarcasm was one area gone forever. Now anything he said that was remotely sarcastic took off on the runway of her forehead, blew through her bangs, and flew high over her head. He tried to avoid her, and walked to the kitchen and opened the refrigerator. Anja came up behind him with the nagging, whining tone that drove him up a tree. "Where you were?"

"I was doing stuff," he said.

"With someone else?"

He shut the refrigerator. "I'm tired of you having a meltdown every time the cap is off the friggin' toothpaste. You forget what I do for you cause your memory is so screwed up."

"It's eight o'clock!" Anja screeched, stabbing at the clock over the stove. "Supper is six, every day, six." She continued to jab at him. "I know what I remember. You . . . non't know everything."

"I'll get your paint tomorrow, AW RIGHT?" He brushed past her, down the hallway.

"No you won't. You forget, all the time." She followed him. "I could drive and I didn't need you. Do it myself!"

He stood in the dark crescent of his room, sloughing off his sweatshirt. "Well, you can't drive, and I have to do that for you too, so get over it."

She stood, fists clenched, and bellowed. "You non't do anything for me!"

He pounded his dresser with his fist and growled. "Leave me alone, Anja. Do you think I like coming home to this? I made fourteen bucks today. And now you're all drove up my ass the minute I walk in the door over a couple of paints? Gimme a break." He bent to pick out a wrinkled shirt from his plastic bait bin and put it on. Anja huffed, trying to assemble the next attack. She was still not up to the rapid-fire verbal challenges of fighting. Her dark pink cheeks blew up with air and she clawed at her bangs. "I can't stand you."

"Goddamn, you think you're fun to live with?" He shoved past her in the hallway. "I haven't slept in THREE years, worrying how we're gonna make it—how I'm gonna pay for everything." He went over to her dry-erase board above the wall phone and erased all over her notes and reminders. He drew a crude boat. "Who's this? That's me." He sketched dollar signs. "What's this? Those are all your bills." He drew a stick figure sitting on a chair watching TV. "Take a guess who that is." Furiously he scribbled round O's to resemble the stick figure eating donuts. "And THAT," he said, stabbing the dry-erase board, "is what you DO all day." He looked at the board, and with the side of his hand wiped away the donuts. "Oh wait, no. . . ." He drew an easel and words coming out of the stick figure, *WHERE IS MY RED PAINT?*

"Go away," she muttered.

"I'm gone," he said, shoving his boots back on.

Anja couldn't help it. "You go away, again. Again! By myself all the time, you don't care—you leave me and you don't care, just go away."

Jamie strode back over to her. "Hey Anja, remember that Boston boyfriend of yours, remember him? How he left you on the side of the road?" Jamie jabbed his finger at her. "Well, guess what? If he was here instead of me, he would've left you a long time ago."

Before he could reach the front door, Anja positioned herself, a dark little fury, in the corner.

"He didn't do this to me—you did," she said quietly. She crouched down even further until she was sitting on the floor.

Jamie stood facing the door. His arms lifted halfway as if to fly, a futile gesture. He let them drop and said no more.

After the door slammed and she heard the Ford pull out of the driveway, Anja remained on the floor, staring at the dark windows.

The fog oppressed the glass. She stared at the canvas of short blue strokes. Staring at different things was better than staring off at that front door. A thread of violence ran through her, somersaulting over the hurt. Looking down at the paints in their dented silver tubes, she snatched at the flattened red one, spun off its tiny cap, and squeezed out what was left of the thick red paste into her palm. *This is for you.* The pastel scene of the ocean on a summer's day transformed under a red, thick smear.

New Year's Eve, Boston, at least four years before it ever occurred to her to move to the rural, wintry state of Maine, she had a pair of chunky black boots, remembered dancing on a fire escape with her friends, a bunch of city boys. The sky was splitting cold, colder than the goblet of champagne she held in her hand. She wasn't dating any of the boys but let each one kiss her at midnight, fired up with the fun of it all. Dancing, doing the funky chicken, doing the shimmy, while car horns blared below with the dropping of the ball, neighboring apartment windows flying open at *five-four-three-two-one, Happy Goddamned New Year!* She was three days away from the Costa Rica adventure. Life was all about Parliament's ripping the roof off the sucka. So black and cold that night, the smeary greens/blues/reds of traffic below. Bursting with the excitement of being alive, with all that lay in front of her.

Where all those college friends were now, she couldn't remember, or those three boys who loved her. Her fingers traced the iron-on cherries across her pajama shirt. Anja stood up, let her one red palm dangle, and stared at the front door. When they were new together, fights were brief. Jamie would come back after a short walk, say something like *That was stupid,* and their thundercloud would have skirted by without much damage. But now too much time had passed; they were no longer new, filled with optimism that they could handle anything as long as they loved each other. All this time she'd tried so hard to convince him she was getting better, to save that precious good thing they had. It was like the water in the tub that drained—the level kept lowering and she could see it draining out. A frantic look came over her face and she stepped lightly down the hall, leaving red handprints on the walls and on the doorframe of her bedroom. Jamie would not be back in a few minutes, or in an hour. She'd been waiting for him to come home all day so she could show him the painting.

TWENTY TWO

The warmth flooded not only from the heat of people all pressed inside, but from the comfort of knowing they'd always be there. If there were an afterlife, he hoped when he walked through that door it'd look like this.

"Ugly—"

"There he is—"

"Waats goin' on, guy—"

The room was almost completely dark, except for two bare light bulbs hanging from the rafters. Cigarettes, like sea smoke, obscured everyone's faces. All eight barstools were occupied. Jeannie handed him a frothy mug of PBR. Big Steve slapped his back as Jamie tipped his mug and slugged some froth. A large crash was heard through the ceiling.

"What's that all about?" Jamie asked.

"Aw, they're all getting into it," Big Steve said, his large belly resting against the bar. "I'm staying down here."

"Why? What's going on?"

"Some conservation group from Washington is suing the Department of Commerce. They want more regulations—"

"Ah Jesus." Jamie pulled his cap down tighter. "Now what?"

"They want to restrict more days we can fish. Get this—they want us to *email* them a report each day how much we catch."

"Yeah, well, they can get a stepladder and jump up my sphincter," Jamie said with foam on his lip. "I don't even own a computer."

"That's why I'm staying down here," Big Steve said. "I go up there and I'm gonna start it up myself." Sitting next to Big Steve, Bill, Chuck, and Phil were florid over the latest story—bragging about the longest they'd gone on unemployment.

"That's nothing. One time," Phil said over the sound of waves crashing below the holes in the floor, "I went on unemployment for four years, 'til my ex-wife got remarried. I just collected bottles, and didn't give one cent to the IRS 'til that wack job got another ring on her finger."

Chuck broke in, sloppily. "It just don't work the way it used to. Remember when my knee went out three years ago? Couldn't lobster, put a claim on my insurance and got through the winter on benefits. So I go moose hunting in the fall, bagged me a goddamned monster, right Bill?"

"Oh yeah."

"No sooner I get home with it"—Chuck's eyes were drowning, his head bobbing slightly—"I get a call from my insurance company that they're cutting my benefits. They said they had me on *videotape* hauling that moose right outta the woods!"

"Who the hell got you on tape?"

Chuck's rosacea was like a smattering of fire coral as he leaned in. "Come to find out they checked a list of names—people who was claiming benefits against names of people with moose permits. Every time they found a match, they sent one of their spies out to the woods with a video camera, how 'bout *that*? Goddamn."

Next to the bathrooms, a stairway ran up to the Fish House. A sign on the door said "Authorized Personnel Only." Each fisherman who went up those stairs knew exactly whether or not he was authorized. Up there, not one blessed trace of femininity peeked through. Although Churchie's widow, Jeannie, technically owned the place and could have done whatever she wanted with it, she left that space to the men who fueled her bar.

The narrow board-and-batten stairway opened up to a large open room filled with smoke. The low-ceiling room was a yard sale of scraggy edges—dartboard in the corner, a hanging cluster of Grundens on wall hooks, on the floor, dozens of boots. Charts, like jack straws, rested in the rafters, next to hanging buoys, hog's rings. A coil of heavy orange extension cord hung under a bare light bulb. Along one wall ran a rustic workbench, under which lay fat, truck tire–sized coils of float rope and sink rope. A small paint-splattered boom box lay on the workbench next to mismatched coffee mugs, Diet Coke cans, and a half-empty bottle of peach schnapps. A stinky dog bed had been stuck underneath the workbench, next to a bowl of moldering dog food.

Up here were couches, a large-screen TV with VCR, a woodstove, a table with cribbage boards, chess games, cards. In the corner, Susie Q. bent over the pool table, her long brown ponytail draped over her cue. Her smile was a balmy day in the tropics—pure sunshine. She let forth a booming laugh as she pocketed a solid ball. The room was a mix of whoever might be up there on any given day, whether they were stowing gear in their lockers or making a sandwich in the kitchen. Up here, if someone wanted a beer, he took it from an icy barrel perpetually stocked with cans of Bud, Coors Lite, and Miller Lite. A buck a can was the rule. No one monitored the barrel, but the cashbox was always full.

Behind the bottle of peach schnapps on the workbench, a framed picture of Churchie's bleary face beamed out into the room, his curly red hair and glazed half-lidded smile a monument to his legacy.

Tonight, there was a hard feeling in the room. In a loose circle stood Newall Watts, doing all the talking, a family man with three kids and one of the loudest to grumble about any tiny inequity in the harbor. As a counterpoint, the single men standing around Newall were the hotheads, like Cheyne Batty, who was 18 and not too bright. Last summer, when Cheyne's nail gun jammed, he attempted to test it out on his skull to see if it worked; it did. Toby Ellis was another one of the hotheads, and a wicked drunk. Ryan Nutter was another. Nutter was going through his third divorce, which made him ready to blow. The others patiently listening to Newall Watts were the highliners—Paul Santerre and Don Thatcher, who not only had been a highliner for close to fifty years, but was the godfather, the one everyone went to with their problems.

Jamie maneuvered past the tight throng of men with their fore-fingers in one another's faces. Newall Watts had the group fired up, as usual.

"They're using old data—listen to me, they're using old data!"

"Well no shit, there, buddy, tell me something I don't know," Paul Santerre said, easily. People counted on Paul to be the calm mediator in any debate. "The problem is that we've had two or three just absolutely off-the-chart years and this year is just going back to the way it used to be."

"Nobody knows what the landin's are," broke in Don Thatcher quietly, his pronunciation indistinct. Don spoke with only half a tongue—the other half had been eaten by cancer. "That's the problem. You got twenty-year-old estimates that don't mean shit in the real world—"

"All I'm saying is," persisted Newall, red-faced, eyes almost panicked whenever he got excited, "whatever new model they come up with still ain't going to help with the problem now. We've got a soft industry this summer and if something don't change soon, I'm gonna go bankrupt."

Jamie walked past them and sat down at the end of the room on a plaid couch that used to be in Churchie's hunting cabin. There was a baseball game on that no one was watching. He had come up here only to get away from the tired topics downstairs.

"I didn't pull diddly-squat today." This came from Toby Ellis, who'd wandered out of Newall's circle. He could hear Newall persisting with his point, trying to outrank Don with some statistic he'd recently read. They all did that up in the Fish House, the big blowhards. Once they got a couple of beers in them, some clown had to always be the loudest, the most knowledgeable, the biggest man in the room, whereas people like Don Thatcher always allowed those lower on the lobster scale to speak their minds. If Jamie had been a highliner as long as Don had been, he'd never allow Newall to talk down to him as much as he did, but then that's why Jamie would never be a Don Thatcher. He didn't have the patience for the egos and the politics. Jamie drummed his fingers restlessly on the arm of the couch, not in the mood for the bitchfest that was permeating the Fish House tonight.

Emmett Smith, an older man who had buzzy eyes and a face children didn't like, sat down on the couch opposite from Toby and Jamie. No one was watching the ball game because no one could *hear* the ball game. Emmett commented on the topic of the night.

"Hell, I made forty-seven thousand dollars last year and I haven't a goddamned clue as to where it all went!" Emmett turned to Jamie with his super-direct gaze. "How about you?"

Jamie shook his head, his way of saying *Don't ask.* Newall Watts had it partially right: here it was August and nothing was coming in. People were starting to panic. For fifty years, lobstermen in this state had set the standard in preserving the lobster stocks, the only state to self-regulate, limiting the size of lobsters caught and not allowing any egg-bearing females to be caught. Jamie suspected, as always, that men had nothing to do with the problem. When a female dropped her eggs, ten thousand of those little sea monkeys traveled as far as hundreds of miles with the Gulf of Maine currents, searching for safe places along the craggy bottom to develop. He'd read that it was possible the currents were changing and pushing the larvae offshore or else the water temperatures were warming, killing them off. If the ocean was the problem, it didn't matter if lobstermen raised the ban on one restriction or clamped down harder on another. The ocean was fickle and unreliable. One day a shoving mosh pit, the next, flat as a fallen house of cards. And Newall could pump his chest like a squeezebox day and night in the Fish House for all the good that would do.

"Well, something better friggin' change soon," Toby groused. "I just bought a new boat and I don't know how the fuck I'm going to pay for it." This was hardly a surprise, as Toby always took his morning coffee with sugar and Jack Daniel's. Not exactly a dub, but damn close.

"Well, don't start getting yourself all wound up about it. You go there and your night will be shot," said Emmett, who looked like he could grin through a tornado.

"Yeah, but they take my boat away, they take my job. But I can't pay for the feckin' boat if I'm not hauling anything."

The young guys, particularly the ones just out of high school, always made this mistake. Jamie closed his eyes, not caring how a dub and his money were soon parted. Toby was 18, just a year into the business, and to prove his worth he'd used all of his cash to buy a new one-ton Dodge Ram Dually Hemi and a thirty-eight-foot Beals Island boat rather than use old equipment and work up to good gear. Toby was still riding the wave of Jamie's generation, who right out of high school had seen nothing but phenomenal landings, huge paychecks. From '89 to '99 the landings had nearly doubled, to 53 million pounds. He remembered when one crazy summer everyone was getting eight dollars a pound and assuming that's the way it would always be. But Toby had salted nothing away under a mattress, and now he'd probably be the first one to fall. It was normal.

"Yeah. Well, at least you don't have a wife in your ear every night going 'Where's the money?'" Emmett said. "We got another kid on the way and she wants me to quit and start working for Dragon Cement, where her brother works."

"Not friggin' likely," Jamie quipped, and instantly regretted commenting on another man's business without being invited.

"Yeah, so, that's what I mean," said Emmett, glad to extend the conversation to Jamie. "At least you don't have a wife and two kids adding pressure."

As if having a wife and two kids was the only kind of pressure anyone understood. Jamie rubbed his nose with both hands and held his hands to his face. Wouldn't that be the worst irony, if those pencil-pushing scientists were right, after nearly fifteen years of histrionic predictions, that the lobster stocks were going to crash? It seemed impossible, like waking up to find that the entire sea had evaporated. His family had been lobstering for hundreds of years—it was Maine's most profitable export, a $400 million to $500 million industry. How in one summer could the lobsters just completely disappear?

He had a little money stored away, but it was scrape-the-bottom money, for when his back went out or if he ever needed to be hospitalized. He already had a late truck payment; had to put down what he could on the boat instead. Things had always been good on the fishing side of his life. Like Toby, like all of them, he'd taken for granted that the sea was plentiful, that lobster would always come in full-bore. Or, difficult as it was to admit, maybe he'd just been cocky to consider himself a damn fine lobsterman. But now, like everyone else, Jamie was facing the fact that if the lobsters hadn't come in by late August, maybe they were never going to come in. He rubbed his eyes, hating to get back on this thread—thinking about the same weighty problems that plagued him all day. He'd come here specifically to forget about it.

The sounds of tree peepers were like distress calls in the heavy woods, plaintive chirps. A shroud for a midnight sky, rips for stars. Jamie killed the Ford's brights against the garage. He was sober and walked into his dark house. Threw his keys in a tin ashtray with a beanbag bottom.

A tiny seashell of a night light burned in the hallway and right off he noticed the red hand prints along the wall. He inspected the ragged, slightly smeared prints, concerned at first they were blood. He went immediately to her room. It was quiet in there, completely still. He knelt down by the car tent and unzipped it.

The faintest light from the window warmed Anja's face. Her eyelashes were stuck together, dried streaks ran down her cheeks. The zipper had woken her up and she blinked at him. Her mouth contorted and she reached for him. Jamie knelt awkwardly and leaned into the tent, which smelled like baby blankets and her own sleepy smell. Anja burrowed her face into his neck. He rubbed her back, could feel her fingernails digging into him through his shirt.

Her words were like the tide itself, rolling in, sucking back. "I won't yell no more. I don't want you to go."

"I'm not goin' anywhere."

The pain in her face was testament to everything he was bad at, every little failing. He let Anja go and knelt by her bed. In his chest lay a heavy, horrible sorrow that dragged him down, pulled him under. It flooded his chest, up to his mouth, to his eyes. He leaned forward on his knees. He was a lousy person and she was innocent, a casualty of all his selfishness.

Anja lay on her side watching him.

"Anja," he said wearily, realizing even as he spoke that he was making a decision more permanent than marriage. This was it, then. "I'm never going to leave. If I have to go off, stomp around a bit I'll always be back, okay?"

She closed her eyes, the tension in her face easing slightly, but her small mouth remained sad. He saw her face from years before—that buoyant expression that she had when they'd first met. And this. What had he done to turn her mouth into this tattered line?

"Come on," Jamie said, and reached in to pull her out of the tent. "You're sleeping in my room tonight."

TWENTY THREE

In another shift of time, Anja had stayed home that October day he went out on the water. And a year later they would've been married as planned on a sunny day, a reception for 200 at Churchie's. Married to a girl he loved, he never would've felt the loneliness that propelled him to go to a party at a castle. And Happy Klein would have been a pirate with a sharp wit and sword, challenging the passengers of a schooner to sing the chorus of a ballad forty minutes away in a town he had no reason to frequent. Further, Jamie would never have known her presence or felt such grinding deprivation. On a regular day, he'd just be looking forward to going home to his wife, cooking up some salt pork and beans, and laughing about the town gossip. That would have been more than good enough.

On the sea, his thoughts ran with the currents. Anja's drive to get better this past year had put such a strain on them both, made her into a person he didn't really want to be around. Of course it was more growth, a new phase of development, that carried with it unpredictable behavior—he was used to that. What nagged him at three in the morning was that her personality had changed so much over the last three years that he wasn't sure if he even liked the new person she'd become. But when he thought of her face, how she hopped up and down in her slippers when he came home at night, he couldn't stand the thought of a separate life. What happiness would there be if he knew she was miserable? These were the dark thoughts that slipped in during the wee hours and were cast out before they even had a chance to root. Of course it was temporary. She'd get better; she'd be like her old self. She would. He had to tell himself this to go back to sleep.

Finally, for the love of Mike, just when it was starting to get colder and the stars at night seemed near, the lobsters started to come in. Harbors up and down in Maine were seeing fuller traps of thin-skinned mottled brown-and-green lobsters. The shedders were shimmying off the old hard shells, migrating inland. Their timing couldn't have been more bumped up against the tidal calendar—just as they started to appear, summer was slipping away.

Jamie was hauling well, feeling lucky, for the first time all summer. The trick was to keep his strings ahead of the lobsters. He'd spent the last two weeks resetting traps further offshore, a canny strategy that always paid off. While everyone else was still fishing up on the rocks, Jamie took a gamble that the gypsy caravan of lobsters would be shivering in their kelp beds and seeking the more temperate waters deeper out. He'd been dead-on. The traps were coming up gorged with them. Within days, guys like Toby Ellis would notice this tactic and start moving their own gear farther out, especially when word got out at the buying dock that Jamie was rakin' 'em in. That was nothing if not predictable.

For now it was a fine morning. The weather reports the night before said fair weather, and nothing in his joints told him otherwise. Dawn opened the near-cloudless sky. Light swells from the northeast were coming from a good predictable haul of wind. The weather settled in, everything feeling slicker 'n a whistle. Jamie loaded bait and gear onto his boat. Straight out of habit he had himself a cigarette, cast a penny over the bow, started the engine and cast off.

The sun crept higher, spreading a marmalade of brilliant dazzling starbursts on the water, the kind of early morning sun that almost causes blindness. Even with UV-blocking sunglasses, Jamie had to raise his hand to his face. He headed for his best strings, the ones that had been fishing well. It was no more than a ten-minute trip out there, and he found his thoughts weightless for once, as he enjoyed the stiff air, Metallica on the tiny boom box competing with the throaty engine. Good rich smells out there, his lungs filled. The sun felt like a mother's warm hand upon his forehead.

He was feeling so good, he'd lost track of time. He'd been motoring out for more than seven minutes. It was the feeling of having driven past the exit on the highway without seeing any kind of sign to verify. Minor irritation set in for having gone past the set. He pushed the throttle to the firewall, churning up a wake, getting impatient. He'd been daydreaming, not concentrating on what he was doing. Minutes passed on the flat calm water. The eastern wash of sun made a diagonal path that should have been brimming with orange and yellow buoys, hundreds of them, but everywhere he looked his territory was bare, not a single toggle in sight. A look at the chart confirmed the coordinates; it was stupid to even check. He already knew. He idled for another mile, until he saw them by the lapping shore of Seal Rock. Every one of his buoys had been cut from its trap, and there they were with their short, pitiful tails, ramming up against the sand beach of a tiny island like a cluster of sperm.

TWENTY FOUR

Until every last piece of coastline was owned and gated, every dotted line on the ocean breeched, every scrap of soil divided among neighbors, there would be war. Like the Maine mafia, the Yakuza, like Indians on a hell ripper—when it came, it would be invisible and swift.

The note on Jamie's truck tucked in under the left wiper said *Saw Courage boys hauling your traps yesterday.*

Jamie scanned the wharf parking lot, his teeth threatening to break the skin on his bottom lip. It was almost two by the time he'd inspected everything and come back. At the end of the dock, he spied his father in a huddle with Paul Santerre and Doug Kane. He gripped the note as if he could kill it and hunched toward them.

"I just got back from Seal Rock, right outside the dry ledge," Jamie broke in. "All my traps have been cut over there."

"Well, ain't that a coincidence," Doug Kane said. With eyebrows like woolly caterpillars and a square white beard that ran down his cheeks, he looked like a kindly Amish farmer. He owned the largest boat in the harbor, yet dressed like a field hand. Next to Doug stood Paul, with dark pointed eyes and a twice-broken nose that sat on his rubbery yam. "Bob Fowlie, Rich Snow, me, Paul, your dad, and others each had traps cut over the weekend, it looks like," Paul said. "Strings that were fishing well."

Jamie thrust the note at them. James Senior took it and held it away from his chest to read it. He passed the note to Doug. "Any of the regattas been through here this past week? Eggenmoggin, New York Yacht Club, any of those assholes?"

"Not that I know of," Doug answered. He passed the note to Paul. "What do you think?"

Paul scratched at his sideburns. "It sounds like Fogerty. Wouldn't put it past him."

"He's probably not pushing enough crack and Oxy on middle school kids," Senior said.

"How many you think you lost, Jamie?" Paul asked.

"Probably close to two hundred."

Paul Santerre pulled his cap low over his dark eyes.

"That ain't no accident," James Senior muttered. "We're getting worked over hard."

"Let's check around some more," Paul said. "I'm gonna get ahold of Don this afternoon—we'll see who else is getting hammered."

Jamie felt the old red haze come over him. It had been hard enough to make a living this summer; now he was down maybe a fourth of his traps. In less time than it took to take a breath, his lip began to sweat. He could feel himself getting wild-eyed, muscles jittery. A hand on his shoulder deflated him. Not his father's, but Paul's. In Paul's eyes, Jamie felt instantly juvenile. Always, his emotions spilled out of him like a woman. "Just take it easy," Paul said, his voice like leather and cigar smoke, comforting. "We're gonna do this the right way. People are looking over here, so don't say anything. We're gonna put together an emergency meeting tonight."

At home, Jamie slouched on the La-Z-Boy with the TV off, just the rhythm of the waves against the rocks outside. He felt all snarled like someone had fouled the gear of his mind. He needed to take the day off, scout around, see what he could find out. He needed to check in with Uncle Normie, a retired seiner who kept the VHF radio turned up in his kitchen from the moment he got up until the moment he went to bed. Sixteen hours a day Uncle Normie might hear nothing but static, weather reports, and banal chitchat until one moment something would inadvertently slip out over the radio. Last summer Uncle Normie was the one to notice someone taking his boat out of the harbor around 10 p.m., an awfully strange time to be out, and not using his running lights. Next morning on the radio, Susie Q. complained that a few of her traps had been cut in the night. Uncle Normie listened . . . and picked up the phone.

Jamie carefully considered what he needed to do. If it had just been Russell Fogerty alone, he needed to calm down before he hunted Russell down and broke his other arm. No, that was wrong, the wrong way to think. That was a punk hothead way of thinking, not a highliner's way. He needed to do some late-night scouting, find out who it was before taking action. Two hundred or so traps; Jamie could feel his neck pump. He would not make the mortgage this month, or his truck payment.

If it was Russell, this would be no simple solution. The Fogertys had already been involved in several major trap wars. They had the money and the ferocity to go longer than anyone, and they enjoyed it—that was the real problem. They'd tanked a newcomer in their own harbor two years ago, Ricky Doughty, who'd been out one day lobstering in the fog when he came across Kenny Fogerty pulling traps. Kenny didn't like his new shiny boat and didn't like Ricky. Without hesitation, Kenny gave him the finger. And Ricky, in foolish retaliation, took his big shiny Novi boat and rammed it right into the side of Kenny Fogerty's forty-foot boat, claiming it was too hard to see in the fog.

Within another week, dozens of people got involved and cut every trap Ricky Doughty had. Then, in the middle of the night, someone rowed out in a dinghy, took a battery-powered cordless drill aboard the Novi, and bored holes in the bottom. Within less than two minutes, the $150,000 boat had been scuttled. When Ricky tried to get his boat off the bottom of the harbor, no company would do it for less than double their normal price. And every lobster co-op within fifty miles refused to buy Ricky's pitiful remaining lobsters rather than risk the enmity of the Fogertys. He gave up, had to move out of state.

Donna's convertible crackled the gravel in the driveway and two car doors slammed. "Jamie!" Anja burst through the door, Donna right behind her, carrying groceries.

Anja knelt down in front of him, clasping her hands. She wore painter's pants, her hair up in pigtails, one skewed higher than the other.

"Jamie, we gone to Stop N' Go and Dee—she needs somebody while she goes down to Boston. And she said I can work the counter for one weekend and I said, Jamie, I said I could!"

He noticed his mother putting away groceries without comment. Anja grabbed his hands and shook them. "Jamie! Know what else . . . know what. . . ." He felt her words glide past him. "Jamie." She lifted his limp hand and shook it again. "Carolyn says my maths is gotten better."

Donna put a couple of boxed dinners in the freezer and turned to face him. "Dee's got pancreatic cancer and she needs to take a few days off to go down to Boston, do some more tests. It's the only appointment she can get and it's short notice. Anja would only be there for a weekend."

Jamie closed his eyes slowly and then leaned forward, rubbing them hard with the back of his knuckles. "Anja, this is gonna have to wait." He spoke to his mother. "I just had about two hundred traps cut today. People are saying it's the Fogertys."

Donna held a gallon of milk in her hand. The refrigerator door remained open. "You are shitting me."

"No."

"Where's Dad? Have you—"

"We already talked at the wharf. Dad had some cut too. So did Paul and Doug." He looked at his watch. "I gotta get going. We got another meeting with everybody in about forty-five minutes."

Anja inhaled slowly. "Jamie?"

He turned warily to her. "What?"

"I'm just gonna train with Dee for two days. She has to go to the doctor on Friday." She could be so annoyingly cheerful, so focused on her own world.

"Wait. Just wait," he said and looked at his mother. "I can't deal with this right now."

Donna nodded. "Anja, let's just put this idea on hold for—"

"You know what we got you? Corn dogs—and they the kind that got no stick." Anja grinned, and got up to fold the paper grocery bags.

Donna jerked her thumb toward the door. "Maybe I ought to let you guys talk about this for a bit. I'm gonna scoot out and find Dad—" She shot him a kiss with a grim expression. "Call me after the meeting."

After Donna left, there was a slam of the refrigerator door. "Know what else? We bought you the Pibber," Anja said happily from the kitchen. She popped the tab on one and walked over to shove it in his hand.

TWENTY FIVE

Ten people could fit in Don Thatcher's work shack, if two sat on the dirty canvas chairs and the rest crammed in on fish totes or the tool bench. Don had been the harbor leader for as long as Jamie could remember, despite some attempts in the 1980s to unseat him by highline fishermen who'd tried to start their own factions. But Don's slow, deliberate nature and his skills as an intermediary made him the man people went to with disputes. He had Mount Rushmore for a face, all ledges, with tight, shingled gray hair. He'd survived tours in Korea and Vietnam, along with tongue cancer from years of stowing a plug of dip between his lip and teeth. A tumor the size of a golf ball had been removed along with most of his tongue, so when he spoke the words came out slurred, as if he were deaf.

It was a meeting of highliners only, no young kids, no assholes except for Newall Watts, who made it his business to be on top of every little thing. Doug Kane, Paul Santerre, Emmett Smith, James Senior, Bob Fowlie, and Rich Snow sat around an overturned wooden crate in the middle of the shack poring over sheaves of charts. Thongchai squeezed next to Jamie, whose back shifted uncomfortably against Don's work table. The hooks on the walls held trap head netting, coils of float rope. The place smelled like buoy paint.

The anonymous note from under Jamie's wiper lay on a splintery crate in front of them, smoothed out. The room swam with heat and the stink of bodies just off the wharf. Jamie could feel sweat trickle down his armpits, and he ground his elbows into his ribs. He glanced at his father's blue flint expression.

Don turned to James Senior. His words came out smothered; everyone always had to listen close to pick out what he was saying. "Your family has been hit the hardest on the border. We'll back you up. What do you want to do? You want to call Fogerty up?"

"Well, given that Jamie just lost about five grand worth of gear today, it's not like we're gonna call that fucker up and give him something to lie about," James said, as if it were obvious. Someone scoffed. James continued, "He'd just deny it anyway. This has been going on way too fuckin' long with them. And no matter how many times we double back on them or send them to jail, they keep coming back. He needs to get the message this time."

Don looked around the room. "Do we have any other proof?"

Boots scraped against the shack floor. But no one offered anything.

"I don't know if you need anything more than this," Senior said, wresting the note. He flipped it with his wrist and dropped it back on the crate. "They've been pushing over our lines for years, and now that fishing's even tighter this summer, there's no doubt it's them."

A silence met this comment.

"They went after us last week," Thongchai offered. "Kenny, Russ, and Ev at the Lobster Weekend."

"What are you talking about?" Don Thatcher said, eyes stabbing.

"During the blessing of the fleet, they just came right up and Russell started swinging—" Thongchai shoved the air as if back in the moment, his mouth tight. "And Jamie friggin' housed Russell in the arm just to keep him off."

The small room began to smell of everyone's breath.

"Well, that's just great," Senior said and slapped his knee. He rolled his eyes as if he'd just discovered the dog had wet the rug again.

A new perception flooded the room. "That's kid stuff," Don said, the fissures of the skin around his eyes like prehistoric rock. "Why didn't someone mention this before?"

The disapproval, the eye roll from Senior, caused Jamie's facial muscles to jam up. He grew hot, embarrassed. And this made him angry.

"You better be careful," Newall Watts warned. He was the kind of guy who always said things like that. Whenever he spoke at a meeting, everyone mentally shoved his words to the side. "You'll put us all at risk of a full-scale cut war if you go off and do something." Emmett Smith nodded along with him. Jamie swiftly surveyed the head nodders. The family men whose wives and kids dictated their decisions. As if either of them had been in a fight in twenty years. They had no idea what it was like to be threatened.

The next suggestion came from Emmett. "I think we need to have a talk with them. It's stupid to just retaliate without knowing if it was them or not."

"What more do you need?" Jamie said, finally. In that tiny room, the force of the words coming out of his mouth startled everyone. "They leveled me in just one day. And they're gonna keep coming over the Point once I'm out. No one's catching anything, they're going to take whatever they can." He turned to face everyone. "So you can all let it be my deal." He stared at Newall. "And go ahead— keep your head in the sand pretending they're not going to drive you out. Be my guest."

Newall Watts flashed back at him. "You don't just cut the Fogertys and walk away. Tell Dale Fogerty unless someone comes forward—"

"No way, you'll tip him off," Jamie said, shaking his head.

"You think Andy Anderson didn't already do that last summer?" James Senior commented. "Fogerty *loves* when people try to be reasonable. He uses it against them, goes for the soft spot, just like what he did to Andy after—"

Newall waved him off. "You start a trap war with them and it's not just you, Jamie. They'll come back on all of us."

"Are you worried about what you have to lose?" Paul Santerre said.

"Hell yeah!" The crease between Newall's eyebrows sharpened. "I don't need to be hauling my traps out of the water in early September cause somebody might be coming around to cut my gear."

"That's the business—" Paul looked away. "You don't stay in the business if you're just in it for yourself, my friend."

The implication didn't faze Newall; he turned to Jamie. "I understand you're upset over your gear, but we can't be starting it up with the Fogertys before we've had a chance to set up a discussion. We're gonna have to set up a Marine Patrol–sponsored meeting and start a dialogue with the Courage folks. We'll get a conflict resolution team of their people and ours together. We can discuss this at the next meeting." This was the right way to do things these days, the politically *right* thing to do. This was the kind of meeting that made the papers.

Don Thatcher watched everyone. The room was suddenly so full of heated talk and dissent, it was hard to hear. At co-op meetings when tempers buzzed like this, someone was going to get shoved. A fluttery sensation appeared in the periphery of Jamie's vision— everything whittled away. Jamie reached for Thongchai, who'd said nothing the whole meeting. Jamie found his arm.

"Keep it together," Thongchai whispered.

Jamie stood up and pushed his way out of the shack. He whacked his hip on the work table trying to step over Thongchai.

"Where the hell are you going?" James Senior demanded, but Jamie wouldn't give him the satisfaction of an answer. He could feel the blood rushing to his head, as if any second he'd blow an O-ring and seize up right there on the floor.

TWENTY SIX

By eight that evening, only two sounds came from sea: the lowing of a foghorn off Tick Island and the heavy rumble of the surf as it broke against the stones along the beach and dragged them tumbling back. The singing of the sea.

Jamie dropped his keys on the kitchen counter and sat in the silent living room, splayed in the La-Z-Boy, his Carhartt jacket still zipped, boots still on, messily unlaced. Jamie aimed the remote. The TV's picture filled the screen. His attention remained on nothing as a commercial barreled on, its cartoonish plot jangling. He toed off the back of one boot, then the other. His neck cracked to the left and right. Another commercial looped up— what was this, five in a row? He clicked again and the TV zeroed off; he wasn't in the mood.

Though it looked bad, he'd had to leave Don's shack. If he hadn't, it would have looked worse if he'd smacked Newall's stubbly gray face, like a mother slapping a child in a grocery store. His hand to his chest, what was that, *a sharp pain?* Hey, right on time, a pending heart attack. His father had had one when he was 38. The evolution of a lobsterman's health: first the back went out, then the heart attack, then, if you were lucky, a stroke. He had to find a way to calm down, and obviously the PBR was not a long-term solution. He thought of Happy, who had recommended something about yoga.

He'd just looked at her. *You're kidding.*

253

No, I'm serious. It's unbelievable what it can do for you.

He didn't want to hurt her feelings, but there was no way he was going to walk around in a beret and a pair of fag pants in order to calm down. All the girls in his life had tried in some way to get him to control his anger. Anja had always harped on counseling; Pia had wanted him to do something ridiculous called biofeedback.

Anger was fuel: without it, he'd be useless. And he'd already had a frosty cold one going over the fact that they were all going to leave him out to hang—Bert, Doug, Bob Fowlie, Rich Snow, even his dad and Thongchai after all the hollering they did over their own traps being cut this summer, all the bluster they gave about what they'd do when they found who did it. Jamie looked out at the moonlit water. The fog was an ashen will-o'-the-wisp hovering at the edge of the rocks. Nobody had the guts. Now they all wanted to appear "reasonable" when it wasn't their gear. Newall could easily lose 200 traps and not miss the income. It bored a hole in Jamie's stomach. When it came down to this kind of personal, political turmoil, when the catch was low, the dock price low but the cutthroat competition up, it was time to cut loose.

He picked up a mandolin in the corner, by the hutch—it was Maynard's, a delicate instrument with mismatched nylon and steel strings. Jamie smoothed the dust from it and plucked a few notes. Wouldn't it be great to spend the day learning how to play this thing and sail three times a day off the southern tip of Florida? He allowed this idea—no one to look after but himself, and if he lived in a dingy apartment, who cared? The bums were happy in Key West and they had nothing. To live as a deckhand, day in and day out, playing music and earning tips. Maybe he'd run into the yachties from the *Wet Dream* and buy them a beer at the ole raw bar. *Hey, this oyster's on me, Smitty, bud-day, why don't ya go tell the steel drum guy to play some of your favorite Kenny G there.*

Cones of light splashed across the walls, and the sound of idling engine brought Jamie to the window. Two trucks emerged from the fog, sitting in his driveway with their lights off. Jamie stepped back behind the curtain, unsure of who was out there. James Senior got out. Behind him, in the second truck, Paul Santerre. Jamie opened the door before they could knock and wake Anja. He stood in the doorway.

"Get your gear ready," his father said. "We're getting two boats together now—weather's coming in with this fog. Perfect conditions. We're going do a little *patrolling*."

Patrolling—now there was an old-fashioned word with an underground meaning. Come to find out there'd been a *meeting* after the meeting. Everyone sat around, chewing toothpicks, swapping advice on where to repair a Cummings engine, until Newall Watts and Emmett Smith left to go home to their wives. That was when Don Thatcher calmly closed the shack door, latched the eyehook, and rolled out old marked-up charts of Fogerty's territory. Over the years, Don had compiled charts on every harbor rival in every area—Port Clyde, Pleasant Point, Tenants Harbor, Georges Island. Dale Fogerty's territory hadn't changed much in the last ten years, but that didn't stop Don from getting his charts updated on a regular basis.

Behind Senior the two trucks idled, the exhaust in red mingling with the heavy air. "What do I need to bring?"

"It's all set," Senior said, walking back to his truck. "Just be ready to go in about five hours."

TWENTY SEVEN

Prior to 1492, sailors and ship captains believed the earth was flat, the dark closets of their imaginations festering to consider what was beyond the edge of the horizon. Was it a beckoning water wall, a hellish plunge toward infinity? In the slim crawlspace between dreaming and fitful consciousness, Jamie found himself reading a chart in the wheelhouse of *Delores*. Only it wasn't a sea chart, strangely enough, even though its course ran past Jeffrey's Bank, heading northeast toward the Bay of Fundy; it was hand-drawn with some thick sludgy crayon of sienna on parchment like a pirate map leading to a treasure. A cold, fingerless wisp hovered around the map and suddenly he found he couldn't breathe. The way the night comes on, slowly, creeping blue, that's the way the fog was coming in, the warm southerly shroud covering the still, cold body of the coast.

The fog became an army of vapor liberated from the water, a phantom roaming the lowest sockets on land and flowing like lava across the waves. In his dream, his chest pumped and pumped—he was drowning in the liquid fog. He woke up on the La-Z-Boy, unable to let go of it.

At quarter to two, Jamie walked through the rain to meet everyone at the wharf. He was hunched in his jacket, cold needles pricking his earlobes. His breath billowed out in front of him, fading into the dense fog all around. Down by the dock there were no trucks, no lights. He knew all the guys were down there because he could hear low murmurings. He could hear the boats' fenders creaking against the floating docks.

In less than twenty minutes, Paul Santerre, Bob Fowlie, Rich Snow, Doug Kane, and James Senior had a boat packed and ready to go. Thongchai, The Kid, and Jamie were at the kiddie table on the *Maisie May*. Both vessels had been cleared of gear; only the hot tank stood to the side. Each boat had a cooler of sandwiches, bottled water, Gumby suits, flare guns, a walkie-talkie, and a detailed chart of Fogerty's territory. Lying carefully upon each boat was a stockpile of weapons: six hockey sticks with serrated machetes swaddled with duct tape, several gaff hooks, Red Ripper knives, and two .22 rifles. Thongchai would be the shot on his boat if it came down to it, and Doug Kane on theirs.

The Kid bumped up against Jamie, just like when they were in high school and someone pulled the fire alarm so they all had to stand out on the school's back lawn. Everybody used it as an excuse to smoke a cigarette and socialize.

"So I forgot to tell you," The Kid said, his hands in his sweatshirt, "if you need some extra cash, I know somebody who's looking for a flagger on a construction crew. It's like fifteen dollars an hour and you can just stand there and get stoned all day, nobody cares."

Jamie looked at him. "Thanks."

At two sharp they lit out, engines gurgling, running lights off. The ocean was a vast smothering blanket of white with a light mist coming down on tottering waves. Ben and James Senior exchanged words over the walkie-talkie, checking headings while Thongchai pushed the throttle forward. He opened the window and screwed down the nuts to keep the window horizontal. The two boats slowed out of the harbor side by side.

Between the space of groaning foghorns, the bow smacked against waves. Only twenty feet away, James Senior's boat was barely visible. The Kid told a joke he'd heard last night. No one looked at him. Jamie lit his second cigarette, watching the radar. The fog was evasive, melting at the bow. The sea peeled open, its wake the same bloodless color. After ten minutes, they reached the long bar, the entrance to Courage Bay. The depth finder began flashing beeps and Thongchai kept his gaze on it while Jamie hung way out over the grab rail, trying to see. "Go port, go way port." They were in tight shallows several fathoms deep. "Oh, you got it," Jamie soothed. "You got all kinds of water."

Fog, the mother of all shipwrecks. Even birds with the finest sense of direction slammed lighthouses, killing themselves in its curdled pockets. Jamie stood inside the wheelhouse checking the electronics every few seconds, alert to any changes on the Loran. The heavy moisture clung to the raised hairs on his arms. Being out in the fog was fun only when he was young, like ghost stories and campfires. One summer evening on the river, he'd gotten The Kid good (when he was still called Ben); he was only 9 or 10. They had been lolling on inner tubes on the river in the fog after supper, the air giving off the same damp clinging sensation. Same kind of sky, a depthless washout of slate blue and dim gray, smoke on either side of the river. Their inner tubes splashed around in the still, smoke-wispy water. Everything around them was motionless; no lapping ripples, no splashing—not even the sound of birds.

"Get your feet up in your tube," Jamie warned, his voice expansive across the water. "The fog brings out the eels."

"Shut *up*," Ben said. It had been only a year since a man was found drowned in that river, a pediatrician who'd been out swimming at dusk when he had a heart attack. His family found the man hours later, bobbing by the dam. Snapping turtles had taken off parts of his nose.

"I'm serious, the more you splash around like an injured fish, the more you attract the eels and snapping turtles."

"Screw you," Ben said, not buying this game, and flopped around in his inner tube to prove he wasn't scared. In the dying slate light, Ben's little nipples stood at attention, along with the rest of his goose-bumped chest. Every time they stopped joking and jostling, all they could hear was the little lick of water, of dripping. Even to Jamie it was unnerving. Suddenly Ben jerked and screamed. "Something touched my leg! Something touched my leg!"

Jamie laughed out loud. "Oh *right*. That was so. . . ."

"I'M SERIOUS, DOUCHEBAG!" Ben's voice had shot to a squeak; his eyes were skittery, and Jamie realized Ben really had been touched by something, probably a fish. It was too perfect an opportunity to waste. For a second, he pretended to be concerned. "You sure?"

"Yeah I'm sure!" Ben's eyes were fierce as he piled as much of his body on top of the inner tube as he could.

"Maybe it was the dead guy," Jamie said.

Ben stared at him. "No—it wasn't. Shut *up*, Jamie."

Jamie slowly brought his arms and legs up in the inner tube and stared into the slate water. "I don't know. Pappy says if you die in the water, your soul stays there and it can come back." Maynard had said the first part, but not the part about coming back—that was for effect.

"I never heard him say that. You're just making it up."

"He said that to me—the summer they found the dead guy in this river," Jamie nodded soberly. "Maybe we should go back."

"*No*—it was just a fish."

"Let's just go back."

"Aww, are you scared?" Now Ben's voice turned smug, oddly tinged with a little hysteria. "I bet you are now, hah!"

Jamie didn't answer, let the stillness of the river fade the smile right out of Ben. Earlier that summer they'd seen a horror movie about a small New England town overtaken by a bluish, sinister fog, and what crept out of that fog had died in the ocean. That movie had scared Ben wicked hard, though he would've died rather than admit it. Jamie found out from his mother that Aunt Francine didn't want them watching stupid horror movies anymore, because Ben hadn't slept two nights in a row.

"Look at that fog," Jamie said. "Look down by the dam. Do you see it? Ben, look! It's almost . . . bluish." The current was taking their inner tubes closer to the dam, closer to where the dead guy had been found. At the moment Ben looked, Jamie screamed and fell through the inner tube. His hand clawed up through the center of the tube, slapping at the rubber. He was working it, his hand making frenzied motions. After seconds, he let his hand limply drop down into the water. He dove down to the bottom of the river and found a rock to hang onto. Jamie held the record for holding his breath underwater—they'd spent so many hours having contests that summer, and Jamie had learned to hold his breath the longest. The trick was to calm the heart and breathing and not think of anything, not be conscious of time. At first he wanted to laugh. Little bubbles escaped his nostrils as he tried to quell thoughts of Ben above, getting more and more agitated as seconds passed. At first, Ben would think it was a big joke and yell at him to quit it. Then, when Jamie didn't come up, with the slate of the night sky and the breath of mist over the water closing in, Ben would give the water a futile slap. He'd look around and find no one out there.

After nearly a minute underwater, Jamie's arms and legs began to feel itchy. He fought the panic that came with wanting to breathe, knowing how to calm himself right into a trance just by closing his mind and letting images slip in and out. That was the trick. He thought of the darkness of the water, let that darkness flow over him. He saw swaying reeds, brown sediment, shadowy minnows like choreographed buckshot. The calmer he grew, the less he thought of breathing. In the murky darkness, there was a larger shape resting on the bottom of the river, blending in with the slick fluctuation of the water. Jamie imagined it, let his mind run the length of it—it was a log. The current of the river was strong, pushing against the reeds. It pushed against the log too, lifting it slightly. It rolled slowly, until it was not a log, not anymore, for he could see buttons, mother of pearl glints in the darkness. On one splayed branch was a tarnished silver wrist watch. It was a man, whose open-necked oxford shirt was dingy as the brown sediment, whose black hair swayed liked the reeds. His skin was brown, like bark. It was the pediatrician, whose name he never remembered, whose funeral he never attended, and underwater, a foot away from Jamie, the eyes opened, glowing against a blackened face that looked like a bubbling burnt pizza, with patches of nose missing.

The doctor's gentle hand gripped Jamie's ankle. The pumping

started and Jamie choked, feeling the need to take in anything through his nose, even water, just to stop the burning. He broke the surface with a real cry and began thrashing toward shore. His inner tube was gone, all the way down by the dam, and Ben—Ben should've been there, but he was gone. And for a blind second, he thought that the dead man had come up with the sediment, for the water was brown everywhere and he couldn't see if Ben was underneath. Every kick in the water felt as if it were about to make contact with a soft decomposing body. He thrashed his way toward shore, little screams in his throat. What was Aunt Francine going to do when he told her Ben drowned? Where the fuck was he?

He swam closer until he saw Ben on the shore, bent over and pointing at him. "I knew it! I knew you were faking!" When Jamie finally dragged himself up on the darkened sand beach, he shoved Ben, who stumbled backward.

"What did you do with my towel?" Jamie yelled.

Ben's smile vanished. "I didn't . . . I didn't do anything."

"The fuck you didn't," Jamie snarled and stomped off, back toward the road. It was finally dusk, the river greasy in the distance. He didn't even know what he was pissed about, but he wanted to get away from the river, Ben—all of it.

The depth finder kept beeping. Thongchai radioed James Senior. "Where are ya? We just passed by the bar."

"We're about fifty yards ahead of you," James said. They agreed that Senior's boat should head for the western side of Fogerty's territory; Thongchai's boat was to skim the inner harbor, up by the rocks. They'd be lucky if they didn't run aground in this gray mess. Small wonder people didn't fish on days like this. Jamie loathed working in it. As they pushed through, the fog gave them enough berth and closed up after them. He hated the way it erased all signs of life, all color and detail from the world. He'd work in the rain, no problem, even if it drove like penny nails into his skull, before he'd ever go out in fog. But his big mouth had gotten him where he was now.

The chatter over the walkie-talkie turned to whispers, now that they had rounded Courage Bay and were approaching Fogerty territory. The walkie-talkie spat. "Let me see that chart," The Kid said, up next to Thongchai.

"All right, listen," James Senior said. "We're looking at three or four square miles. We're not going for all of it. We'll go for a hundred-fifty, two hundred, that's all, so stick to the plan."

Jamie sat on an overturned bait tub, staring out, not listening. Thongchai and James Senior continued plotting points in low voices.

"Hey," The Kid said, noticing Jamie's silence. "What is it?"

"Nothin'." A crush of awful feelings squeezed Jamie's chest, making him feel panicky for feeling panicky.

"It's gonna be fine," The Kid said.

"Dow," Jamie scowled and got up off the bucket. Bad enough it looked like he was afraid of the mist, but damned if he'd give his cousin the impression he was afraid of the mission.

Jamie squinted, trying to make out anything beyond the bow. Behind him, he heard the familiar flick of a lighter and the short intake of breath—Thongchai passing a bowl to The Kid, who sucked at it. Jamie stared at both of them. Neither one was paying attention to the electronics, or the charts, or even the wheel. "Hey," Jamie said to Thongchai. "Think you might want to take a day off from your fuckin' habit in case we actually need to fight?"

Thongchai burst out laughing, smoke oozing from his nose and mouth. The Kid passed a ripple of flame over the bowl. "Nothin's gonna happen," he said.

"Oh, you *sure* about that?"

"Nobody's gonna be out here."

Jamie lit a new cigarette off the old one, pitched the butt off the rail. His lips clamped down; the crease between his eyes deepened. Both of them were fucking morons at times, particularly The Kid, who'd never been in a trap war and always looked to Jamie and Thongchai to fight his fights for him. Neither Thongchai nor The Kid had ever had more than twenty traps cut. What did it matter to them but to go along for the ride? There they were, popping a beer at 3:30 a.m., smoking weed as if this was just another day out on the water.

Jamie bit down on his cigarette, stared at his cousin. "Let me ask you something. What would you do if Dale Fogerty was out here waiting for us?"

The Kid shrugged, less certain. "He won't be."

Thongchai turned from the wheel. "Relax, precious, this'll go fine."

"You better be right, cause if any of Fogerty's friends or family are out here, they won't write us a ticket, so *look friggin' sharp!*"

Thongchai turned back to the wheel, unconcerned. "Eugley, just sit back and let me take care of it."

To not question your life from time to time, to glide along oblivious to the fact that the twitch road was turning into a deer path, was to Jamie the crowning trait of harbor life. His two best friends had nothing more going for them than good strong backs and the unquestioning faith that nothing bad would ever happen to them. What did The Kid ever do but buffer about on his good looks and cheerful nature? He had no idea what it was like to always fight through life, or what it was like to forcefully board a scab's boat and press his thumbs to a man's neck to convey *This isn't a good place to fish.* For the first time, Jamie considered that The Kid might've simply let his traps get hauled by others from time to time, or resigned himself to thinking that they got cut for natural (or maybe unnatural) reasons. That's why he could sit there on his fat and happy can with veiny red eyes each day and look so staggeringly complacent. And Thongchai, the closest Thongchai got to questioning whether there was anything more to this life was when only four beers remained in the cooler. Thongchai's big goal was to own a bigger boat, with a twelve-disc CD player and Bose speakers. And here he was, a lobsterman, on an ocean that got smaller and smaller every year, with every passing regulation, every new guy with a trap license, every summer that shrunk in landings. There would be no more freedom or escape after what they were about to do. Taking on Fogerty was like unleashing the Kraken—the seas would never be free and open again.

Jamie stared past the stern, watching the burble of water curl white onto gray and fade. The drive to retaliate only hours ago had faded away, leaving him wrung out. He didn't feel like fighting. He closed his eyes, imagining sunken boats, torched wharves and docks, cars and trucks vandalized, dumped into quarries, and thousands and thousands of traps severed, stomped flat, cut loose. An entire town in economic devastation, banks denying trap loans, newspaper stories, Marine Patrol investigations, more fines on top of Chapter 11, repossessions of houses, more retaliations, hospitalizations. No one in his generation had ever seen a big trap war, except for the one the Fogertys got into with that yahoo back in the '80s. That guy's livelihood was cut to pieces in less than a week, with no hope of ever starting from scratch. This was going to be ridiculous. How the hell was he going to be able to take a vacation from all this if he had no money or livelihood? How would he keep his truck, his house, keep up with Anja's bills without collectors, if every one of his traps went missing in action?

This was bad, bad, bad. Good time to think about it—*now*. Jamie rested his head between his hands, grabbing at his forelock, wanting to rip hair out of his skull. Who had the big mouth? He did. Oh yeah, *What more do you need? Are we going to let them put us out of business?* Brilliant. The fog was going to get them. Just like in that horror movie with Adrienne Barbeau, who they called Adrienne Bar-boob in middle school because of her enormous rack. They'd run aground against some giant rock, radio for help, and of course the electronics would go all flooey in the fog (because of some mysterious short-out) and they'd run out of beer. Being on a boat with Thongchai this long would cause them to run at each other like a couple of stags—knock the piss out of each other—so inevitably there'd be bleeding. And Thongchai didn't carry a first aid kit on his boat, nor a lifeboat, not even a rescue suit. *Hey, if my boat ever goes down, I'm going down with her,* he always bragged. Jamie was on a friggin' death cruise with Laurel and Hardy. He could feel the sinking already, feel it in his joints. *Relax, precious, nothin's gonna happen.* Jamie pounded his forehead.

"Precious having a flip-out?" Thongchai asked.

"Looks like," said The Kid, who turned to face the windshield.

Out of the white wake it emerged, as if stepping out of a doorway. The running lights were off. In the bare light beyond the stern, a figure emerged, seemed to be walking in the trough of gunmetal water, steadily forward, without making progress. It seemed the fabric of fog itself, dripping, taking the form of coarse oilskin trousers, a leather apron, a tattered sou'easter hat, clothing from an earlier century. It walked toward Jamie, boots seamless in the white wake, face downwind, hat flapping against the wind. It was an old man. He had a nod for Jamie as if they were old friends passing on the road, as he stepped up on the wash rail of the *Maisie May*, his sou'easter hat flipping back to reveal a papery face like peeling birch bark, before continuing to walk toward the wheelhouse and back into the fog.

Jamie looked over at The Kid and Thongchai, their backs to him. He hadn't breathed. In his memory, still fresh, the moment that sou'easter rim flipped up, he saw the man's face. It had been long dead, a greenish face with film over the eyes like cataracts.

Jamie got up and stood behind Thongchai close enough to whisper. "You need to turn us around right now. I'm dead fuckin' serious. Right now."

"What?" Thongchai checked the readouts, ascertained they weren't about to hit anything.

"I don't care. Let me off—here—over on that peninsula." Jamie reached to grab the wheel. Thongchai shoved him away. "What the fuck are you doing?"

"Let me off. There's gonna be some serious trouble."

"Jamie—what happened?" The Kid said, suddenly frightened. "What the hell is going on?"

Jamie shook his head and would say no more. He felt hot inside his two sweatshirts. His hand stayed fixed on the rail, his eyes wild. He'd heard stories about them out there all his life, and he'd just seen one. Everywhere around them fog—

Thongchai eased the throttle, slowing into someone's private dock, and reversed expertly alongside as Jamie stumbled off the boat. There wasn't a skiff tied to the dock. It looked like a personal dock for grandkids to jump off.

"Are you gonna be sick?" The Kid asked.

Jamie shook his head.

"What then?"

The Kid stared at him, profoundly disappointed. "Jesus, guy. Just have a couple of beers. You'll be all right."

Thongchai ran a rough hand through his thick pointy hair, embarrassed for Jamie.

"I saw something out there. . . ," Jamie said.

"What?"

"Was it Fogerty?"

"No." The way the old sailor had nodded to him with such familiarity was a sign straight out of the books. The information was all there—if a man had enough sense to read it. "Something really bad is gonna happen. I'm telling you, I feel it. You guys should just turn around, right now."

The Kid's eyes fell to his beer. Thongchai scowled. They both doubted him. "I can't turn around. I don't know why you're. . . ." Thongchai's lips pinched. "Shit, man, your dad, Bob, and Doug are relying on us. We can't just *stop*."

"Call them right now . . . get them on the two-way," Jamie urged.

"They're too far away."

"Use the VHF then."

"We *can't*."

"I don't care. Blame it on me—just tell them—"

"Forget it," Thongchai said. He worked up a spit and hucked it out of his throat. "Whatever you say—they're not gonna give a shit." He moved back to the wheel, preparing to go.

The Kid looked like a boy who just dropped his ice cream cone, his loyalties divided. He didn't know who to go with.

"Be really careful," Jamie said, backing away, and immediately got hot inside his clothes again. Could he be any more of a housewife? The way Thongchai smiled made Jamie cringe, as if he was no longer relevant. The Kid stared open-mouthed at Jamie, completely dashed. Thongchai reversed the throttle and Jamie watched them both slip away from the dock, as if plunging into cream.

Are You There, Pappy? It's Me, Your Nutless Grandson and other novels that Judy Blume never got around to writing. Jamie stood on the disembodied dock. The wretchedness of that moment felt like all the times Jamie peed his bed as a kid, lying in it all night, waiting for Senior to leave at 4 a.m. so he could get up and change the sheets. Oh, this was going to be a funhouse when The Kid and Thongchai explained to Senior what happened. It would confirm everything his father had ever suspected. Hotheaded, all talk, no guts. Jamie sunk lower into his collar, now sick that he'd done the wrong thing. Off the boat, things seemed less dire. Fog still around, but not that panicky itchiness. Maybe he lived with too much fantasy. All those stories Maynard used to tell him about the pirates and phantom selkies, the shipwrecks and ghosts, pass-the-winter-by-the-woodstove stories. They'd been absorbed in his bones—saying there was so much more out there on the sea than a fisherman could know—all those stories that allowed his mind to wander in the blind routine of his days.

How stupid could he feel in one 24-hour period? Jamie felt each new emotion sack him like a punch. It was just a panic attack, over silliness—and now it looked like he bailed on the mission. This was going to be brutal—talk would spill out among the close circles that Jamie lost his nerve, big tough guy. Like a game of telephone—the way all gossip started. He could just imagine everyone at the Beach Store sitting around at the breakfast counter and someone saying, "Oh, did you hear how Jamie Eugley cried so hard to be let off the boat that an ambulance had to come and give him oxygen before they took him away?" When he walked into Churchie's on Monday, all the chatter would go silent. Thongchai and The Kid wouldn't rib him about it, and everyone would pretend it never happened. Until he got up to go to the john—then they'd ride him like a Palomino behind his back. *Tell Eugley to come back when his balls have dropped!*

The fog clotted around him and he walked gingerly, his toe tapping a semicircle out in front like a blind man; the dock made a racket of loose boards and chains clanging with each step. He had no idea who this dock belonged to or how far it went. He tried to guess where he was, maybe a mile or two over the Courage Bay harbor line, smack in the middle of Fogerty territory.

The only sound was hollow dripping, moisture clinging to the air. The birds remained silent. Another sound sent a spike through his nerves, the outboard motor of a skiff coming up the coast, not Thongchai's boat coming back but a smaller one approaching, its motor nice and clean, like a commercial bus purring at a stop light. It was way too early for anyone to be legitimately fishing. The skiff came closer. Jamie settled quietly down on the dock; he dared not risk walking, as the rattle of the boards would give him away. If he could hear the skiff, whoever was aboard would hear him. He guessed it was not more than forty feet away. He sat in a protective stance, thinking hard—who'd be out there now? It might have been Fogerty himself, checking his traps, sitting right pretty with a twelve-gauge shotgun by his feet. They were so stupid. Someone had tipped Fogerty off, as Jamie had feared. Thongchai and The Kid, clueless as usual, out there cutting traps. *Nothin's gonna happen.* His system spurted adrenaline and it was making his stomach sick. His luck, he'd pass out a mile behind enemy lines. He'd be known not only for ditching a trap raid, but for fainting in the fucking fog. With any more luck, his head would come down on a rock and he'd wake up with a head injury. Then he and Anja could tell each other jokes that neither of them would get.

The outboard was skillful, muttering around, stopping to attend to traps. It moved in closer, another twenty feet. If the fog had cleared away in that moment, they'd be eyeball to eyeball. Jamie dared not even crouch, as the sound was so drippingly quiet, so amplified, even the cracking of his knee joints would sound like the snapping of dry twigs. His mind worked hard: somehow

Fogerty had found out about the trap raid and was pulling up traps to save them. But why would he do that in a skiff and not his own boat? It sounded like a brand-new Yamaha engine—one of those hot new models with the throaty burr. A whistle came from the man in the skiff, freezing Jamie. The whistling was strangely cavalier, a vague tune that carried hollowly across the water, reminding Jamie of some nagging eighties song or a commercial.

The man grunted, hand-hauling the trap and pulling up the wet slop of warp. The wire of an aluminum trap scraped horribly against the hull of the skiff. Then there was the unmistakable sound of cutting, the sawing sound of float rope—and a splash. Jamie bent down to the dock until he was lying flat, his cheek against the wet boards.

TWENTY EIGHT

Within a day, all along the back roads the sagging telephone wires began to talk. When big news in a harbor town surfaced, it didn't come from the police logs or the paper or the radio. It first came through the VHF, then the telephone lines, then a hasty dock meeting. It came on like the lawn chair–flipping winds of a typhoon.

Colleen Marshall, owner of the beach store, had heard it from Greta, Don Thatcher's wife, that Dale Fogerty discovered two hundred and twenty hundred traps cut late Monday afternoon. The whispers in grocery store aisles grimly announced that a trap war had started, a big one this time. And this wasn't just an interesting item for the stitch n' bitch, something to perk up the town, like a bit of sizzling gossip.

Within an hour of Greta's call, the beach store began filling with locals well before the lunch rush. Colleen scrutinized the orange stickers on the items as she rang them through. A line of ten people formed in front of the counter. Colleen glanced to see what they were holding in their hands: duct tape, canned goods, bottled water, and flashlights. "We're actually having a run on duct tape," she told Kelly, the bagger/sandwich maker. "We might have four rolls left. Can you see?"

Kelly strained her neck to view the far-end shelf. "Yep. That's weird."

"What are they going to do, tape their boats to the moorings?"

Everett McAdoo had to finally come out of the bait shop and direct traffic at the wharf himself. Sunny-faced, he supervised the road—one finger up to halt the bottleneck of cars, the other waving a gray GMC truck through. The wharf was glutted with vehicles, keys all in the ignition. Not even a spare patch of grass left to wedge half a back wheel into. "Can you go across the street, squeeze her into that last space on the library lawn?" Everett asked the owner of the GMC. A reddened arm swung out of the cab window; the hand gave him the thumbs-up. Another truck maneuvered into the lot. Everett watched as older lobstermen, one after another, came zipping down to the wharf, jumping in their skiffs.

Someone called to him, "You hear anything new?"

"I imagine you'll know more than me when you get out there," Everett said.

When the telephone rang in the Petit Point town manager's office Tuesday morning, Don Thatcher was sitting in mud-stiff jeans on the corner of Roger Powers's desk. Little clots of hay stuck to his back pocket. Newall Watts looked like a pinched hen, the way he paced. Paul Santerre lounged in the red leather chair by the window, a toothpick on his dry lip. Roger Powers, a slender man who'd been a co-op manager in the 1970s before someone had pitched him over the dock, glanced at the three highliner fishermen who had been camped in his office since five that morning. He had no love for lobstermen and wished they'd handle their own problems. And he didn't like the way they'd taken over his office to put him in the middle of something that they traditionally handled on their own. He flashed them a strained look before picking up the phone.

"Roger Powers," he answered.

On the other end was Fogerty's rake-thin voice. "What do you hear?"

Roger took a breath; he cleared his voice twice, a nervous habit. "Well, uh, like I said, Dale, we've been trying as hard as you to get hold of them. The phones aren't answering at either of their houses, and we've got some people looking for them out on the water."

"Well, it's pretty obvious, wouldn't you say?"

Roger struggled to balance his loyalties. "We're just as anxious to hear from them as you are so we can straighten this out. To be fair, we need to hear their story."

Fogerty was silent.

Roger stumbled more. "Listen, I can certainly appreciate how you've got to be pretty ripshit about this. . . ."

"Fuckin' right."

"I mean, I'd be too, no question. I'm just asking for a little more time so we can. . . ." Roger's voice muted as Fogerty talked over him. "You know what? I've never believed in phone calls for something like this. This was your deal, not mine. If you and your guys are colluding to hide Eugley and his kid, I'm going after all of ya."

"Now wait, cause we're not. . . ."

"I'm already so fucking past the end of my patience."

"I understand, I just. . . ."

"No you don't. You have no idea what's about to happen."

Roger let out a weary sigh and hung up the phone. "Well," Roger said. "That's just great, now I'm going to have to call Marine Patrol."

Paul and Don held a silent meeting in the span of two seconds. Don chewed a scab on the tip of his thumb and looked out the window. "No you won't."

Roger stood behind his desk. "Look—you guys got me involved. Fogerty's calling me at eleven at night, waking up my wife, who just got our one-year-old to sleep, all right? And I was up all night trying to get in touch with you, but because none of you were around, you made it my problem. So now I've got to do my job."

"You're not calling Marine Patrol," Don said, his ledgy smile favoring Roger. Paul Santerre got up from the leather chair and opened the town manager's door. Newall went out first. "You did what you had to do and now your part is done," Don said with a wave as he left. "We'll take care of it from here."

Roger Powers watched them go. He knew he wasn't going to call Marine Patrol and he sat down in his desk chair, helpless.

TWENTY NINE

On the baking paved blacktop stood two corroded gas pumps, regular and diesel. Within the greasy pump windows, the manual numbers ran up like a slot machine.

They belonged to the Stop N' Go, the only convenience store in the Point. Inside was a labyrinth of dusty aisles. Boots and shoes crossed the dirty, cracked tile, across the rubber floor mat. Hands self-served at the convex dome of the shaved ice machine, pulled sticky plastic coffee lids apart. The back cooler opened—hands reached in, pulled out twelve-packs of Bud, Miller Lite. Motor oil was hefted, scrutinized; cans of Dinty Moore were turned over in calloused palms. Fingers poked at the hard, flat racks of stale candy, flipped nimbly through the pegboard displaying emergency rations of aspirin, deodorant, tampons. From the center aisle, a little girl in a Girl Scout uniform stared at Anja. She'd been there for minutes, feet planted, her green beret over one pigtail.

Anja stood behind the counter with Dee as her fingers clacked at the cash register. Dee's soft blond helmet contrasted with her weary mouth. Without having to look, Dee knew how to reach up and coax the right pack of cigarettes out of the overhead rack. Under the counter were multicolored rolls of lottery tickets. Beyond the glass doors, Anja could see pickup trucks continuously revolve around the two lone gas pumps. Anja saw money pushed across the worn counter, pennies, nickels, riding the bills. Heard Dee's advice between ring-ups.

"You don't have to do the math anymore. All you have to do is check their license and key in their birthdate, right here, see? It does the work for you."

Anja picked up the Stop N' Go training manual and looked up at the ceiling, trying to memorize the Five Customer Service Guarantees:

Give a friendly greeting with a smile.

Be available for assistance.

Be knowledgeable of related items.

Ring up merchandise quickly and accurately.

Thank the customer and invite them back.

Two coffee cans had been placed on the counter, decorated with construction paper, their plastic lids slit to accept bills and coins. One was for a local boy who needed a spinal operation following a tragic football injury. The other was Dee's, which she made herself. HELP DEE MILLER GET A NEW PANCREAS, it said. She'd nudged her coffee can out in front. Every time someone handed her money, she slowly pushed the change toward her can.

A man with worn eyes and a sullen frown hefted a cardboard box onto the counter. "Six-pack Bud, pack Mahboros, two slots, and a queen of hahts."

"If they want the Black Fly ticket, it's this one," Dee said to Anja as she snatched off a square from the lottery roll for the man. "Not this other one, which looks the same. You getting this, hon?"

Anja scratched down in her notepad. "Black Fly ticket, not the other one." Later she'd have no idea what that cryptic note meant. "Um, is there a bathroom?"

Dee pointed to a small door behind the counter. "Need to go?"

"No. . . ," Anja said, her face reddening.

"Listen, hon. Maybe you oughta start talking to the customers, you know? I'll just stand back and let you do some transactions."

"Carton a Camel Lights—" The woman at the counter looked rough: black Aerosmith T-shirt, skinny shoulders, skinny legs, and a mound of fat from her belly to her crotch. Her hair was a grown-out perm, a zipper of gray at the roots. Her face looked as if it'd been raked with a clam hoe and her teeth looked bitten off.

"And how is *your* day going?" Anja flashed her a man-eater of a grin, mindful of the first customer service rule.

"Fine." The woman fingered wadded dollar bills from her front jeans pocket, distracted.

Anja handed her the cellophane package. "Cigarettes can kill you, you know," Anja said. "My grandma smoked a carton a day. When she died, my grandpa said her lungs were so—"

"Let me take care of that for you." Dee sidled in, playing the register like a piano. "She's *training*," Dee said, which didn't erase the annoyed lines from the woman's brow.

"Are these your kids?" Anja asked. A shy boy and girl, each with longish hair, dirt and cereal around their mouths, stood oblivious to their mother, fingering the candy rack. The Girl Scout with the blond pigtails stood slightly apart from them.

"Yeah?" the mother answered, as if it was a challenge. There was some mewling from the kids as she got her change. "Oh all *right*," she hissed, plucking the candy bars from their hands and slamming them on the counter. "Ya happy now?"

Anja glanced at the little girl in the Girl Scout uniform. She was adorable, really, two blonde piggies under that beret, a sweet, pink-cheeked face. Obviously knew how to keep herself clean, unlike the other two. "Did you want me to ring up one for her?" Anja said.

The woman looked behind her and then back to Anja, scowling. Dee also gave her a warning look, which Anja took to mean she'd overstepped some customer service rule. The little Girl Scout followed the woman and her children out the double doors of the convenience store, her blue eyes on Anja as if *she* understood what Anja was trying to do.

The rest of the morning was exhausting. Between enormous amounts of information that Dee was expecting her to write down and understand, there were always people coming in, interrupting them, wanting gas, to-go sandwiches, milk, coffee, dirty magazines. The working guys always seemed to bring to the counter the same things, as if there was a code among working men. A blue or red soda-type drink and two stacks of candy bars. Anja wanted to chide them: *Is this your lunch?* But she'd picked up from Dee that "Give a friendly greeting with a smile" wasn't supposed to extend to more than "Canna help you?"

At noon, Donna Eugley breezed through the door and Anja felt a combination of excitement and relief. She just wanted to get out of there. "Hey, kiddo," Donna said, leaning onto the counter. She was wearing a business suit with a leopard collar. "How's she holding up there, Dee?"

Dee nodded, took a second before answering. "We definitely need to keep covering some things before I take off Friday."

"We'll whip her into shape. Listen," she told Anja. "Grab your stuff, I'm taking you to my place tonight."

Anja reached down and gathered her day planner and notebooks and placed them into her book bag. "Why?"

Donna looked at Dee. "Tell ya in the car."

In Donna's convertible, Anja sat with her combat bag on her lap. Donna got in. "Jamie and Dad are gonna be out on their boats for a couple of days—and we think it's best if you stay at our house."

Anja's brow furrowed. She didn't understand. "Why non't he answer when I call the radio?"

"No one's talking right now. Trust me. You're safe with me. You trust me?"

Anja nodded, but looked out the window. She wanted to be home.

THIRTY

As *Delores* skimmed under a cracked sky of Easter-egg colors, her windows became the muted orange of an electric burner. The bawl of blackjacks reached across the bay; up close to the hull there was the light slap of waves. Crazy light bounced across the windshield and canopy ceiling, making prisms of the screens, instruments, and dials, lighting across the salt-coated VHF radio. The signal of urgent radio waves undulated lazily from shore to ship, voices slipping down the trough and scooting up the crest to find contact, anything.

"Jamie, Jesus, if you're hearing this, you need to call me right away . . . there's a. . . ."

"Hey there, monkey spank, hey, ya on theah? Stopped ovah at the house. We've got some business to take care of. . . ."

"Delores, come in, Delores. Can you give me a reading on where you are. . . ."

". . . this is why you need a friggin' cell phone, retard. . . ."

". . . friend of the Fogertys. And man, you'd better get back here soon is all I can say. . . ."

The radio remained off. He'd not heard any of it.

Even on the water, his most favorite place in the world, too much time alone made him crazy. He only liked solitude when he knew he could get off the boat and go home again. But this lying-in-wait strategy, hour after hour on aching calves, staring out at the water in every direction—this was a haggard way to make a living. Earlier he'd

278

eaten cold beef stew from the can, crackers that had gone soggy from the sea air. The skin around his mouth became a whitened crust. Hours upon hours passed as he scanned the blank horizon, his pulse quickening every time he heard a lobster boat nearby.

In the middle of the night, a large white ring surrounded the moon, swallowing the sky over his boat. When he got up to urinate over the rail, he took his shotgun with him. As he stood there, he wondered who was involved and how far this would go. Every other harbor was a rival: Rockland, Owls Head, Spruce Head, Friendship, Cushing, Tenants Harbor, Wheeler's Bay, Martinsville, Petit Point, Port Clyde, and Courage. Friendship generally had no wars with Tenants Harbor and would side with the lobstermen of Petit Point, but if Courage and Port Clyde got involved—there would be some big head-banging there.

No one had seen anything this big in years. Sure, small arguments every summer, maybe a blow-out every decade. Going back eight summers, a lobsterman named Lunt had discovered the pennant line of his vessel cut, his boat set adrift. When the tide brought his boat back onto soft shoreline without a scratch, Lunt considered himself lucky, until he went aboard and found that all of his electronics had been smashed. When he got home, he discovered all the tires on his truck were slashed. Lunt started a war with his neighbors that dragged four families and sixteen individuals into it, a nasty, back-and-forth skirmish that had built up over the course of a summer until thousands of dollars of property were destroyed and Lunt and his son got arrested.

Near seven the next morning, pockets of low-lying vapor burned off with the sun. The birds, sensing it coming on, cranked up with a mazurka of cries. Jamie sat up in his sleeping bag, a knuckle swept across his bloodshot eyes. By the time he'd finally fallen into an exhausted sleep at three in the morning, he realized he'd been dreaming of arguing with Amanda over painting her car the same color as his buoys. A ridiculous dream. His neck hurt to move. The last two nights he'd slept on an air mattress the thickness of a waffle down forward in the bunk. And to call it sleeping was inaccurate, when lying in the dark for hours until the slightest sound, a flap of wings in the night, a bump against the boat, sprang him up on deck.

With the tender peach light, the pearly waves, he lay there, rolling with the waves, half sleeping, half thinking, until the sound of approaching boats jerked him upright. Jamie stood up in the cramped space and speared a foot into his Wranglers.

His father's boat came up from the west, just beyond the Point. As it came closer, Jamie could see Rich Snow, Paul Santerre, and Ronny H., his father's sternman, on deck. Jamie shoved his matted curls under his cap and knelt over the rail to throw some salt water across his face. He waited for them to arrive. He'd known this was coming.

As the boat approached, none of the guys would look at him. They were too busy adjusting their hats, scratching their ears, scanning the horizon with their hands as visors. Paul was the one Jamie wanted to get a read on first. He already knew what his father would have to say about ditching the patrolling raid the other night, but he wondered if Paul would be reasonable. Rich Snow, another highline fisherman, was one of his dad's old fish shack pals and would be on his side, would think what Senior told him to think. Senior jockeyed his boat right alongside *Delores*, twirling the wheel, and reversed expertly up. He brought one foot casually up on the rail of *Delores*.

"Why didn't you keep your radio on?" his father asked. The rest of the men looked uncomfortable.

Jamie raised an arm and held onto the roof of the wheelhouse, bracing for it, knowing he'd have to take it in front of Rich and Paul, even Ronny H., the 21-year-old, who looked as though he wanted to be anywhere but there.

This is where it starts. Jamie looked at his father. "I just didn't want to keep it on."

"Smart thinking," he answered sharply. James Senior hadn't slept either; the skin under his blue eyes was puffy. He bent forward, resting a hairy forearm on the leg that kept Jamie's boat anchored to his own. "You know something? We got ourselves a little problem."

Jamie tried to stand up straight, keep his face as square as his father's. "Yep."

James Senior raised his index finger to his mouth. "Because you kept your radio off, you didn't know what happened this morning. Kenny Fogerty went looking for us last night and found Thongchai instead."

Jamie stared at Senior and tugged off his cap. "What happened?"

James Senior rubbed a grease spot at the knee of his jeans. "Kenny beat the shit out of him with a bottle of scotch, fractured his skull, took out his fuckin' teeth—that's what happened. Thongchai got airlifted to Portland last night."

"WHAT?"

Senior stood there, infuriatingly silent, contempt curling his lip.

"We don't know how bad it is." Paul stepped in. "All they'll tell us is that he's in stable condition—and Kenny has been arrested—but it's not good, whatever it is, so they flew him down."

Jamie turned toward the wheel, gazed uncomprehendingly at the scratched glass.

"What *was* the fuckin' problem the other night, by the way?" Senior said. "Thongchai stood up for our family, but you couldn't even go through with the mission *you* wanted to happen. You get scared, PMS—*what?*"

Jamie shook his head. He looked to the others, Senior's words flowing past him. "No. . . ." He was thinking of Thongchai in raging pain over what, dotted lines on the water? He couldn't say anything and looked away, a feeling swamping him like he wanted to cry or give up. *If he ends up dying over this. . . .* Jamie turned away, his head dropping.

"Too fuckin' late now!" James Senior spat. Rich nodded, hands jammed in his pockets. They all seemed to agree with what Senior said. Only Paul's voice held any understanding: "Jamie, the point is, we're all in it now."

In the span of a remote horizon, a speck appeared against the sun. Everyone turned, the sun in their eyes. "Who is that?" Rich muttered. Coming on like a quarterback, all hunched shoulders, growling, was an oncoming boat, a mile off, white wake spilling off both sides. "It's them," Paul said. Rich went down forward, came back with his shotgun.

"Oh, fuck," Ronny H. said.

"Calm down, Ronny," James Senior said. "I'll knock you overboard if you act like that. Everybody shut up." He set his own shotgun down by his feet.

As the oncoming boat slowed from a high whine to a low growl, white wake falling away, the dark, spindly face of Dale Fogerty came into view. Behind Fogerty stood Ev and Russell. Fogerty's cheeks held a familiar scowl. That lifeless face, like deer jerky. He looked runty in proportion to his sons. No one said anything as the boats bobbed ten feet from each other doing a delicate dance, a bow and curtsy against the waves. James Senior set his foot against the rail and his gun flat against his knee. Guns skyward like antennae, engines churning. Rich's cigarette was gone and Paul stood, arms crossed. Ronny H. stared as if his eyes had been burned out by Zeus.

Jamie tried to reconcile in his memory the big man Fogerty used to be with this ropy, skinny brute. With that thin, lackluster smile, Fogerty spoke. "It's pretty *poor* I had to come all the way out here to find where you been hiding out."

James Senior scoffed. "Nobody's hiding from you."

Ev and Russell cackled. "Oh no?" Fogerty said. "That's why you're way the hell out here?"

"Good thing Kenny can't run and hide," James bit back. "Not this time."

Somebody was going to get shot; Jamie could feel it coming on, his collarbone aching. It propelled him to say something.

"Somebody cut about two hundred of my traps the other day."

A sour expression came over Fogerty's features. "Oh, you trying to say I had something to do with that?"

"Yeah, *somebody*," Senior said.

"Prove it."

Each time words were thrown out, the party on the other boat made a collective sound like a full tire punched by a knife. Dry, humorless snorts.

"Your father stole from my father's traps in 1959, and your

whole family's been scabbing around our gear for the last hundred years. . . ."

The way Fogerty suddenly laughed made Jamie cringe. Senior pressed. "You wanna talk about working someone over, I can give you. . . ."

"Aawww. . . ." Fogerty threw James Senior away with a wave. "You know what? You know what, Eugley? I love how high and mighty you are, like your father never did nothing wrong, when your fuckin' family was the one who got mine put in jail. And for the last thirty years, you all been nothing but a little whiny bitch every time one of your traps gets cut. So," he said to Jamie with a flick of a nod. "You got your traps cut and I got mine. You think that's a coincidence? What do you have to say about it?"

"It wasn't us," Rich said.

"Bullshit," Fogerty said pleasantly. "Jamie, why don't you tell me the truth."

"The truth is I didn't. . ."

"*Right*." Fogerty said with a hard, slack smile, as if that was entirely expected. Water ripped around their boats, a school of sardines passing through. A steady rumble of silver fins. This sparkly, splashy disturbance momentarily distracted Fogerty. "I'm not gonna dick around anymore," he said, staring at the water. "You got one chance to tell me. . . ."

The water began to churn madly, a violent pelting like hail coming down. "Whoa," Ronny H. said. It turned the hot oppressive morning wavy with confusion—everyone looking at the water, where below, mottled gray snippets of darting fin cut the surface. Bluefish were hurling out of the water, blood-mad, after a siege of sardines. The fish made plunging splashes like violent exit wounds everywhere around the boats. Above, a screaming flock of gulls descended upon the water, hysterical to get the dying fish. It was impossible to stand there and come off as threatening, guns poised, while sardines gyrated out of the jaws of bluefish and seagulls whipped like a dust storm around them. The ripping cries of the seagulls sounded like screams in a burning building.

A shotgun blast scattered the birds, dropped the frenzy of the water back to smooth, flat ribbon. Jamie jumped, as did everyone else. In two seconds, it was as if nothing had happened. A plume of smoke seeped from James Senior's gun. The gulls flew away, complaining, in high, short strokes. It was so stupid to be firing a weapon like that, not knowing if it would trigger the Fogertys to let loose. He already knew how little Ev and Russell needed to be provoked.

Fogerty smirked. In his hands, he held his own ten-gauge loosely against his thigh, his finger by the trigger. "You trying to scare the fish or me?" Ev and Russell held their guns pointed to the deck. Jamie looked at Ev and Russell, who would someday have children as strangled in the face.

He faced Fogerty, desperate to change the course of things. "Listen, this whole thing is stupid. Nobody needs to get shot over it. All I need to know is if you cut my traps first—then we can settle this."

James Senior snorted, as Jamie knew he would. There was a code for how a confrontation worked, and Jamie didn't care that he was violating it. "Don't even bother," Senior said. "He'll never tell you."

Fogerty turned his weathered neck cords towards Jamie. "You want the truth?" Dale Fogerty had the dead eyes of a small man who had long been angry and disappointed. "I didn't pull your traps," Fogerty finally said.

Slurry rolled back and forth on Jamie's deck; he watched the briny water toggle back and forth, from stern to bow, not sure where to go from here. Fogerty could have been lying, but Jamie didn't sense that he was.

Jamie turned to his father and the others on the boat. "That's all I needed to know."

There was a low murmur from Ronny H. and Rich, who were far from happy with the way this was going. "What the hell are you doing?" Rich said. "Just shut up and let your dad talk."

"What are we gonna do?" Jamie said. "Stand here until the sun goes down? They didn't do it—end of story." Everything he was doing, he couldn't explain; he was trying to think fast, throw everybody off.

"Jesus Christ," James Senior said in his throwaway way. He gave Paul a look as if it was typical. *My stupid kid doing something stupid.*

The entire morning had been a ton of bricks. Everything from his traps getting cut to this; he'd redlined so far up in the last week, he thought one more thing might trigger him to blow. Thongchai in the hospital, now Fogerty smirking—Jamie's breath became shallow. He stared at the slurry on his boat rolling back and forth and thought something would break—he was a bag of fluid, dripping heavily at a strained seam. "Forget it," he whispered. He talked to the deck. "I said what I had to say."

James Senior lifted his shotgun, stiffly pointing at Jamie's chest. "Why can't you just do what I tell you?" He wore a pale, washed-out expression. "Always got to fuck it up."

Jamie felt cold, a small knot spreading out from the center to the rest of his body. They stared at each other and nothing in his father's devoid expression reminded him of family, or of loyalty. Jamie saw by the way his father's mouth twinged, by the way his finger was bent on the trigger, that Senior was close. His collarbone felt it. The others felt it, too. Paul cleared his throat. "Jim."

The twitchy feeling in Jamie turned to sweat; his armpits felt damp. He looked once again to the Fogertys as the shock began to recede. He looked at Senior. "I can't do this anymore." He didn't care how he sounded; he was wrung out. "You can all stand out here as long as you want with your weapons, waiting for someone to cross the imaginary line. You can take each other out 'til there's no one left. I'm fucking *done*."

Dale Fogerty's familiar scowl disappeared. Jamie looked back to his father, whose flat, devoid eyes had not changed. Jamie turned to start *Delores*.

A blast jolted from Senior's boat. Everyone on both boats crouched. "Hold it—hold it!" Paul yelled amid the smoke. Everyone remained in a crouch, as if in a game of Freeze Tag, afraid to stand all the way up.

Jamie saw it first in Ronny H.'s expression and looked to the side of his boat where the lettering of *Delores* had been blasted through. Everyone looked at Senior, whose demeanor had finally reached a degree of tight serenity. He never could stand being talked back to.

Jamie turned the engine over. He didn't give a crap what happened after that. He didn't look at his father or his friends. He was done protecting nine generations of this crippling excuse. He cranked the wheel and throttled down, *Delores*'s engine thumping past the others.

THIRTY ONE

Who's the Chinese kid?

Driving down 295, his mind was everywhere but on the road, spooling back to the first time he laid eyes on Thongchai on a hot, dusty August day at the gravel pit when they were all still around 12 or 13.

There by himself on a BMX, this wiry Asian kid rode ferociously, messing around, skidding down dunes of loose gravel. Before Jamie could get properly worked up about what this kid was doing at *their* gravel pit, he watched, momentarily fascinated by the rich, smooth color of the boy's skin, like the caramel in a Snickers bar. He had a wide, flat nose and black prickly hair and was wearing a red-checked plaid shirt with the shoulders ripped out the way all the local kids did. Jamie's cousin The Kid was on his own bike behind him, followed by Kevin, another local they hung around with. They pedaled up to the exotic stranger, drawing arcs in the dirt with their knobby tires. Jamie took charge, speaking for the group. "What are you doing at our pit?"

The Asian kid didn't respond right away or engage in any of the reactions they were hoping for. Instead, he pedaled around them lazily, sizing them up, making fresh tracks in the gravel silt. The silence was so pronounced that Jamie felt compelled to say something. Not until much later in his life would it occur to him that any time he'd ever had that itchy impulse to clash, it was out of panic. He had begun to burn in the hot sun. He stared down the stranger, irritated at having to force a provocation.

"Who's the Chinese kid?" Jamie said, looking to his gang. Kevin and The Kid didn't really laugh, but rather grimaced and looked aside, clearing their throats. The Asian kid continued to pedal around the three of them, shark-like.

"I'm not from China, fool," he scoffed. "I'm from Maine."

"Bullshit. Where?"

"St. George."

"So?" Jamie said, craning his neck as the kid circled behind him. "You weren't born here."

The kid wove in closer, fishtailed, spitting gravel on Jamie's spokes. "How do you know?"

Jamie squinted, thrusting out his toughest retort. "'Cos I never seen you before."

"Yeah, well," the kid said over his shoulder, "I seen you"—he let the pause draw out—"riding the banana seat on your sister's bike." That sparked laughter from Jamie's gang, startling him. *Was that a double slam . . . riding the banana?*

Jamie took in his square face, all shiny golden like a dinner roll. This kid had the whitest teeth Jamie'd ever seen. Even if he were standing in a whiteout with snow slashing to and fro, those teeth would be like the goddamn Fresnel lens of a lighthouse. "What's your name?"

The kid continued to do figure-eights around the three of them. "What's yours?" he challenged back.

"Jamie Eugley. I'm ninth-generation around here. You?" Of all the cocky things he'd said as a kid, this was the signature comeback.

"So? You still ain't too bright, now, is ya?" The strange kid said, expertly mimicking the local dialect.

The Kid and Kevin snorted again, and that began to piss Jamie off. He fired a look back at his small gang, trying to wrestle back control. "So, what's your name then?"

"Thongchai." It came out as *Tongchai.*

Jamie tilted his head, armed with his own twitchy smile. "What's your last name, *Wang?*"

THE GHOST TRAP

Once, in their early twenties, sitting around with a bunch of other people in somebody's dumpy old apartment, baked out of their minds, Thongchai said after a long silence to Jamie, "What's your last name, *Wang*?" That story was legendary and everyone fell onto the floor. But face-to-face in the gravel pit, it took Jamie by surprise when Thongchai picked him up off his bike and dumped him in the dirt. As Jamie lay there on the ground watching Thongchai's arm cock back, he had a disjointed thought— *You only get that kind of arm from hauling traps*—as a fist whaled him twice in the stomach.

How familiar was this, walking into Maine Med, down a sallow corridor, looking for intensive care? He already hated being here— just walking these corridors pushed old fears into his throat. Jamie finally found Thongchai's shared hospital room and he stood, teetering at the doorway, staring at the white curtain that separated the patients. An old man nearest the door slept in an elevated bed, his head swaddled in bandages. Beyond the edge of the white curtain, Jamie saw Thongchai's feet under a yellow blanket. As he came around the white curtain he held his breath.

Thongchai was awake. Upon recognizing Jamie he smiled, and Jamie's mind had to fill in the blanks of where that flashbulb smile should've been. Instead there was a dark, yawning gap where the upper teeth used to be.

"Hey, buddy," Jamie said, close to a whisper. At that moment, he was trying very hard to process what he was actually seeing. *Don't act like there's anything different*, Cary told him at Churchie's. But as Jamie's eyes took in each detail, he knew that would be impossible.

Gone was the shock of black hair. Thongchai's shaved head appeared grotesquely misshapen, swollen to twice its normal size as he lay against the pillow. From his left jaw hinge, a livid scar furrowed with black stitches rode up over the top of his forehead and back down to his right jaw hinge. Another scar wound around the back of his skull. Both of his eyes were swollen, but bright.

"Eu-lely," Thongchai said with a guttural grunt. Witnesses said that as soon as Thongchai walked out the door of the Time Out Pub, Kenny stepped around the bar and palmed a full bottle of Maker's Mark. By the time people heard the screams and began rushing out the door, all that could be seen was a broken figure on the sidewalk haloed by blood. His teeth had scattered like a broken necklace. The doctors had told Thongchai's parents to picture his fractured skull as "a hardboiled egg that had been dropped to the pavement."

"Waa goin' on?" Thongchai said as best he could without teeth. Jamie leaned upon a hard-backed chair next to the narrow bed. Everyone at Churchie's had told him to be prepared, but *this* . . . to see this distorted creature staring back at him . . . this was not Thongchai. It looked like monster movie makeup, the kind one would have to sit in a chair for six hours to achieve. All kinds of falsely cheery greetings that flitted through his mind as he was driving down 295, the ho-ho jokey crap people said to cover their discomfort visiting friends in the hospital—all of that dissipated the moment it became clear that Thongchai would never be normal, would never have his vibrant good looks again. Never, ever, would he have his former life back after this. Jamie clamped down on chattering teeth, too dizzy to keep standing. He pulled a cold PBR out of his jacket—yet another coping mechanism, bringing a beer to a friend in the hospital. But this did nothing to disguise his trembling. The way vomit comes out uncontrollably, beyond control, Jamie's eyes filled. He slumped into the chair next to the bed.

"I'm so fucking *sorry*." He covered his face with both hands, too far gone now to pretend everything would be perfectly okay.

"Ahhh." Thongchai smiled again. He rested a hand on Jamie's downturned head, giving it a couple of gentle pats. "S'aw 'ight, Eu-lely. I'm aw-live." He cracked open the PBR.

Jamie smeared the back of his hand across his damp eyes, nodding fiercely. One hand he placed on Thongchai's bed, the other dropped to the knee of his Carhartts.

"*Mmmm,*" Thongchai murmured, taking a sip of the beer. His eyes appraised Jamie. "You look like suh—hit."

Jamie snorted. "Yeah. Been a great couple of days, let me tell ya." They both smiled.

It was hard to understand Thongchai without teeth to form a barrier for his tongue, but Jamie's ears filled in where the consonants should have been, so he could pick up most of the news. As they sat together, Thongchai told him that a new dental bridge was being made and that Big Steve, Cary, and The Kid had already been down to see him. His parents were in Portland, at a nearby hotel, and James Eugley Senior was footing that hotel bill.

"I . . . can' bu-lieve all the 'hit that's been gawin down," Thongchai said slowly. "Your dad said it's been ah *hu*-uckin' nightmare."

Jamie rubbed the knee of his Carhartts with a savage movement. He didn't feel like talking about his father or how justified everyone felt about this trap war.

"So, listen," Jamie said. "Everett's working with a bunch of guys who are gonna donate a percentage of their catch for you, and Jeannie's roughing everyone up at Churchie's for tips. Every buck they give her, she's putting in a big jar for you. She's been bitching at Chuck, Bill, and Jimbo to put a crowbar to their wallets and match every tip they give her to the jar. We got you covered, buddy. No matter what, we got you covered. All you have to do is get better."

"Damn." A pervy light gleamed in Thongchai's swollen eyes. "Maybe I should pay Heannie a li'l visit when I get out of the hospituh. . . ."

This had the intended effect and Jamie snorted again. Churchie's widow was a lovely person, sort of a surly den mother to them all, but as a woman she was a dried sinewy husk, charred inside and out. "Oh, God. . . ."

Thongchai chuckled.

"Don't do that to my mind," Jamie said, rolling his eyes.

"I'll take huh up on the bah. Under Churchie's pict-tuh. . . ." Thongchai's hips under the covers humped up and down.

"Stop it."

Thongchai was silent for a moment. Then a queer look came

over his sallow face and he sneezed twice, wincing hard. "Ah, He-sus," he said, blinking. "Dat hurt."

"What do you need, buddy? I'll go get the nurse." Jamie surveyed the nightstand to see if there were any medications; it held nothing but a grimy TV remote and tissues.

Thongchai checked that his IV tube was still attached his wrist as he lay back against his pillow. "Naw." He swallowed, closing his eyes. "S'okay." But the strain in his voice was evident as he lay, weak, against his pillows. "You go if you want. Ain't no good to stick around he-ah."

Jamie stayed put. His boot played with the wheel on the IV cart. "What else am I gonna do? I'll be here as long as you want. I'll just make sure a nurse is around to fix you up if you need something."

Thongchai's swollen eyes opened, regarding Jamie for a second before they closed again. "You know waat sad, Euleley? You're probably the best guhfriend I ever had."

The cash register kept ringing like a child's bell on a training wheel bike—the echo of its shrill chime in the air. Southend Marine was jammed with fishermen, guys looking for tools to repair traps, cleaners to scrape the scum off the bottoms of boats.

Jamie had gotten back from Portland around two. Not wanting to go home, he searched the cavernous aisles, craning his neck to see items on shelves fifteen feet high, looking for Bondo, bilge cleaner, and a few other supplies. He was pulling out *Delores* next week. Didn't care that the lobster fishing season still had about two good months left. He was going to have to fix his boat anyway, rip out some ribs and resheathe that shotgun blast to her hull with new fiberglass. *Nice shot*, he thought. It wasn't the physical damage to the hull that bothered him the most (Senior had known to shoot high enough above the waterline not to sink her), but the deliberate violation of the most sacred part of her. You didn't mess with a boat's name; you didn't strip it off or rechristen it, and you sure as hell didn't blast a hole through the heart of it.

Jamie scanned the small hand-lettered signs above the aisles: Boatbuilding and Maintenance; Dinghies and Accessories; Batteries and Chargers; Tools, Switches, Inverters. There was still so much to do. He had to find his missing traps, haul the rest out.

He ran into his sternman, Toby, on his way to the register, carrying a box under his left arm.

"Hey," Toby said affably. "Glad to see you're still kicking."

"Yeah." Jamie ruffled the back of his hair with his hand. "Hey, listen, I'm sorry how this all worked out this season. I can get you hooked up with another boat right away. I've just been . . . everything just went to shit."

Toby shrugged. "I'm picking up some other work in the meantime." Jamie waited for Toby to elaborate, but he just stared beyond Jamie to the registers. The kid never did have much to say.

"Whatcha got there?" Jamie could see a high-end weather band radio in Toby's arm, which was interesting, as he probably had no money.

Toby smiled. "Yeah, it's got a DVD and CD player too."

"Those ain't cheap."

"Yeah, well. . . ." Toby repeatedly kicked the toe of his boot into the concrete floor. "I know where you can get three bucks over boat price right now."

"Where?"

Toby pulled out a rolled-up copy of *The Working Waterfront* from the back pocket of his Levi's. "You know that guy Ames?"

Just the mention of that name clenched something within. "What about him?"

Toby handed Jamie the paper. "Well, he just bought Quinn's Lobster Pound, including the wharf. He's gonna reopen it and it's gonna be bigger than Eastern Lobster. Ames is only asking *select* guys to come to him." The way Toby said that, his head cranked back, all proud as if he himself were in that league. "He's got big plans, and bigger money backing him. He's talking about hiring select fishermen, you know, like full time, benefits, none of this self-employed shit. He's got buyers lined up in different countries and he's got Jerry Eaton talking to everybody for him—and you know how Jerry is, people are gonna listen to him."

Another high school fisherman passed them—gave Toby a fist

that Toby gently punched back in greeting. "What's up?"

"You realize this is a bunch of smoke up your ass, don't you?" Jamie said, scanning the news item. There it was all right, left column. So Ames had purchased the lobster pound in Port Clyde with the intent to renovate it to accommodate 50,000 pounds and sell to wholesalers in Europe. It was just simply unbelievable how determined Ames was to get in, one way or another. Jamie scanned the article for his background, which revealed little; he'd managed a Boston wholesale business for a couple of years before moving up here. But if he thought he could win the locals away from their dealers, he was arrogant beyond measure. This guy needed his nuts back-tied. "Don't abandon the co-op, man," Jamie said. "It's been there for you for years."

Toby made a *Yeah, right* face. "Everett ain't paying shit and everybody's sick of it."

Jamie shook his head slowly, staring at Toby. "Toby, I know that guy Ames. He's a fuckhead and he's only out for himself. He'll change everything. He's gonna *incorporate* an industry that belongs to the people who live, work, and die here, not him. Do you friggin' get what I'm saying?"

The box shifted to Toby's other arm. "Yeah, so Ames is paying big money now to build up his stocks and maybe that's the way we're gonna have to go to survive. I mean, I don't like him either, but I'll use him."

Jamie shook his head. "Don't get sucked into it. You're turning your back on everyone if you do."

"Well, you really left me no choice, did ya?" Toby snapped, the only time in two years sterning with Jamie that he ever showed the slightest flash of anger. Jamie stood mutely, watching Toby move into line with his weather band radio hugged awkwardly in his left arm. He didn't think he could feel any more like shit, but right now, what Toby just said felt like a stick stirring his guts. Jamie turned abruptly so no one could see his face and walked down the Maintenance aisle.

So round and round it went. A conglomerate had tried it first in the 1970s, explored the possibility of buying up a number of boats, dealerships, pounds, hiring fishermen, making lobstering a corporation, but with lobstermen fiercely protective of their families' fishing grounds, nobody with a corporate logo was ever going to own the water. Now, twenty-some years later, there were kids like Toby, a different generation screaming about the money, the same shallow kids who wanted all the best boats, equipment, gear, wanted it without the hard work but felt it was *owed* to them just for being alive, changing the industry from the inside out. And face it, the industry itself needed some long-term solutions. Jamie walked to the checkout line churning on Neal Ames's latest underhanded move.

In a frightening way, the conditions this summer were in Ames's favor. The young kids coming up had the knowledge and the resources, but a lot of them were so easily manipulated and ignorant of the politics. The only thing to stop Ames would be the highliners, the ones with the history. As Jamie left Southend Marine, he threw his plastic bag of hull and bilge cleaners into the cab of his Ford and stood, one foot on the running board, thinking. What better way to hobble the power of the highliners than to start an all-out trap war among multiple parties? What a way to clean out the competition. If someone was clever enough. He thought of those expired ski tags, that choir boy smile. Of Fogerty's spindly face when he said the truth. *I didn't cut none of your traps. Not one.*

Oh, you poor, sorry bastard.

Jamie parked three doors down, close to the road. The Parker Snow cottage sat tucked among the pines, its deepwater shorefront just visible beyond the driveway. The sun was low on the horizon. Ames's Jeep was parked down by the garage.

Jamie took out a hammer and his Red Ripper knife from the battered red toolbox in his truck bed and hooked them to his belt. He kept out of sight, walking beside the tall hedges down the driveway, crossing the tight, trimmed lawn to the left of the house.

When he got just below the kitchen window of the cottage, he stood to the side and peered in. Found it dim and empty, everything sparkling clean, retrofitted with modern appliances and an enormous stainless hood. He could see Ames in the living room on the phone, pacing the room. Jamie slipped away from the window.

All those years skunking his cousins in cribbage, lying awake nights thinking of new ways to maneuver his traps into the best possible position, and Jamie hadn't seen this one coming. If he was right, this had been one major drubbin' by a minor player. He moved quickly down the left side of the lawn, staying close to the hedges, and shambled down the stone steps to the wooden pier next to the weathered boathouse. The Novi was tied up on cleats to the pier, as spanking clean as a picnic yacht. But he wasn't interested in the Novi. The boathouse was locked. Jamie looked up to the roofline of the Parker Snow house. The house was out of sight, a good three hundred yards away from the boathouse, but water carries sound. He made a decision. The hammer came down twice on the lock of the boathouse. It was unmistakably loud; he'd have to do this fast. He used the claw to rip the door handle off and pushed his way in. Hollow, echoey sounds of the pushing tide filled the boathouse. A Boston Whaler with a deep V hull and a Yamaha engine bobbed in the dark water. Jamie maneuvered around the Whaler and knelt down next to it, his fingers tracing the gunwale down to the hull. Even in the dim afternoon light from the greasy windows, he could see visible drag marks, black cross-hatched scars everywhere on this brand-new skiff, made from reefing a trap over the edge. Scuff marks, dried algae matted all over the gunwale—there was no question. It was the one Jamie had heard in the fog, the awful scraping of someone hand-hauling Fogerty's traps. He knew it had been a Yamaha engine. And knowing this, he trembled, not sure why.

Neal Ames smiled at first, curious. As if it was perfectly normal to see Jamie Eugley at his sliding door, barging right into his living room. The smile was a filament, streaking away. At that moment,

Neal seemed like a teenager caught in the act. He forgot he was speaking on the phone when Jamie strode forward, hammer in hand.

"Hang up," Jamie ordered.

Neal's frozen gaze broke. He seemed aphasic, not sure what to do with the phone. He did not say anything to the person on the line—just did what he was told and put the phone back on its cradle.

As Ames backed away, something in Jamie threatened to leap up—he felt a tickle at the back of his throat like he might vomit. Jamie strode forward, shoving Ames until he stumbled back and, finding nowhere else to run, crouched like a child in the corner. It was an effort not to take Ames by the back of his red hair and break his fine straight nose.

"I know you started the trap war between us and the Fogertys."

Neal shook his roundish face. His arm jerked up protectively to cover his head. "Don't, don't," Ames said.

Jamie looked down at his hammer, and without breaking his gaze slipped it back into his belt loop. Ames watched him, blinking rapidly, and just when his body seemed to deflate slightly with relief, Jamie moved forward and punched Ames across the jaw. It gratified him to see Ames's head whip back and his cheek turn white, then red. The desire to punch Neal again was almost irresistible. Jamie jerked the hammer out of his belt and Ames cried out. It angered Jamie even more that this little man couldn't fight, could only crouch there in the corner, making him feel he was attacking a woman. He bared his teeth, breathing hard.

"Look at you—in this house. Look at that fucking granite counter top. Your little game has ruined my friend's life."

The blood returned to Ames's face. He held his arms over his face. "I'm sorry. I'm sorry. I was just trying to make a living. The law told me I could. . . ."

Jamie moved in close and Ames's eyelids fluttered behind the protective circle of his arms.

"Shut the fuck up," Jamie whispered through his teeth. "I don't care what you have to say. I just came here to beat the shit out of you." Ames crouched even lower to the floor, to the point where he lay on his side, protecting his head. The little boys with the cell phones and the big money never seemed to know how to face a man with nothing but intent. It made Jamie long to kick him in his soft stomach, but it would be like kicking an injured dog.

Jamie stared down at Ames. He whacked the hammer in his reddened palm. This produced a moan from Ames. "Please, please, please," he whispered.

"Do you *know* what a dub is?" Jamie said, and waited until Ames slowly peeked through his arms. "I'm giving you a chance to answer this question," he said. "Since you know fucking everything about lobstering."

Ames's voice croaked. "It's a . . . uh, somebody who doesn't know how to place traps."

Jamie moved in and whacked Ames across the head with his open hand. "Good try. It's more than that." He stood there for a moment, staring down at Ames. "I'll let you find it out for yourself what a dub is and what that means around here. All I have to do is go to Fogerty right now, tell him the whole situation. You'll be lucky just to find your truck shot the hell up. And your brand-new Novi's gonna look right fancy sitting at the bottom of the bay. But you'll be lucky if that's *all* that happens to you."

Ames was silent, watching him.

When the implication of what *more* Fogerty and his family could do to him sunk in, Ames blinked rapidly again.

Jamie had to smile. "You really have no idea what you started, do ya?" He turned away and sat down on the plush arm of Ames's tailored off-white couch. "Once word gets out that it was you who started the trap war—oh, they'll definitely hospitalize you. They might kill you." Jamie looked at a greasy thumb- and fingerprint he left on the white couch. "Right now, I'm probably the only one who can save your ass. And I hate *you*." Jamie stared at him. "I really hate people like you. I'd rather just sit back and see you get what's coming to you."

"What should I do?" Ames asked quietly.

Jamie gave him a sour look. The choirboy was just *now* looking to absolve his sins? He resented the truckling tone in Ames's question, as if he was trying to curry favor by asking Jamie's advice. Jamie looked around for a moment at the modern kitchen, the overstuffed off-white sectional couch. The white framed paintings, the giant soapstone mantle over the fireplace. "Well," Jamie said. "Get out your famous checkbook, buddy. You're gonna write out a check for twenty grand to Dale Fogerty right now. Then you're gonna fuckin' write me a check and everyone in my harbor that Fogerty cut."

Neal's eyes scanned as he thought about this. "I'd have to move some cash from a couple business accounts over. . . ."

"Whatever." Jamie shook his head, disinterested. He stood up, looming over Ames. "Just write those checks. I'll deliver Fogerty's and tell him you were just this fuckin' idiot who cut his traps thinking you were cutting ours. And after this"—Jamie aimed his finger straight at Neal Ames's nose—"I'm gonna tell every one of your *select* lobster fishermen what you did. And before you reopen your pound, everyone is gonna know how you do business around here."

He drove the 1.4 miles south to Courage, one town over from Owls Head. In the last twenty years, he'd probably set foot in Courage only a dozen times, so ingrained it was in him to avoid it. In the early 1980s, there was a drive-in next to the hot dog stand in Courage that ran triple-X movies on Saturday nights in plain sight, regardless of who was driving by. "The Hot and Saucy Pizza Girls" or "Lesbian Thunder." Banana schnapps stowed away in a backpack, he and Mike Mailman and The Kid would pedal out to Courage late Saturday nights and shimmy under the fence to watch.

Jamie held his breath as he drove past the graveyard, whose headstones had an unobstructed view of the sparkling sea. He passed the one-room post office and turned by the boat yard, his truck jangling all the way down the dirt track of Fogerty Lane.

A slam of the truck door brought Dale Fogerty out of his enormous gabled barn. Fogerty stood in the dark rectangle of the door, rubbing paint off his hands with a rag. Without his hat, his head was pointed and bald at the crown. Jamie's finger and thumb snapped a greeting off the brim of his cap. "Mr. Fogerty," he said. "I come by to talk to you about a couple things. Got a minute?"

Fogerty didn't say yes or no, just stood there rubbing paint off his hands. Jamie walked toward him and, at a certain distance, stopped. "I've got some money for you, to settle the loss of your traps."

He looked to Fogerty for any reaction, but Fogerty continued to watch him.

"This idiot from Boston who just moved here this summer—well, him and me got into it earlier in the season, and anyway, he was the one who cut my traps and then he cut some of yours too, thinking they were mine. It. . . ." Jamie chose his words. "It came to my attention that maybe you were the one who'd cut me initially, but now I know the truth."

Fogerty rubbed his hands. "So, you didn't think to come to me first and ask?"

"Right," Jamie said, feeling foolish. "Okay, so here it is. I really did think it was you and I went out to double up on you, but in the end, I didn't," he said. "Swear to God, that's the truth."

Dale's eyes narrowed as he wiped his hands slowly. "So, how do I know you didn't come over here to set this Boston fella up to take the blame?"

That caught Jamie off guard. What did he think he was going to do, bring the news to Fogerty like a shiny apple to the teacher? Jamie took off his hat and held it. "I know what you think about my dad, but I don't operate that way."

Fogerty's head tilted; he looked impatient. Jamie continued, tightly. "When I found out how many of my traps got cut, I just went nuts. I wanted to get back at somebody and I wasn't thinking straight. I just thought because of our history. . . ."

Fogerty interrupted. "I never cut you personally, ever notice that?"

Jamie stared into the dirt. "Well, what about that one time. . . ."

"There was *no* time, not one. My father and your grandfather—we got into it. That was our fight. Your *father* kept it up all these years with his big mouth, but not once did I ever personally go after you. If my son or nephews got into it with you—that ain't my problem. The point is, I never cut you personally. Do you get it now?"

It was tough to meet Fogerty's eyes. "I guess that's what you're telling me."

"That's right. That's what I'm telling you. Now who else besides this Boston fella cut me?"

"I can only speak for me." Jamie reached into his pocket. His eyes met Fogerty's briefly and dropped. "I'm sure you know, but . . . anyway." He pulled out a folded check and approached Fogerty with it. "The name on the check is Neal Ames. I took care of him about a half hour ago. He's just a damn fool and he's paying everyone back. So you don't need to go after him."

Fogerty took the check, but didn't look at it. He scrutinized Jamie in his withering way. "So, what is this—some kind of apology?"

Jamie looked at him. "Yeah, I'd say it is."

"For your whole family?"

Jamie chewed his cheek, weighing this. Oh, wouldn't Senior blow an O-ring. "Especially my father."

"Hah!" Fogerty looked up to the clouds and smiled.

THIRTY TWO

The white plastic bag moved slightly, greenish brown claws sticking out among a tangle of brown, bubbled seaweed. Happy kept her eye on the bag, which moved slightly on the small narrow counter. "Do they know?"

On the dim two-burner galley stove, a large stainless pot began to boil. "Nah." Jamie reached into the bag and extricated one of the lobsters. Its feelers and walking legs made slow movements, as if it was still swimming. Its black beady eyes were close together. He held the lobster up to Happy, who instinctively backed away. Its curled, mottled tail muscle flapped suddenly.

"Ooh, she's a feisty one," Jamie said. "Knows she's going hot tubbing soon." Jamie laughed at how far Happy had moved away. She had no room to back up in the tiny galley. "Come on, touch her. She can't hurt ya, she's double banded."

"I don't need to touch it," Happy said, checking the lid on the pot. Jamie settled the lobster back down on the counter, where it tried to crawl. Happy's mouth distorted, watching it.

He leaned in. "Are you my tough little sailor? Or are you a squeamy little tourist?"

Happy took off her glasses, which were fogging up from the pot steam, and frowned. She tentatively touched its crusher claw and withdrew her hand. "Holy Moses, I'd have nightmares if I had to work with these things all day."

"I brought them over for you to try. Come on, at least once

before you leave Maine."

"All right, I told you I'd try it."

He picked it up again and held it out to her. "If you're gonna eat it, you're gonna drop it in. That's the rule, hippie."

"Jamie—just do it. You do this all the time. I just don't want to hear it scream," she said, rubbing her hands.

"They don't scream."

"Yes they do. They make this high-pitched *eeee.*"

"Oh my God."

"Oh, don't be using our Jewish accent like it's yours now," Happy chastised. "*Oh my Gawd.*"

All afternoon it had been drizzling, the galley and crew quarters of the Sea Hair damp and musky with the smell of work clothes, pungent spices. Nick and the crew had taken advantage of a day of no sailing to go to a movie. The grubby sky spilled into the kitchen porthole. Warmth from the pot steam seeped through the cold, dark quarters, washing over the lockable cupboards, the bracketed shelves that held coffee cups. Jamie held the lobster up to Happy. She shook her head. He shrugged and pulled the yellow rubber bands off the lobster's claws. Unsnapping the porthole window, he pushed it open. The steam from the kitchen escaped through the round window. He looked at Happy and dropped the lobster out the window. They heard it splash below.

He pulled another lobster gently out of the plastic bag. "You know we can always go get a pizza, it don't make no difference to me." His fingers unwound the seaweed from its walking legs. He held up the second lobster and made its crusher claw wave to Happy. "Bye, nice meeting you."

"Bye, you nasty prehistoric spider. Have fun bottom feeding from all the bilge tanks that have emptied into the harbor!"

Jamie talked for the lobster in a high voice. "I'm gonna go join my friends now!"

"Great, I'll see ya at the next clam bake."

"You sure you don't want to kiss me?" Jamie held up the lobster to be kissed.

"Rather kiss a slug. Bye now," Happy said and wrapped her arms around herself.

Jamie dropped it out the window.

Happy smiled, all freckles and red lipstick, and moved in closer. She settled her chin upon Jamie's chest. "Two more days and we're casting off."

He nodded.

"Before you know it, we'll be sitting on the beach watching men go by in teeny ball-hugging thong bikinis."

"What?"

Happy laughed. "So much you don't know about the Keys. . . ."

"It'll just be, like, a week going down, and then we're there, right?"

"A week, give or take." Her tanned face looked up at him.

"Okay, cause I can't stay longer than a couple of weeks."

"You sure?" She stared at him. "You know, Nick plans on paying you a little something for helping us take the boat down. But I've got plenty to keep us in style." Her mouth was glossy, like a shimmery, hot coal, and he felt her fingers on his belt, pulling it loose.

A sound in his throat gave him away. With her glasses off he could see her dark blue eyes, and she had a cocky smile.

"What are you doing?"

"Shut up for once," she said.

Earlier, at the park, he watched a skateboarding teenager with wide pants ollie up onto a green park bench and bite it on the way back down. The kid lay there, curled up, grabbing his crotch; it was what he and his friends used to refer to as a good old-fashioned *raunching*. The heat in the kitchen and the Happy girl curling around him like a creeping vine—this, too, would be a severe raunching when he thought about it later. But right now, it was that hot coal mouth and a dark, damp galley. And he was not going to think about anything.

THIRTY THREE

At 4:30 a.m., Anja unzipped her red car tent and swung her legs out. She heard Jamie's truck pull out of the driveway. A kitchen timer buzzed, one of her little tricks to stay on track. Anja dressed deliberately, working herself into a gray business suit that she'd pulled out from the back of her closet. Something she used to wear in Boston. The waistband, uncomfortably snug, allowed the zipper to come up only so far. She buttoned the jacket so that it wouldn't show.

Jamie had not remembered that this was her first day and she was glad for that. It left her free to concentrate on what she need-ed to do. She frowned, applying makeup in the mirror. She hadn't practiced this at all. The mascara had clumped and feathered on her cheeks; the blue eye shadow looked hideous; she wiped the lipstick off with toilet tissue.

The sun had not yet risen. After Anja left the house in heels, it occurred to her a mile walking on a dirt road that sneakers would have been better.

"Next time, sneakers," she said into her hand-held tape re-corder. By the time she arrived at the Stop N' Go, the blisters on each pinky toe and the sunlit horizon both had the same infuri-ated hue.

The store advertised its hours as 6 a.m. until midnight; she was a half hour early. Anja dug the brass ring of keys Dee had given her out of her courier bag. Once inside the store, she switched on the lights and pulled out her training notebook and laid it on the counter. Each section had color-coded stickies: *Cash Reg; Gas Pumps and Procedures.* Beside the notebook, she placed her tools: a calculator, two sharpened pencils, an orange highlighter, and Stop N' Go's Five Customer Service Rules. She set to her tasks, feeling good, in control, opening the staff restroom, unlocking the beer cooler, measuring out coffee for the twin air pots. As she worked, she pretended to be a customer, choosing random items off the shelf and placing them on the counter. Her fingers danced above the register keys, practicing ring-ups. Methodically, she placed Post-it notes all along the inside edge of the counter.

KEEP SMILING!

BUY 1 COOLANT, GET 1 FREE—REMEMBER!

LOTTRY TICKETS $3.25 EA. ADD .07 TAX!

THEY JUST PEOPLE!

HIT RESET BUTTON ON GAS PUMPS—EACH TIME!

CREDIT CARD, SWIPE ONCE, ENTER CODE, THEN #

YOUR DOING GREAT!

Anja tucked in her shirt, made sure the gray jacket was covering her open skirt zipper. She surveyed the store in the early yellow light. The Frosty machine whirred. A wee feeling of disappointment nagged at her. So maybe this wasn't the greatest ambition, to start working in a convenience store. But each task she mastered would lead to better things. And customer service wasn't only one of Stop N' Go's top five rules; it was the key to her future. So, it would start here. When Dee came back, she'd realize what an asset Anja was. "My God, woman, why don't you work for us full time?" would be the inevitable question. She'd revolutionize the hot dog roller, turning them on a spit, like rotisserie chicken, so that they wouldn't look all sweaty. She'd change out the fluorescent lighting with pink-tipped bulbs, so the place wouldn't look like a meat locker. She'd make them play classical music rather than country. Anja bit her lip as the marmalade light washed over the rusty gas tanks outside. Her rapid heartbeat took over with all the possibilities. She looked spanky in her charcoal suit, and she smoothed her blond bob in the bathroom mirror, reapplied the red lipstick carefully inside the lines. At two minutes to six, Anja walked over to the glass doors and unlocked them for two fishermen, one in a wool cap and muddy boots, the other in work worn jeans and a old Bean windbreaker. Each poured black coffee, selected caulked donuts from under the glass lid, and placed the items on the counter without a word. The coffee was 79 cents if Styrofoam, 89 cents if paper—easy to ring up. By 7:30, Anja'd done enough gas-coffee-oil-plastic-wrapped-sandwich-Hershey-bar combinations on the register that a new ripple of lucidity had dug a trench in her brain. Multiple combinations, like the violent pull of a lawn mower cord, tripped new lights, grooves of sequential learning. She had this job down.

Closer to eight, the store began to fill up with more people. A line formed at the register. She knew Fay, one of her neighbors, who was in the line, and a man she used to work with at the high school, but couldn't remember his name. The rest were working men. Two people, then three, then four, entered the store at the same time, swarming the coffee kiosk. She glanced at them nervously, estimating maybe sixteen people in the store, which made her forget what she was doing. She squinted at her notes. "Coffee/breakfast sandwich discount 1.60!" The gas pumps beeped every time they needed a reset. The guy at the head of the line, in a Carhartt jacket and jeans, put a chocolate milk, a candy bar, and two breakfast sandwiches in front of her. He had a tight, acrid expression. "Look, it's seven fifty-four. I just gave you a twenty and four pennies," he said.

Customer service! *Friendly greeting with a smile.* Anja forced a smile. "But the change on the register says twelve forty-six."

"Yeah, but I just gave you four pennies, see? So that means you give me twelve fifty back. See?"

Anja didn't see, not at all. Her brow knotted. She pawed at the bills in their respective compartments as if an answer would come.

"Just give me twelve bucks and fifty cents," the guy said. "Come on—I don't have all morning—I gotta be at work." People behind him in line were shifting their weight, glancing at their watches.

The gas pump had been beeping for several moments. Outside, a man knocked on Stop N' Go's window. "Hey!" He jerked his thumb toward his truck. Anja turned and pressed the reset button.

"Let me make this easier for you," the next woman in line said. She brought a waft of gardenia perfume to the counter. "I just need to pay for gas." She handed Anja a credit card, which Anja studiously swiped. She was panicking, trying to understand why the man had handed her $12.50 instead of $12.46—where was the mistake? The credit card machine beeped and Anja peered down at the LCD. The numbers didn't come up like they were supposed to and she felt her chest constrict. She flipped rapidly through her training notebook to the credit card section and scrutinized the different highlighted lines. She looked up at the woman blankly. "The, uh, numbers aren't coming up." Mumbles came from the back of the line. Even Fay, her neighbor, had the raised eyebrow look of "What the hell is going on?" Anja asked in a timorous voice, "Do you have cash?"

"No, this is all I have." The woman reached over the counter and tried swiping the card herself. The LCD remained blank. She plunged her card into her wallet. "Look, uh, I know this card is good and I already put in twelve dollars worth of gas and I have to go. But I'll call later on and figure it out. I promise."

"I don't know if. . . ." The gas pumps beeped and Anja swung around and pounded the reset button. Upon turning, she saw two teenagers smuggling six-packs under their sweatshirts, almost making it all the way out the door. "Hey! Hey! You need to pay for that!" Anja called, feeling hot and flushed.

"We already did, remember?" the teens shot back, and left the store. Anja couldn't remember if they had or not. Soon, people were leaving the line with coffee and donuts in their hands and just putting money on the counter. "Just keep the change," one guy snarled and slammed a five on the counter. "And tell Dee to get her ass back in here. Cause you SUCK."

A man she used to work with at school, the one whose name she felt stupid for not remembering, came around the counter. "Hi Anja, let me see if I can help you out here."

"Oh my gosh." Anja's hands rubbed at her temples. The line was not getting any shorter. More people kept coming into the store. "Now here's the five dollar bill that guy gave you for gas. So ring that up as five." Anja followed his directions. "Okay, and I think these three dollars were for a pack of cigarettes. And that's a check—I don't know what for, though. Oh man, this is a mess."

Anja blinked rapidly.

"I wish I could help you—but I have to get to school. Can you call someone to help you out?"

Anja hit the wrong keys on the register and it jammed. "Oh shoot, oh shoot. Oh my God." The gas pumps beeped. Someone opened the door. "He-llo? Think you could reset pump number two?" The spangles of the Monster Truck Headache were beginning to come on. She backed up to the wall and sank to the floor.

The man bent down. "Are you okay? Anja, what can I do?"

She shook her head, feeling the Wash-Out coming on next. This was a nightmare, a nightmare; she'd had everything under control. It was coming on, like the headache, the panic, nothing stopped it. It was too early to call Carolyn; Jamie was long gone. She couldn't wrestle it; it was coming on. The periphery of her vision began to feather away.

The man looked at the line of disgruntled people. "Folks, you're gonna need to give this woman some room." Some stood around her. Others slapped more piles of loose bills and change by the register, which looked like a piggy bank had been emptied out on the counter. "Look," the man said, turning to Anja, "I hate to leave you here. Maybe you should call somebody, the owner. Or the manager? Is he around?"

Anja's eyes were saucers. "She's . . . in . . . Boston."

"Do you know the owner's name?"

She shook her head, staring ahead.

"Wow, they should have never left you alone today. Okay." He punched numbers on his cell phone.

By the time the owner showed up twenty minutes later, Anja's former colleague had gone. Gray, full hair, a big belly, the owner looked as if he'd just been interrupted from his favorite football game. A small herd of people were standing around her as he strode in. "Who's hurt?" he said. A customer pointed behind the counter. "That woman there—nobody knows what's wrong."

Behind him, someone said, "Hey—you the owner? Can you switch the gas on to number one?"

The owner walked to the counter as Anja slowly rose up like Nosferatu. "Right here." Small voice.

"What's wrong?"

She stared at the counter piled with money and shook her head.

"Did we get robbed?"

"I . . . I don't know."

"What?" He lumbered over to the register and pressed the button to spit out the cash drawer. "Did we get robbed? Simple question."

"No."

The owner gave an exasperated sigh. "Dee told me you were qualified. She told me she trained you this week." Already people were streaming in and lining back up at the counter. A man pushed a packet of peanuts and a beer across the counter. Anja stood with her hands at her sides.

"Well?" the owner said. "Go ahead and ring him up."

The rapid blinking returned, contributing to her dizziness. "I can't."

"Yes you can, now come on. Just ring it up. The peanuts are ninety-nine cents and the coffee is seventy-nine cents."

"I SAID I CAN'T!" Her fists rose and slammed her hips. She dumped her notebooks and calculator and day planner into her courier bag. There was a hot, dry spot in her throat. Her chest pumped as she plucked the yellow Post-it notes from the cash register, counter, cigarette rack, credit card machine. They stayed stuck to her fingers as she hoisted the bag over her shoulder. At the end of the ice cream aisle, the little girl in the Girl Scout uniform stood watching her. She was four feet tall, clutching a blond doll with square glasses. She wore the same green beret as two days before. The beret was tipped jauntily, exposing a curly blond pigtail tied with red ribbon. Unlike the others, who moved around Anja in grainy images as if on a surveillance tape sped forward, this one watched Anja with grave eyes, still as a lake. Her Clara Bow lips did not move.

The blisters popped and her heels in her black pumps became sticky with pus. The red dimes of torn, new skin sent waves of pain with each step. Her suit was dirty from sitting under a tree for so long—and when Anja finally walked the dirt road all the way back to the Captain's House, dusk has already come. It crept along the dirt road as she walked under the shadows of pine trees. Long tall shadows.

Anja stopped just short of the dirt driveway to their house. Jamie's truck wasn't there. No welcoming lights inside, no flickering blue of the TV. No Jamie in the kitchen cooking up sloppy Joes like he used to do when she came home from teacher meetings. This was a house that didn't like the dark, and she stood staring at it as it stared back, with cowled windows for eyes.

"Aaahhh. . . ." The sound dribbled out of her mouth. She hunched, her arms dangling, one lower than the other, holding her courier bag.

A year ago, she'd begged Jamie for a dog, but the doctor didn't think it would be good for her fragile nerves, the way they barked. She desperately wanted a dog now, just to have something soft to touch and press her face into. She pushed the door open. There were no groceries to drop on the counter, no lectures to give. "Jamie—wouldja pick up all your nasty socks out of the mudroom?" Just a light switch, and the slightest pop of flipping it on. And what poor light it gave off, infusing the neat kitchen counter and the wide planks of the floor with an enervated sheen.

Anja shuffled into the house as if she'd been dead for years and was coming home, seaweed hanging off her lank, colorless hair. No note, no "beer in the fridge for you." He hadn't said anything about staying out tonight.

She was startled by the thought that maybe they'd had a fight, because it seemed that for days now, for weeks, he wasn't coming home at the normal time. Was he mad at her? Or no, that was a few weeks ago, when the red paint had to be scrubbed off the walls. The more she squeezed her memory, the more it burrowed. The brain fog was back; so frustrating not to remember. She dropped the courier bag, overturned it, and shook out her day planner. Turned the pages. All her notes in the last week had been about the convenience store—there was nothing about Jamie. She unclicked the lock on her Princess diary and rubbed the pages backward, trying to find anything pertinent. More notes about the convenience store, what she intended to buy with her first paycheck. She put a fist in her mouth, thinking hard.

She opened the door to Jamie's room—their old room. The bed was a riotous tumble of musky sheets. The dresser was dusty, covered with beer cans, a coffee cup, deodorant, a Leatherman, some junk mail, and a Mason jar of change. Jamie's clothes, stacked in fish totes all along the wall, seemed like people jumping out of a burning building. In this room was careless energy, but its messiness gave her some strange comfort. She could feel Jamie in here. She moved to the dresser, wiping a gray streak of dust with her finger. She picked up a small white plastic bottle, squinting to read Jamie's name on the medicine label, painkillers for his back. She did not see his watch or his wallet, and another note of anguish plucked at her. Where was he? Why was he never home anymore? What had happened? Anja opened his dresser. It was a mahogany lowboy, part of Maynard's old furniture from the 1940s, with brass pulls. Her fingers curled around the pulls on the first drawer. It was where she used to keep her lacy underwear and see-through things, with sachets. Anja's head jerked to the hallway with that memory. Where was all that stuff now?

The drawer contained boy junk. Car magazines, a pile of change, matches, crumpled cigarette packets, a silver frame. Anja touched the only pretty thing in there, the silver frame, and pulled it out from beneath unopened credit card offers. In the picture, she and Jamie stood with their arms around each other's waists. A friend's wedding. She couldn't remember whose, but Jamie looked the same, with his rumpled curly hair, all dressed up for once in a dark suit, a long-neck beer in his hand. Someone must've said something funny the moment before the camera snapped the picture, making them both tip their heads back with laughter. Anja scrutinized herself. She'd had long hair back then, all piled up in a loose bun, framed with daisies, no bangs. She looked so much better back then, thinner. Her dress was a stick-straight line of butter yellow.

Anja caught sight of herself in the mirror over the dresser. A fat girl in a rumpled, too-tight business suit. She placed the frame on the dresser, on the far right, where it used to be. Then, in doing that, her throat heated up, with the realization that the picture had been deliberately stored in a junk drawer. That picture was junk to him now. He was no longer that man with a goofy happy smile, with an arm around her waist. All she could recall now was strangled impatience: *Anja, wouldja just put your friggin' shoes on? We're late.*

Tonight, if he even came home, she'd have to tell him the job didn't work out. She wouldn't have to explain; he'd already know. *I told you, Anja. I told you the damn job was too much for you. Why wouldn't you listen to me?*

Her nose was running and she wiped it with a sleeve of her charcoal suit. The plan had fallen apart. She'd planned to help him with the bills again, buy her own clothes. It was only a stupid convenience store. She looked at the girl in the silver frame. "Aaahhh. . . ." Anja brushed her palm against the light switch in Jamie's room, killing the dim light.

The wall phone was marigold yellow with a dirty, gummed-up plastic rotary dial. The sticker in the center for emergency numbers was out of date—numbers relevant back in Maynard's time. Anja stuck her finger in the number 2 hole and pulled the dial around. It wound back with a clunk.

"Hello?" The voice was bored.

"Is . . . Mumma there?" Anja murmured.

"Jesus Christ."

The phone dropped away on the other end and Anja heard Amanda's husband say in a faded tone, "Who is it?"

Amanda answered him: "Who do ya think?" And dimly, Anja heard through the line: "What does she want now?"

"I just wanted to talk to Mumma," Anja said.

Amanda's voice came back on. "*Mumma?*" She was chewing gum. "Anja, she ain't your mother. And anyway, she ain't here."

"Is Jamie there?"

"No, he ain't."

"Do you know where he is?"

"Probably out with his girlfriend. I don't know." There was a sharp comment from Jeff, Amanda talking back to him. "I can say what I fuckin' want, shut up." Back to Anja. "And I guess you're gonna be staying here while Jamie goes down to Florida with her, so I'm gonna tell you right now, you can sleep in Jamie's room, but I don't want nobody sleeping in my room. All right? Just so you know."

And a click, and a dial tone.

Anja pulled the back of her hand against chapped lips. Leaned her forehead against the wall, feeling the fog come in on silent rollers. All the work of all her days coming to this. Her fist tightened and she pounded her temple, seeing bright flashes. It was coming on, a twisting, a charley horse of a headache, her brain writhing. Mumma. Flashes—of a gorgeous, verdant island; of a grand, graying Hispanic man and his short, swarthy companion in a white suit. Of a sand beach, of a barefoot dad and his little boy, whom he called Sport. An ornate stage, a look-alike brother and sister in purple jumpsuits, lavender scarves, intense white teeth. Of the beach, of the island, back to the Manhattan apartment, where she shared a room with the twins. . . .

A hand took the phone from Anja's slack wrist and hung it up on the wall for her. It was a man's hand, with the creases and valleys of older skin.

Anja stared at the wall. "It's never going to get better, is it?"

"Now, now," came Uncle Bill's soothing voice behind her. It was the same as the singing of the rocks, that voice, the gravelly kindness of smooth stones brushed up against the sand. The hand snapped its fingers, and when Anja turned around, Mr. French had a steaming pot of tea on a silver tray waiting for her. Anja shook her head, no. Uncle Bill smiled. His square face was a shelter for his kind blue eyes. Anja wanted to fall into his chest, put her miserable chin, wet with tears, against his neck. Mr. French stood stiffly in the dim living room, round as his employer was square, uncomfortable with such a display of emotion. He cleared his throat.

"Perhaps, sir, she might care for a hot bath. Shall I draw one?"

"I'm okay," Anja said. Uncle Bill's smile warmed her. He really had the gentlest eyes. He wasn't going to tell her to "snap out of your fuckin' mood," the line Joe, her mother's husband, had made his signature all through her high school years. Those sympathetic eyes were for her. That sad, sweet smile: hers.

From the hallway, the little blond girl with the Girl Scout uniform came out holding hands with her red-haired twin brother. Her other hand held the limp, blue polka-dotted doll with glasses.

The little girl spoke in a squeakier version of Uncle Bill's gravel voice. "We had a dream about you. . . ." The green sash across her uniform displayed the rewards for her efforts, and from the noble angle of her green beret, one cute, curly pigtail tied with red ribbon stuck out.

She and her brother turned on their heels at exactly the same time and headed back down the hall toward Anja's room. Uncle Bill nodded that she was to follow them.

Anja's room had taken on the quivering light of dozens of lit votives, as in a church, swaying underwater light refracted across the walls. The red VW car bed was bright pink, lit up within. Two small children sat cross-legged in there. A small hand reached outside the zippered door. "Come in."

Whoever thought this day would end in a party? How her spirits lifted to have all four of them in the car bed with a bottle of tequila Mr. French had taken from way back in the cupboard over the refrigerator. There was even enough room in the car tent for

315

big old Uncle Bill and his square shoulders and round French and his ovoid head. The twins provided much of the hilarity. Anja found herself talking in complex sentences—unbelievable. "I was going to pursue my master's in art therapy before the accident. But even then it was very expensive to try to work and go to grad school at the same time."

"Were you still painting?" the girl said, with the doll on her lap.

"Oh sure, all the time, but there was no way I was going to make a real living with painting."

"What if you didn't"—the twins started to say together, and giggled—"have to worry about it?" The girl finished the question.

"I . . . actually, I've never thought about it."

Uncle Bill crossed his arms. "What would you do with your life, Anja, if you had all your options open?"

Anja ran her fingers through her hair; these were questions no one had ever asked. "I would just work with kids, teach them how to paint. I would sit with them and find out who they were, and every day I would give them something to feel good about."

"Would you take them to fairs and let them go on scary rides?" The girl sat up, excited, her grin exposing a missing tooth.

"Yeah, and buy them corn dogs and soda pop?" asked the boy.

"Of course! I . . . I would love to. You know, we could all go do that sometime. I could take you two and we could . . . would that be okay, Uncle Bill?"

Mr. French and Uncle Bill tipped their heads toward each other, conferring in a paternal way.

"Uncle Bee-yoll!" wheedled the boy.

Uncle Bill rubbed the boy's crest of red hair. "Let's not forget, children, why we're here. Not to think of ourselves, but to think of Anja." Something passed between him and the boy; the boy nodded and crawled out of the tent. "I'll be right back!"

The girl clutched her doll. "Anja," she said soberly. "We're orphans, you knew that."

Anja nodded.

"There have been many times I thought Uncle Bill might leave us—or send us back. A bachelor does not have time for children, and it's been very hard on Uncle Bill at times."

"Not that hard," Uncle Bill gently reminded.

"Certainly not," said French.

"Still," she continued, "sometimes we've done things to make them want us more. Let us"—she indicated herself and Anja—"be truthful."

"Okay."

"Cause we're gonna love you no matter what."

The little boy crawled back into the tent with a flushed smile and emptied what was in his fist into Uncle Bill's hand. Anja watched all of them, compelled by an aching need to be whatever they wanted her to be.

"You understand," the girl continued, "we're not going to leave you."

"Yes."

The twins looked at each other. "We're going to help you get better," the girl answered for them both. "There's a way you haven't seen. You've been trying so hard to get to it, but we've got a better way."

Anja's forehead laddered. She tried to speak, but the words felt used. "What about Jamie?"

A dimple seemed to tighten in the girls' cheek. "When you come out of this, Anja, picture the way you were, the way you both were."

"Yes."

"The hand around your waist at the wedding. Do you remember?"

"No," Anja whispered.

"That night at the wedding, he told you he wanted to marry you."

Anja found it hard to swallow.

"So, are you ready?"

Her breathing quickened; she looked to each of them. "I don't wanna die."

The twins found that funny and erupted in a simultaneous giggle that rose up and out of the tent. Uncle Bill shook his head, and Mr. French chuckled too. Of course, how silly did that sound to say that. The red tent burned bright pink.

THIRTY FOUR

With twilight he could see his own breath as he let the tide scrub up against his boots. On the back end of his property, right up to the water, he sat in an aluminum beach chair. The chair was mildewed, several long yellow bands torn and hanging to the ground. At his feet were smooth bluish-black stones that clacked with the tide, surging up and dragging back. The brown air sacs of seaweed mingled with the stones. The last week of October, a few days before Halloween. He burrowed his cold hands into the pockets of his dirty blue sweatshirt.

Six thirty-nine in the evening softened everything up, put a champagne fizz on the water, made it undulate in supple, wide ripples. Above, a fantastic feathery sky. To the right, Tick Island, with its jutting pine trees sharing space with a lone outbuilding near a rock wall.

He wasn't aware of the odd way he was breathing or the nasty and lovely reek of the harbor, like wet wool and clam flats. From his property, he could see only the horseshoe-shaped harbor of Petit Point, the board-and-batten summer houses across from his, silvering with each year. In the harbor, the water seemed a tight, gray color. Beyond the lip of the bay, the outer water slipped into some sort of vivid deeper green, like fish scales on a mermaid's hip. That's where he kept his eyes. His breath was shallow, the feeling in his chest as if every rib had been cracked.

For a few seconds, he could see it way beyond the harbor, its sails creamy smooth, erect with the spindles of rigging, a tiny ship on a yellowing page. He'd been sitting out there wondering if he'd see it before she sailed down to the Keys. With the rise and fall of his chest, the schooner stayed on the horizon, barely seeming to move, before it disappeared beyond the point.

Inside Churchie's, Jeannie closed her eyes, smoke drifting up past her leathery face. Watery green eyes held him. "Some girl came down here the other day looking for you," she said.

"Yeah?"

She put her cigarette down on a tin ashtray and mixed up a rum and Coke, pointing the soda gun into the glass with a limp hand, and plopped a lime in. "She just asked me if I knew you— wanted to know if you were okay."

"What did you say?"

"I said you were fine." Jeannie picked up her cigarette. "She just left after that."

"You didn't tell her anything else?"

"I didn't know her, so I didn't say nothin' else," Jeannie said. "Oh, by the way—" She pulled a small newspaper article from the cash register and slid it across the bar. Jamie saw the headline, *House Fire, Arson Suspected*, but didn't feel like reading any further.

"They can't find him or his boat either," Jeannie said. Jamie slid the article back to her but not before noticing the newspaper image of what used to be the historic Parker Snow house, now some gutted shame like a rotten, hollowed-out tooth.

"He probably hauled his ass back to Boston," he mumbled, more to the empty bar than to Jeannie. An image flashed across his imagination, of Neal Ames duct-taped, bug-eyed, in the forward hold five fathoms below. Or maybe the ocean had done her thing, came forward on a furious roller and slapped his boat to splinters. Or maybe, if Ames had been smart, he would've simply hauled his boat out of there, away from Maine waters, in the middle of the night. In any case, Jamie wished for no more news.

He got up to leave. "Well, we'll see ya, then."

"Good enough," Jeannie nodded.

He got there before visiting hours were over. Broken gurneys sat around the outside of the building. Inside, barren hallways led to corridors of sterile white tile, with the occasional salmon or leaf green to break up the monotony. The rooms were dark boxes, revealing raised, motorized beds. Why would no one think to cheer up the rooms with fuchsia and flaming orange and azure blue or murals of the beach? As if people healed any faster staring at flat white walls somewhere between milk and vanilla ice cream, no pictures, just the ever-present TV mounted in the corner.

For the second time in three years, Jamie walked through the air-conditioned corridors with humped shoulders, knowing exactly what to expect. Smells of urine and stale forced air permeated the place. He trod the corridors, passing doctors in blue scrubs, nurses in white sweaters and white sneakers, orderlies in eggplant uniforms. He stepped out of the way of tiered food carts and passing wheelchairs. Each room he went by was open.

"Don't rush me," he heard an irritated older man say to his wife as he walked by.

"But honey, I'm just trying to get you to put your leg in here."

Anja had a shared room, just like last time. She looked like the back of a computer. Cords, tubes, and wires snaked out from her neck and wrists, twisting from the ones in her nose and mouth. He looked upon her dough-slack face, her closed eyes and chapped open mouth. There were machines to feed her and machines to remove her waste. He hadn't really eaten in a week.

Donna acknowledged him standing there and went back to stroking Anja's hand. There was not one time he'd come to the hospital that she wasn't there, stroking Anja's hand, talking to her. To the right of Anja's bed, a metal tree held her IV bags. Little plastic hoses hung from the tree, looping down to the bed. The net over her wrist looked like a bleached bait bag.

The day before he'd missed visiting hours, late from working. Down by the dock, the air had been sharp like New York cheddar, deliciously tangy, fishy and sweet. He'd been diving, looking for his traps. Biting into a regulator, he rolled backward into the water, feeling the awful chill inside the suit. Everywhere the powerful flashlight illuminated, there was a solid wall of green with floating particles. He found a few traps hung up on rocky outcrops, the pulse in his ears beating loudly. He secured a heavy clamp to the wire of the trap and swam up with it, watched The Kid wind it up to the rail and stack it with the others.

Down there in nocturnal limbo, where the ocean bottomed out and the pressure became oppressive, he knew he'd never find all of them—he just couldn't go down that far. But he'd seen what the ocean floor looked like, the way the moon looked with its desolate pebble fields and whitish rocks. He knew they were down there like so much other debris that would never be found—crumpled plane wings and shattered hulls of submarines and boats, beer bottles and diamond rings. He couldn't stop thinking of those discarded traps, like clumped child's blocks, but how else was he supposed to escape the grief? Jolted out of a hot damp sleep, he'd opened one painful eye and remembered nothing. Paid for it dearly at the sickening hour of three. If he were to find any relief, it would be on the southernmost tip of Florida, where baby salamanders darted out of bushes, begging to be picked up. There would be the sea, winking, the color of 1950s hot pants, the color of true blue eyes. This was what he wished for, a clean start.

Jamie felt the rushing; the ocean chop, hurling starboard and portside; felt the stench of herring in the back of his throat. He was on dry land in the same hospital, the same cafeteria where he'd been eating a Baby Ruth bar when Dr. Nayar summoned him up to Anja's room the first time. Now it was three years later, the doctor's face gaunt with the news that the combination of the tequila and his prescription pain pills had put her into a deeper coma than the one from her original injury. Grave brown eyes told him that she might never move beyond a vegetative state.

A female orderly in pink scrubs came in, with the standard half-knock and "Hihowyadoin?" She was obese and had an air of efficiency. She proceeded to flip up Anja's johnny to check her catheter, exposing Anja's naked thighs, her pubic hair. The orderly hummed as she worked. This was just flesh to the woman, who worked with sickness and death as naturally as Jamie could shove a fist into a maggoty bait bag and think nothing of it. Still, the draining fluids, the blood, the urine, the IVs of insulin, potassium, medications, the bandages, monitors, nasopharyngeal tubes, the strangers coming through the room to visit the girl in the next bed, the janitor, the repairman with the power drill hanging up a picture—all of it sifted in and out of the room like effluvia, quick darts and glances, while this fat orderly had Anja's cunny flapping in the wind for all to see. Jamie reached forward, yanked viciously at the dressing gown, pulling it back down.

"Jamie!" Donna snapped.

"Oh honey," the orderly said, chewing gum. "I see this all the time, don't worry about it."

THIRTY FIVE

Now that the sun was at a lower angle in the day it gave the harbor a lingering, dispossessed feeling. Lobster boats shared lanes with tugboats, all grimy black, flanked with tires like oversized barnacles. One or two sailboats, despite the late season, tacked about in their pretty, useless way like delicate butterflies.

The day was absurdly warm, the last siege of Indian summer. He'd tossed his blue sweatshirt down below, worked in a white T-shirt yellowed under the pits. His back hurt, but he worked through it, baiting and shoving traps overboard, hauling, selecting. The skin under his eyes seemed bruised from lack of sleep.

He was grateful to be alone. He didn't know how people could stand this pain and still show up to work every day, interact with coworkers and clients. Some stupid friend of his mother's tried to be well-meaning the other day. "At least you are finally free," she said, as if this was *freedom* that made him wake up each night or lean on the doorframe of her room looking at the forlorn hump of her red car tent.

On top of her dresser he'd placed the silver frame of the two of them at Jack Hallowell's wedding four years ago. Anja had her long hair up in a bun; he had a rumpled suit, a beer in his hand. He knew exactly why they were laughing in the picture. Just before the picture was taken, someone implied that it was their turn to get married next and Anja joked, "I'm waiting for somebody better to come along." That silver frame, along with the tequila bottle and pills, had been in her hands when he found her in a dirty gray suit. Later, he'd torn up her room for any sign of a note, anything. He'd found her voice recorder and played it back. "Next time, sneakers," she said, something only she would understand.

By ten, the rich, sunny day and cool, blustery wind invigorated him to press on, keep hauling traps over the rail. He gaffed the buoy, lifted the line over the snatch block, and watched it bridle the surface. It had been a week of incredible landings—the gypsy caravan had finally come home. He found himself catching what they used to catch in the 1990s heyday. The traps teemed with flipping muscle, clenching and unclenching claws. Feelers whipped like downed wire. By noon, he'd filled his lobster tank and made mortgage for the next month. He idled ahead, cutting through silky wake toward the next string.

The seagulls swooped and cried, long long, short, short short, like Morse code. All those Friday night clam dip and cribbage parties they used to have with Cary, The Kid, and Thongchai. Enough dandelion wine flowing to get somebody doing something foolish, like the time somebody turned up the stereo and he started gyrating to Styx's "Come Sail Away." It got her laugh going, which always started low and rose up, flying over the rest of the room in a high siren. Anja's eyes would squinch up; she'd be cackling and trying to speak at the same time, the kind of laugh that made people helpless. She'd get going, and then that would get everybody going, stomachs hurting, tears rolling.

He thinks of her routines, all her hassles, thinks of what she said after he tried driving away from her that one afternoon when they first started living together, her arm resting casually on his window while he gunned the motor. "I'm not leaving you over the fact that we fight. So what? Everybody fights. So fuck you, Jamie, I'm not leaving you over that. To break us up, you're gonna have to leave first." From that day to this—three years.

The waves roll in, and he thinks of the singing of the rocks. He tries to recall the exact moment when she knew, even in her badly lit brain, how she somehow managed to grope for the truth of their relationship and found it—even when he could not—and gripped it in her hot hand in the dark. Why did he not feel this in his collarbone? Or smell it? He, who could divine the direction of the wind on the flight of a shitepoke. Until now, he did not know himself when he'd truly left her, but deep below the roiling surface, down where one of his algae-covered traps made its home, he saw a wraith peel out from one of the broken ribs and slide up through the night to collect Anja from her bed. Back down it took her, turning that baby pink face blue, down through those bitter, snatching waters. He cursed the sea out loud for the first time in his life. What could he possibly lose now?

On a curling wave, the afternoon shoots through a wall of bottle green, flecks of foam surging before the wave somersaults and becomes nothing. In the end, he stares out at the sea and stares, just stares.

THE AUTHOR

DRAWING BY WURGE

K. Stephens is a Maine arts and entertainment writer who has written about schooners, food and wine, teenagers, and the creative economy. Most lobstermen she knows are only too happy to share a crazy story after a beer or three.

ABOUT THE TYPE

This book was set in ITC New Baskerville, a typeface based on the types of John Baskerville (1706-1775), an accomplished writing master and printer from Birmingham, England. He was the designer of several types, punchcut by John Handy, which are the basis for the fonts that bear the name Baskerville today. The excellent quality of his printing influenced such famous printers as Didot in France and Bodoni in Italy. His fellow Englishmen imitated his types, and in 1768, Isaac Moore punchcut a version of Baskerville's letterforms for the Fry Foundry. Baskerville produced a masterpiece folio Bible for Cambridge University, and today, his types are considered to be fine representations of eighteenth century rationalism and neoclassicism. This ITC New Baskerville was designed by Matthew Carter and John Quaranda in 1978.

Composed at JTC Imagineering, Santa Maria, CA
Designed by John Taylor-Convery